BURIED AT SEA

Nancy
The Greatest
Stories Are
Still, Being
Told.

Buried at Sea

A Sea Story

by

R. Kenward Jones

www.Penmorerpress.com

i

Buried at Sea by R. Kenward Jones
Copyright © 2019 Toni Bird Jones

ISBN-13: 978-1-957851-09-9 (Paperback)
ISBN-13:978-1-957851-10-5 (e-book)

BISAC Subject Headings:
FIC014000FICTION / Historical
FIC032000FICTION / War & Military
FIC031020FICTION / Thrillers / Historical

Address all correspondence to:

Penmore Press LLC
920 N Javelina Pl
Tucson AZ 85748

Buried at Sea

A Sea Story

by

R. Kenward Jones

www.Penmorerpress.com

Buried at Sea by R. Kenward Jones
Copyright © 2019 Toni Bird Jones

ISBN-13: 978-1-957851-09-9 (Paperback)
ISBN-13:978-1-957851-10-5 (e-book)

BISAC Subject Headings:
FIC014000FICTION / Historical
FIC032000FICTION / War & Military
FIC031020FICTION / Thrillers / Historical

Address all correspondence to:

Penmore Press LLC
920 N Javelina Pl
Tucson AZ 85748

Acknowledgments:

My mother gave me a love of reading. My father could make a game out of anything. In me these two things combine as the ability to see stories anywhere and to play with them until they work. I'm married to a unicorn who is so full of magic that she made it make sense to dream and to risk. I have kids who live so authentically it makes me know I can't live (or write) otherwise. And I have a community who elevated me to a height of eye that lets me see beyond the horizon. All of these people created the environment in which I wrote this book. I gratefully acknowledge them all.

Dedication:

To all the characters I've met in my life who've swirled around in my imagination and created the new friends and acquaintances who inhabit my stories and...

To the Spirit who taught me how to speak worlds into existence.

Chapter 1
Berth of a New Era
August 1976, at anchor, Naples, Italy

USS *Redstone* swung gently to her anchor. A hint of a breeze carried the odd blend of sweet and foul scents of the ancient city a quarter mile away. The sun rose in a blaze of red-orange flame over Mount Vesuvius as she kept watch over the smooth, gray-green waters of the basin at her feet. A sailor leaning on a lifeline of the ship's fantail took a drag on his cigarette and reflected on the silent volcano. He pictured an ancient sailor standing here witnessing a different fire blazing there: a violent explosion ripping away the mountaintop, throwing it down on the surrounding cities and the sea like a giant, gray fist falling from heaven. He muttered grimly to himself, "Red sky in the morning..." and flicked the spent cigarette into the water below.

Redstone was on the burnt end of a grinding nine month deployment. According to her original orders, she was due home tomorrow, and should have been, as sailors liked to say "one day and a wake up" out of her homeport of Norfolk, Virginia and its stinking waters, instead of the eerily similar-smelling Naples. At least here you stood a chance of catching the scent of the lemon trees on the Amalfi coast, their yellow fruit shaped like women's breasts and so large *Redstone* sailors referred to them as sour tits. It wasn't beyond the range of possibilities to glimpse real Italian breasts on the sweet young things who liked to ride around topless in the summer heat, circling ships in the harbor in their sporty little boats, tantalizing sailors with a call louder than the mythical siren song.

Yeah, Naples had its advantages, but Norfolk was on his mind. This deployment had dragged, not at all like his last ride to this side of the Pond two years ago. The pace of repair work and the fairly good material condition of the old ship back then had left time to explore every port they hit in the southern Med. This go-around they'd been ridden hard and put up wet, and were getting a special kick in the ass on their way home: an outchop Operational Propulsion Plant Exam— OPPE— a word used by the ship's engineers with the vehemence of the foulest curse they could imagine. While the rest of the crew anticipated rest and an easy ride home across the North Atlantic, the snipes would be trying to prove their World War Two vintage ship could still operate her engineering plant safely. He had his doubts as to whether or not the old girl *was* actually safe, but he'd seen enough Navy chicanery to know that in the end, although the OPPE inspectors would drag the plant and her engineers through a knot hole backward, the powers that be would not down check *Redstone*. They needed her to be safe, so, by definition, she would be pronounced safe.

But they weren't lying at anchor here in Naples, delayed two weeks because of an engineering exam or any other problem under the control of the crew. No. It seemed the Old Man had volunteered them for a special mission. The old bastard was just like the other skippers he'd sailed under in his six years on *Redstone*. They came aboard talking about morale, team, and rah rah rah, but he'd never seen one of them in the main spaces for longer than ten minutes. Too hot, too loud, too grimy for their gentle dispositions. To a man, none of them had a clue what it took to keep the old girl going. He came to believe they didn't care. The entire engineering department and every man in it was nothing more than a light switch. They expected it to work when they flipped it on, and gave it no further thought when they flipped it off. Two extra weeks steaming the plant, waiting for whatever special assignment to play out, was nothing to them. But it was something. It put hours on machines more weary than the sailors who operated them, and the combination of weary machines and operators added up to things going wrong and things getting broken. Things getting broken on the eve of an OPPE sucked.

The special mission? Rumor was they were delayed because an admiral wanted some boxes full of his old junk hauled to Norfolk.

"Like a damned mail man," the sailor said to himself, as he wearily stretched and got ready to return below decks.

The sailor was a hull technician second class (HT2); a welder and "'A' Gang-er" who worked some of the most unpleasant duties aboard *Redstone*. Cleaning out toilets and drains on one end and crawling down into collection and holding tanks (CHT) where the things deposited in those toilets and drains made a temporary appearance before being pumped into a waste barge or, depending on where the ship was at the time, over the side and into the ocean. It was an especially nasty job in this old ship and there were changes coming that would make it even nastier.

Admiral Elmo Zumwalt, youngest man ever to serve as Chief of Naval Operations, was turning the Navy into a place where Navy tradition and social norms were questioned. One of the oldest questions was the place of women. Did they belong in the workforce? In the military? In combat? The answers were all falling in one direction, and the Navy, with Zumwalt at the helm, was grudgingly beginning to adjust. *Redstone* was the place where the wheels of change were beginning to move.

In anticipation of women coming to the fleet sooner rather than later, the repair ship was directed to discreetly refashion a large set of spaces amidships and make them into a berthing compartment. It was a win-win for the Navy. *Redstone* had the ability to carry out the work on her own, at a low cost and out of the view of the public. The brass didn't want to create a self-fulfilling prophecy by making one of their ships ready for women at sea, but they also saw the handwriting on the wall and wanted to be able to claim the initiative, when and if called upon to accommodate women. So HT2 Jasper Phipps spent a great portion of his Med deployment hacking away bulkheads with an acetylene torch and running the plumbing for a head that would service at least 100 female sailors, if they ever materialized. It had been hot, dirty, thankless work with too many chiefs and not enough Indians. The floor plan changed daily and many times, multiple times in a single day. The result was many mornings when Phipps cut a hole through a thick steel bulkhead in the smoky, ill-ventilated belly of *Redstone*, only to be ordered to weld the hole shut in the afternoon. It was demanding work, sapping his physical and mental energy. Being jerked around daily, even hourly, by an endless stream of khaki-clad meddlers exhausted and demoralized Phipps and his crew more than the work itself. Two weeks swinging at anchor in this harbor, without even the prospect of a brief jump onto the beach to drown his sorrows, was pushing him beyond his limits.

"Phippsy!" The familiar nasally northeast twang of his one and only topside buddy rang out. It was Radioman First

Class Joey Russel. The man always had the inside scoop on what the ship was doing and about to do, and what the Captain was telling the greater world outside *Redstone*'s gray metal skin. Every message in and out of *Redstone* passed through his hands. He and Phipps shared an unlikely love for the Red Sox; unlikely for Jasper because he was from Kentucky, unlikely for Joey because he was from Boston.

"You're not gonna fuckin' believe it, Phipps. Not gonna fuckin believe why we're fuckin' hangin' here in Naples like an old man holdin' his limp old dick in the shower," Russel said.

Phipps wearily smiled at the man, who waited for him to take the bait. Russel looked disappointed when Phipps said, "Too tired for twenty questions Russ. Just give me the dirt."

"No fun there, Phipps. You look god awful. You need some sunshine... maybe one of those Frenchy beaches we visited last time we rode this merry-go-round."

"It was a nice view," Jasper sighed. "But that's about all. Too rich. All them women were just too rich. Take a million bucks make 'em look up from their drinks. Probably have to own a beach of my own to make time with them. I'm never gonna be a hundred miles from money like that."

"Not true," Russel said. "You're gonna be a lot closer than that to a lot more than a million dollars." He arched his thin lips and eyebrows, a look that reminded Jasper of the weird old banker on the Andy Griffith show.

When Jasper passed on the bait a second time, Russel gave him a disappointed shrug and continued. "Just got a look at the latest from COMSIXTHFLEET to the Old Man. Want to know exactly why we're swingin' here holding our collective dicks?"

Jasper nodded unenthusiastically. "Sure Russ. Why?"

The Radioman smiled broadly, savoring the tidbit for a moment as he did all the little morsels he served up around *Redstone*. "We are soon to be the camel that ole' King Tut rides across the Atlantic."

Jasper's face stayed as slack as his mood. "Not in the frame of mind to solve riddles, Russ," he said.

"Fine," the man pouted. "I'll spell it out. From what I can tell, the President has been trying to get the Arabs a new image in The States. Thinks it will help with the Middle East peace plan or something or other. They came up with the idea to get the Egyptians to send a bunch of the treasure from King Tut's tomb for a tour around the country. Stuff that's priceless. Irreplaceable." Russel paused for dramatic effect. It was lost on Jasper, who looked on blankly. "Well, they got the deal done, all but one snag. The Egyptians wouldn't let the stuff go in an airplane—afraid of a crash. And they didn't want to send it on a commercial ship because they didn't think it was secure enough. So at the last minute somebody in the Pentagon caught wind of the problem and volunteered the good ole' US Navy to save the day! The *Milwaukee* is in Cairo right now picking up the stuff. She's gonna come to Naples and hand it off to us!"

Jasper sniffed. "That's just great Russ. Glad you think it's so interesting. I could give a rat's ass about King Tut and everything they buried with the sum bitch. I just wanna get home and get off this tub." He paused and added, "Do you think they realize *Redstone* is held together by rust and terrazzo? All that stuff might just fall right through the bottom like a ball bearing dropped in a rusted out oil can."

Russel said, "I overheard the skipper telling the Cheng, the Repair Officer, and Suppo they'd better make damn sure we're ready for the shipment. Big argument. None of them wanted to give up any of their space to house it. Guess where it's going?"

"I told you Russ, I'm not in the moo…"

"In the spaces you and your guys have been rehabbing for the women's berthing compartment," Russel cut him off.

"You've got to be shittin' me."

"Nope. Expect you'll be hearing about it shortly. Sorry for the bad news, but I have a silver lining for you."

"What's that?"

"We've got to go to the commercial piers for the transfer. They don't want to risk it at anchor. We'll get some liberty at least."

"We?" Jasper said glumly. "You topsiders kill me. This only means I'm gonna be working my twelve-a-day where I can see the town for the few hours they leave me to come up for air and watch you and the other no-loads scurrying down the gangway, like the rats you are."

Russel started to protest when another sailor interrupted them. It was one of Jasper's crew, a scraggly looking HT in a set of coveralls so soiled they appeared more brown than their original dark blue.

"Cheng's looking for you, HT2," he said. "Think we've got another alteration to the "plan." He mocked the last word with clawed air quotes.

Russel gave Jasper a knowing look. He said, "Here we go."

Chapter 2
Sea Change
May 1989, Barren Ridge, Augusta County Virginia

Machinist Mate Fireman Apprentice Maggie Freeman reported aboard USS *Redstone* (AR-20) in the fall of 1989. She had joined the Navy to get away; away from a perpetually sad house, away from a life hurtling through Fishersville, Virginia, going nowhere, away from THE PLAN everyone else seemed to have tacked to an invisible bulletin board in their unimaginative minds. Away.

She'd decided upon a change in scenery at the end of a Saturday night with Dave, the latest in a string of boyfriends —key word being "boy." While Dave bowled, consumed a pitcher of beer, and hit on a flask of vodka stashed in the side pocket of his monogrammed ball bag, the night bled away at the Staunton Lanes. Afterwards it was a burger—her money —and a drive—her car—to the pullover up on Barren Ridge. Dave's idea of romance was telling Maggie he wanted to make the inside of her car look like a washing machine. Maggie said "yes" to Dave, because... she didn't know why. It hadn't occurred to her to say "no." So the inside of her car did end up looking like a washing machine; clothes scattered on the seats, floorboards and dash, windows fogged over with breath and sweat. He finished with nothing to spare, not exactly falling asleep or passing out, just... gone. He uttered a slurry, 'I love...' as he eased out of consciousness. The sick, sweet smell of beer sweat became unbearable, emerging on cue as if it purposely hid until the wash cycle ended.

She struggled out from under Dave, pulled her scattered clothing together and got out of the car naked. She got dressed in the late summer moonlight. She could see the lights of Wilson High School in the valley below and the outline of the two familiar little mountains, Betsy Belle and Mary Gray, further out on the horizon. Sitting on the hood of her car, she lit a Marlboro to clear her head. The incongruity of smoking a stinking cigarette to get over the lingering smell of her lover hit her on the second drag and she dropped it, still burning, on the ground. It's nice up here, she told herself, really nice. A pleasant smell drifted to her as the cigarette smoke distilled into the night. It connected to a forgotten memory. Magnolia? No. Honeysuckle. The vine grew along the rusty barbed wire fences on either side of the road. She saw herself as a child, picking the delicate white and yellow honeysuckle flowers, her mother showing her how to pinch off the end and pull the style through just so— not too hard and not too soft—to get a tiny drop of liquid to fall on her tongue. Her heart stirred at the memory of the nectar on her taste buds, intense and sweet, but only a tease, like an unkept promise. The contrast between the inside of her car and the Barren Ridge night grew clearer.

Dave. Sweat. Vodka. Stale.

Awake. Sweet. Honeysuckle. Breeze.

A chasm opened. It grew wider with each breath. The image of her mother and the remembered taste of honeysuckle was the final snowflake touching down on some unseen mountainside in her heart and mind. An avalanche of thoughts and emotions slid, unbidden into her world. If Dave had been watching, he would not have seen much, only her eyes closing slightly as she lifted her face into the night air. But he wasn't watching. He didn't know it, but Maggie Freeman was gone, even before she dropped him off to stagger up the steps to his house. She'd left him up on Barren Ridge along with Fishersville's expectations and a half smoked Marlboro.

She didn't go home after she dropped Dave off. A sense of mindfulness swept over her. Sleep seemed ludicrous. She drove, enjoying the bassy growl of her '68 Pontiac Catalina. The power in the machine's rebuilt V-8 400 cubic inch motor —she'd done it herself in her father's garage—was always ready to answer any question the local punks in their souped-up rice rockets wanted to ask at a red light. Fast enough? Try me. The Catalina's headlights spilled onto Route 250 as she cruised and thought. She was out in Monterey, Highland County when the sunrise caught her by surprise. She wheeled around at the Union 76 gas station and headed back east, hurrying to get home and catch a shower before work. Her mind hummed.

She was 21 years old. If she could have afforded college, she would have already been there. No relatives or friends lived far enough away to get her the kind of change her heart was calling for. She was not particularly pretty or particularly bright, but neither was she bad looking or dumb. Just an average girl. That was her assessment.

Cruising back through Staunton, she caught the light at the corner of Churchville Avenue and North Augusta. Straight ahead was the old Coca Cola bottling plant, abandoned in the 50's and converted into office space. It housed the Armed Forces Recruiting Station. Each pane of the first floor office windows sported a colorful poster. The center window displayed the classic white-bearded Uncle

Sam, finger outstretched, announcing that it was "YOU" he wanted. Right next to him, another poster, also a classic, showed a girl with a fetching smile, dressed in a sailor's cracker jack uniform with a white Dixie Cup hat perched coyly on her head. It read, "Gee I wish I were a man; I'd join the Navy." It was a lightning strike, the perfect image at the perfect moment. She'd driven past this place dozens—hundreds—of times on her way to and from Gypsy Hill Park. That's all it was; another sad old place in this sad old town. In the growing light of this new day, the nameless place became the doorway she would take to a new life. It clicked like the smell of honeysuckle on Baron's Ridge. The Navy. That would be a ticket to a whole new world. That would be a big enough change.

Her father was unimpressed. "Girls don't join the service unless they're sluts." he said matter-of-factly. And, "You ain't going nowhere. You're Fishersville... you'll always be Fishersville."

But she had gone somewhere. At lunch that day she drove back to Staunton and the recruiting center. She talked with a sailor wearing the same uniform as the girl in the poster. While the girl made it look sensual and inviting, the fresh faced young man made her feel like if she touched the creases in his pressed blue blouse it would cut her. A row of colorful ribbons on the left side of his chest were topped with a silver device consisting of two odd looking fish facing one another. The whole effect upon someone seeing this up close for the first time was mysterious, and exotic—a thought Maggie would laugh about a few short months hence, when she realized the recruiter was exotic the way the palm tree her wacky neighbor brought back from Florida was exotic: two hundred miles from the nearest naval facility, the recruiter was an island of Navy in a sea of farmland.

Buried at Sea

MS1 (SS) Ricky Cowen, Mess Management Specialist First Class, was quick to contradict Maggie's father. More and more women were joining up as the Navy offered new opportunities for them. No, she couldn't serve aboard submarines like him (that was the funny looking pin tacked to his chest, his "dolphins," and the ominous sounding "SS" tacked to the end of his title), but seagoing billets were opening up on a select number of surface ships for women who were willing to go to sea. When he asked Maggie about her vocational experience, the recruiter smiled broadly to learn she was a mechanic, the daughter of a mechanic.

"Ships need mechanics more than squirrels need nuts," he said. In a blur, Cowen drew up paperwork for her signature and set an appointment at the Armed Forces Examining and Entrance Station in Richmond.

Two days later Maggie rode a Greyhound east to the state capital and spent a restless night in the General Robert E. Lee hotel, a decrepit, roach infested establishment the Navy used to house its potential recruits, because it was equidistant from the bus station and AFEEs, and because, by the time a potential recruit made it this far, the Navy felt no need to impress them. She spent a long day taking aptitude tests and being paraded, poked and prodded by a set of doctors who looked as old and ramshackle as the General Lee. At the end of the day, when the Navy was finished with her, she felt like a package of meat wrapped in paper, stamped, and sitting on the butcher's counter at the Kroger.

The list of jobs she was most qualified for, matched against the current needs of the Navy, pointed to three ratings: Machinist Mate, Engineman, and Electrician's Mate, not surprisingly, all engineering jobs. Each of the ratings sounded like a good fit to Maggie. Before she got on the chartered bus back home, she signed what felt like 5000 documents, committing her to a four year enlistment, and a guaranteed billet in Machinist Mate Apprentice school at the Great Lakes Naval Training Center north of Chicago. Bootcamp would be in Orlando, the only place women recruits did their initial training, and was set to start the last week of June, only 8 weeks away. She returned to Fishersville feeling like she was a rocket on a launch pad and the countdown was running.

Bootcamp turned out to be a joke. All the images the title conjured up in her head—running till the point of falling down, drill instructors screaming obscenities in her face, marching in the rain—none of that happened. There were a lot of mind games, a lot of hustle and bustle to get her and her fellow company of recruits to the next training evolution on time, only to stand in formation for 45 minutes or an hour, motionless and silent, and an actual series of lectures where she was required to take notes on the precise way to fold every piece of clothing she'd been issued. It seemed to Maggie that the women who struggled the most with recruit training, struggled because they missed home, or a man, or both. She didn't miss either. She was here to get away from both—to go in a new direction and start a new life, and if the new life included a new way of folding clothes, well, it was tedious, but it wasn't Fishersville and it wasn't Dave's socks she was folding.

Maggie chose machinist because it was the best fit for her and it was the one thing she didn't want to leave behind. She loved working on anything with a motor. Blueprints and mechanics' manuals made sense to her in a way nothing else did. Finding your way around a problematic machine was easy; eventually the pieces would fit, the problem would yield, and the process would be over. Success. It frustrated her no end that other things didn't work the same way machines did. She had no feel for what a Navy Machinist Mate actually did, and since boot camp had nothing to do with any particular Navy job, she didn't think about it again until week four of recruit training, when her company attended a lecture on Navy ratings. It was then she realized machinists worked in ship's engine rooms, and it was then she learned that 99.3 percent of all Machinist Mates were male. If joining the Navy to get away from men had been a questionable proposition (and it was), choosing an engineering rating would shine a light on the point.

Maggie was the only person from her recruit company of 73 women who opted not to take leave following recruit training. She hadn't joined the Navy to go away for eight weeks and back home for two. Everyone else seemed desperate to run right back where they came from, but she wasn't. She drove to Great Lakes Naval Training Center north of Chicago for "A" school in a new Pontiac Firebird she bought as a 22nd birthday present to herself. Her birthday had come on the third day of boot camp, but she had not remembered it until a week later while writing down the date on another of the endless forms the Navy was always making them fill out. The powder blue Pontiac was her first new car, and the trip from Orlando north was the first time in her life she had ever felt totally free.

The nine weeks she spent learning the Navy's version of what a mechanic should be and do passed quickly. Orders came out for the class during week six. Everyone was going to ships. Destroyers, frigates and cruisers were the destinations of her male classmates. She was the only female in her class, so she had no idea what to expect for her first duty assignment. She opened a manila envelope stamped with her name and rate and pulled out a stapled sheaf of papers: her first set of orders. They read:

Report not later than 30 NOV 89 for permanent duty afloat USS *Redstone* (AR-20) report for duty as ship's company. Thirty days' leave authorized en route.

On graduation day from 'A' school, Maggie packed her Pontiac with the entirety of her possessions. Everything she owned fit in her dark green sea bag and a beat up Samsonite suitcase she'd picked up at a thrift store in Orlando after recruit training. The MM 'A' school graduation ceremony ended at a quarter past ten. She was on the highway, a hundred miles south of Chicago, before daylight faded.

Chapter 3
USS Redstone
November 1989, Pierside, Norfolk, Virginia

USS *Redstone* would have shocked anyone expecting to see the version of the Navy portrayed in "Join the Navy—See the World" advertising campaigns. She stuck out on the Norfolk waterfront, berthed among nuclear powered aircraft carriers and sleek cruisers and destroyers like a prehistoric creature exposed at a construction site, a relic of a bygone era. Her keel was laid down in 1939, and her construction was the sort requiring separate hull plates, individually riveted together to form her outer skin. Each plate aged differently, leaving bulges in some places and pock marks in others, giving the impression the old girl needed a girdle. Her bow came to a rounded gray point, pitted and dented, looking like the nose of a used up second rate boxer. Overall, *Redstone* looked as if every day of her 50 years on the Navy rolls had left its mark; she looked sad, tired, and ready for a long rest.

Maggie took in her first ship, walking up pier 7 of the Norfolk Naval Base. It took another stack of paperwork and several hours at the base pass office to get a sticker for her car so she could get on base. There she discovered that the military hierarchy extended to the parking lot. E-1 to E-3

16

parking was half a mile from the ship. It was an unusually cold and blustery afternoon for November, but she broke a sweat hauling her seabag, like a Plains Indian lugging her entire existence on her back. She carried a half-eaten apple in one hand and the manila envelope containing her orders in the other. She stopped several times to pull her hat down in a tug of war against the frigid wind blowing off the gray green water. She reached the gangway and started to climb. The sweat and the cold and the wind did not keep her from thinking about the significance of the moment. She flashed back to the night on Barren Ridge. What a change. I really did it. My first ship.

While she was very interested in her first ship, Maggie's first ship was indifferent to her. *Redstone* buzzed with activity. The ship was hours from getting underway for a three week cruise to Mayport, Florida, where she would provide maintenance services for the destroyer squadron homeported there. Maggie climbed to the top of the gangway all but unnoticed. The sharp salutes she gave, facing aft to the ensign and then to the Quarterdeck watch, were returned by a young-looking petty officer wearing a heavy green foul weather jacket and grungy blue ball cap with the ship's name and hull number across its front. He wiped a salute off the brim of his cap and quickly stuck his hands back into his jacket.

"Request perm..." she started.

"C'mon, c'mon aboard," the petty officer said. "Throw your bag over here for a minute and I'll get the duty WINS to come get ya. What's your rate?"

"Machinist Mate," she said.

The man arched an eyebrow at this. "Must be going to Repair Department," he said.

"I don't know," she said.

"Lemme see your orders," he said, taking the manila envelope and looking over the first page of the document, which seemed to be written mostly in a foreign language to her.

"I'll be. Well Freeman, says here, you're ship's company. Looks like you're going to be a part of MP division. First female that's gone there, that I know of." His tone didn't fill Maggie with confidence.

"What's MP division?" she asked.

He smirked. "Ohhhh man, are they gonna have a time with you. MP division? It stands for 'Mostly Pennsylvanians' 'cause all of them folks up there can't find work. Billy Joel. Allentown. Steel mills closed down. They end up in the Navy."

Maggie looked puzzled. The petty officer laughed. "You'll see. It's 'Main Propulsion', but it's mostly Pennsylvanians."

"Martin!" A man in khaki pants and the same heavy green coat stepped onto the Quarterdeck.

"Sir?" said the petty officer.

"Go get me the Bos'n, and tell him he better get his ass up here in a hurry. Who's this? Get the duty WINS up here to take care of her, and get her off the Quarterdeck; the crane's gonna be pulling this brow in about five minutes. What'r you looking at? Move your skinny ass before I start kickin' it."

Martin looked like a man tied by the wrists and pulled in two directions. He started to step forward, looked back over his shoulder at Freeman and changed his mind. He addressed the officer.

"Lt. Hiller?"

"What, Martin?"

"Freeman here is going to MP division...."

The officer looked at Maggie. He was short for a man, perhaps only an inch taller than she was, and he slouched, making him even shorter. Plain brown hair inexpertly hacked to Navy regulations by ship's barbers stuck out from under his khaki piss cutter officer's cap. His eyes were not unfriendly, but shiny, black, and intense. He reached for the same set of orders Martin had just interpreted for her and scanned them.

He grunted. "Main Propulsion division, eh? Where are you from, Pennsylvania?"

"No sir. Virginia, sir," she said, remembering what Martin had told her, half a second too late.

Hiller smirked. "Well, Freeman, you're going to be the first woman in MP division. I'm the Chief Engineer, Lt. Hiller. You'll need to get a place in WINS berthing to stow your gear and then we'll get you checked into engineering department. BM3 Martin is going to help you get there now." Martin, get a move on, and don't forget to send me the Bos'n." He paused and beamed a smile on her. "Welcome aboard!"

Martin glanced at Hiller, then Freeman. A looked passed over his face that Maggie couldn't read. He pointed toward a watertight door with a flick of his head. "Let's go," he said.

Once inside the door Martin led Maggie through a maze of passageways and ladderwells she was sure she would never be able to retrace. Lugging her seabag kept her off balance and on edge, expecting at any moment she'd go for a spill down the hard steel steps. Finally they arrived at a gray door stenciled with foot high white letters, reading WINS BERTHING. Below this, also in white, was the warning: no men admitted without escort.

Martin said, "WINS. This'll be where you get your rack and stow your gear." He rapped the door rapidly three times and waited. He looked at Maggie and said, "Let me give you a heads up, Freeman. You be careful of Lt. Hiller. You're...

well...." he looked down at his shoes. He seemed embarrassed. In an instant, she was transported to a hallway in Wilson Memorial High School, conversing with some fumbling, nervous boy.

"I'm what?" Maggie said.

"Never mind," Martin said.

"No. You started it. I'm what?"

He hesitated again. Maggie frowned and pursed her lips.

"You're kinda pretty. Ok?"

Kind of pretty. Maggie considered this. She flashed back to the hallway again. She saw in an instant that small town pretty and Navy pretty were close relatives. She knew she'd never be the prettiest girl at the party, and was reconciled to the fact. What this might mean aboard the *Redstone* was a mystery to her. Maggie began to flush, unsure if this was a warning or a come on. At the last instant she decided there was a sincerity in Martin's tone that kept her anger in check.

"I don't know what you're talking about," she said. "And what would an officer be doing, looking at me? Isn't that against the rules? Isn't it against the rules for anyone here to get involved like that?"

Martin rolled his eyes. "You've got a lot to learn. Don't you know what they call this ship? They call it "The Love Boat." There's more hanky panky goin' on on this ship than a soap opera. Officers hookin' up with officers, enlisted with enlisted, officers and enlisted. You name it. They got a sayin' around here: 'what goes on on deployment stays on deployment.' Not many of 'em round here stay out of the game, especially when we're on the other side of the Pond. Stuff goes on you wouldn't believe." He hesitated again and looked either way. When he continued he spoke so lowly Maggie had to lean in to hear. "But I never saw the Cheng treat anyone, especially a newbie and an engineer, like he just treated you. Folks in his department say he's too much in love with his self to notice anyone else. Maybe I was just seeing stuff, but...."

The door to WINS opened. A woman dressed in a khaki uniform with Chief Petty Officer anchors on her collars stood in the open doorway. Martin took a final glance at Maggie's face and addressed the Chief. "Chief, this is Freeman. Cheng told me to get her down here so you could get her a rack."

The woman gave Maggie a cursory up-and-down sweep with her eyes. "I got her, Martin," she said. "Freeman, grab your seabag and follow me."

Chapter 4

Haze Gray and Underway

December 1989, sea and anchor detail,
outbound Hampton Roads

Maggie barely had time to stow her gear before *Redstone* got underway. She hustled up to the main deck and found an out of the way corner of the foc'sle to watch, as Martin and the other sailors of Deck Division took in all lines. From her vantage point she saw a cluster of khaki clad officers scurrying back and forth on the bridge wings. Two of them wore blue ball caps with gold scrambled egg braiding of senior officers. One, an unassuming little man, she guessed was the CO.

Captain Ralph Shumate, Commanding Officer of *Redstone*, observed the well-orchestrated moves transforming his ship from "building 20" on the Norfolk waterfront, to haze gray and underway. Building 20. He mused at the moniker given *Redstone* in the early 80's when she fell out of the regular deployment schedule for the better part of four years and languished at pier 5, more an immobile repair shop than a US Navy ship. Not anymore. The ship was underway all the time. Shumate strolled to the opposite bridge wing as two tugs swung her into the channel. Chief Warrant Officer Pete Baber, the "Bos'n" and Dive

Officer, approached him going the opposite direction, speaking orders calmly into the walkie talkie clipped to his green foul weather jacket. The squirrel-like Executive Officer scrambled to keep up with him; she wore the bewildered look Shumate was growing familiar with in his second in command. Baber rolled his eyes as they passed each other. Shumate smiled. They were old dogs in a new world. The clock would run out on their careers before they learned any real new tricks, like how to get along with women aboard their ship.

Shumate was a career Navy pilot. He flew A-6's and had diligently worked through the career progression, which should have led him to command of a big deck aviation platform— a helo carrier or full sized aircraft carrier. He took orders to *Redstone* because he saw the candle of his career flickering and guessed it would be his last opportunity for command at sea and a longshot chance of getting a carrier, making flag rank, or both. It wasn't looking good. Cuts in the number of conventionally powered carriers in favor of their nuclear powered sisters left him one wrung short on the ladder. He had never checked the nuclear power box. God knew when he would have managed to get that done in a career that included combat missions over Vietnam and two tours at the Pentagon—everything his detailers told him he needed to do. It wasn't fair, he thought. I did everything right, and I still won't have a chair when the music stops. He leaned on the wall of the port bridge wing as *Redstone* passed Elizabeth River Buoy 3 and headed for the channel opening over the Hampton Roads Bridge Tunnel. Looking out he saw a massive haze gray object materializing in the vicinity of Thimble Shoals light. At the same time the Officer of the Deck called out, "*Nimitz*, sir. Pass the word to render honors?"

Shumate nodded. This was rubbing salt in the wound. The two ships closed fast. The Boatswain's Mate of the Watch sounded attention as the huge aircraft carrier's sleek bow came even with the battered nose of *Redstone*. All hands stood and saluted. Shumate craned his neck looking up at the con of the mighty vessel far above him. After what felt like an impossibly long time, the carrier's stern appeared. The Boatswain sounded 'carry on.' Shumate dropped his salute and went back to leaning glumly against the wall of the bridge wing.

Half a mile further along the channel a fisherman near the Chesapeake Bay Bridge Tunnel called *Redstone* on the bridge to bridge radio channel 16. Shumate heard the cackle of the radio and a salt encrusted voice:

"Hey, Navy vessel 20, outbound, this is Fishing Fly, Channel 16.".

The Officer of the Deck nodded to his JOOW, telling him to answer up.

"Fishing Fly, this is Navy vessel 20, go ahead."

"Yeah, uh, is that the old *Redstone* I see? That old girl still seaworthy??"

The JOOW smiled. "Yes sir this is *Redstone*," and feeling the power that for no apparent reason accompanies mouths near amplifiers he added, "Yes sir, *Redstone*... Fast Attack Repair Tender 20."

Fishing Fly keyed up their mic and laughed into it. "OK, *Redstone*, I got it, yeah, Fast-Attack-Repair -Tender 20, FART 20! Haww!"

Shumate listened to this from just outside the open door of the bridge wing, his hands gripping the half bulkhead. Yes, here he was, one wrung short on the ladder and bound to be here forever. His career, which included bombing runs over Vietnam and night landings on carriers, would end on an ugly remnant of a boat, a floating piece of refuse. The OOD noticed too late his captain's proximity to the radio and all that had been said. He misidentified the slight upturn of the Old Man's lips as humor. Actually, it was a pained grimace at the sun of his career setting, shining its dying rays in his eyes.

Below, Maggie Freeman's career was just dawning. She adjusted to life on *Redstone* quickly. She forgot about the ominous conversation with BM3 Martin in the frenetic pace of checking aboard and the excitement of being at sea for the first time in her life.

The open ocean turned out to be something altogether different from what she expected. Maggie had been near the ocean only once in her twenty two years—a week's vacation in Myrtle Beach the year before her mother abandoned them. The water crashing onto the beach there was green and opaque. It smelled and looked like something malevolent; a veil over something dead or dying. When she emerged from swimming in it, she immediately wanted to shower to get its essence off of her.

The first time she went topside, after *Redstone* passed Chesapeake Light 13 miles off shore, she stood at the lifelines, hypnotized by the deepest blue she had ever seen. The taste of salt on her lips and the sun playing through clouds like a thousand spotlights on an infinite stage, held her fast. The sea. It didn't fit in her mind. It spilled out. *There is nothing like it,* she thought. She felt it and tasted it more than she saw it and smelled it. She felt small in a contented way. Appropriately small. It was like God opened a curtain and invited her to look at something everyone didn't get to see. Vastness and motion. From the first time she stood on the weather decks underway, Maggie was in love with being at sea. She found a secluded set of bitts near the ship's fantail which served as her deck chair where she took any and every opportunity to sit and let it wash over her.

Working in engineering turned out to be both harder and easier than she imagined. Easier because the work was interesting and her mechanically inclined mind quickly grasped the fundamentals of *Redstone*'s antiquated 400psi steam plant, harder because standing watch four hours at a pop in the whirring, clanging, hellishly hot main engineering spaces felt as if she was not working *on* an engine as much as she was working *in* one. Even with yellow foamy ear plugs rolled up and stuffed in her ears underneath blue plastic hearing protectors, the noise was apocalyptic and resonated in her body a minimum of thirty minutes after getting off watch. To beat the heat, her male counterparts slipped their arms out of the tops of their dark blue coveralls and tied the sleeves around their waists, leaving their dingy, white, sweated-soaked t-shirts exposed. Maggie resisted the urge to join them. She was not self-conscious about her body—had never been—but swimming in this sea of men, it felt wrong. She proved herself the equal of any of the other five engineering newbies—all men—who were also making their first cruise on *Redstone*. She mildly resented the feeling of being a mascot, which accompanied being the only woman in MP division, but in the manner of all sailors, the ship, the officers and life at sea gave them common enemies, challenges and rhythm that quickly blurred her gender and theirs and tended toward the camaraderie of shared suffering and adventure.

Maggie also discovered she was not inclined to seasickness. Many of her shipmates battled it during the brief jaunt to Florida. Their pale, dead-eyed look reminded her of the last few hours of her grandmother's life before she passed. It didn't look fun at all. If anything, she enjoyed it when the ship moved more than its usual gentle fore and aft, side to side pitch and roll. Everyone else might not want it, but she hoped they'd get into some heavy weather. But the trip from Norfolk to Mayport was a smooth one, and after a leisurely three day cruise, *Redstone* turned into the St. Johns River and tied up at the Naval Station destroyer piers.

Mayport was sleepy and hot compared to Norfolk's chilly weather and congestion. Things moved slower here; the very weight of the air insisted upon it.

"Ain't nothin' to do in Mayport except drink," one of her fellow engineers told her.

Maggie had never been much for alcohol, and most of the crew of *Redstone* still retained the bonds of friendship forged during her recent deployment. That left her without a natural liberty buddy. This was not a problem for her. A single beer in a koozie and a walk by herself along the beach suited her just fine. Having the recent experience of the sea, the real sea, under her belt made the beach seem different. She knew what was out there now and it made her more genial toward the beach and the waves scratching the edge of the great blue garment. She walked every afternoon the ship was there, appreciating more and more the contrast between where she was now and where she had been just six months ago. Remembering the ominous warning from Martin, the sailor who'd escorted her to WINS on that first day, well, she had not even seen the Chief Engineer. She liked her new life, immersed in men but attached to none of them.

Redstone left Mayport after a week of repair work on the destroyers homeported there, and made her way back to Norfolk. The second day out, the ship passed through the edge of a small storm. Maggie awoke to the increased heaving of the ship and got dressed quickly. Making her way aft, she surfaced from mine shaft darkness into a gray so complete she had to hold onto the handle of the water-tight door until she oriented herself. It seemed the sky and the water and the ship were all one thing; only the sound of the sea and the movement of the deck underfoot contradicted her eyes. She moved to the port side life lines, feeling her way as if walking to the edge of a cliff, and made her way to the stern post. She peered over the stern, attempting to see the ship's wake. Bits of the gray sky broke off in the wind. She blinked to keep her eyes clear. In minutes she was wet to the skin, but had no thought of going below. The isolation of the fantail and the gray morning loosed her from being either a sailor or an engineer. She felt like she was flying. The whoosh whoosh of the ship pressing against the water, pushing it aside, and the steady thrum of the propulsion plant, conducting rhythmically through the hull up and into her feet, were the sense of power in her airplane. Standing with her back to everything, facing the ocean's blankness, she smiled. It was good to be here.

A form materialized at her elbow, startling her. She stifled a gasp and drew in a sharp breath. Saliva, rain and sea foam caught in her throat and choked her. Her eyes watered.

"Whoa, there... y' all right? Need a slap on the back?" the figure said, gesturing.

"No... No...," she hacked, "Just... went... down... the wrong way." Maggie's eyes were streaming. Her vision was blurred.

"What went down the wrong way? You aren't drinking anything."

"My, my, uhh," she didn't want to say it but wasn't swift enough to think of anything but the truth. "My own spit, I guess," she said, finally looking up into the eyes of her visitor. It was the Cheng. "Ah, ohh, uhh, sir."

"Sir what?" he said.

"I mean I swallowed... ahh... my own spit, sir."

28

The Cheng looked at her for a moment and then a long, snorting laugh erupted from his face. "I swallowed my own spit... *SIR*. That's pretty good, Freeman. Glad you got your 'sir' and your 'spit' sorted out."

The Cheng remembered her name. She had not seen him since coming aboard. Her man-boy collision avoidance system went off. She told it to shut up.

"What 'r you doing out here all alone?" he asked.

"I woke up and noticed we were moving differently than last night, sir. I wanted to see why, so I came out here."

The Cheng looked forward. "Not too smart to be out on deck alone. Fall in there with no one to see it and you're pretty much done. Better to have a partner."

"Yes, sir. I'll be careful, sir." Avoidance system again. Something in his inflection on the word 'partner.' She told it to shut up again.

The Cheng slung an arm around the sternpost. Maggie thought for an instant he was going to sling it around her and she moved slightly to avoid it, feeling stupid when it became obvious he wasn't making a move toward her. She had dressed and come on deck so quickly she'd forgotten to grab a hat. Her hair whipped around her head like a sail loose in the wind. She'd let it grow out since the trimming at boot camp, and long black strands flayed her eyes and smacked the Cheng's khaki jacket. At the same moment she realized this was happening and started to restrain it, he reached out a hand and brushed a strand of hair into place behind her ear. His hand lingered on her face for an instant.

Fixing her with his dark, intense eyes, he said, "Better get yourself below and dried off," and walked away.

Her man-boy collision avoidance system would not turn off this time. Nope, not shutting up. The Cheng touched her. She was accustomed to being touched by men. She knew touches and she knew touches. She knew looks in the eyes and she knew looks in the eyes. This was not a friendly gesture. It was not violent in any way but it violently upset her and... intrigued her? Excited her? No. Yes. The storm, which had attracted her to the weather decks and made the ship come alive with its motion and noise was now inside her head. She felt dizzy. Seasickness? Not a bother. This? This was a problem. Her face was hot. She felt exposed, naked. She looked around her to see if she really was alone; feeling someone must be watching. Scanning the structure before her, she realized how isolated this spot was from the rest of the ship. No one who had not been within the fifteen foot radius of the teakwood deck making up the fantail could have seen her and the Cheng together. She retreated to the superstructure and quickly entered the skin of the ship, dogging down the watertight door behind her, shutting out the wind and rain and sound.

Making her way back to her rack through dark passageways, she touched the place where the Cheng's hand had been expecting to feel something. A mark? It didn't make sense to her. She wasn't a school girl. Why was her head spinning? An avalanche of unwanted, disconnected thoughts slid into her mind: the first fumbling boy she'd let lie on top of her; the day her mother left her father, their home, her; the tenth grade English teacher who told her she could write well, but looked at her breasts instead of her eyes. It made her head hurt. Suddenly, she wasn't so sure she'd gotten away from anything when she left Fishersville. It was all here and she was still the same girl she'd always been.

Reaching her rack and dropping her wet clothes on the deck, she scrubbed herself dry with a coarse white Navy towel that smelled like bleach and felt as if it might crack if she folded it too quickly. She drew on dry underwear and a t-shirt and laid down under the scratchy gray blanket they'd given her when she checked aboard.

The ship still moved violently. No one had stirred when she got up or came back. No one noticed her. She was alone in a room with a hundred other women—that was familiar. That felt normal. That made her head slowly begin to stop spinning. She realized she'd always been alone in the world of women. Men? Men were easier to navigate. They wanted one thing. Once you knew what that one thing was and how you felt about it, you could find your way around in the world of men. Having a man was like having a car—a way to get where you wanted to go. She didn't think this, so much as she wore it like a suit—a way of protecting herself in a world full of confusing, unanswerable questions: who am I? how did I get here? where am I going? That night up on Barren Ridge, the suit had ripped momentarily. Now, in the dark, swaying, berthing compartment of the USS *Redstone*, Maggie wondered why she felt so naked. The old suit was still there. Maybe the Cheng would mend the rip.

Chapter 5
Different Road, Same Vehicles
December 1989, Pierside, Norfolk, Virginia

Maggie and the Chief Engineer became lovers less than a month after *Redstone* returned to Norfolk from her stint in Mayport. The holiday stand down, which began the day the ship pulled in, created the perfect conditions for the two of them to connect. One of them had no interest in going home; the other had no home to go to. It left them living on a ship with a bare minimum of people, none of whom had much in the way of gainful employment. It was quiet and boring, and most of the officers and crew occupied themselves with card games, board games, and, in a few select berthing areas inhabited by nerds with too much time on their hands, Nintendo.

Maggie played her own game. It had been too easy for her. The Kabuki dance of movements designed to communicate interest to men was transparent to her; as unthinking as putting on her clothes, yet also deliberate. It was a pattern she had discovered at fourteen years old, the first time she discovered her power to attract the male of the species, and she was guilty of exploiting it, always with plausible deniability, even to herself. She never stopped to question if she was the one being played, or that here on

Redstone, the game might have different rules and a different goal line.

She and the Chief Engineer were like iron filings in a magnetic field, showing up in the same spaces of the ship at the same time. It didn't surprise her when the Cheng made an appearance at a bar she and several engineers hit up the day after their duty day. She pretended not to notice, a week later, that she was the only one of those same engineers not tasked with a project that kept them onboard, leaving her free to make her way to that bar. She managed to keep up the charade when the Cheng walked through the door, but somewhere between her barstool and his glossy black Camaro, she dropped the pretense.

At first it had been fun in the way the beginnings of all love affairs are fun; novelty, secret knowledge, seeing things from a set of relationship bifocals. The thrill of flaunting the Navy's rules for good order and discipline and of keeping a big secret, she admitted to herself, added to the otherwise unremarkable sex. But soon she found herself in an uncomfortable bubble, protected from many of the harsh realities of life as a *Redstone* snipe by her lover's patronage, but feared by her fellow engineers for the same reason. In the everyday life of the ship's engineering department, she became a caste of one, an untouchable leper. Budding relationships with the men of her watch section that had begun to form during the Mayport trip mutated from camaraderie and jovial conversations into cold shoulders and stunted one line exchanges, followed by knowing glances behind her back.

The process of becoming a qualified watchstander, and thus a useful human being instead of a no load, also mutated. Maggie was truly interested in learning about the engineering plant, how it worked and how the individual members of the main space watch did their part to keep the ship hot, lit and moving. Becoming "the Cheng's woman" compromised her ability to talk with the people who could teach her the most.

Learning to be a shipboard engineer begins at the same place, regardless of whether you are officer or enlisted; have a master's in engineering or a high school equivalency: tracing systems. You're handed a diagram of say, the Auxiliary Steam system, and off you go to locate each pipe, pump, valve and gadget from one end to the other. On *Redstone* the hunt was intensified by years of modifications, some appearing on the diagrams, and some not. If the outside of the ship looked like a plump woman in need of a girdle, the insides were a fantastic voyage inside the old girl's guts. Maggie was one of the few who didn't mind the looks of *Redstone*, inside or out. As the New Year came and went and the crew returned to their normal in-port routine, she took on system tracing like a kid playing a greasy game of hide and seek.

Her effort and enthusiasm for tracing out systems got the attention of the leading enlisted man in MP division, Senior Chief Boiler Technician Sam Snell. Snell, a thirty year veteran, was no fan of women in general and women in the Navy specifically. Maggie didn't know it, but she single-handedly broke down an iron door in Snell's attitude by simply paying attention to what he said and working as hard as any man he'd ever seen. It was true that she needed help lifting things most of the guys could carry on their own, but not often, and she never waited for anyone to tell her that something needed to be moved in the first place. The salty old Senior Chief couldn't help but admire her initiative. She also knocked over his barriers by taking all the shit dished out by everyone to the only girl. She didn't turn into a blubbering mess and she didn't back down.

The more he saw of the girl, the more he saw her fitting into a plan. Snell was convinced of the value of having both of the ratings in MP division: the Boiler Technicians and the Machinist Mates, being able to perform each other's underway watchstanding duties. He saw how it would have benefited the division during the last deployment. Sometimes one of the ship's four boilers needed the attention of extra BT's to perform maintenance. It would be a great advantage to use MMs to stand the boiler watches, to free up more men to do the work. The same held true for doing maintenance on the MM's equipment.

There was a lot of resistance to his idea. He got nowhere with the snipes. An old hand who knew his idea was no place to pop his collar and pull rank, he saw a different way to skin this cat in the person of Maggie Freeman. She was eager to learn and didn't care whether it was boilers or turbines. He would train her in both areas and use her to shame the boys into doing the same. So MMFA Maggie Freeman was indoctrinated into the duties of both the Machinist Mate of the Watch (MMOW) and the Boiler Technician of the Watch (BTOW), and her first eight months aboard *Redstone* flew by.

She felt at home in the ship's main spaces and was amused at how much it reminded her of her father's garage. It was like wearing a familiar set of clothes. Sweaty men, salty language, dirty jokes. All normal, all native to her except for one thing; this garage sometimes moved to the other side of the world. And *Redstone*'s next trip to the other side of the world was closer than anyone aboard the old ship knew.

Chapter 6
Proposition
August 1976, Pierside, Naples, Italy

Jasper was wrong on one count. The trip to the commercial piers did get him and his fellow engineers a brief stint of liberty. True to the normal course of Navy tasking, the present crisis overrode and pushed out the previous crisis. In this case the debate about how to stow the treasures of the long dead Egyptian king snuffed out all but some relatively simple work on a few temporary bulkheads in the women's berthing compartment. Once Jasper and his crew completed the work, which took only half a day, the Cheng and the Suppo deadlocked over who was responsible for the incoming precious cargo. In a move meant to convey how little he cared about this silly distraction to his preparations for the outchop OPPE, the Cheng called his welders together and sent them ashore for a forty-eight hour liberty. It was a middle finger to the Suppo, who had been acting like a pharaoh himself, tasking the engineering department from on high with demands to build a metal tomb within *Redstone* to house the treasures. No welders, no fabrication. Let the womanish old bastard figure out how to get things done with his manicured posse of Storekeepers. His snipes would be enjoying Naples.

So it was that on the Wednesday and Thursday of the week following his conversation with RM1 Russel, Jasper Phipps found himself at his favorite bar in town, a famously seedy establishment run by a Brit expat named Riley. Riley claimed he had no other name, first or middle; that whatever nomenclature he'd started out with in life had rubbed off in hard living and harder drinking. Riley's was in a section of the oldest, narrowest streets in the ancient city and had no sign directing patrons to its front door. The clientele found Riley's like flies find decay.

When the Cheng cut him and his men loose, following quarters, Phipps walked directly off *Redstone's* gangway, caught a cab, and slipped into the bar. He didn't shower, brush his teeth or change clothes. He intended to get filthy drunk and had no misgivings about letting his personal hygiene reflect it.

Certain establishments—mainly those serving seagoing men of the world—don't have operating hours. In a real port town there are always enough customers looking to slake their thirst, even at the most pedestrian times of day. Phipps was settled into the dimmest corner of the bar, nursing a third generously-full glass of whiskey long before the populace of the city woke up to their first cappuccinos and began bringing their ancient city to life.

Street sounds barely reached Riley's. The only noises were a faint screech of steel on steel from a distant rail car, and a cat making much the same sound in the alley, just outside the door. Phipps ignored both. He concentrated on the single ice cube in the tumbler, giving up its watery shape a single drop at a time as it diluted his spirits.

The door opened, a weak beam of morning sunlight tried reluctantly to penetrate the bar, then fled as it clunked shut.

A *Redstone* sailor stepped in and scanned the room with sun-blind pupils. Phipps kept his head down, trying to remain unseen, but the man spotted him. The sawed off, stocky blonde from California, with the unfortunate name Richard Richards came to his table and stood. Phipps had introduced Richards to Riley's the first time the ship touched land in Naples, over seven months ago. The man happened to walk off the brow at the same time he did and asked where he was headed. Without thinking, he'd said Riley's, and Richards came along like a stray cat.

The man reminded Phipps of the guys in cheesy television info-mercials; always louder than the background; always smiling about something they knew but you couldn't figure out. His round face was pock-marked with tiny craters, remnants of a bad case of teenage acne. Disproportionately large, bulging eyes of glow-in-the-dark blue hung over his face like they were about to drop out and roll around like marbles. He was a Shopkeeper Chief Petty Officer, a topsider who, like Phipps's friend Russel, knew more about the daylight world of ship's tasking and timing than the snipes sentenced to get the ship to her tasks on time.

Double Dick, or DD was how Richards was known, behind his back by his sailors and to his face in the Chief's Mess. DD was an equal opportunity drinker on the beach, and was one of those people whose level of inebriation magnified an already annoying personality to the point of being unbearable. His favorite topic was money; the value of any object in his field of vision set him into an endless stream of words like "monetization" and "depreciation" and "cash flow." When he was into his cups, Richards frequently explained to waitresses how prostitution made more sense than being a table jockey; a practice which killed his tablemate's chances with the waitresses and made him the most unpopular liberty buddy on the ship.

"Phipps!" Richards bellowed. "Knew you'd be here, boy." He slapped both hands down on the table and leaned into Phipps's face, elbows craned out, eyes bulging. He paused waiting for an invitation Phipps wouldn't have given his own mother. Ignoring the ignoring, he lowered himself into a chair. "Round on me!" he yelled over his shoulder.

"Richards," Phipps said, forgoing the use of the man's rank—SOP for Riley's, "you're using a seventeen hundred voice at Oh nine hundred. Tone it down, man."

Richards leaned away from the table and pushed the protesting chair back onto two legs.

"Aw, Phippsy, are we sore about somethin'? It's drunk-o-clock and a great day away from haze gray." He cocked his head to one side and curled his lips into a sneering grin.

A waitress materialized out of the gloomy far side of the bar with a tumbler and a bottle of bourbon. She poured for the new customer silently and gestured to Phipps for a refill. He waved her off. She ambled back into the shadows at a sleepy pace. Phipps had a pace of drunk in his head like a marathon runner timing his miles. He didn't expect these two to be around when he pushed through the wall where the amateurs turned back or went flat.

Richards looked hurt. "Something wrong with my money or my booze?" he said, still too loudly.

"Nothing at all Dou... Richards," Phipps answered, barely slicing off the nickname before it escaped his lips.

Richards squenched his eyes to slits. "Good. Phipps, good." He flipped the chair forward onto all four legs. It thudded on the wood floor. He rubbed his mouth with the back of one hand and then the other before gulping down the generous glass of whisky.

His eyes watered and he sputtered a bit. Phipps gave him a contemptuous look. Richards scooted his bulky frame as close as he could get to the table and said in a whisper as annoyingly low as the loud voice he'd been using; "What do you think of the cargo we're gonna haul back to the States? Guess you know all about it, having to cut and weld a space for it."

Phipps didn't come to Riley's to talk shop. He didn't come to Riley's to talk. He tried to make this fact come out of his eyes and expression. Richards either didn't get it or didn't care. He persisted. "You know it's priceless stuff. Any single item in the shipment is worth more than both of us will earn in our lifetime...." his whisper trailed off into the gloom like the waitress.

Phipps, growing more annoyed by the minute at the intrusion into his drinking, said, "The hell should I care? Think they're gonna give us a bonus for carrying the shit to Norfolk? Now how about either shuttin' up and letting me drink or finding yourself someplace else to run that mouth?"

Richards was nonplussed. He got up and Phipps thought he'd won, but he only moved his chair closer; so close Phipps could smell his Brute aftershave mixed with his whiskey breath.

"I know you call me Double Dick," he said, with an odd little grin, inches from his face. "I know. But don't let what you think of me get in the way of being rich." He leaned back and cocked his head to one side. Phipps could see his face in full. The look wasn't the smarmy infomercial man. It was crafty and intelligent and somehow compelling. He sighed.

"Go ahead, Richards, I give, but for God's sake, give me some space. Can't even bend my drinkin' elbow with you sittin' so close."

Richards looked pleased as he dutifully scooted his chair back a full half inch. "I can't let too much space between us,

Phipps. What I've got to say can only fall from my mouth into your ear and nowhere else."

Phipps sighed. "Get on with it, man. Spare the drama."

"I got called into the Suppo's office just after quarters this morning. You know, the guy is the most laid back of all the khaki in the ward room. Always been that way. Easy to get along with. Leaves me to run my shop. But today he was nuts. He's stressing over this Egyptian stuff like nothing I've seen." Richards paused and smiled the sly smile again. "So much so that he's given me a blank check... a free hand to do whatever needs to be done to make sure the transfer goes off without a hitch. From what he said, this deal goes way beyond just sending some stuff to US museums. This is about US—Arab relations. The *President* himself is involved. It's a big, big deal, Phippsy."

Phipps took a swig of whiskey. The ice cube clinked. It was still more interesting to him than this conversation.

"Suppo gave me the job of tracking each item we receive. I know every piece that will come aboard and every crate. I've got the list. I've got the numbers. As I went through it, a thought came to me." Richards leaned in close again and lowered his voice even more. "What if one of those crates was numbered wrong? How do we really know what's in them? We're being asked to sign for things—priceless things—that we may not ever put our eyes on. I started to bring it up to the Suppo, but then I had another thought. If one of those crates goes missing, who's gonna tell the Arabs? And if the Arabs did find out one of those crates went missing, what are they gonna do about it? You see?" He wiped one hand and then the other across his mouth again, greedily. "Then I saw it! No one's gonna do anything! No one's gonna want to admit it! That would be an international incident! The Arabs would keep their mouths shut and so would we!"

His eyes gleamed with the glint of an ancient grave robber. "I mean it can't be something major, something obvious. But if it was something small; something most people don't even think about when they think of King Tut... well maybe it could disappear. So I went through the lading list to see if there was anything that fit the bill. And there it was. One crate. It only contains three things. They have to be small because the dimensions of the crate are listed. It's the size of a sea chest. In it there is an amulet, a ring, and something called a pectoral necklace. I looked up "amulet" in the dictionary. It's a good luck charm... something to protect you against evil."

Phipps said, "Richards I've got exactly 48 hours of liberty. It's the first 48 hours I've been off that hulk in a month. I'll be damned if I'm gonna use another minute of it on your little social studies lesson. Now you either piss off or shut your pie hole while you watch me drink." He paused and added, "Or there ain't no am-a-lat that's gonna keep me from putting a fist in your yapper."

Richards smiled the same stupid smile. "I'll finish the lesson in less than a minute. One minute to make you and me rich. I'm gonna alter the lading list. The chest will officially cease to exist. I will make it disappear on paper and you will make it disappear into the belly of *Redstone*. Simple. A few extra welds, a false bulkhead wide enough to stow the chest and it's done. Fifteen minute's work between the two of us, for a million dollar payday. How's that for an hourly wage?!"

Phipps began to squeeze his whiskey glass. His anger; anger at sitting in the toilet bowl of Naples Bay for three extra weeks, anger at thirty straight days choking on acrid weld smoke without a liberty or a simple thank you from any part of the chain of command; anger at having his work reordered and rerouted half a dozen times, all of this found

42

its way into his hand around the glass; all this and now this idiot who wouldn't or couldn't shut up. A weaker vessel would have shattered in his working man's strong hand, but the thick old tumbler took it, the only sign of the energy flowing into it, a rattle as his hand shook.

Without putting the glass down, Phipps raised a thick finger to Richards's face, ready to make good on the threat to throttle the man. As he raised the hand he saw two things at once— the angry red streak of a fresh burn running across his wrist, the result of a bit of slag nestling down between his welder's gloves and coveralls long enough to add to his collection of scars and, momentarily glistening in the light reflected from the mirror behind the bar, the smooth gold surface of Riley's best whiskey in his glass. It sloshed out with perfect aim, wetting the fresh wound. The alcohol stung like a yellow jacket from his Kentucky youth. The pain momentarily interrupted the anger, and gave it a different focus than the man sitting in front of him.

The insanity of Navy life, the system that took you in as a human being and recreated you as a cog, a function, no longer a human being but a human doing, dawned on Jasper Phipps. It wasn't the first time he'd seen it, but for some reason this time it was more clear than it had ever been.

Hand still shaking, he dropped the glass back on the table. He took a questionable looking cloth napkin and dabbed at the burn. *Why use a napkin?* he thought. *I'm just an animal. I should lick my wounds like a dog. All I do is exist.* In a flash the insanity of Richards's scheme to steal the treasure and the insanity of continuing to do what he'd always done collided. A shadow crossed his brow. Richards mistook it for rejection and started to get up.

"Ok, Phipps. Ok. Let's forget about this," he said, "no need to mention it to anyone."

Phipps looked into Richards's blue bulging eyes and laughed. His mouth compressed into a tight-lipped line. He wiped his face again nervously.

"Don't drag anchor on me now, Double Dick," Phipps said. "Just how big is that box we need to tuck away?"

Chapter 7
The Chief Engineer
December 1989, Pierside, Norfolk, Virginia

Mal Hiller wanted Maggie Freeman immediately. He didn't spend much time analyzing why. He was a man who reserved analysis for things with engines. Everything else was either too hard or too stupid to burn brain cells over, especially women. His first (and only) wife had divorced him after a long five years. If asked about it, he would say he was married for eighteen dog years, and there was no doubt in his tone who the bitch in the relationship was. The woman didn't understand the two things that mattered to him: the Navy and motors. When he volunteered for back to back to back deployments on ships that needed a good engineer, she packed up and moved back home. The last stretch was seventeen straight months when he walked off his ship's gangway in Rota, Spain—the last stop on her Med deployment—and up the gangway of another ship arriving for her own stint in the Med. He didn't give it a second thought. They needed an engineer. He was an engineer. Logic.

When he finally arrived in Norfolk, he found no one waiting on the pier, and no one answering the home phone, only a "this number is no longer in service" message. He took a cab to his apartment in Larchmont, and found it occupied by a hacking, middle aged woman who looked and smelled as if she'd smoked so many cigarettes she'd become one. Between deep, wet coughing spasms she told him she never heard of him or his wife and said she had been living there just under a year. She did know the number to the real estate company managing the apartments and let him use her phone. They only confirmed what Smoky told him; his wife didn't live here anymore. She'd let the lease run out and moved about a year ago. Hiller tried to remember the last time he'd spoken with his wife or received a letter and realized he couldn't recall either.

On the ride back to the ship in the cab, he came to another realization, one much harder to bear—all his tools were gone. A week later a notice of divorce proceedings came in the mail. A month after that, he signed and returned a document agreeing to a no contest divorce. He hadn't communicated with his wife in the five years since. *Over is over*, he thought. Of course there was the little matter of the tools he was out. He'd done some detective work to find them: ten thousand dollars' worth of Snap On hand tools in two separate rolling boxes, plus the tools he'd earned, one by one, working at his grandfather's garage every summer and every day after school since he was twelve. The combination of the Snap-ons and the hand-me down tools, which were made of better stuff than anything any company made these days, had been sold in Bress's pawn shop on Granby Street for the tidy sum of one thousand dollars. The dollar amount confirmed his ex's motives as vengeful rather than financial. He knew she knew what they were worth. The only good thing about it was, they all went to the same buyer, the owner of a one man garage in West Ghent. He decided he could live without the newer stuff, but he had to have his grandfather's tools back. They had the man's name scrawled on them with his old hand engraver. It only cost him two thousand dollars and a lunch full of grease monkey stories salted with plenty of commiseration about she-devil women who would not only sell a man's tools, but sell his soul if given half a chance, to get them all back.

Grandfather's tools in hand, he decided the account books did not balance. He drove the brand new black Camaro he'd bought with three deployment's worth of sea pay, up to the little town in Connecticut where she was living with her parents. He stopped at a hardware store in White Plains, well away from his destination, and bought three items: a pair of thick leather work gloves, the longest flathead screwdriver they had, and a roll of duct tape. Luring the lame old family tabby through the fence behind their house was easy; so was the quick snap of its neck. Some thought went into how he wanted to use the screwdriver: through the heart wasn't the right message; through the head was. He wrapped the lifeless pile of fur with the entire roll of duct tape leaving only the gruesome head sticking out, and placed the sliver gray clump on top of a galvanized trash can near the back gate. She loved that cat. He was back in Norfolk before ship's muster the next morning. Over is over.

His only regret in the whole affair was that it had turned him into a counter puncher. His Grandpa warned him; told him over plenty of beers—never trust anyone; if you think of doing something to somebody, assume they already thought of doing it to you and get the first shot. He'd applied this maxim his whole life. He was amused one night watching Hill Street Blues when the precinct sergeant sent the cops out the door with his grandpa's warning: Let's get out there and do it to them before they do to us. His ex-wife had been an exception. He wouldn't let that happen again.

Buried at Sea

After the divorce he satisfied his human engineering needs in various mechanical ways, but never with prostitutes, although he sometimes believed it would be the less expensive route. But he had his standards, and paying money outright for sex was one of the few lines he would never cross. He went out with half a dozen women he'd met in bars. He followed the same pattern: copious amounts of alcohol before, during and after dinner, and a hotel room, usually on the no-tell motel strip of Military Highway near the airport. He gave them fake names, left before midnight while they slept off the drinks, and didn't go back to the same bar for a minimum of two months. There were plenty of bars and plenty of opportunities for Mal Hiller, but since the divorce, he'd noticed a change. Sex made him feel vulnerable, more naked than naked, not completely in control. It was not a feeling he enjoyed at all.

Women, even thoroughly intoxicated women, always wanted to ask questions. Where are you from? What was it like? What do you do? He always thought the same thing when these inquiries started: what does this have to do with taking off our clothes and making the proper connections? And besides, when he did try to tell them what he did—how he could tear down an engine and rebuild it blindfolded—or how he was the only person, officer or enlisted, who could hear things in a ship's engineering plant that were about to break. Well, it didn't go anywhere. Like the time he walked through shaft alley on his first ship and knew a line shaft bearing was going to give up the ghost just by standing there and listening. The Chief Machinist Mate with him at the time, a 15 year veteran, laughed at him when he explained that he better let the Chief Engineer know. The Chief wasn't laughing when the bearing wiped, less than 24 hours later, leaving the ship barely able to limp into port and costing the whole engineering department a weekend of liberty in Saint Thomas because they were working around the clock to fix it. The woman he told that story to actually dozed off before he finished.

The answers to the other questions they asked were even less interesting to the women. He came from a small town in Pennsylvania. How small? Small enough to escape the attention of Triple A. His life growing up? Mom who'd left him and his drunk father, when Hiller was young and she was still young enough to get a new life with a new family. Grandfather who helped him get away from his son, in the manner of an old man trying to atone for his sins. In other words the man who'd bent his father wanted to be the one to keep Hiller from getting bent the same way. But Gramps was his own worst problem to start with, and going from a drunk young man to a sober and bitter old man wasn't exactly salvation; it was more like a stay of execution. He did learn something valuable from his Gramps though. He learned motors. His hands found pleasure in the precision of the room temperature steel of a stripped down engine. Here was a place where all problems had precise answers if you just had enough time. Predictable. It became the only thing he cared about. The only thing he related to. It also became his ticket into a whole different world when he discovered he was one of those rare individuals possessing both a practical and intellectual talent for something he loved.

It was his high school physics teacher, Mr. Gringwold, who'd convinced him to go to college, where he could pursue engineering without having to worry about all the other subjects he hated. Gringwold was a retired tin can sailor who sailed the Pacific with Halsey in WWII, and he managed to pry open the doors Hiller needed to get into the Navy ROTC with a full scholarship. Hiller lasted less than a year. For one thing Gringwold had lied. They made him take courses in literature and writing which he promptly failed, not out of stupidity, but out of apathy. One of the guys in the NROTC program turned out to be a fleet Machinist Mate with a desire to become an officer. He and Hiller found out they had grease monkey blood in common. He regaled Hiller with sea stories from a real snipe. When it became apparent he was going to fail English Comp for the second time and he'd been told he'd lose his scholarship if he didn't pass, he quit instead. Over is over. He got a ride into Philly, found a recruiter's office, and enlisted in the Navy. Through some magic loop hole in the normal bureaucracy and by lying about his NROTC status, he was on his way to boot camp two weeks before spring semester classes ended.

Life as an engineer on any Navy ship is one of the most difficult in the modern Navy. Vessels pushed to their limits and beyond by the security needs of the nation, the whims of politicians, and the egos of men atop the chain of command are always in a state of brokenness. The questions Navy engineers answer every day sound like those you'd hear in a thousand neighborhood garages across the country: what's broken, how long will it take to fix, and how much will it cost? The difference is your local mechanic doesn't live in the car and his boss isn't breathing down his neck and threatening to take away his birthday if he doesn't fix the problem.

It suited Hiller. He liked living in an ongoing, hands-on engineering project. Broken things intrigued him rather than frustrated him. He advanced in rank as a matter of course. He wasn't paying attention to it, and before six years passed he found himself on the border between enlisted man and non-commissioned officer. Machinist Mate First Class didn't sound any better or worse to him than Machinist Mate Chief Petty Officer, as long as he got to do what he loved doing. His desire to own more tools and cars with bigger engines made a bigger paycheck attractive enough to listen to the opportunities the Navy offered. After several engineering officers he worked for had tried convincing him to pursue the position of limited duty officer—LDO—with an engineering specialty, it finally occurred to him that becoming an officer might have the double advantage of more money and more control over his own schedule.

Getting accepted as an LDO was as easy for Hiller as filling out the right forms. He was exactly the type of man the Navy always needed to feed to the decaying, conventionally powered, maintenance needy portion of the fleet. No top notch line officer in their right mind wanted anything to do with ships like *Redstone*. For them, anything outside the cruiser-destroyer world was taking a career Quaalude. The Navy didn't want to send their best officers to auxiliaries, but guys like Hiller? Perfect. The powers that be practically set a record, getting him through the administrative hoops. They sent him off to 'knife and fork' school, where in eight short weeks, vulgar enlisted men are transformed into equally vulgar officers with better table manners.

Now, after three years as an officer, he was wearing lieutenant bars and holding down his first of what would be several chief engineer billets. He liked his job. He liked it for all the reasons everyone else in *Redstone's* engineering department hated it. Some vital part of her fifty-year-old engineering plant was broken, seemingly every day. He was pushed to the edge of his abilities and he took his department along with him on a regular basis.

Since a Navy ship is, for all intents and purposes, a series of interconnected engineering systems there was nothing in the ship beyond his touch. From the most advanced electronics, which on this old tub were admittedly not too advanced, to the toilets in the CO's cabin, to the shafts and their huge screws, they all needed him. A decent Cheng in the Navy is godlike inside the skin of his ship. Hiller's position on *Redstone*, with a tired out Captain limping toward obscurity and an Executive Officer dog paddling in her role, neither of whom knew enough about engineering to challenge him about any significant decision he made, exceeded a normal Cheng by many degrees. And as often happens, for no reason other than playground brute strength, the inability of anyone to challenge him in the one area he knew led him to an overarching sense of invincibility. Mal Hiller held absolute sway on *Redstone*, and he did as he pleased inside the bubble he'd created.

Lately he'd discovered a new way to satisfy his sexual needs in a much less expensive and much more convenient manner without leaving his bubble. Hiller had begun identifying and pursuing a certain type of enlisted woman. It was instinctual, predatory. A wolf's eye for strays. They had a look—a way of talking and carrying themselves that may as well have been a neon sign over their heads. He was nervous the first time he made a faltering attempt to persuade a buxom 18-year-old Seaman Apprentice from Deck Department to sleep with him, but it turned out to be too easy. The girl jumped into his rack. She was insatiable in bed, which was fun, but she was indiscrete and clingy, which was not. She was also three months away from a medical discharge, which saved him a lot of trouble getting rid of her. The Navy did it for him. He gained confidence and experience from this first foray into free, convenient, shipboard sex and had since made it a policy to check a woman's personnel file before bedding her. Ideally, he wanted a girl within 6 months of rotating off the ship. He had no use for any of them, long term. They might as well have been the cans of Pennzoil he poured into his Camaro and drained back out after 2000 miles.

Now in his third year aboard *Redstone*, he had a well-established routine of identifying and carrying on with enlisted women. Occasionally he juggled more than one woman at a time, but he preferred to leave that to the ship's real champion gigolo, CWO3 Pete Baber, the ship's Bos'n and chief diver. It was Baber who gave him an idea for keeping a rein on the women he seduced.

Hiller went to the Bos'n's stateroom one day after a meeting to talk over a leaky steam line running through the Dive Shack. It was a relatively easy fix, except it involved cutting out a length of pipe and shutting down an auxiliary steam line that fed the CO's galley. The leak was a nagging item that kept coming up on a hit list and Hiller was irritated to hear about it regularly at the weekly Department Head meeting. He had a lot of leaks on the 50-year-old ship and this one was not critical. The Bos'n brought it up week after week for the simple reason that the leak was directly over his desk—a desk he admittedly hated, and avoided sitting behind as much as possible. Hiller knocked on Baber's door hoping to work out something between them until he could spare a man to get into the Dive Shack and take care of it, hopefully while the Old Man was ashore and not needing his galley. While talking with Baber, he noticed a polaroid camera hanging from a strap next to his rack.

"Whatcha got there, Bos'n?" Hiller asked.

A sly look bloomed on Baber's face. "This? I like to do a little amateur photography. I do some *sightseeing*. Like to keep some pictures of the places I've been. The people I've seen."

Hiller nodded, picking up the emphasis in Baber's face and voice. He said, "All of them? They let you do that?" He'd never thought of this before.

"Let?! Mal...." he glanced around conspiratorially in the cramped stateroom and lowered his voice as if there might be a bug planted in a corner stanchion. "They loooove it. Turns them on. Turns me on. It's nuts."

Mal Hiller left the Bos'n's cabin with an agreement to leave off mentioning the leaky valve in the Dive Shack and a plan to buy his own polaroid camera. Taking pictures of the women he seduced might be a turn on for the Bos'n, but for Hiller it was the ideal way to keep their mouths shut. A little reminder that he had a photo locked away somewhere did wonders for the few women who got out of line. A promise to destroy the pictures when the women left the ship placated most of them, although it was a promise he never kept. In this one particular, Maggie Freeman was the exception. She flatly refused to allow him to snap a photo and never left him an opportunity to catch her in an unguarded moment. It was as if she always knew she was swimming with a shark and never let him bite. He hated and loved this about the girl. She was different. She was dangerous. But how dangerous can the biggest mouse be to the cat? Not very. She was still just another plaything in Mal Hiller's world; even if she had teeth.

Chapter 8
Kissing Your Own Boo-Boos
July 1989, Pierside, Norfolk, VA

Maggie looked both ways before stepping into the passageway outside the Cheng's stateroom. Satisfied no one was around, she walked fifteen tense paces down a corridor of white doors tagged with brass plates naming each of the ship's officers. She didn't belong in officer country and would not have a good explanation to give anyone she might meet, especially at this hour. Turning right, she took the fastest way out onto the port side weather decks. The ship was stern in and starboard side to, leaving the port side in relative darkness, away from the stark glow of orange-yellow security lamps lighting the pier. Once outside the skin of the ship she continued all the way aft, a shadow in shadow.

The Cheng, or Mal, as she now referred to him in their private, duty night meetings, enjoyed these rendezvous. They were nerve wracking for her. She scarcely thought of anything other than being found out; caught like high school kids making out on the sofa. She heard every opening door and every footfall within two decks fore and aft of the Cheng's stateroom. She waited breathlessly for them to come to a sudden halt outside the door to be followed by a hasty knock. As with all the staterooms on *Redstone*, there was only one way in, and it was through that door. They would be trapped. She would have no place to hide. He laughed at her fear. No, it was more than that. He enjoyed her fear. It heightened the experience for him somehow. There was a growing uneasiness in this for Maggie. The man had a thread of cruelty in him she had not seen at first. Not that he had ever been openly cruel to her. The most she could pin on him was the usual inattentiveness of all men she'd known intimately. But she noticed something new growing inside herself—an unwillingness to overlook either his cruelty or his inattentiveness.

In the darkness, making her way aft, her ears and nose worked over time filling up the sense void of the semi-blindness. Norfolk had its smells. Briny water, a hint of fish and the lingering smell of maritime industry: paint, fuel oil, and rubber; steel rusting as the Chesapeake Bay steadily chewed away the hulls of ships and anything else she could get her teeth into. It was a quiet night. In the greatest naval base of the most awesome naval fleet assembled in the history of the world, Maggie heard the ripples from a light evening breeze lapping at the gray metal sides of her ship like a cat drinking water from a bowl.

Instead of taking the midship ladder down and cutting into the interior of the ship and her berthing area, she felt the sudden urge to go to her place of refuge on the fantail. The same vantage point which let her look into the clear blue eyes of the Atlantic for the first time in her life, now gave her only a panoramic view of the parking lot and, beyond it, the supply buildings known as Servmart, where sailors handed over chits in exchange for the things the modern Navy ran on: pens, yellow pads, reams of copier paper and reams and reams of forms.

She leaned on the top of the life lines and held her face with both hands. She glanced at her watch and lit a cigarette. It was early. Hiller liked to have his fun between midnight and 0400 which suited Maggie. She wanted to be well clear of Officer country before any early birds arrived for work. She had a flashback to her first day at sea—the view from this very spot, the overwhelming sense of gratitude she felt for the beauty, the freedom, the change. The change. A whole new life had opened up in that view. The ocean seemed to reach out and embrace her and invite her into that life.

A stray ember from her cigarette broke off and burned her fingers. It stung her into the present. She shook her hand and flicked the still burning cigarette into the black water lapping against the side of the ship below. What change? *Here I am attached to another man who falls asleep on top of me. And this one I can't get away from, because no matter where I go, he's never more than 500 feet away from me.* She sighed. *Maybe I'm just not made for freedom,* she thought. *Maybe my father was right. Maybe I am Fishersville, or maybe I'll just make wherever I am into Fishersville.* And what's wrong with that? a voice inside her head tried to say. Nothing. Fine place. Fine people. It ain't small town living that steals your life... it's small town thinking and small town dreaming; that's what leaves you without a horizon—without a view of the ocean. She held her fingers to her lips and kissed the burns before she realized what she was doing, then laughed. "Kiss your own boo-boos." Something her father told her to do, one lonely gray day after her mother left. She saw his face. Saw the moment. Little girl crying in the garage; her father rolled up under a car, legs sticking out. The disembodied sound of his voice seemed to come through the motor and upraised hood. "Ain't got time for hurts, little girl. Life hurts. You gotta learn to kiss your own boo-boos now."

She had tried, but that boo boo was on a skinny little elbow. She had gone to the grimy front desk, slid out a creaking drawer and found the equally grimy tin box of band aids. It took two tries but she got the scrape covered. The second try, she kissed the little white gauze square before she placed it over the wound. There was always more than one way to get something done.

Maggie sighed. Hiller was a boo-boo. No one was going to kiss it away but her. He was only one of many she'd made with boy-men. If she'd learned anything about herself lately it was that mistakes were not fatal, and starting over again was only a breath away. She headed for WINS berthing, feeling the same as she had the night up on Barren Ridge. There was a way out. She'd find it.

Chapter 9
Tuts Treasure Arrives
September 1976, Pierside Naples, Italy

The USS *Milwaukee* came alongside *Redstone* on schedule. Sailors swarmed the decks of the ships like ants on two haze gray anthills. Amongst the bluejackets, every officer from both ships scurried back and forth, trying to look necessary, but generally making a nuisance of themselves while the real working men completed the transfer of crates filled with King Tut's priceless artifacts.

Jasper remained below decks. Normally he preferred his sunless haunts inside the skin of the ship to being topside; in this instance he had extra motivation to keep away from the chaotic movement topside. *The less they see of me*, he thought, *the less likely anyone will associate my face with the disappearance of one of those crates*. And that's what he and Richards planned to do—a disappearing act so good, Houdini himself would be proud. He smiled at the thought. Not that the plan didn't have its drawbacks and pitfalls. In the three days since their confab at Riley's, Chief Richards had worn out his welcome in the unfinished WINS berthing compartment where Phipps was surreptitiously constructing the paraphernalia needed for their magic act. Richards was tiring on a good day; "trifling" was the word his mother would have used to describe the man. More than once Phipps threatened to trash the deal if Richards didn't stay away.

As with most plans, what appeared simple became more complex as time went on and details emerged that they'd overlooked. The lading list Richards depended upon was wrong on several points. Different items were in different containers. The inload took longer and the stowage plan was adjusted many times by the Egyptian Bureau of Antiquities curators chosen to travel with the treasures, fussy little brown men in sweat-stained white shirts and khaki pants, who barked at each other in streams of Arabic and at everyone else in halting, barely understandable English. The head curator—distinguished from the others by being the sweatiest and the loudest, seemed determined to single-handedly hinder any progress at getting the crates secured and getting this show on the road. He oversaw their placement and re-placement four separate times before agreeing that the load was seaworthy. He and the other curators worried Richards half to death with their chattering and changes, right up to the moment *Redstone* cast off all lines, steamed out of Naples harbor, and pointed her nose westward for the trip home.

Phipps and Richards's plan hinged upon identifying one small crate they'd noted in the lading list. They needed the crate to end up in a location where they could easily move it into a section of the unfinished WINS berthing compartment and seal it into a hidden compartment. Before anyone was the wiser, Phipps would weld up a wall so perfect it would appear to be just another bulkhead. There was so much new work in the future WINS berthing compartment, one new wall would look like ten other walls he'd installed in the last month. On paper—sitting in Riley's under the influence of four or five generous glasses of whiskey—it was simplicity itself. But in the belly of the *Redstone*, it wasn't simple.

The few days before *Milwaukee* arrived in Naples had afforded Phipps plenty of time to create the false compartment. No one questioned him when he continued work in the future WINS berthing and no one watched as he methodically welded in two steel plates, deck to ceiling, near the entrance to what would one day be the women's head. He had worked out the location as the least likely to draw attention and had a cover story ready, should anyone ask what he was doing. It was the location of electrical runs that needed to be isolated. He procured spare lengths of conduit to lend credibility to his story although it would only take a cursory glance to see there weren't any penetrations in the deck or the overhead where real electrical runs would be installed. A third steel plate, cut to fit the remaining opening, leaned against the far side bulkhead in a darkened corner, ready at a moment's notice for the quick tack welds that would complete the secret compartment. The result was a cunningly disguised space about eight feet tall, four feet wide and seven feet long.

The one complication came when he realized he would need to reroute an auxiliary steam line and run it through an abandoned space, one deck below. It wasn't a complicated job, but it required him to lug his gear up and down the ladderwells between the second and third deck several times while trying to stay as invisible as possible. In the end he got it done, although he was not satisfied with the welds on the new run of pipe. No time to worry with it. He'd fix it once the ship was through OPPE and the treasure was concealed. Plenty of time then.

On one of his visits, Richards commented on the size of the compartment.

"That's damn big, Phippsy!" he said. "I pictured a little box along a bulkhead. You know, something out of the way that didn't draw any notice."

Phipps smiled. "Best place to hide somethin's always in plain sight, Richards. Trust me. When I button this up, no one's gonna give it a second look. You just worry about your end. Get me that box and fifteen minutes alone and it will disappear faster than fifty bucks at a roulette table in Vegas. You and me are gonna be the only souls on earth that's gonna know where to find it and we wouldn't find it ourselves if we didn't know where to start lookin.'"

When the treasure crates came aboard, those 15 minutes proved impossible to find. The morning *Milwaukee* arrived, Phipps was summarily banned from further work in the WINS berthing. He went back to his regular "A" Gang duties, repairing various bits of machinery throughout the old ship. He kept a spare acetylene welding rig stowed in a locker near WINS berthing, ready for a quick plunge in and out to finish the theft, but it became obvious as soon as the treasure was stowed and *Redstone* sailed, that no one could enter the space. Masters at Arms stood watch at the only entrance and the only personnel allowed in were the CO, the Suppo, and the half dozen Egyptian curators traveling with the treasure. Soon the excitement over the treasure diminished as the excitement of crossing the Atlantic and getting home replaced it. Phipps put thoughts of the treasure away and returned to being a cog in the routine of a Navy ship at sea. There was still the dreaded outchop OPPE to complete, including engineering drills at all hours of the day and night. The second day out from Naples, after a long day of basic engineering casualty control exercises, lolling under a sputtering hot shower, he decided the whole plan had been a drunken delusion and he was well shut of it. Richards be damned.

Chapter 10
Mal Hiller's World
1989 Pierside, Norfolk, Virginia

As was his long habit, Mal Hiller rose well before reveille. The girl was gone. He combed his short brown hair and splashed water onto his face from the sink in his stateroom. Duty nights were a lot more interesting since he'd bedded Maggie Freeman. There had been a couple month's lull in his Navy-sponsored sex life, when a brief pregnancy scare had required quick thinking and a word to the Admin Officer to rid himself of a Signalman Seaman Apprentice who liked to smoke reefer. Ironic. She'd popped negative for being preggo on the same day she popped positive on a "random" urinalysis.

He smiled at himself in the mirror. It had been easy to get Maggie. He knew what to say to her type. It was like putting money in a vending machine; the right combination of coins, push the button and out comes the snack. He laughed at the analogy and he laughed at the memory of the look on her face the first few times she'd been with him and a door opened near his stateroom or they heard footsteps in the passageway outside. Her eyes went wide. It was a turn-on for him as much as a terror to her. He had to admit she was right to be afraid, getting caught together in his stateroom would be inexplicable, and possibly career ending for both of them, but only possibly. What Maggie didn't know, couldn't know, was how many of the officers on this ship were sleeping with her crewmates. He knew two female junior officers who had boyfriends paying visits to their apartments. One was sleeping with the newest diver assigned to *Redstone*, a buff blonde California dream, and the other was hooking up with an old broken down, and very married, First Class Dental Technician, which was convenient because she happened to be one of two Navy dentists assigned to the ship.

Hiller enjoyed the fact that he knew all of this; he more than enjoyed it, he took an obscene pride in believing he was the one officer on *Redstone* who saw the intricate web of illicit relationships honeycombing the chain of command and that he alone knew how to turn this to his advantage. For instance, it never hurt to imply to the Operations Officer, a self-proclaimed family man, that he knew about a certain busty, brunette eighteen-year-old Hull Tech from Repair 1 who liked to talk a lot when she drank. The hint would be enough to keep Ops from pushing Hiller about the low numbers of engineering department Enlisted Warfare Qualifiers at the next Department Head meeting. He also knew the indiscretions of another four or five members of the wardroom, some more significant than others, and of at least 13 members of the Chief Petty Officers' Mess, including three of the four most senior enlisted men on the ship. He had obtained his information through various means, but mostly he obtained it because it is what people like him were made to do.

There's always a low spot in every yard where water pools and there is always a low spot in any group of people where nasty information does the same. Hiller was *Redstone's* natural low. He held every bit of his collected *Redstone* dirt at precisely the right distance above each person's head to give himself the leverage he needed when he needed it. Because of this he was simultaneously the most feared and hated person on the ship, from the lowest ranking deck seaman to the Old Man himself. To the lowly he was a predator to be avoided at all costs, to the more powerful he was a necessary evil, like a mud sucking fish in an aquarium. It was Mal Hiller's world, and he ruled it with brutal efficiency.

Chapter 11
The Duty

"Hey, Steve..."

"Yeah."

"What'd ya do last night?"

Machinist Mate Second Class Steve Carter looked up into the steel gray top of the box twelve inches from his face. He was in his bunk, affectionately known to sailors as a 'coffin rack'—sometimes at night when the ship was in port with most of its machinery cold and dead, the berthing compartments got to feeling like graveyards—the only spot on the ship he could call his own. With the curtain drawn across the face of his rack, he had a cube of privacy approximately three feet by seven feet by eighteen inches high, unless Mark Hayes was aboard ship. In that case privacy went out the window.

"You know I had the duty, Mark." Steve sighed.

"Yeah... I know," said Hayes, as he pulled back the curtain on Steve's rack.

Steve yawned. He did a fire drill getting out of his bottom rack; stop, drop and roll. Easier than trying to sit up. He got to all fours and slowly stood, stretching and yawning as he did.

If politics made strange bedfellows, the Navy was its match. The two sailors were a prime example. Steve Carter joined the Navy to get enough money to finish college. He moved with the easy grace of an athlete, and he was handsome in an understated way. He attracted people like flowers attract bees—something he took for granted as normal and natural without attaching too much pride to the fact. It was just the way things went for Steve. Make the grades? Make rank? Be the captain of the team? Of course. Running out of money for school was a nuisance, not a major setback. He was the son of a bi-vocational pastor in Damascus, Virginia, a couple hundred miles south of where Maggie Freeman grew up, and money had always been tight for the family. His father liked to say it was God's job to keep a pastor humble but it was the deacons' job to keep him poor, and the deacons at Damascus Holy Spirit Harvest Church did an exceptionally good job. His dad worked hard, but there was always more month than money in their house.

Like father, like son, Steve worked hard but came up short on funds. His money ran out two and a half semesters into an engineering degree at Virginia Tech. There was no college fund set aside for him—he'd never expected there would be. He worked two part time jobs trying to keep ahead of the registrar's office demands for more cash, but it just didn't add up—not enough hours to work, go to class, and sleep.

Much like Maggie Freeman, he ran into Navy marketing at the exact time it had the greatest impact: the day his third semester bills came due and his bank account hit zero. For Steve it was a TV commercial instead of a poster, but the effect was the same. Before that summer was out, he was marching around the black asphalt parade grounds—the "grinder"—of Great Lakes Naval Training Center. Machinist Mate "A" school followed recruit training, and here he was, grist for the *Redstone* millstone until he achieved exit velocity. He had risen to second class petty officer, and had almost saved enough money to ensure he could complete school. Another year and he'd have just enough, if everything went according to plan.

He was proud of himself for keeping true to his course in spite of everything. His family had not been wild about the idea of the Navy—to be fair, they loved the military, but reserved their affection for the Army, where three generations had served with honor. Tattoos seemed to be a real problem for Navy men, and loose women in foreign ports, and weren't most of them heavy drinkers? Steve didn't bother pointing out that all these vices were evenly dispersed across the spectrum of military men, basically since the beginning of time. His family were good God-fearing, Bible reading folks. They loved him and meant no real harm. His dad pointed out that, on balance, the sea stories in the Bible ended badly for sailors; the Apostle Paul's shipwreck and Jonah's ordeal to name a few. He signed up anyway.

After spending three years aboard ship, Steve would admit Navy life challenged a young man. There was a current running through the sea service that pressed against you, a current that ran through the history of men going to sea in ships and included many of the things his family feared would sidetrack him. But so far he'd stayed on the straight and narrow. The current seemed to work the most on the folks who had the least idea where they were going in the first place. To Steve the Navy was a stone in the middle of a stream he was crossing. He had no intention of standing on it any longer than necessary, and so far he hadn't fallen in.

Mark Hayes literally fell in step with Steve during their time in Great Lakes. Steve was his squad leader in the company formation; Hayes the first recruit in the column behind. It was perfect for him. He was as natural a follower as Steve was a leader. Joining the Navy was also a financial necessity for him, but for another reason. Mark was an example of the MP division motto: "Mostly Pennsylvanians." Hailing from the tiny berg of Lititz, in Lancaster County, Pennsylvania, Mark found nothing but fast food restaurants waiting for him upon graduating high school, jobs which would not allow him to accomplish the one and only thing he had any true determination to accomplish: to marry his girlfriend. He wasn't unattractive but neither was he particularly noticeable to the opposite sex. His rounded features were welcoming and disarming to most people he met. While Steve would consider a good quiet afternoon with a book something to be savored, Mark had little to do with books and preferred extended periods of playing the latest version of his favorite video game, Super Mario Brothers.

These two, whose paths would never have crossed in their civilian incarnations, had become, through the peculiar magic of naval society, not only shipmates but friends and roommates out in town. In spite of the fact that it made no financial sense for two single Navy men, they'd rented an apartment in Ocean View. It was their declaration that the Navy did not completely own them, and they were willing to pay for that statement, even though they spent one out of four nights a week in port aboard ship and about half the year underway. The apartment had been Steve's one concession to unnecessary spending, but he justified it in the name of mental health. It was a haven from the metallic harshness of *Redstone* and, since Hiller had come aboard, his tyrannical reign. He had no regrets.

"What time is it?" asked Steve, still unfolding himself from a night in his rack.

"Oh five forty."

"Ok, Mark, I've gotta hit the head and get ready to muster with the duty section."

Mark started to say something, stopped, then stammered, "Steve, I think I'm the Cheng's new target."

Steve raised an eyebrow. "Target?"

"Yeah. I think he's... he's just got it out for me."

Steve let out a long sigh. "Mark, if you haven't noticed, the man has it out for all of us. What makes you think you're special?"

Mark grinned one of his stupid, disarming grins. "Special. Yeah, I don't like being special when it comes to him, but I think I am. He's been pinging Peary over my cold iron logs. Nobody else's—just mine. Peary asked me what the hell I did to piss off the Cheng."

Steve looked at his friend's worried face. "Take it easy, man. It's part of the game. The Navy's a game and this ship is a game inside a game. That's all. He gets off on stuff like this —like knowing he's under your skin. Just chill. He'll move on to the next one soon enough." He grabbed a towel and his shave kit. "See you at quarters."

But Mark didn't move. He looked over his shoulder to see if anyone was listening and stepped in closer to Steve so he could speak in a whisper.

"You do any more of that, whadya call it... slooping?" Steve made a face. Mark went on, "You know. Looking for clues? Evidence of what he did to Lambert, or you know... pictures?"

Steve said, "Sleuthing. Mark. It's Suh-looth-ing. And no. No way I'm poking around in his stuff when he's aboard." When Mark's face fell, he added, "I wouldn't hang my hat on that anyway. Who knows what will turn up and when?" He slapped his friend on the back. "Take it easy, shipmate. This too shall pass."

"Hmmm?" said Mark.

"Something my mom used to say whenever I got down. We won't be on *Redstone* forever. And... " he gave Mark a warm smile, "...remember, they can't take away your birthday."

Duty sucks, Steve thought to himself for the millionth time, as he washed the soap from his face. It was one thing to spend months on end aboard a ship on deployment. Hardships like that were to be expected. Drinking water tinged with the taste of jet fuel, stale fried fish sticks for dinner, shower heads you could never turn your back on without fear they might spew scalding hot water on you, and a tiny, rock-hard rack to sleep on, all that didn't seem so bad in the middle of the Mediterranean Sea or in a foreign port. Those same things in home port, when you were a twenty minute drive from your own apartment, your own dinner, your own shower and your own bed, well, they sucked. But someone had to stay onboard this old tub each night and keep her safe and sound. Someone had to have the duty.

He smiled, thinking how people talked about having the duty like women talked about having their period – just something that happens to us in the course of living. For the rest of the ship, duty nights consisted of little more than an involuntary night in a hotel you had to clean yourself. During the hour or so between liberty call for everyone who was going home and dinner time for those who weren't, most of the ship's duty section hustled to clean up its spaces. After dinner they settled into various lounges in front of TV's, fought over the questions on Jeopardy, and watched whatever sports they could find. Some read and some actually studied rate training manuals, but no one worked too hard. The worst thing to happen to the average crew member on a duty night was standing the mid-watch on the Quarterdeck, and realistically, that happened only once in ten or fifteen duty days. Right now the ship was 'fat.' She had enough people to keep the minimum amount on board and stay in five section duty, so you only stood duty every fifth day. Other ships on the waterfront weren't so lucky. Steve had a friend a couple of piers over standing duty every third day. 'There is always something that sucks worse than the way your life sucks,' he thought. But no one on his ship had it worse than his department.

Engineering was the exception to every rule. On a regular work day, when the rest of the crew was knocking off for liberty call at 1530, the engineers were lucky to leave the ship at 1700. When the rest of the ship got off half a day on the Friday before a three day weekend just because the Old Man was feeling good and wanted to get on the road himself, the engineers worked a full day. And when everyone else was spending their duty nights in front of a TV and complaining about pulling a watch, the engineers were working on lists of maintenance items the Chief Engineer left for them to get done.

The first thing the Cheng did each day was call the duty engineering officer to his cabin for a report on what the duty section accomplished. God help the guy if there wasn't a healthy dent in the list. The Cheng's view of duty was simple: more hours on the ship equaled to more man hours' worth of work. A typical duty night for the engineers was more like extending the 12 hour work day to 18 hours and adding in cold iron watches, sounding and security watches and fire party training, as well as having to participate in the ordinary watches everyone else had to stand. The demands upon manpower sometimes stretched the department so thin, the Cheng would threaten to tell the Captain he didn't have enough people to safely keep the fire party manned and insist that the ship go to four section duty. So far they had avoided that actuality.

Toweling off, Steve wondered if the rumor he had been investigating was true or just another sea story made up to pass the time on a boring watch. He had heard some first-class tales in the past, some rising above the run of the mill 'how many women I've slept with and how much they want me' type. His personal favorite was told by a kid from Alabama one night in the middle of the Med in the middle of the mid-watch. It involved his grandfather's church in rural Tennessee, some rattlesnakes, and a bunch of folks filled with the Holy Ghost. The kid told it in spurts, between spitting long streams of tobacco juice into a steadily filling coke bottle. It got a good laugh and passed the time. But the story about the Cheng—it was a story with the potential to change things.

Contrary to what he'd told his friend, Steve had, in fact, done some sleuthing last night, despite the fact it was crazy to go poking around in the Cheng's personal stuff when the man was aboard. He was damn near a ghost sometimes, and Steve had witnessed personally one of Engineering's most enduring ghost stories about Hiller.

He was relatively new himself on *Redstone* when Hiller arrived. On the lower level of the forward engine room, aft of the massive main engine reduction gear, he and several newbies were getting a run through of the layout of the steam plant. They were standing on a steel mesh walkway that connected the boiler front to the main shaft side of the space, when a grease smeared arm appeared from below and hooked itself around the walkway, like the leg of a dinosaur trying to escape the primordial ooze. A few grunts later, as the surprised group of sailors gaped, Lt Malcolm Hiller clawed his way out of the bilge onto the diamondback steel plates of the walkway. He looked at the tour group as if he were a troll and they had walked across his bridge without permission, but he said nothing. He pulled the oil smeared remnants of a red mechanic's rag from the back pocket of his coveralls, more black than their original blue, and wiped his hands slowly as he walked toward the cluster of sailors. They parted, squeezing against the walkway rails, letting him pass through them like a sushi knife through tuna. He was gone. The whole incident took less than a minute. The new engineering rates looked nervously at each other, eyes wide. What the hell kind of ship was this?

Noting the effect this tale had on the engineering department, Steve wondered if the man staged the incident. The more he got to know Malcolm Hiller, the more feasible he thought it was. The Cheng enjoyed his Darth Vader aura and depended upon it to get things done. Adding a sense of omnipresence to the fear he engendered fed straight into Hiller's dark lord mind game.

All Steve knew, as he got dressed to face another day, was something had to give. People were starting to think and talk about the man as if he had supernatural powers. He permeated the engineering spaces, whether he was onboard the ship or not. It reminded Steve of trying to wash away the smell of spilled gasoline; no matter how hard you scrubbed, the smell lingered. You had to live it off. The name "Cheng" had its own dark cloud. All the engineers unconsciously lowered their voices when saying it, as if he might materialize straight out of a steel bulkhead. Steve wondered how one man could make so much misery with so little effort and so much indifference.

But Steve didn't buy into any of it. He wasn't given to fear in general and he wasn't easily intimidated. He had come to a decision; he didn't know how, maybe he came to it a little at a time or maybe the thought arrived fully cooked like a frozen dinner that only needed heating up: Hiller was a bully and needed a taste of his own medicine.

Well, he thought, *like my mom always said to me and my brothers, "Evil leaves footprints."* The Cheng was evil, therefore there were footprints. He didn't think of the word 'blackmail' and probably would've argued against labeling what he had in mind as blackmail anyway. He was going to get evidence of the Cheng's evil, and when he had it, Hiller was going to either straighten up or pay up, and it didn't matter which. Last night he began looking for the footprints. He didn't realize at the time that he might leave some of his own.

Chapter 12
Collision at Sea

Steve dressed hurriedly and made his way to Damage Control Central, the nerve center of engineering. It was a habit he developed over his years on *Redstone*. If something was shaking, there would be news in DCC. It was bisected by a stainless steel table to the left as you entered, outfitted with five positions for sound-powered phone talkers connected to various command nodes of the ship during battle stations. Centered on the wall behind the desk, a huge rack of ship's drawings was mounted on a frame that swung on a hinge. Each drawing showed a different deck and vital systems, such as fire mains and electrical supply runs, and was covered with a plexiglass shield for watchstanders to mark up with red, yellow and black grease pencils during engineering drills or actual casualties. On either side of the rack were bookcases containing *Redstone*'s operation manuals, Navy regulations governing maintenance and all aspects of the safe operation of the ship's steam plant. Opposite of the desk, tucked away in a corner, was the Damage Control Assistant's office. It was more like a cave than anything a landsman would call an office. Three walls were filled with rack upon rack of more manuals and, due to the current DCA's proclivity for bodybuilding and his unusual pecuniary habits, cardboard cases of protein powder and tuna fish filled in any leftover space. *Redstone* snipes referred to the office simply as "The D Cave."

During normal operations the desk in DCC was the front desk of the engineering department, the place where topsiders sought answers to their engineering questions like; why is 250 degree steam coming out of our shower heads? Or, can someone fix the stay on the water tight door near my workspace that bangs back and forth every time we get underway? Or, can you send someone up to fix the shitter that keeps backing up in WINS berthing? But that would be later in the day. At turnover of the duty section in port and at the beginning of a work day at sea, DCC was where the machinist mates, boiler technicians, electricians and hull techs who'd been abroad long enough to accumulate some responsibilities gathered to get the dope on their departments and divisions. There was usually a lot of jawing and grousing—a happy sailor is a complaining sailor—and greasing of skids, to get something done for a favor owed or repaid before everyone but the watch headed out for quarters.

Steve caught up with HTC Mulligan and asked about borrowing a small welding kit for a job in the forward mainspace—he was a self-taught welder and a good one, good enough that Mulligan regularly let him use gear he was hesitant to let out to many of his own welders. They agreed that he could pick up the rig after quarters and keep it until the following day. Steve said his goodbyes and checked his watch. The Navy had drilled into him that fifteen minutes early was late and it was already 0645. Quarters was on the fantail at 0700 for engineering. He stepped through the door into the passageway outside DCC with his head down and all but bowled over a sailor headed in the opposite direction.

"Whoa!" he said, grabbing the flailing sailor to keep them from falling flat. He was surprised instantly. Instead of handfuls of the stringy, stinky *Redstone* engineer he was expecting, he found he was holding a slender arm in one hand and something distinctly feminine in the other. Before this could fully register, he pulled the body towards him to keep it upright. He found himself face to face with a gasping girl. The moment was frozen, a snapshot he remembered for a long time, not for its sensuousness, although the girl felt nice in his arms, or for its awkward humorousness, but because, as he later reflected on this time of the Cheng's reign of terror, a human moment. Completely and utterly human. He also remembered—and this was central to the memory, the way the brain catalogs and stores memories in file cabinets marked "smell"—she smelled delightful, unlike anything or anyone below the main deck of *Redstone* ever smelled.

The freeze frame ended with Steve snatching his hand away from her right breast as if he'd placed it on a hot stove, while at the same time trying not to drop her. As his hand came away he saw her stenciled name: Freeman.

She said, "I'm so sorry! I was... I forgot my cover and I'm going to be late for quarters!"

"You all right?" Steve stammered, still feeling her softness on his hands.

"Yeah," Maggie said. "Thanks for keeping me on my feet." She didn't seem self-conscious about the scene, which in another context would have looked like a couple of teenagers groping each other.

"No problem," Steve said, and added stupidly, "my baseball coach always told me I had good hands!"

"Yes, you do," Maggie said with a girlish grin. "I'm Freeman. I work forward."

Steve knew this. It also occurred to him that this was the girl everyone said was currently sleeping with Hiller. He tried to keep this information off his face but he saw instantly that he had failed. Freeman's smile faded like it was on a dimmer switch and she stepped back and turned away. "Thanks again," she said, and walked away rapidly down the passageway.

Steve stood an extra second outside DCC, then picked up his own cover, dropped in the collision with Freeman, and headed in the opposite direction. He never noticed the open door to the Oil King shack or the man standing silently just inside it. Hiller waited until both sailors were gone. His habit of popping into the various nooks and crannies of his engineering plant always turned up interesting bits of information. Yes it did. And this bit was very, very interesting. The heat behind his eyes burned bright red. Anyone who saw him at that moment would have drawn back at the intensity in those eyes, but there was no one there. He pushed the door to as Steve passed by, oblivious.

Chapter 13
The Missing Valve

Steve emerged into the pale light of the main deck and another Norfolk morning. Someone was cursing.

"You'll find the valve, Hayes. I swear you are going to find the valve and you're gonna do it before lunch. You're gonna find it and I don't care what you have to do." Mark Hayes was trying his hardest to stand at attention, but his round frame just didn't do attention.

Machinist Mate First Class Alvin Peary, the leading petty officer of Main Propulsion Division was delivering the message. Peary habitually pointed with his middle finger instead of his index finger, so under the best of circumstances, his gestures bordered on vulgar. Because of a recent crewcut, the angry red of his face could be seen spreading all the way to the top of his head. His middle finger was stabbing the air in front of Hayes's nose.

"All MP division is staying on this ship till that valve is found. All of us! Cheng said he wants it on his desk by close of business today! And you're the one who signed off the job, Hayes. You're the one. Now where is it?" Mark's mouth opened and shut like a fish out of water. Nothing came out.

Steve eased up to the two of them. "What's the prob, MM1?" Steve asked.

Peary wheeled around on him. He laid out the problem point by point with his crude finger stabs. A valve that MP division had replaced during *Redstone*'s last deployment had been designated as a 'turn in' item, meaning if it was replaced, the old valve had to be packaged up and returned to a maintenance facility. No one had known about the special case valve until now, a half year since it had been replaced.

"Cheng must've gotten a message from Supply asking where the valve was. He wants it on his desk by knock off today. He's promising to keep the entire division here until it shows up. I've got to be home tonight or my wife says she's had it. It's just getting to be too much. Sick kids, broken cars, overgrown yard and I'm here. I'm in port. She just can't understand why I can't be home to do stuff, and you know what? I don't blame her. I've done back to back to back sea tours and no ship's ever been like this. Not in port. Not every single day."

Steve looked into Peary's red face and tired eyes. He saw panic. The look of a man losing something he couldn't afford to lose.

"Me and Mark 'll take a look around MM1. If it's on the ship we'll find it and if it isn't we'll figure out where it went. Give me till chow and I'll come find you."

Something like hope edged into Peary's eyes. Carter was a good one. Maybe there was something he could do. He grunted agreement and returned to herding his sailors into formation for quarters.

The rest of MP division meandered toward the spot on the main deck designated as the division's fair weather mustering place. Uniforms and ranks were out of order and the Cheng would arrive shortly to point this out in excruciating detail. Peary screamed for the stragglers to fall in and moved up and down the rows with admonitions to tuck in, button up, and straighten hats. Steve and Mark took their regular spots near the front right of the formation.

"Mark?"

"Yeah."

"Do you remember working on the valve? Do you remember what you did with the old one?"

"I'm thinkin' Steve, I'm thinkin'. I know it was a valve in one of the chillers in WINS berthing—the older unit. I remember that 'cause of the hassle it is every time we work on gear in there, makin' sure we don't see anything. I don't know." Mark's round face clouded up. He shut his eyes tightly trying to see the past. The weight of the division, imprisoned by his need to recall an otherwise unimportant detail from months ago closed in on him. "You know, there were a lot of valves replaced in that old piece of junk while we were in Naples. Who would think something that old and wasted would need to be a turn in?"

Steve smirked in agreement. With Peary's curses ringing in his ears he said, "Why would anything on this ship start making sense today? I do remember that job. Didn't we take a bunch of old stuff and dump it in the scrap bucket in the MR's shop?"

The Machinery Repair shop was *Redstone*'s version of a junk drawer. Things that didn't fit anywhere else ended up there. A good MR could often either fix or scavenge together parts no one else on the ship would think twice about.

"Steve..."

Mark's latest thought died on his lips with the appearance of the Cheng in front of the formation. He gave a swipe at his cap, passing a salute toward the division's two chief petty officers, who arrived only a moment before he did.

"All present or accounted for, Cheng," the Senior Chief Boiler Tech said, with no idea if it was the truth.

Mark moved slightly, adjusting his position to avoid the Cheng's line of sight. His method of coping with this daily ordeal was to try to keep himself as invisible as humanly possible. Today it looked like the Cheng was in a good mood, and that always meant bad news for MP division.

Hiller stepped around the two khaki clad Chief Petty Officers and Peary, propped one hand on a hip and took a sip from a white styrofoam cup, the same cup he would use to spit his tobacco juice in as soon as he finished the coffee currently steaming in it. *If ever there was a set of beady eyes*, thought Mark, *these were it*. They looked like they had been cut from the face of an old teddy bear... or a great white shark... black, shiny and lifeless. Under his overgrown mustache his lips curled into a smile. Yep, not good.

Chapter 14
Sister Ships

MP division on the USS *Redstone* (AR-20) consisted of 108 sailors. The ship, originally laid down in 1943, was designed to serve as a tender for the hundreds of destroyers combing the Pacific for Japanese submarines in WWII. At the end of the war she had been one of only four ships of her class to escape the massive cutbacks in the rolls of active Navy ships. Two remained in the Pacific Fleet. *Redstone* and her sister ship, USS *Seahook*, were reassigned to the Atlantic Fleet.

Two months after the war ended, due to the spaciousness afforded by their many repair shops, both were pressed into service as transport ships for soldiers coming home. During the three week long transit from Guam, through the Panama Canal and north to the debarkation point in New York City, every square inch of space in the ships had been taken up with folding cots hastily taken aboard from the Quonset hut barracks abandoned by the victorious allied forces. New York was not just the place the two ships parted company with their passengers, it was also the place their paths diverged.

Seahook spent the next fifteen years hopping up and down the east coast as the duty tender for Atlantic Fleet ships in port. *Redstone* was thrown into a rotation of six tenders, taking turns on deployment to the Northern Atlantic and the Mediterranean Sea. Perhaps the visibility of working with ships of the line on the other side of the world helped *Redstone* survive longer than her sister. In the late 50s, the ax fell on *Seahook*. She was sent up the James River to the ghost fleet, left in suspended animation, neither dead nor alive, swinging at anchor in a crook of the river within sight of the Jamestown fort, history gazing upon history. The reason for keeping her there was the same as any ship of the ghost fleet: the country may need her again, so she isn't scrapped, but she's too expensive to keep operating and maintaining right now. Mothballs.

Mothballed ships are stocked with everything they need to be put back into service expeditiously. Their engineering spaces have every piece of gear lubricated and sealed in full working order. Dehumidifiers are placed throughout the ship's interior to retard the advancement of rust. Every part of the ship is given a fresh coat of paint. In the case of *Seahook*, because of her unique mission as a repair ship, each one of her 47 repair shops was stocked with every tool and spare part she would have needed, if she'd been sent on deployment. And there she sat, like a spare toolbox, ready to go if she was needed.

Redstone, her keel laid down six months before her sister, was anything but mothballed. She was only a few short months removed from a six month deployment to the Med, and Fleet HQ called the CO and told him to get the ship prepared for another deployment in less than six months. Normally the number of tenders in the Second Fleet rotation would keep a ship in port for eighteen months between deployments, but the failure of a major engineering inspection on one of the newer tenders in the rotation pushed everything up six months. It was no consolation to the engineers on *Redstone* to know they were keeping a fifty-year-old WWII vintage ship deploying when a ship less than half her age was broken down.

Mark looked down at the teakwood deck and failed to appreciate the rich history of his ship. In fact it didn't make any difference to him at all. His world was revolving around a point in time not fifty years ago, but a point only six months ago. At least the Cheng hadn't told everyone who was responsible for the missing valve. Mark knew that wouldn't last. When everyone found out he was the one who lost it and he was the one who was keeping them all on board because he couldn't find it... it wouldn't be pretty. He thought of the stories he'd heard of guys disappearing from ships underway, guys who just never showed up for morning muster, and he thought he had an idea of what might have happened to them. They screwed up so bad someone wrapped them in their own blanket and threw them off the fantail in the middle of the night. *That's what happens*, he thought. Filled with these gloomy thoughts, he almost walked into Steve, coming down the port side ladderway near the MR shop.

"Watch out, Mark." Steve said.

"Sorry Steve. Can't think of anything but that valve." Mark said.

"Well, the story ain't gettin' better." Steve said.

"Why's that?" Mark asked.

"I checked with the MR's and they said they remembered the exact time we were fixing the old WINS chiller. They remember the valve, and they remember you bringin' it to them. They also remember the valve getting put in a scrap metal bucket which got emptied about three days after we left Naples."

"Where'd it get emptied?" Mark asked, not wanting to hear what he knew was coming.

"Over the side, Mark. They dumped it over the side. That valve is at the bottom of the Med."

Mark sat down on the lowest ladder rung, and took this in. He put his face in his hands.

"I am so screwed," he groaned.

Steve looked at the eyes of his friend and saw the despair. It angered him. Mark was a good guy. He wasn't the brightest bulb, but he worked hard, did a good job and actually cared about what he did for the Navy. And here he sat like a man who just got diagnosed with terminal cancer because he knew what was going to happen when the Cheng found out where the valve was. It wasn't fair.

He said the only thing he could think of, which had also become his catchall descriptive phrase since coming aboard *Redstone*, "This sucks."

"No, Steve, this is worse than just sucking, this is like, my life. These guys, you hear'm just like I do, man. The guys are gonna find out its me that's lost this thing and they're gonna snap. You can feel it buildin' up—another deployment, the Cheng... this is gonna be the thing that busts it all loose." Mark looked up at Steve with hopeless eyes. "What can we do Steve? I mean what can I do...? don't want to pull you into this with me. I guess the only thing is for me to go tell the Cheng what happened and explain it all and let 'm do whatever he wants to me. Maybe he'll just take me to mast and have the Old Man bust me or restrict me to the ship."

Captain's Mast on a Navy ship is a subset of the legal system which most normal people would never hear about. Steve thought going to Mast must be like standing before a local sheriff in the old west. The sheriff might be working under a broad legal system to which the accused could appeal, but the next higher authority was miles away and the sheriff had the authority to keep the peace and enforce the laws the best he saw fit. Sailors who were guilty of day to day breaches in ship's discipline were mostly driven back into line by someone in their chain of command at the divisional level. A division leading petty officer, chief, or the division officer himself could make most offenders sorry enough to keep out of trouble a second time when they messed up. Repeat offenders, episodes involving multiple parties where the facts were in question, or more serious matters such as theft, suspected drug abuse or sexual harassment (*Redstone* was the first ship in the Navy with a fully integrated contingent of women in her crew) were sent up to Mast. Cases for Mast would accumulate over the span of a couple weeks and then on a designated day following morning muster, a line of the accused formed outside the Executive Officer's cabin for the Executive Officer's Inquiry (XOI). Sailors in their best looking dungarees and cleanest white hats were called in, one case at a time, to give their explanation of the charges brought against them. The Exec decided if there was enough evidence to refer a sailor to the Captain or to drop the case. Depending on the phase of the moon, pay day, or length of time out of home port, the line for XOI could be anywhere from a handful of cases up to twenty or more.

On high case load days, the well-dressed victims of the Navy's legal system had the extra humiliation of their shipmates passing by and ribbing them about being in line with the other scumbags, because the line formed in a high traffic area where almost everyone onboard walked past at least once a day.

Mast usually took place the afternoon of XOI, and each sailor facing the XO and Captain had to be represented by their leading petty officer, their chief petty officer and their division officer, not to mention any witnesses necessary to the case. It was a manpower intensive event and Hiller hated it, because it cost him man-hours, which could be better spent working on his precious maintenance lists. On the other hand, he knew that a day standing in line for Captain's Mast could give him a sailor restricted to ship for thirty, sixty or even ninety days, a sailor who could then be worked harder, without having to worry about sending him home at all. When anyone from MP division went to Mast he could count on the Cheng being there asking for the maximum punishment for the given offense, and often the Cheng came out of the Captain's cabin fuming mad when the punishment was less than what he asked the skipper to give.

Steve didn't like the idea of Mark going to Mast, but he had to agree it was a likely outcome.

"Well we gotta start with Peary. You gotta go and tell him what happened and then you'll be goin' to see the Cheng because Peary ain't gonna go tell him this on his own. C'mon, I'll go with you and tell him what I found out."

Mark gave him a pitiful look of gratitude and stood up. The 1MC keyed up at that moment and four sharp rings of the ship's bell divided into two strokes, a pause and then two more were followed by the voice of the petty officer of the watch.

"*Redstone*, departing."

"C.O. must be getting an early start on the three day weekend," said Steve, looking down at his watch to see it was just past ten am.

"Yeah, guess he's got a long drive ahead of him."

The current skipper of *Redstone* was a thirty plus year Navy veteran who was serving out his 'twilight' tour in Norfolk. Like quite a few of the senior captains on the waterfront, he hadn't moved his family to town. It made sense for these officers to become geographic bachelors for the eighteen months to two years they would spend on their ships, because the amount of time they would typically be home wasn't enough to justify the expense and trouble of finding a new home and resettling their families. Most Fridays the *Redstone*'s C.O. left shortly after lunch for the drive to his home on the outer loop, just north of D.C. and most Sunday evenings he arrived back in town around nine pm, to spend the night in his room at the bachelor officer's quarters. Thankfully the current CO kept a room in the bachelor officer quarters where he retired each night. The previous CO was too cheap to spend the money to get a place ashore, opting instead to live on the ship in his in-port cabin. The effect of having the CO aboard non-stop was like keeping too much air in a car's tire. The thing still worked, it just didn't work the way it was designed to work. A ship needed to exhale once in a while, and none fully let her breath all the way out while the Old Man was aboard.

Steve and Mark moved out to the port side weather deck and stood at the rails watching the captain descend the brow. In civilian clothes he would never have been taken for a Navy officer, much less the commander of a ship. Slightly built and balding, his appearance was much more akin to the cartoon figure Mr. Magoo than lord and master of a Navy ship. He was unaware of the comparison, but the better artists in the crew had taken to writing their boss into comic strips of their own, and in unguarded moments, the crew referred to him as "Magoo."

"Magoo's sure got a dumpy ride for as much money as he makes," Mark said.

The captain threw an overnight bag in the back seat of a 1972 Volkswagen bus which had once been red but with oxidation had taken on the color of a worn out hot water bottle.

"Guess he likes to spend it on other stuff than cars," said Steve. The distinctive Volkswagen sound fired up and echoed between the thirty foot high steel canyon formed on either side of pier 7 by the ships tied up end to end.

"Gonna be a long weekend," Mark said.

Chapter 15
Richards Pushes the Plan
September 1976, North Atlantic Ocean

The 1MC blared, "This is a drill. This is a drill. General quarters. General quarters. All hands, man your battle stations. Fire in the main space. Make manning reports to the bridge. This is a drill." The Bos'n of the watch sounded anything but excited. It was 0200 on the third day out from Rota, Spain. The ship had secured from GQ barely four hours ago.

Bleary eyed sailors scrambled from their racks, throwing on clothes as they hurried to their battle stations. Jasper Phipps reflected, as he made his way to the aft engine room repair locker amidst half naked men, that these drills would certainly be more interesting after women became part of the crew. He suppressed a wry chuckle. Yes. Much more interesting.

His job in a main space fire drill depended upon which main space was affected. In this case, with the fire called away in the forward engine room, he was the lead of the backup firehose team, held in reserve against the possibility that the primary hose team failed to make it to the scene, got wiped out or needed extra manning. In this scenario, scripted by the OPPE inspectors, he could expect to sit in his

92

repair locker picking his callouses for the next two hours, while the primary crew ran through their paces. Rarely would the inspectors call for backup. Like all good sailors, Jasper and his gang in the non-engaged main space, worked out their own informal watch bill when the idiots topside insisted on stealing their well-deserved sleep. Two men stayed awake while the other ten found suitable nooks and crannies in which to nap. As soon as all the men made it to the repair locker, dressed out in firefighting gear, and reported the locker manned and ready, Jasper settled down on a nest of piled-up life preservers. He quickly dozed off, anticipating an uninterrupted hour of sleep.

He awoke disoriented. Someone was shaking him. Opening one eye, he glanced at his watch. It was 0220.

"Wha?" he mumbled.

"Phipps!" A man hissed in his ear. "Phipps!"

He shook himself and looked into the bulging blue marbles of Richard Richard's eyes.

"What the hell?" he slurred.

Richards bent over him, too close for comfort. He pushed him away with both hands.

"Get off me, man. What'r you doin' down here?"

Richards was sweating profusely, his usually big, crazy eyes, bigger and crazier than normal. He plopped down next to Phipps, glancing over his shoulder like an escaped convict looking for pursuers.

"I think I know a way we can do it." Richards said. "A way we can get in there!"

The fog cleared. Phipps raised his eyebrows. He hadn't given a second thought to stealing some of *Redstone*'s precious cargo since his last hot shower the day the ship pulled out of Naples; hadn't had a moment for thinking or hot water since. Phipps tried to convey this with his face, but

Richards wasn't looking at him, he was continuing to look over either shoulder to ensure their privacy.

"It came to me just now." Richards said.

The man was maddeningly slow witted, Phipps thought. It was like talking to a kindergartener who needed to check each sentence with teacher before proceeding.

"Just spill it," he exhaled, knowing he didn't care, also knowing there would be no ridding himself of Richards without hearing him out.

"GQ! No one's guarding WINS berthing during GQ! Everyone has to go to their battle station including the MAAs. I thought it was true, so I made an excuse to the SUPPO just now and came down to check it out. No one is there!" Richards let this out as if he'd made the most brilliant case in a closing argument.

Phipps rolled his eyes. "You're an idiot, Richards. A topsider idiot. I know you don't come down here much, but you'd think you'd know that we don't sit around sucking our thumbs during GQ."

It was Richards' turn to look incredulous. He spread his arms out, indicating the makeshift couch Phipps lay upon. He grinned. Phipps realized the incongruity of what he'd just said.

"Yeah, yeah. But this ain't the norm. And we can get called out of here any second. If they switch it up at all, it's gonna be elbows and assholes getting to the fire drill. I can't come up missing if that happens. Forget it man. It ain't gonna go."

Richards didn't change expression. "It's worth the chance, Phipps. What's it gonna cost you? You said yourself, all you need is 15 minutes alone and we've got it."

As if on cue, a sailor in firefighting gear stumbled to the back of the repair locker. "Phipps! They're calling us away!"

Phipps stood up and gave Richards a withering look. "Thanks Rogers," he said. "I'm coming." As he hurried to the door he turned and said to Richards, "It's over, DD. Go back to whatever it is you bums do topside and forget about it. It was a crazy ass plan anyway."

If he'd been looking at Richards's face, he'd have seen that at least in one man's mind, the plan was anything but over.

Chapter 16
Cheng's Demand
November 1989, Pierside, Norfolk, Virginia

Mark Hayes and MM1 Peary stood in front of the Cheng's desk and waited for him to look up from the mound of engineering logs he was reviewing. He hadn't acknowledged their presence since shouting "Enter!" in response to their knock at his door. The office smelled like oily gas station rags, sweaty locker room and burnt coffee. Rows of file cabinets tack welded to brackets on the walls lined either sides of the space. The desk was a gray standard Navy issue type with a semi-rubberized top, the kind that looked as if the edges had been chewed by rats before it ever reached the fleet. A greasy ball cap sat facing away from them on top of the nearest pile of papers on the desk. Across the back of the hat in grimy yellow embroidered lettering the word CHENG was barely visible. As Mark watched, Hiller opened the desk's middle drawer, took out a can of Copenhagen chewing tobacco and proceeded to stuff half of it into the space between his left front cheek and gum. The mound of tobacco was so large it was as if a small black rodent had crawled into his maw for slow consumption. He picked up a Planter's Peanut can, held it to his lips and spit a mouthful of amber-brown tobacco juice. He let out an elongated sigh and said, "Speak."

Peary stepped half a foot closer to the desk. "We know where the turn in valve is, Cheng."

Hiller didn't look up, didn't stop marking sweat shriveled logs with his red pen, didn't give any indication he heard him at all. Peary licked dry lips and made the plunge.

"We know what happened to it, Cheng. Hayes here did some tracking after quarters and found out it was given to the MR shop by mistake. There were lots of valves replaced in the WINS chiller. The turn-in valve got thrown in with a bunch of stuff, and, well, the MR's threw all of it overboard when we got far enough out from Naples. The valve is at the bottom of the Med, about 30 miles south of Naples."

Mark moved forward enough to be even with Peary to see what would happen.

The Chief Engineer spat again without looking up. Sighed a 'I have to work with this bunch of idiots' sigh, and said in a deadly calm voice, "I said that valve is going to be on my desk before close of business today or nobody's going home. That's what I mean. Don't bring me any more excuses...bring me the valve."

"But Cheng..." Peary started.

"On my desk. Close of business. Get out."

Peary and Hayes tried to beat each other out the door. Peary won. Mark shut the door, feeling like he'd just escaped a venomous snake. In the passageway outside the office, Peary gave him a "keep it shut till we get out of earshot" look. Mark was glad to oblige, having no response he could think of to what he had just heard. Peary took him aft and down the main ladder into the number two engine room. Steve, who was working on a blown gauge on the back of the main control panel, stepped around it and met two bewildered faces.

"What happened?" he said.

"Cheng says he wants the valve on his desk by C.O.B.," Mark said.

"You told him it was at the bottom of the Med?" Steve said.

"Yeah," said Peary. "He didn't bat an eye. He didn't even look up. What're we gonna do? It's a three day weekend, and he's serious, he'll keep us all here all weekend."

"And we don't have anyone to appeal to either," said Steve. "If the Old Man was here at least, we could get someone to tell him what's going' on and maybe he'd call off the Cheng."

"Carter, you're talking dangerous stuff there, going around the chain of command."

"We can't just let Hiller do anything he wants to us MM1! We've got to get some help. He's killing us. Since we've been back from deployment, how many times has he pulled something like this? You aren't the only one who's got a wife that's gonna split if they don't get home... and kids who ain't seein' their dad. And this is while we're IN port!"

"More than likely you'd just end up with the Cheng on us worse than he already is. He'd find out who ratted on him too, Steve, and I wouldn't want to be the rat in his cage. Remember what he did to Lambert?"

Everyone in MP division knew what had happened to Boiler Technician First Class Raymond Lambert, a five year veteran of *Redstone* and 18 year veteran of the Navy. He had been aboard longer than any other engineer and even though he wasn't the ranking enlisted man in the division, he had enjoyed a somewhat privileged relationship with the previous chief engineer, acting as a buffer between the Chief Petty Officers, the Chief Engineer and the rest of the division.

During the first month after Lt. Hiller relieved the old chief engineer, Lambert had tried to talk with him about the way he was riding one of the young BT's at quarters every day. "He's just a kid," Lambert told the Cheng, "lighten up a bit."

When the Cheng intensified his criticism of the kid, picking apart his uniform, haircut and weight, putting the kid through a non-stop Navy regulation hack job, Lambert asked the ship's senior enlisted man, Master Chief Boatswain's Mate Muzzey to get involved, by coming to quarters a few mornings to see what the Cheng was doing. Somehow the Cheng must have been tipped off, because for the next two weeks of morning quarters he never came near the man. The Master Chief showed up and hovered near the MP division formation every other day but there was nothing to see.

On the first day of the third week, the Cheng informed the division he was going to do a random locker inspection following quarters and to stay out of their berthing areas until it was done. The ship's Master at Arms accompanied the Cheng and the two divisional Chief Petty Officers to the engineering berthing space, where the inspection turned up, among enough porn mags to stock a city library's shelves, a baggie of white powder, which was turned over to the base police for analysis. The source of the baggie was Lambert's locker. It turned out to be 75% pure cocaine, cut with a few non-toxic boiler water treatment chemicals from the water shack where Lambert had worked for the past two years as the ship's 'oil king,' keeping the chemistry right in the water running through the two ship's boilers. No one had ever seen Lambert high or drunk in the time they had known him—not on the beach overseas and not in the states—but with a 'zero tolerance' policy for drugs or drug abuse, he was taken off the ship in cuffs, court martialed, and given the Big Chicken Dinner—Bad Conduct Discharge, as well as a year in the brig. They said that, by the time his legal struggles were over, he had nineteen years and six months in the Navy, six months shy of his pension. He never saw a dime of it. Lambert was gone, the Cheng ignored the kid he'd tried to protect and no one in the division ever felt safe again. Yes, Steve knew about Lambert.

"We've gotta figure something out," said Peary, but his tone betrayed a total lack of insight into what they could do to produce a valve which may as well have been on the moon. He rubbed the side of his nose with his pointing finger. "Why the hell did you have to throw it away," he said to no one in particular. To Steve he sounded more like a teenager whining about not getting the car keys than a grown man who was himself charged with taking care of the bunch of teenagers who made up the majority of MP division.

"Steve..." Mark hesitated, "Steve what if we could find the..." Steve shot Mark a "shut up" look at point blank range. It was enough to kill the words about to spill out of his mouth. Peary didn't seem to have noticed. The First Class Petty Officer didn't look like he was aware of them at all. His eyes were as far away as the cursed valve.

"C'mon, Mark," Steve said. "Let's go take a look at the bilge pump. Think it may be acting up by the sounds of it. MM1?" Peary looked up as if waking from a dream. "Me and Hayes are gonna go down aft a minute."

Peary nodded. "OK. I guess I'll go find chief and tell him what's going' on. We'll have to have an all hands meeting for this." All emotion was draining out of him like an oil can tipped on its side, glug-glugging out its contents. He left without turning around.

Mark and Steve found their way to the port side ladder and down to the lower level of the engine room, passed between the two boilers and on to the darkest, loudest corner of the engine room near a reciprocating bilge pump which looked like it belonged on an ancient, coal-fired ship. The arms on top of the pump's cylinder cried out as if in pain each time they lifted it up, protesting against the continuing weight they had to lift. Then rising to the top of the stroke, the whole machine let out a steamy mechanical exhale. The effect here in the dim light of the lower level shadows of 1C boiler was like listening to a cat digging in its claws and being dragged across a tin roof and then dropped from the roof in full voice, all this with a microphone taped to the cat to amplify the sound. Only an engineer could understand a word spoken within twenty feet of the thing, and only an engineer would be able to tolerate the heading splitting noise long enough to have a conversation.

"Mark... you... can't... say... anything... about... me...checking... up... on... Cheng!" Steve mouthed.

"I... know..., I... know," Mark nodded, exaggerating to show Steve how earnest he was.

"Don't talk to anybody about it!" Steve said, his right hand clenched into a fist, his eyes open to their limit for extra emphasis.

"OK, Steve! OK! Do we have to stay here next to the pump? I'll keep my mouth shut. Promise." Mark's eyes were wide. He looked like he was about to cry.

Steve immediately regretted the look he'd put on his friend's face. *Can't become a bully to fix another bully*, he thought. His fist relaxed back into a hand and his face softened with it. He didn't say anything as he walked back toward the boiler front, away from the bilge pump. He could feel Mark on his heels. He was tired of the gut shot feeling he had over this mess, over this ship, over the Cheng and over a stupid missing valve and a stupid mistake that was costing people their freedom. Steve wasn't the kind of guy who hated people, and he never had thought of anyone as an enemy, but walking away from the depths of the engine room, he felt he was coming to understand both.

Chapter 17
Ghost Ship

Steve looked at the ship's clock on the bulkhead of Damage Control Central (DCC). It was approaching 1300. The engineering spaces all shared the same black cloud atmosphere he felt in here. No one made eye contact as they walked to their various tasks, head down, resigned. During a follow-up attempt to move the Cheng from his no liberty mandate, Peary and Mark had been told not to show their faces in his presence again unless they had the missing valve with them.

Steve sat on top of the DCC desk reviewing the daily message traffic on a ringed clipboard. The third message down in the pile caught his eye. The header read: STRIP SHIP ANNOUNCEMENT. A strip ship meant one of the old tubs sitting up in the James River had been towed down to the shipyard in Portsmouth where she would be opened up for active Navy ships to come and take whatever parts they needed.

Strip ship was the last stop before a hulk was handed over to the ship breakers to scrap it or sold to a foreign navy. It was a good deal for active ships because the parts and materials taken off the old ship were not counted against any budget. It was essentially a free trip to the hardware store and whoever got there first generally took anything and everything in sight. The next line of the message had to be wrong, Steve thought, it was just too miraculous to be true. It said the ship being stripped was the USS *Seahook*, and it was available for active ships to come aboard as of 0700 on the 9th. That was yesterday! How could *Redstone*'s sister ship be stripped and they not know about it? Steve ripped the message off the clipboard and headed aft looking for Peary. He ran into Mark two steps outside of DCC as he continued reading the message without looking up.

"Watch out, Steve!" Mark said.

"Sorry, Mark, c'mon, I've got to find Peary."

"Why, what's up? I think he's back in engineering berthing." Mark said as he fell into step behind Steve.

"*Seahook*. Strip ship." was all Steve said. His mind was going over the possibilities and improbabilities. There was no way the *Seahook* came down from the ghost fleet and Cheng didn't know it. There had to have been messages coming to the ship at least a month ago, telling about the move. Why hadn't he organized a work party to go check it out? He couldn't think about that right now. A more important question was: would any other ship on the waterfront need the same kind of valve as they were looking for? What a cruel joke this would turn out to be if he got to *Seahook* and found out the valve they needed was removed in a refit fifteen years ago, or worse, someone got to the ship yesterday and took it. He swallowed that thought. No. He was going to go there and he would find that valve. And when he did...

Once when Steve was thirteen or fourteen years old, his dad got on him for not working hard enough, gathering firewood for the family. Steve went into the woods near the house and found a 25 foot tall dead tree, standing like an ancient telephone pole, its limbs rotted off. Hitting it like a football blocking sled, first one side and then the other, he rocked it off its rotten roots enough to make it fall. With insane determination, he dragged the entire tree a foot at a time all the way back to the house where he deposited it on the front porch. The look his father gave him, the grudging admiration, the admission of getting something done he didn't think his son could do, that was the look he was going to put on the Cheng's face. He did it to his dad because he loved him, he was going to do this to the Cheng for the opposite reason.

***

Convincing Peary to let the two of them off the ship took some work, but the prospect of finding a way out of MP division's predicament overrode his fear of whatever problems would arise if the Cheng discovered that two of his sailors had left the ship in defiance of his orders.

"You have a problem, Carter," he said. "You know *Seahook* went upriver at least 15 years ago?"

Carter, itching to get moving, didn't register the significance of this information. He raised an eyebrow. "So?"

"So, women didn't start ridin' ships till '78. That means she never got women. Never got women's berthing. No WINS."

It dawned on Steve. "No WINS." he repeated. "Our valve. Our chiller."

"May not even be one on *Seahook*." Peary said.

Steve shook his head. "It'll be there. I know the unit is at least that old. That's one of the things about this that doesn't make sense—why there's a turn-in valve on a busted down old chiller unit."

Peary grimaced. "Never know, Carter. I did an addition on my house last year and the dude doing the work freaked out over the old studs he found. He said he couldn't get lumber like that anymore. Actually paid me for them. I was happy to. I'd of thrown them in a dumpster or burned them. Maybe the chiller valve is the same way."

Steve nodded. "Guess that's possible." He had an idea. "Don't we have the *Redstone* master blueprint book in DCC? Those prints would be before the WINS mod, and *Seahook* is the same class as *Redstone*. That'll at least give us an idea where to look."

Peary agreed. A few minutes later they had a musty smelling leatherbound book spread out on the stainless steel desk in DCC. The book fascinated Steve. The fine blue lines etched on fold out folios of thick linen paper made him feel he was looking at an intricate picture book rather than reading some lifeless industrial document. It was like the book belonged in a museum, not a shelf in DCC.

"This is a cool book," Steve said.

Peary grunted and rifled through several plats before he found the layout of the deck he was looking for. As he spread the book open, the print underneath it pulled free from the book. Peary tried to shove it back in the volume but Steve stopped him.

"Let me see that a sec," he said.

At some point in the long history of *Redstone*, a single folio had been torn from the book, and returned to its place. There would have been no way to properly affix it again, because the tome was stitched together, so it had sat here loose, for who knew how long? The binding edge was slightly frayed and upon closer inspection Steve saw creases in it where someone had folded it back on itself. While the rest of the book's pages had a pristine look, as if they'd never seen the light of day, this sheet had been roughly handled. There was writing on it. Steve tried to take a closer look. Peary swept the sheet aside impatiently.

"You can come back and look through this some other time, Carter." He poked his pointy middle finger into the fine blue lines of the deck drawing. "Right here's the chiller before any mods were made for WINS. If this is the bulkhead near where they put the women's heads," he said, tracing a line with his finger, "then it looks like it never got moved when they gutted this area. It was in," he leaned closer and squinted at the fine writing on the print, "the aviation instrument shop. Always forget these old tubs were outfitted with seaplanes."

Steve nodded agreement. "*Seahook* should be laid out like this and I should be able to get at our valve easy enough."

Peary said, "Here, take this with you so you have a map," and unceremoniously tore the page from the book. "And take this other loose one too." He handed both sheets to Steve. The tearing of the page from the book felt sacrilegious to Steve, but he accepted the sheets, rolled them up like posters and pocketed them.

"Don't come back without that valve," Peary said.

Steve started to retort something about Peary doing a poor imitation of the Cheng but when he looked in the man's face he saw desperation, not a tyrant.

"If it's there, I'll get it, MM1," he said, putting more confidence into his voice than he felt.

Steve and Mark joined in with a working party carrying trash off the ship, so they wouldn't walk down the brow exposed and alone, in case Hiller was watching. They took Steve's truck instead of the ship's van. Steve, true to the bone snipe, had his own portable welding gear and tools. They were counting on his gear to do any salvage work they needed, if they found the valve. The only evidence that they weren't on the ship was their missing bodies.

They drove along the stop-and-go of Hampton Boulevard to the shipyard. How different the world looked from the cab of the truck! There were people going about their business out here, oblivious to what went on in the Cheng's universe. They went home at night. They went to lunch at McDonalds. They smiled. Steve and Mark drank it in, in silence.

Passing through downtown Norfolk onto I-464 Steve took them across the old Jordan bridge into the shipyard through the back gate. The blackened steel bridge reminded him of the bones of a tyrannosaurus rex thrown over on its side. Glimpses of ships sitting at the yard's backside piers flashed between black ribs as they crossed. Many of these ships were dinosaurs themselves, going extinct, their original coating of distinct haze gray paint, was now faded and chalky, as if their very image was blurring away into the past. The white hull numbers were all but gone from these ships, making it near impossible to distinguish their identities, but *Seahook* was there. They would find her and find the valve.

He asked the rent-a-cop gate guard where to find her. *Seahook* had been towed up into a slot near several active ships undergoing normal yard periods. *This wasn't good for them*, Steve thought. A day's worth of picking through the ship by the crews of four or five destroyers would take a toll. Having driven his personal truck, Steve couldn't park on the pier. He found a parking space on a dirt and gravel lot half a mile from the ship instead. After making the trek to the ship, he discovered a hitch: in their haste to get going, neither he nor Mark had thought to obtain the necessary paperwork to remove anything from *Seahook*. The petty officer in charge of the gangway was adamant— they weren't going to get on without it. Steve finally convinced the gatekeeper to let them on by offering to give up his military I.D. card in exchange for a promise to bring the paperwork back for anything they scavenged off the hulk, as soon as they returned to *Redstone*. This was the equivalent of giving up his passport in a foreign country, but Steve had nothing else to bargain with, and he reasoned, if they obtained the missing valve, coming and going from the *Redstone* would no longer be a problem with or without an ID. Mark, who had been listening to the negotiations, interrupted them.

"Let me do it, Steve. I'm the one who got us in this mess. I'll give up my card." Mark's face was too sincere to ignore. It was obvious he needed to do something to regain some self-respect. He handed over the card and they started up the brow of the abandoned ship.

They carried portable yellow battle lanterns borrowed from the petty officer who took Mark's I.D. card. The lanterns cut into the dark of the ship's interior. A musty smell met them as they stepped inside. It reminded Steve of an old leather boot which hadn't been worn in years, well used yet long vacant. They found discouraging evidence of other strip ship crews along their route; wiring harnesses dangling into passageways, and random bits of partially deconstructed pieces of machinery littered the decks. In the dim light of the borrowed battle lanterns, walking through the interior of *Seahook* felt like walking through a morgue of autopsied robots.

Picking their way along in the dim light, Mark and Steve became disoriented. They had not realized the extent the modifications for WINS berthing had required on *Redstone*. After making several wrong turns leading to dead ends, Steve remembered the rolled up blueprints. He pulled them out.

"Here, Mark, shine your lantern on this so I can get an idea where we are," he said. Mark complied. Steve unrolled the blueprints on the deck in the passageway. Running his finger across the platt of the third deck he murmured, "This must be the location of the aviation instrument repair shop... and..." He looked over his shoulder in each direction to orient himself. "...I think we are here." he tapped the print. "That means the chiller ought to be at the end of this p-way in the last space on the right. Let's check it out."

The last door on the right leaned askew in its frame, the blackness behind framing it like a single crooked tooth. Above it a brass plate, green with corrosion, read:

Aviation Instrument Repair

They stood in the passageway and read the plaque silently. To Steve, it felt like he was at the entrance to an ancient tomb. A childhood memory flashed through his mind. His mother had given him a book about the discovery of King Tut's tomb. He was obsessed with it. He read and reread it until the cover fell off. That same summer the boy king's treasures came to the Smithsonian Museum in Washington, D.C. He begged and pleaded to go. His mother surprised him when she took him for his birthday. Now he envisioned the explorer—easy enough to remember his name —Howard Carter, standing just outside the stoned up entrance to the tomb, gazing in with his light, to see if it was intact or if it was plundered and empty. He sensed Mark staring at him. He shook himself and pushed the door inward. It squealed and swayed in on the one remaining rusty hinge.

Steve shone his lantern into the space and saw what he was looking for immediately. "There it is, Mark!"

The chiller unit stood on the far bulkhead, a six foot by eight foot box with piping running in and out of it. The front cover of the unit had lost its grip on one side at some time in the last twenty years. It sat slanted, giving the chiller a lopsided look, but other than that, the unit appeared to be undisturbed. They approached it silently, playing the beams of their battle lanterns across its face, neither realizing that he was holding his breath. Mark took out an adjustable wrench and removed three stubborn bolts remaining on the cover. It came off suddenly with a clang that reverberated in the enclosed space. Both men shined their lights into the interior of the unit. There it was—the valve whose twin slept at the bottom of the Mediterranean. They looked at each other with kid-like grins. In his mind's eye Steve saw Hiller's smug face. He knew he was going to enjoy erasing that look.

Chapter 18
Phipps Trapped
September 1976, North Atlantic Ocean

The outchop OPPE continued, dragging the old ship and her weary engineers across the Atlantic like an old west wagon train. Simulated casualties requiring the ship to go hot, dark, and quiet made for sporadic progress west, as the engineering department proved they could extinguish dreaded mainspace fires, reroute electrical circuits around damaged distribution panels and control flooding in both shaft alleys at once. The topsiders did their usual complaining when the drills interrupted their meals and lounging time in front of the ship's CCTV, which played a continuing stream of movies everyone aboard had watched half a dozen times already.

The loudest complaints came from Repair Department, a department filled with engineering rates who viewed themselves like TV personalities on the set of a show. They were the talent that made the whole ship important, not like the lowly ship's company engineers who merely got them to the places where they carried out the ship's mission. These divas often found ways to skip going to battle stations altogether, congregating in out of the way repair shops, playing spades or poker or partaking in a sailor's favorite pastime at sea—sleeping. And so the majority of *Redstone*'s crew grumbled at time spent on a few extra watches and their disrupted schedules while the engineers sweated out the Navy's version of an engineering colonoscopy.

Jasper and his repair locker crew were running on three hours sleep over two days. Between drills, bleary eyed and too fatigued to keep to his feet without leaning against a bulkhead in DCC, he was summoned to the phone.

"Phipps?"

"Yeah. Go," he said, wondering at the effort it took, just getting his mouth to work.

"Can you come up here to the Supply Office? I know how we can get our job done."

"Job? Wha? Who the hell is this," Jasper slurred.

"It's Richards! Come up here. I've got something to show you!"

Phipps held the phone away from his head, looked at it and at the duty HT of the watch, who appeared to be asleep sitting up at his post. He swayed slightly on his feet, more with fatigue than *Redstone*'s rocking. He put the phone back to his ear and hissed in it.

"Listen dumbass, if I come up there it'll only be to stuff you in a locker... if I can find one big enough for your fat ass. If I..." Phipps was like a helicopter spinning up; ready to unleash pent up anger; glad to have a convenient place to let it all out. Richards cut him off with his own flood of invectives.

"Shut your pie hole, you hillbilly dip shit. We're going through with this. It's too late. I've doctored the lading lists. The box doesn't exist anymore. If it shows up on the pier, there's no getting around it. I'm the only one who has touched the paperwork. I'm done. So shut up your sad sack, 'cry me a river' snipe story and get your ass up here. Do it or

I swear I'll sing a song for the Suppo. I'll tell him about the secret compartment. How I heard you and... and who's that silly son of a bitch that hangs around you like a little sea pup? Carns. Yeah. You and Fireman Carns were hatching a plan to steal one of the crates. I'll take him to the spot. I'll show him the conduit you laid that ain't attached to anything. And Phipps, there ain't nobody else but you could've done that work. Now," Richards paused. He let the temperature of his voice fall. When he spoke again he could've been offering Phipps a piece of gum. "hang up the phone and come see me in the Supply Office."

Jasper realized he had slowly tightened his grip on the phone as Richards spoke. With an effort he unclenched his fist and hung up.

Chapter 19
Return to Redstone
December 1989, Pierside, Norfolk, Virginia

The drive back to *Redstone* felt like a holiday. Mark popped a Huey Lewis and the News tape in the cassette player, and they butchered *Hip to be Square*, laughing at how badly they sang. Steve noted how Mark sat up straight. The droop in his shoulders was gone. He was reinflated. But as they approached the gate to the naval base, Steve's mind pinballed. What if Cheng knew they were off the ship? Was he sure it was the right valve? How were they going to explain where they got it? Who could he get from supply to write up the documentation for the strip ship? When could he get back to *Seahook* to retrieve his I.D. card? Once his brain got going he had a hard time stopping it. He was tired by the time they parked the truck and crossed *Redstone's* brow.

The petty officer of the watch welcomed them back aboard with a deceptively cheerful, "You guys are in a world a' shit."

Steve felt the blood drain from his face. "Why's that?"

"Cheng told the OOD about two hours ago, wasn't no one from MP division supposed to leave the ship for no reason unless he personally OK'd it."

Steve looked at his watch. "We were gone before he said that."

"Yeah, but you were also gone when they mustered MP division and did a body count. We passed the word for you two twice on the 1MC since then."

Mark's shoulders resumed their hangdog angle.

Steve said, "Come on, Mark. We were gonna end up in front of the Cheng one way or another. We've got this," he indicated the green canvas bag holding the valve, "and we'll see what happens." He said this with more confidence than he felt, realizing again, as he stood on her deck, the weight of *Redstone* gravity.

The labyrinth of stairwells and passageways leading to the Cheng's office felt like descending into a dungeon. Steve's vision of wiping the smugness off Hiller's face faded. Now he only wanted to make the man's latest outrage go away quietly. Mark subconsciously moved behind Steve as he knocked on the door. For the second time today he heard Hiller's shrill "Enter!"

Steve took the lead. "Cheng?"

"Ohhh, so here's the two of you. I've been looking for you." The smug look. The condescending smile.

"Yes, sir, Cheng, ah, we went to get the missing valve," Steve said. "Show 'im Mark."

Mark unzipped the canvas bag with unsteady hands. He took out the recovered valve and laid it gently on the desk, like an offering on an altar.

Hiller stared at it, expressionless. He said, "Where'd you boys find this? Thought you said the thing was at the bottom of the ocean?"

Steve briefly explained their trip to *Seahook*, omitting the part about leaving Mark's I.D. card in exchange for getting onto the ship.

"So *Seahook* is at strip ship, uh? Wonder how I missed that. I guess MP division will be happy to know they can go home tonight. Why, you two are heroes aren't you?" There was a warning note in the man's tone. It made Steve more uneasy than he already was. This was going too smoothly.

The Cheng was still talking: "...the supply petty officer up here and get the paperwork we need to get this turned in."

He looked up at the two of them. Steve realized he must have missed something requiring a response. He defaulted to "Yes, sir." Turning to go, he and Mark were at the door when Hiller spoke again.

"And after you get the supply guy up here you both can head down to the Master-At-Arms Shack to sign your report chits."

Mark looked at Steve. Steve turned back toward the Cheng and said, "Report chits?"

"Oh yeah, Carter. You and Hayes have been off this ship for over three hours. You disobeyed a direct order. Unauthorized Absence. Both of you are gonna see the Old Man." *Now* the Cheng was smiling. "In fact," Hiller said, opening a drawer and pulling out a sheaf of papers, "I've got quite a file on you, Carter. Had a little talk with Peary and BTCS Snell, and wouldn't you know, they remembered some talks they've had with you about your performance." He picked up the top sheet of paper. It was white and crisp, obviously a recent deposit on the Cheng's desk. "MM2 Carter counseled about appearance of his uniform. Here's another: MM2 Carter failed to turn in required training before it was due...."

Steve stared into the face of a snake and not a man. Hiller riffled the papers in his own face. "Smells like reduction in rate to me. Maybe thirty and thirty, too."

Steve felt as if a thick wool blanket had been pulled around his head. Hiller's words became muffled. He remained frozen in the doorway. Mark poked him in his side to get him moving. Numbly, they found their way to the supply office. Steve regained his senses enough to remember their I.D. card problem and asked the SK2, a frumpy dirty blond female named Martin to write up the paperwork he would need to get it back.

On the way to the Master-at-Arms shack, Mark spewed worried questions. "Can he really say we were UA? Weren't we doing Navy business? Can we still get off the ship tonight? Why didn't Peary tell him where we were?"

Steve kept his head down. One step. He told himself. You only have to take one step at a time. He heard all of Mark's questions. He had no answers. He was going to the MAA shack. That was the next thing to do. After that he would do the next thing. *Maybe*, he thought, *the Cheng was trying to get a rise out of them.* Maybe there were no report chits waiting for them. He was the kind of guy who would relish the awkward situation created by doing something like that. If he sent them looking for a chit that wasn't there, what would they do next? Would they come back to him asking if he was only joking? Would they pretend they never had a discussion about report chits? Steve smiled grimly to himself. Yeah, Cheng would enjoy putting someone in a tough spot and watching them writhe. He was a cruel man. But when they got to the MAA shack, he wasn't surprised to find the real things waiting for their signatures and MAC McBurney handing them a Navy issue black ink pen to officially acknowledge being on report.

"The Cheng said you two gotta give up your ID cards to me," McBurney said apologetically. He wasn't a bad guy, not a cop wanna be like most of the underling Master at Arms who worked for him.

Steve raised an eyebrow. "Can he do that, Chief?"

The Chief Master at Arms shrugged. "Tell you the truth, it's kind of a gray area. Technically he can't make you surrender your ID card, but he told me he gave you an order to remain on the ship until he says you can go, and without your ID's, you can't go anywhere. He's the CDO, and the Old Man and the XO are already gone for the weekend, so...." He shrugged again. "It's his ship right now."

Steve pulled his wallet from his back pocket and extracted his plastic coated military green ID card. The half-ounce card felt heavy in his hand. McBurney accepted it without comment and held out his hand to Mark. "Sorry, bud. Give it up." Mark stared at McBurney's outstretched hand, blank faced. He started to speak. Steve cut him off.

"Chief, let me explain all that's happened today." He summarized the events of their day. When he was done, McBurney gave a long "hmmm," as if debating what to do next. The missing ID card presented its own set of problems. Hayes was not supposed to be without it and McBurney couldn't give an viable explanation to Hiller if asked for it. He could write Hayes up for not having his ID, or let the man go and claim it was lost, but neither of these solutions felt like a good one. McBurney felt no love loss for Hiller and, like most of the khakis in the Chief's mess, avoided crossing swords with the man. Steve's story reinforced the picture he'd already formed of the Cheng as an out of control tyrant. The Chief Master at Arms was a man with strong ideas about justice, and this wasn't the first time he felt that an engineer was being railroaded by Hiller. It was McBurney and his men the Cheng had forced to conduct an extremely questionable locker search, leading to a drug bust and Big Chicken Dinner for a Boiler Tech named Ray Lambert, just over a year ago. He was pondering this when Steve ventured a solution.

"You could let me take the paperwork back over to the shipyard, Chief. It'd only take me an hour and a half round trip. If I left right now, I could be back before liberty call. The sally port is open till then for load out."

McBurney considered this. Steve sensed both his hesitation and sympathy. "Chief, you know me. You know I won't screw you over. I'll get over there and back before anybody knows I'm gone. You can send one of your guys with me. You know what Cheng's gonna do if he finds out Hayes gave up his ID. It'll be another report chit on top of the ones you already have to deal with." For a second Steve thought his appeal to the Chief's dislike of paperwork had been too condescending. McBurney didn't say anything, but looked at Steve's ID, still in his hand. Shaking it gently in the air for emphasis he handed it back.

"Get back here ASAP. If I find out you did anything besides go there and back...."

"I'm gone, Chief. See you in two hours, max," Steve said, accepting the card like a baton in a relay race. "Thanks."

The Chief stopped him and looked him in the eye. "Carter, I'll keep an eye on the sally port till they close it at liberty call. If you come back later'n that and have to come up the main brow, you're on your own. Same thing if the Cheng comes lookin' for you or asks about you. Got it?"

"I understand." Steve said.

Chapter 20
Back in Time

The drive back to the shipyard crawled. The traffic on Hampton Boulevard accordioned along, finally coming to a halt at Terminal Boulevard. A train blocked the intersection, easing forward and back in slow advances and retreats across the road, never quite clearing the way. Steve stared ahead numbly, barely noticing. Thoughts of XOI, Captain's Mast, and the stack of counseling chits Hiller had produced like a magician pulling a rabbit out of a hat, buzzed around his head like flies. He was certain the XO would refer the case up to the Captain for Mast. Hiller would intimidate her into forwarding the case.

The current XO had spent her entire career ashore, working with reserve centers. Although holding the rank of full commander, the woman was woefully lacking in experience. A wispy woman with dirty brown, chopped hair surrounding a face too small for her coke bottle glasses, she looked more like a fifth grade boy playing dress up than the second in line to command a Naval vessel. In order to be considered eligible for command and her next promotion, she needed to check a lot of boxes during her 18 month tour on *Redstone*. One of those boxes was qualifying as an engineering officer of the watch. That was the catch. Hiller controlled every qualification in the engineering department and he could make it very difficult for her if she didn't see things his way. Steve doubted the XO had the stomach for a fight with the Cheng even if he didn't have any leverage over her career. With engineering quals hanging over her head, Hiller could make her do backflips and say 'thank you for the exercise' when she was done.

The train moved. A red faced man in a Ford F-150 brought Steve back to the here and now with a too long to be friendly blare from his horn. He rolled off, still lost in thought. It was a foregone conclusion; XOI was a formality. He would go to Mast. Amazing. He had never been in the slightest bit of trouble in the Navy. On a normal ship, under normal circumstances, for a first offense, he and Hayes would have had to pull a little extra duty or gotten an ass chewing from their LPO or Chief. But *Redstone* was a different animal. The engineering chiefs were scared of the Cheng and convinced he would ruin them at the drop of a hat. They avoided confrontation with him and wouldn't think of getting in his way. The stack of doctored counseling chits was evidence enough of where they stood. Of course the chits were made up out of thin air. Hiller intimidated Peary and Snell the same way he would intimidate the XO: provide me with some dirt on Carter and Hayes or else. And they did. It wouldn't do any good to point out to the XO or the Old Man that he never saw those chits in his life until the Cheng dropped them on his desk like a miniature cluster bomb. It was strange to Carter, though. Why was Hiller hedging his bets? He knew the man was mean and that Hayes had lately become one of his targets, but why me? He got a cold shudder when he considered the possibility that Hiller knew about his late night sleuthing expeditions. The more he thought about it, the more the idea grew. It was the only explanation. How did the Cheng know? Hayes? Probably. Mark wasn't the brightest bulb and tended to use a lot of words. If it turned out that Hiller was on to him, Captain's Mast might be the least of his worries. He might be the next victim of a locker search that turned up drugs. Regardless, this was serious. If he got busted in rank and forfeited half a month's pay for two months—the max punishment he could receive—he would miss going back to school on schedule. He would either have to get out and find a job or reenlist another four years. Four years! He and Hayes had been UA for less than four hours and it was going to cost him four years??

His mind swirled as he drove up to the shipyard gate. The security guard waved him through. Fifty minutes had elapsed since McBurney had walked him to the sally port and secretly escorted him across the auxiliary brow, giving him a final warning not to be late getting back. He felt the clock ticking like his own pulse. He heard it in his ears. Felt it in his chest. 'It would be fine,' he told himself. *Seahook* loomed up at him from her berth pierside. Afternoon sunlight shone dimly on her port side, absorbed by her chalky gray hull. The shipyard shift change was fifteen minutes away. Finding an open parking place near the ship would be a miracle, but he drove along the front row of the crowded lot anyway. There was no time for the hike from the outback he and Hayes made earlier.

He spotted an open space at the head of the pier and dove into it, whispering a prayer of thanks before he noticed a sign sitting at the head of the space. In runny black spray paint it read: *Seahook* Strip Ship Supervisor ONLY. Guy's gotta be gone for the day, Steve said to himself. I'll be outta here in three minutes.

He locked the door and stuffed his keys into his pocket as he strode toward the small guard shack at the foot of

Seahook's brow. The sailor who greeted him was not the same as the one he and Hayes met on their first visit to *Seahook*. That guy had been a tall blonde HT named Billings. This guy was a short stumpy sailor with a Marine buzz cut that made him look shorter than he was. His name tag said Harding and he wore the crow of a third class machinist.

He nodded a greeting and said, "Where's the guy who was here earlier? I left an I.D. with him and I need to get it back ASAP."

"Billings? He's making a tour around the ship before we close 'r down for the night," Harding said. "Got to make sure no one gets locked up in there by mistake."

"He say anything about the I.D.?"

"Nope, not to me."

"Man, I've got to get that card and get going or I'm in big trouble. Can I go on and try to find him?"

"Go ahead. Billings is a pretty thorough guy, he takes a long time and does a real inspection. He may be down in shaft alley, for all I know."

Steve felt time passing like a leak from a holed tire. "If he comes back before me would you ask him to leave the card? Here's the supply paperwork I promised him I'd bring back," he said handing the forms over. "Can I borrow one of those battle lanterns?"

"Sure shipmate," Harding said, handing him one of the dingy yellow box lanterns and flipping the switch on and off to make sure it worked. "I'll tell 'im. You awright? Look a little stressed."

He started up the brow. "Yeah, I just gotta get back to my ship," he said over his shoulder.

Steve went aft, guessing the engineering spaces would be the best place to find somebody who was making a real inspection and not just gun decking it. The battle lantern light was weak. It spilled reluctantly from the front of the box onto the deck in front of him in a barely discernible yellow puddle. He flicked the switch on and off and slapped the side as if the light was in a box of Rice Crispies and he was shaking the very last bit of it out. It was cold inside the skin of the dead ship, noticeably colder than it had been earlier in the day. He could see his breath in the failing light.

The ticking of the clock in his head grew louder minute by minute. If he didn't return to *Redstone* in time to slip aboard using the auxiliary gangway at the sallyport, he'd have to cross the main gangway—and the thought of that terrified him. McBurney warned him about that; the Cheng had alerted the watchstanders on the main to look out for Steve. Crossing there would be as good as turning himself over to the Cheng.

Twenty minutes passed with no sign of Billings. His stomach was doing backflips. He was on the third deck, as far away from an external source of light as he could get, when the battle lantern expended its last bit of juice. He was in complete darkness. Disgusted, he threw the worthless plastic box down the passageway. It bounced off one side of the narrow corridor and then the other, coming to an abrupt halt when it hit a door and bounced back onto the deck, a beam of strong white light spouting from its face like a water fountain pointed up at a crazy angle. Steve said, "I'll be," as he went to it and retrieved it. "Guess I didn't slap you hard enough." He laughed. It was a good laugh. All the tension built up over the last few hours spilled out with the laughter. He looked at the door the lantern had banged against before coming to rest and realized he was one deck down from the chill unit where he and Hayes had retrieved the lost valve only hours ago. Curious, he pushed open the door and swept the room with the now brightly shining light. It took a moment but he saw that not only was he one deck down, but he was precisely under the spot where they got the valve. He could see the pipes feeding the unit disappearing into the overhead. Orienting himself further, he pictured where he would be if this was *Redstone* and not *Seahook*. The Dive Shack. Yes. This would be the Dive Shack on *Redstone*. Funny how a few alterations to bulkheads here and there changed how the place looked. WINS berthing didn't exist on *Seahook*, just as Pearcy told them it wouldn't, and the maze of spaces up there was enough to make his head spin. He remembered the old blueprint book he found in DC Central and resolved to trace out the changes when he got back to *Redstone* so he could see where he'd gotten lost.

As he stood contemplating this, he heard the distinct clank of a watertight door opening nearby. Simultaneously he heard, "Yo! Anyone in here?

He stepped out of the space he'd been exploring and nearly bowled over Billings.

"Sorry 'bout that, man," Steve said. "I was looking for you."

"Looks like you found me," Billings said good-naturedly.

"I just need to get that I.D. back I left with you earlier today."

"Yeah, I got back to the guard shack after my rounds and Harding told me you were looking for this," he held up Hayes's card. "Too bad he didn't look up. It was right there over the bulletin board. Left it there in case you came back while I was gone. Guess I should've told him, but I forgot." He handed the card to Steve.

He looked at the card in his hand and checked his watch. It was 1515. He could still get back to *Redstone* before the sally port closed. It would be close, but he could make it. Billings led the way back to the main deck. They emerged into the afternoon daylight and crossed the gangway in time to see a yellow flashing light receding from the parking lot. Harding was standing at the foot of the brow with his hands tucked into his green foul weather jacket. He nodded toward the yellow lights.

"Some idiot parked in the ship sup's spot," Harding said. "I called the tow truck to come get 'em."

Steve stopped dead. He looked from Harding and Billings and back again. His face felt hot. All the tension the laughter had drained away sprang back into place.

"That's... that was my truck!" he said. "Why'd you have to do that? Dude...." He flopped down on the last metal step of the brow and put his head in both hands. He thought it might explode. He groaned and threw his head back.

Harding and Billings watched the meltdown with a mixture of military indifference toward the troubles of anyone not in your own unit, and concern for the suffering of another human being. They fell on opposite sides of the issue. Harding shrugged and insisted the truck needed to be towed because it was what the watch rules told him must be done, and anyone stupid enough to park there deserved whatever happened to them. Billings got Steve up off the step and walked him to the guard shack. A call to the base Command Duty Officer's office located the towed truck.

"I'm off watch in fifteen minutes. I'll run you over there and help you get it out of the impound lot." he said.

The passing of more time, which had been so important to Steve only moments before, no longer had meaning. The tow truck towed away any chance of making it back to *Redstone* under cover of Chief McBurney's excuses. The sally port would be closed. He would have to pass across the main brow. The race was over. He'd lost. The realization calmed him.

He rehearsed the worst punishment he could expect once he was discovered UA a second time in one day, and explained the situation to Billings and Harding. The two sailors made the appropriate groans and curses at the particularly unfair parts of the story. By the time he finished telling it, he felt lighter again. Shared woes were always better than private ones, he heard his mother's voice again, and again wondered at how many of her words were caught in the tangles along the stream of his thoughts. He was even able to laugh over Harding's need to tow his truck away, less than an hour before quitting time on Friday of a three day weekend. Billings laughed along, Harding did not.

Fingering the I.D. card in his pocket, he pulled it out and held it up to Billings. "Hey, show me where you left this card. I want to see just how close I was to finding it before my life got towed away."

Billings took the card and leaned it on top of a weary cork board to the left of the tiny guard shack's entrance. "It was right here," he said.

Steve stood up to simulate where Harding stood when he first approached him. Seeing the card there now he understood how Harding had missed it. The card was visible, but it was only visible if you were looking for something beyond the upper edge of the board, beyond the edge of where the normal messages were to be found. He reached up and plucked it from its perch. He placed it back in his pocket and sighed. So clear once you knew what you were looking for and where to look.

"Come on, man. I'm secured now," said Billings. "Let me run you over to the tow yard and get your truck."

Billings drove Steve to the base impound lot and talked the tow guys into giving his truck back. It was 1600 when he drove out of the yards. Liberty call on *Redstone* was going down right now. The sally port was closed.

He stopped at the 7-11 at the corner of Effingham and Elm and sat behind the wheel trying to gather his thoughts. It would be a miracle if he got back aboard without being missed. A car pulled in next to him with its stereo blaring. It jarred him out of his catatonic state.

"Don't Stop Beleevin'. Hold onto that feeelinnn'..."

He watched as the car exhaled five passengers. He realized he had been squeezing the steering wheel, staring straight ahead lost in another world. How long? He checked his watch—ten minutes—felt longer. He flexed his fingers to get the blood flowing again and decided to get a cup of coffee. The earthy, rich aroma of the steaming liquid filled up the cab as he gingerly took the first few hot sips. The smell and the taste cheered him. No use trying to get back on the ship right now. The best bet was to wait until dark. If their secret was still safe and he hadn't already been discovered, it was the one way he could get up the pier and across the brow with the least exposure. And if the jig was up, might as well take an hour or two at the apartment and grab the things he would miss if he got restricted to the ship; mainly, for Steve, that meant books. A foxhole or a prison wasn't so bad if you had a paperback escape hatch. Never get caught without a book. He started the truck and headed for Ocean View.

Chapter 21
Richards Finds a Way
September 1976, North Atlantic Ocean

Every ladder on the way up to Supply felt like pitches on a mountain climb to Jasper's weary legs. Every rung made him regret the day Richards cornered him in Riley's bar; every step was a deposit in the account of growing ill will he felt for the man. He decided the best way to handle Shopkeeper Chief Petty Officer Richard Richards was the way you handled any khaki who "got too big for their britches," as his dear old mother would've said. You nodded your head, smiled, and waited for them to trip over their own pants legs. Meantime you carried on as best you could and did as little of what they told you to do as possible. This had served Jasper well in the Navy, which was full of men promoted above both their ability and sense; men who too often reached further than their grasp, making the sailors under them suffer for it. This was no different. Richards was no different. It reminded Jasper of why he'd gotten into this ridiculous situation in the first place—too many years of too many of these men treating him like a human back scratcher, picking him up to scratch their itch, throwing him back down when they were done.

The door to the Supply Office was open. Several sailors in too clean dungarees and chambray shirts sat at tidy desks topped by metal trays of forms. One looked up disdainfully as Jasper entered. He was playing solitaire.

"Help you?" he said, with no help in his eyes or voice.

"Chief Richards?" Jasper said.

Before the sailor could move, a door behind him opened and Richards strode out; prince of this little domain.

"HT2! Thanks for coming up to see me," he said without the slightest hint of irony. "Come on in. Mallory, go get us some coffee," he said to the sailor, who looked anything but pleased at having his game interrupted.

They entered his office and he closed the door. The tiny space barely contained a standard haze-gray desk and two chairs, but any private space in a Navy ship marked its owner as a class apart. Before they could settle in, Mallory knocked and entered with two paper cups filled with steaming black coffee. Jasper sniffed. It was real coffee, not the noxious brown water common to the mess decks.

"My own stock," Richards said, nodding and smiling. "Traded some old useless foul weather jackets we were going to survey out with a supply chief on that Italian destroyer that was alongside in Naples. Got a five pound bag of genuine expresso beans and a grinder for ten of 'em." He looked pleased with himself and disappointed when Jasper's face remained impassive. He changed tacks. "Of course, when we've sorted out our little problem, fine coffee will be easy enough for us to come by."

Jasper decided to match Richards's diplomatic tone. "Chief, I'm right tired. Let me in on your solution if you don't mind, so I can get below and rest before they call away another GQ. OPPE says we failed the last main space fire drill and things aren't gonna go well for any of us if we fail the next one." He managed what he hoped was a disarming smile that would mask the hatred he felt for this man.

Richards said, "Glad to see we're on the same page now. Guess we can chalk up our little disagreement to fatigue."

He reached behind his desk and pulled a book out of a filing cabinet. The cover was light blue canvas edged in orange brown leather, cracked with age. It was large and rectangular. It looked important to Jasper, like the family Bible his mother kept on its own stand in the living room of their ramshackle home. He said so.

The Chief smirked as he sat the tome on the desk between them, undoing a leather hasp that kept it closed. "Guess you could say it is a Bible of sorts." He opened the cover, revealing a stack of papers folded back on themselves. He unfolded the first sheet. It was covered with a full length tracing of the outline of a ship in fine lines of royal blue. Tiny notes filled spaces around the ship in boxes and over various components.

Jasper's eyes went wide. "This's the original book of *Redstone*'s blueprints!"

Richards looked pleased. "Yeah. I came upon them accidentally in the chief's mess. The book was in the bottom of a locker no one was using. I asked around the mess and no one knew where it came from. Guess some old snipe chief left it there when he transferred. I thought it was cool, so I kept it. Feel this paper. I think it's made of cloth or something." He rubbed a sheet between his fingers and motioned for Phipps to do the same.

The book mesmerized Phipps. The perfectly straight lines, the tiny detail and the boxes of meticulously handwritten titles and descriptions of components and specifications fascinated him. He ran his fingers back and forth on the linen sheet as if it were Braille.

"This is history," he said. "Look, here in the corner, at the label for this plate. It's got the shipyard name and the date the keel got laid down. This book must be valuable!"

A familiar greedy gleam flickered in Richards' eyes. "You think so? I kept it because it seemed like a thing the Cheng or one of you snipes may want some day. You know me. Always looking out for an opportunity to make a good trade."

"That should go in the Navy archives if no one onboard wants it. It's almost 40 years old and probably one of a kind. Besides that, after all the mods that's been done to this ship, these drawings may be the only accurate ones left. They didn't do such a hot job making records of that stuff in the sixties. I run into things all the time that ain't where they're supposed to be."

Richards smiled again. "So you say. And that's why I pulled them out an hour ago. You see, I had this thought come to me clear as a bell." He wiped a hand across his mouth. "Our problem is the door, you see? It's guarded and we can't get in. But then I thought, if we can't use that door, why not use another?"

"There is no other." Phipps interrupted.

"Right! There is no other," Richards said. "I didn't know that for sure, and I didn't want to get caught roaming around down there. But I remembered my book!" He slapped the opened volume on the desk and pawed through it, stopping at a fly leaf marked with a piece of scrap paper. "Here's the original second deck, where you're making all these spaces into WINS berthing. Funny thing is that even back then," he poked a finger in the center of the drawing, "all this area only had one door. The same door that's our problem today."

Phipps tried but failed to keep his contempt for this conversation and for Richards from leaking into his face. Richards didn't notice. He continued, his tone rising with excitement.

"No other doors! At first I was disappointed. Then I thought a little and it hit me! Look at all this. It used to be compartments and passageways and doors... and you and your guys made it one big open space. If you can take doors out you can put doors in! And we can! We can put a door anywhere we want. I've got a door maker!" He glanced up to see what Phipps would say to this.

Phipps comprehended the idea immediately. The coffee, which had been momentarily pressing back the fatigue, was losing its battle. Phipps managed a low, "Hmmm." Then he said, "Don't you think someone's gonna notice it when a hole appears in a bulkhead that wasn't there yesterday? And the entire perimeter of the new WINS berthing is exposed... it'd be like cutting your new doorway next to a highway. Lots of people coming and going through there, night and day."

"True. Thought of that too, Phippsy. But why think one dimensionally? Or even two dimensionally? I was stumped for a while. Then I walked in here and saw Mallory and a friend of his doing a brain teaser. You know the one where you're supposed to connect the dots with a line on a piece of paper without crossing any lines? It's really a trick puzzle with no answer. It's supposed to piss you off. Anyway the guy Mallory played it on looked at it a few minutes turning it all which ways. Then he picked up the paper, poked a hole through it and drew a line on the back side of the paper to the other dot where he poked another hole. Sure pissed off Mallory. He had a 10 on it that the guy couldn't solve it, but he had to pay up."

Phipps yawned. "That's great, Chief. What's the point?"

Richards said, "This is the point," turning to the next blueprint in the book between them. He pointed to a faint circle drawn in pencil on the plat. "This is where we make our door. This is where we poke our hole and solve the puzzle." Phipps leaned over the drawing to see what Richards was talking about. In the original 1939 drawing, it showed a small rectangular compartment labeled "small arms locker." He oriented himself using the starboard side passageway as a landmark.

"That's not a small arms locker anymore." He looked puzzled. "I can't place it. What's there now?"

If it were possible for Richards to look any more pleased with himself, he did now. "It's part of a storeroom now. It's where we keep controlled inventory that has a habit of walking away if it isn't locked down tight. And I've got one of only two keys onboard that open the door. You're the expert. I just roughed it out, but I think you'll find that we can make our door upward right there and come out within a few feet of our false compartment."

Jasper looked hard at Richards. Richards didn't return the look. He was staring at the blue print and his penciled circle as if he was holding a treasure map and "O" marked the spot. His protruding blue eyes gleamed and a stupid grin split his face. It was going to be hard keeping this crazy bastard from actually cutting this hole and carrying on with his insane scheme, terrible hard. He took the only route he could think of to forestall the him. He took the book, folded up the fly leafs they'd been studying and shut it. "Let me have this for a bit. I'll do some measuring and see what I come up with.

Chapter 22
Steve In Chains
December 1989, Pierside, Norfolk, Virginia

Hiller checked the digital clock on his stateroom desk. It was 0100. He finished up his post romp hygiene and dressed in his washed khakis. Tonight he'd bedded the 18-year-old Deck Department seaman apprentice he shared with the Bos'n on nights Maggie wasn't available. He headed to the quarterdeck to check on the watch. One of his special pleasures was descending on unwitting watch keepers at ungodly times from unexpected directions. He exited Officer Country onto the weather decks, just forward of midships, and slid silently down a ladder. He knew the slight rounding of the ship's hull a few yards forward of the quarterdeck would conceal him until he was no more than ten feet from the quarterdeck. The watch wouldn't have time to react. If they were skylarking, he'd have their ass for a midnight snack. This night, however, it wasn't the unwitting watchstanders taken by surprise.

Steve Carter was halfway across the brow, a mere ten steps from slipping back onto *Redstone* and disappearing into the nearest watertight door, when he spotted a figure striding toward the quarterdeck. He caught a flash of khaki and for the briefest instant thought it might be McBurney arriving miraculously at just the right moment to shepherd him safely aboard. The figure's next step brought him fully into the floodlight shining over the Officer of the Deck's stand. It was Hiller. There was nowhere to hide. Steve walked the final few steps over the gangway like a man in a bad dream. His hands went ice cold. He fought to keep his knees from buckling. More naked than the day he was born, Steve stepped onto the ship and stood still. The weight of the bag of possessions he retrieved from his apartment gave him a lopsided, Quasimodo-like posture. Hiller stood in front of him, blocking his advance. Their eyes locked.

"Carter," The Cheng said. The barest hint of a smile creased his lips

"Sir." Steve said, surprised he could keep his voice steady.

Without taking his eyes off Steve, Hiller said to the Officer of the Deck, "Make a log entry. By my watch it is 0105. Under that time, I want you to note Petty Officer Carter's return to this ship. Also note that he escaped from the ship some time after 1400 today when I handed him over to the Master-at-Arms."

Steve flinched at the word "escape." He knew he couldn't argue the point without pulling McBurney into this. He also knew better than to hope McBurney could somehow help him. He didn't know what "escaping" from the ship would cost him in terms of punishment, but he was pretty sure he wouldn't be going ashore again any time soon.

"Carter, you and I are going to take a trip down to the MAA shack. OOD, get Chief McBurney and tell him to meet me there so I can turn over a returned deserter."

Another flinch: *deserter*. He said nothing. Years later, replaying this scene and all that followed, he would always be proud of one thing: I never looked down. He never made me drop my head.

***

McBurney looked at Hiller in shock. "You want me to do what... sir?"

"You heard me, Chief," Hiller said. " I want Carter handcuffed to a stanchion. This sailor escaped from your custody once already. He is a flight risk. If he gets off the ship again, Chief, it won't go well for you. Be a shame to ruin a career over a scumbag like this." Hiller nodded at Steve.

McBurney said, "I see you point Lieutenant, but how's he going to sleep? I can't keep somebody like this."

"Well Chief, you can lock him up here or you can call over to the Brig and see if they'll come get him for you. Of course that is going to take a bit of paperwork on your part. It also would mean Carter here would become a part of the system over there, and his fate would be out of our hands. Not sure the Captain would appreciate that as the first phone call I make on Saturday morning of his three day weekend. If he stays onboard, he stays chained up. Tell you what. You decide what to do about it. I'm going to make a tour of the ship, then I'll be in my stateroom. If you send him to the Brig you can bring the transfer up for my signature." Hiller swept his eyes around the MAA shack. Steve was just another piece of navy issue furniture in that glance. "Looks like you could probably grab a cot out of Medical and fit it in here fine. Easiest thing to do." He closed the door behind him.

McBurney took off his ball cap and rubbed his forehead. "Geez, Carter... what the hell are you doing to me? What happened to you?" His eyes were wide, his stubbly face, grave.

Steve started to speak, didn't know where to begin and let out a long exhale. Finally he said, "Chief, if you'll get a cot from Medical like Cheng said, I'll stay here. I won't make any complaint against you or him for chaining me up, I promise, just don't send me to the Brig. This is my fault. All my fault." He felt a weariness rising up his legs and pulled a chair over to a stanchion. Sitting down he rested his head against it. The cool metal felt good against his skin. McBurney looked at him, sighed and headed to Medical.

The cot, a scratchy green wool blanket, and a blue and white striped coverless pillow wrapped in thin plastic, soon appeared. Steve lay back exhausted. The pillow crinkled every time his head moved. McBurney clamped the cold silver cuff around his right wrist, then to a white stanchion.

In spite of everything, Steve fell into an exhausted sleep as soon as McBurney shut off the lights and closed the door. He dreamed. He was in woods, on the hills out behind his hometown. His favorite creek ran cheerily along; the creek he walked and fished and searched for arrowheads. On an average day the stream was knee deep and clear as it was cold. On the gravel banks in the twists and turns you could let your eyes search the stones for a particular color of quartz and the shape of an artifact made by ancient hands. He walked here for hours that felt like minutes, the only indication of the passage of time, a growling belly he'd forgotten to feed. There were nice lengths of flat water that gave way to miniature slips and falls, feeding into deep holes where the chubs, or small mouth, or maybe a rainbow trout waited to destroy a rooster tail, taking it and running like it was shot out of a gun. In his dream he cast and let the stream take the lure along. It dropped over a six inch shelf. The strike was unmistakable, quick, and hard. The line went stiff and straight. The fish ran. He reeled. The fish broke the surface ten yards away. It flashed in a single ray of sun, silver-bellied, huge, furiously shaking off the insulting hook. Reel, reel, reel. The trout was in his hands. He felt it. It was a pulsing bullet, hard, speckled, and alive with power. The brown, the pink, the black spots, mesmerizing. He struggled to remove the hook, trying not to harm the fish. He stood on the edge of the pool beyond the ledge where he hooked the trout. The slate rocks were wet with spray and the water dripping from his catch. The hook came free of the blunt mouth. Simultaneously the fish became heavier in his hands. It grew like a child's magic sponge doused in water, the ones promising to reveal a creature 100 times larger than the tiny capsule they come in. It grew impossibly large and still more.

He tried to hold it, cradle it, but it was too big. Shifting his feet to support the weight of the fish, his feet slid on the wet stones. He threw his hands up to regain his balance. The trout flew into the pool. Seconds later he was also in the pool, except it wasn't a pool in his favorite stream, couldn't be, for it was much too deep, and he could taste saltiness on his lips. He went under. He flailed to the surface, spluttering. The trout was grown to the size of a whale. He treaded water as the huge creature turned in a wide arc and came toward him. His arms and legs wouldn't work, wouldn't respond to the command to flee. Flee where? Nothing but deepest blue water before and beneath him. As the fish came on, it opened its mouth wide, its black gullet readying for a feast. When it closed to within yards of him, it began to change color. The beautiful pink stripe disappeared and blended into the sliver white underbelly. The speckles pooled together, black with the brown sides. Now all the color faded into the unmistakable haze gray of a naval vessel. The last thing he saw before the huge mouth closed on him was an unmistakable, blocky white number on its side: 20.

He woke up with a start, throwing his arms over his face from the dream. His right wrist jerked to a halt, the handcuff clanged against the stanchion. The cold steel bit into his arm and he cried out in pain. He was breathing heavily. It took several minutes to come back to the MAA shack. The dream had been so vivid that he expected to feel wet—to have seawater dripping off of him—but the only wet he felt was sweat. He stared at the overhead in the dim MAA shack for a long time. A bright line of white light from the passageway outside outlined the shack's door. As his pupils dilated fully, his mind tried to follow suit. He tried to make sense of the dream. Tried to talk himself down. Swallowed by *Redstone* like Jonah? It felt like it; felt like the ship opened its mouth and swallowed him whole. Would he stay here in the belly of this haze gray metallic whale, being slowly digested until there was nothing left?

He focused on the line of light seeping into his makeshift prison cell. Dark in here. Light out there. Five feet away there was a whole different view of things. There was an end to all of this. There was a day coming when he wouldn't be on this ship any more. It was out there. It was. He tried to imagine it, tried to touch it, taste it, smell it, hear it. He imagined the strip of light widening as the door opened. Imagined it opening onto a new day when this present darkness would be the bad dream, or maybe even a funny story he would tell. He felt his heart slowing down on each beat. He concentrated on the line, willing his imagination to play along. Two shadows appeared in the line, breaking it up. Too late he realized their significance, as the door opened and whiteness from the passageway flooded into the room.

"Ahhh!" he gasped, grabbing at the scratchy gray blanket at his chest. His hand came to a stupid clanking stop as it reached the limit of the handcuffs and banged against his wrist again. He tried to screw his eyes shut against the intruding light. He heard the door reach the limit of its inward motion and bang against a bulkhead. He was effectively blind. He could hear whoever it was breathing and sense their presence, but whoever it was did not speak.

"Who's there?" Steve said. He tried to force his eyes open but they refused to cooperate. An icy thought stabbed his heart. The Cheng had come to make sure his little mouse was still securely in its trap.

"That you, Cheng?? He said with as much sarcasm and contempt as he could put in his voice. "I'm still here... you didn't have to check on me. I'm not going anywhere."

Enough light leaked around his blanket defense to make his eyes begin to adjust. The doorway was an upright rectangle of pain he couldn't look at directly, but with his head cocked down and using his peripheral vision, he made out the silhouette of a person. Just an outline.

"Who are you?" he said.

Without a word the trespasser left. The door to the MAA shack slammed, punctuating the return of darkness. Steve lay back and tried to make the square of light disappear from his retinas, but it was many minutes before it faded from view.

While he tried to rest and go back to sleep, he replayed the event. Just before the door closed he thought he had heard a stifled cry and, in the air wafting from the closing door, he swore he smelled a distinctly non-shipboard odor. He was sure he recognized it, because it was the same cheap dime store musk oil his high school sweetheart wore every day without exception. It was also a scent he had smelled recently. When? He strained after the memory, but it eluded his tired mind. He slept.

Chapter 23
The Visitor

Maggie Freeman had departed *Redstone* at liberty call. She checked into a cheap motel a mile outside the base on Hampton Boulevard. She needed room to breathe and to think and to be. Hiller gave her none of these when they were aboard ship together after hours. She felt hunted, suffocated and... heavy.

The drama over the missing valve, the suspension of liberty and the normal intensity of the engineering department workload were too much. Added to the mix were the sideways glances and mutterings of her shipmates, who treated her as a pariah because of her status as the "Cheng's woman." Cheng's woman. That was another bit of heaviness. She was becoming more and more sure she wasn't Hiller's exclusive girlfriend. She heard rumors about others. She was not going to be approached by another man on the ship. Who would be stupid enough to do that and risk getting on the wrong side of Mal Hiller? No one. But one man did like to chat her up; another officer at that, the Bos'n. And something he said set off a tiny bell in Maggie's mind. A single "ping." Something about taking pictures. It was innocent enough on its face, but just the night before, in

Hiller's stateroom, he'd broken out a Polaroid camera and playfully—actually stupidly and clumsily—asked to take her picture. She said no. He pressed. She told him to piss off. It was the first time she pushed back. She could tell from the look on his face he was not expecting resistance. He was used to pliable women. He thought he had one in Maggie—he had had one up to that moment. But the suggestion of a nude photo when she had already told him the stateroom rendezvous made her nervous, made her find her voice. When the Bos'n made his comment, the thin curtain between her willfully unsophisticated version of Mal Hiller and the reality of the man she was sleeping with came down. How stupid to think this was real and even more stupid to think it was exclusive? It bloomed in her mind like a time lapse photo. The bits and pieces of the puzzle fell into place neatly, once she was willing to look at the box top.

At the end of the day, when the missing valve miraculously turned up and liberty was restored, she packed a duffel bag full of clothes and toiletries and fled the ship. She checked into the Bluejacket Inn where the front desk attendant, a toothless old man, gnawed his gums hungrily at her and asked if it was going to be the hourly or the nightly rate. She paid for the night and before going to the room, walked across the street to grab dinner at Long John Silvers. The place was a novelty to her—the only one she ever knew existed. It took convincing by several shipmates to make her believe it was a chain. A bag full of hushpuppies and deep fried seafood accompanied her to her room. She loved the smell of the fried shrimp, but it had competition. The hotel room was smoked like a piece of meat—so permeated with cigarette residue it overwhelmed anything else. After ten minutes in the room, the filet of fish sandwich, even after dunked in industrial strength tartar sauce, had the aftertaste of an unfiltered Winston.

Getting up following her meal, she realized she had been sitting on a discoloration on the bedspread that resembled a urine stain. She had a sudden urge to take a bath. The ship smell that became so normal she only noticed its absence from her clothes after her once a month trip to a laundromat was bad enough; this place made her paranoid that her skin itself might become saturated with its essence. When she opened the door to the tiny bathroom, the scent of Pinesol was so strong it made her eyes water. The message was clear: you don't want to know what this is covering up. It was a testament to her many years growing up in a garage with all its assaults on her senses that she ran a steaming hot bath and stripped off her clothes instead of fleeing the motel room. She discovered that the towels, starched to painful scratchiness, were actually clean and abundant enough that she threw the bed clothes on the floor and covered the mattress with five of them, including one she wrapped around the pillow.

Turning on the television, she found a station playing back-to-back episodes of *McHale's Navy*, a show she had not seen since before her mother left them. It triggered memories of too hot TV dinners served on fold out tin trays pulled up to everyone's seats in the living room. Mom and Dad, Maggie and her brothers gingerly peeling off aluminum foil covers to reveal sectioned off meals while they watched their favorite line up: *McHale's* and *Hogan's Heroes* on channel 7, and if it was a good night, a switch to channel 12 to catch *I Dream of Jeannie*. Maggie was surprised to find herself crying as this scene unfolded in her memory. She tried unsuccessfully to analyze why this had affected her. Why now? Why so many years removed from the events? She fell asleep with no answers and the television on.

She awoke with a start, momentarily unsure of her surroundings. The white towels, scratchy and bleachy, made her heart race. Hospital room? The other predominant smells of the room quickly dissuaded her of that thought. As she lay there re-acclimating to her surroundings, she felt the unmistakable tingle of insect feet across her bare shoulder. She sat up and swept and arm across her skin and heard the faint crackle of a sizeable roach landing on the bed stand before it scurried away. That's all I can take of this, she said to herself. She got up, turned her duffle bag inside out, dumping all its contents on the bed. Not going to give anything a free ride back to the boat. She assured herself it was empty of any insects—at least visually—and shook out each piece of clothing, carefully examining them for further signs of intruders before stuffing them one by one in the bag. Once done, she got dressed rapidly. As she pulled her shirt over her head she thought it already had a whiff of this horrible room. Absently she dug through her bag and found her bottle of perfume. She spritzed herself and the entire contents of the bag. *That'll do for now,* she thought; back to *Redstone.* Hiller wouldn't know she was back and she could rest there. Maybe go for a long drive somewhere tomorrow.

It was cold. Maggie shivered as she made the long walk from the E1- E3 parking lot. She was learning, first hand, a saying she'd heard the first couple weeks she'd been in Norfolk: if you don't like the weather around here, wait fifteen minutes and you'll get a whole new season. The first week of November was shirtsleeves weather. When she left the ship it had been a reasonable sixty or seventy degrees out, now it was a good twenty degrees colder and a sharp breeze swept in off the harbor. Her lightweight hoodie was little protection against wind or cold, but she pulled it over her face and tied it up tight leaving only a slit for her eyes. She made it to the pier, and was reminded of her first time making this jaunt through the valley created by the elephantine sides of the ships of pier 7. Tonight it was

Redstone to her left, and to her right was a fleet oiler, the *Seattle*, just returned from a month underway. She all but ran across the gangway, anticipating climbing into a warm, clean rack. She saluted the empty flagstaff and the OOD and requested permission to come aboard, flashing her ID card.

"Permission, granted; Jeesh, Freeman... couldn't tell it was you. Cold?" The First Class Boatswain's mate on watch said.

She nodded and started toward the nearest door, leading off the weather decks. He said, "What have you guys been feeding that Chief Engineer?" She stopped and turned around. No one talked openly to her about Hiller.

"What do you mean?" she said.

"I mean," he said, "you guys must not be feeding the Cheng enough red meat. He's been on a roll today. Threatening to secure liberty on a holiday weekend was one thing," the man shook his head, "but now he's gone and locked Carter up in the MAA shack!" Seeing Maggie's eyes go wide in disbelief he added, "Oh yes... had McBurney handcuff him to a stanchion!"

Maggie said nothing. She turned and went through the midships breezeway, forgetting the warmth of WINS berthing. She descended the ladders leading two decks down at a speed that would have astonished her just months ago, strode to the door of the Master-at-Arms shack and flung the door open.

It was true. Steve Carter cowered on a cot attempting to keep the light out of his eyes, the metallic ching of the handcuff restraining him was another warning bell, like the one she'd sensed when talking to the Bos'n. The scene left her speechless. It flashed through her mind that the man she had given in to, an officer in the United States Navy, was running his own brothel and sweat shop, and no one on this ship would stop him. He was a king in this little kingdom and did whatever he pleased. Anger and fear choked her. She backed out of the room and slammed the door. The last thing she heard before the door slammed behind her was Carter's voice:

"Who are you?"

Chapter 24
That Smell

Mark woke from a deep sleep with someone shaking him. He was disoriented.

"Hayes! Hayes!" It was MM3 Harper, part of the oncoming Saturday duty section.

"What... what is it?"

"Chief McBurney sent me down. He needs you in the MAA shack as soon as duty section muster is done. Better get movin'; I've been trying to wake you up for five minutes."

"Sorry, man," Hayes mumbled. "Thanks. What time is it?"

"It's 0640. Muster in five," Harper said over his shoulder. "I'm gonna be late myself."

"Right, I'm moving now," he said to Harper's back, "Hey! You know anything about what happened to Carter? I fell asleep waiting for him last night. You seen him?"

Harper stopped and turned around. His eyes were wide. "Oh, man, Hayes, Carter is in deep shit. Story is all over the boat. Last night he got put on report by the Cheng for disobeying a direct order, and when no one was looking he escaped from the ship. Then, this is the funny part. I guess he must've forgot something and came back to get it, but

149

right when he did, the Cheng caught him trying to sneak onto the quarterdeck. He was still dressed in his coveralls like he had been working on the pier. Can you believe it? Cheng is going to have his balls cut off and mounted in his office. He spent the night in the MAA shack *handcuffed to a stanchion!*"

The 1MC blared. "Now muster oncoming and off going duty sections on the fantail."

Harper glanced up at the speaker mounted just over his head. He cursed and retreated out the door.

Mark felt ice in his blood. He shook involuntarily and rolled out of his rack. He threw on his coveralls and sped to the fantail. As the oncoming and off going duty sections went through the formalities of shifting responsibility for the ship from one to the other, he shifted from one foot to the other like a toddler needing to pee and ran to the MAA shack the moment he was released. He tapped on the door. It jerked inward as if spring loaded for his knock. McBurney greeted him.

"Get in here, Hayes," McBurney said, closing the door behind him. The Chief looked as if he had not slept or shaved. Steve sat on a cot near the far bulkhead, his hair tousled and the pair of coveralls he'd been wearing for a solid twenty-four hours looking worse for the wear. A pair of handcuffs hung from a stanchion behind the cot.

Mark looked mournfully at his friend. "Steve...." he started to say.

"This ain't a family reunion," McBurney said, pushing a chair across the floor towards Hayes. "You guys are in deep and you've got me halfway in it with you." He pulled his ball cap off and ran a hand through his receding hair before replacing it. When he spoke again, he muttered to the floor, as if Steve and Mark were not there. "What the hell's going on here? Makes no sense. Got to be missing something." He looked up at Carter. "What am I missing, Carter? What did you do to piss this man off so much?"

Steve rubbed his chaffed wrist and tried to focus. It was a good question. McBurney had tried to help them. He deserved an answer. But there was no answer.

"Chief," he said with a shrug and tilt of his head to one side, "I don't know. I haven't had a run in with Lt. Hiller. For all I knew till yesterday, the man could barely tell you my name without checking out my name tag."

"What about it, Hayes? Nothing? Cheng hates you and Carter for no reason at all?"

Mark looked at his lap. His mouth was dry and tasted like the rags he used to wipe up oil in the engine room. He wished he had taken an extra two minutes to brush his teeth. "Cheng just hates people. He doesn't have to have a reason. Everyone knows it, Chief. Only way to handle him is to get small so he don't even think of you at all. And even that doesn't work. I never did anything to the man, and even before this whole thing with the valve he was getting onto me. Guess he doesn't like my face."

McBurney let out a long sigh. "Still doesn't make sense."

"Can't help offending someone who's already offended," Steve said.

"What?" said McBurney.

"I think he's already angry. I think he wakes up that way. Don't know why. Maybe his dad kicked his ass his whole life for no reason. Now he looks for reasons to go with the feeling."

Hayes and McBurney looked at Steve. They remained silent, unsure of how to respond to this unexpected bit of philosophy.

Finally McBurney said, "At the moment the reason the man hates you makes no difference. What matters is, it'll be

Monday evening at the earliest till the skipper is back in town and the Cheng took duty for the whole weekend so he's basically in command of this ship until then. What am I going to do with you two? He's charging you with desertion and escaping from custody, which means I have to treat you as a flight risk, Carter." He rubbed his temples in a vain attempt to ward off a growing headache. "I should be home already today, but here I am. Three day weekends are supposed to be relaxing... the only way I'm going to get some rest is to send you to the brig."

"Chief," said Steve, "You know I'm not a flight risk. I told you last night. I decided I might as well get my stuff onboard because I expect to get at least thirty and thirty. Give me an escort to the head and to chow and I'll stay in here the rest of the time. I'll stay in here and whenever you can't have a watch on me, you can handcuff me."

McBurney mulled this over. Speaking to himself out loud he said, "I'll be damned if I'm sending one of our sailors to the brig over some shit like this. And I'll be damned if I'm gonna chain up a sailor for nothing. I already lost sleep over this picture," he swept his hand toward the rumpled cot and the pair of cuffs dangling from the stanchion.

"Hayes, are you willing to stay onboard and be Carter's escort the rest of the weekend? If you do, I'll do my best to get a good word in for you when you go up to see the XO for your report chit."

Hayes's eyes brightened for the first time in days. "I'd be glad to do it, Chief. I owe it to Steve."

McBurney said, "This place will have to do for now. Take Carter up for a shower and change of clothes and get some chow." He stripped a key off a huge ring of keys from his desk drawer. "This is the key to the shack. Keep the door locked while you're in here. And when you come and go, stay away from places you might meet Lt. Hiller. If he sees you I'm sure I'll be getting a call."

Steve and Mark made their way back to engineering berthing, using the least conspicuous route.

"What happened to you?" Mark asked. "Why didn't you come back to the ship?"

Steve looked at his friend. Normally he patiently endured Mark's endless supply of questions. Today he'd had half his normal ration of sleep. He didn't respond. When they got to berthing, he propped his coffin rack open and said, "I'm gonna get a shower, Mark. You better get your stuff and stay in the head with me just in case. You and I are gonna have to stay within eyeshot of each other."

Mark looked hurt. "Thanks for trying to help me, Steve. I don't know what to do to make it up to you..." He trailed off hopefully, waiting for consolation like a dog looking for a scrap to fall from the dinner table.

Steve had nothing for him. He was numb and empty. He pulled a towel out of his rack with his shaving kit and started toward the head.

The hot water made him feel almost human again. It was nice. The white steam, the white walls, the white shower curtain. He could be in a make believe heaven if he only had a white robe. Even his soap was Ivory. As he lathered up and let the water run over his upturned face. The outer door to the head slammed as Mark entered and closed it behind him. The sound triggered a memory. The door to the MAA shack, flung open in the night. Who did that? He replayed the scene frame by frame. Nothing stood out. Whoever it was had been a shadow against a too bright background. The last bit of his memory flickered, like the bitter end of a strip of film running through a movie projector before it hit him. The smell! He smelled it now, stronger than the bar of Ivory soap in his hand. It connected. The black shadow at the door had a face that went with that scent. He knew it had been the same person he collided with outside DCC. It was Maggie Freeman! He remembered their awkward embrace. Her soft skin and her friendly eyes. And her smell. Not like anything else below decks, that was for sure. The shower head spit and sputtered menacingly, breaking his train of thought, threatening to begin shooting out steam instead of hot water —a regular hazard of shipboard bathing. He quickly shut it off and grabbed his towel. *I have to see what she has to do with all this,* he thought.

***

"What's in the bag?" Mark asked as they settled themselves for a long day, holed up in the MAA shack. He unzipped one of the two bags Steve had carried on the night before and reached inside. He came out with a couple of books in each hand and a puzzled look.

"It's the stuff I went and got from the apartment last night, mostly books." Steve said.

"This is what you went home for? You put your ass in the Cheng's hands for some books?"

Steve started to answer with something along the lines of "No, I put my ass in the Cheng's hands trying to keep your ass out of them," but thought better of it. "Mark," he said, "there are basically two kinds of people in the world. People who read and people who don't, and I don't mean people who can and people who can't, but people who can't live without reading and people who just read because it is part of life. I am one of the first kind. Since I knew I was going to be confined to this ship one way or another, and since I didn't know when I might get back to my books, I just had to have them."

Mark gave a bobbleheaded, non-comprehending nod and replaced the books in the bag. "Whatever, Steve. I'm gonna go down to the galley and see if I can get us something to eat for breakfast. What do you want?"

"See if you can snag a couple of those little boxes of raisin bran and a banana." He paused, remembering something else. "Hey, Mark, could you go by DCC and grab the old blueprint book that sits on the shelf behind the watch desk?"

"Sure, Steve, but if the Cheng's in there I'm not going anywhere near the place."

As soon as the door closed behind his friend, Steve retrieved the two rolled up prints Peary had forced upon him before his foray to *Seahook*. The more he thought about his confusion in finding the chiller on *Redstone*'s sister ship, the more curious he was. To his well-ordered mind, it wasn't just the gutting of *Redstone*'s third deck to make room for WINS berthing that threw him off; it was something else. Adding what he knew of a sailor's penchant for avoiding extra work and the trouble it took to get an engineering modification approved, *Redstone*'s chiller configuration didn't add up. As he spread out the prints on the cot next to him, the problem of the leak in the Dive Shack came to mind. It was also part of the chilled water system. Once he had the rest of the original prints for the deck, above and below, he could trace out the chill water system and find some answers.

Am I pathetic or what? he mused to himself as he looked over the top of the two prints. Here I am locked up, and I'm still thinking of how to fix this ship. There must be something wrong with me. He folded over the first sheet and studied the second. This print, unlike the one Peary tore out of the master blueprint book the day before, had obviously been removed from the book long ago. It was creased in several places and it was brown and curled at the edges. There were tiny blackened spots on it, which upon closer examination, turned out to be holes burned completely through the linen paper. Steve immediately identified them. The print had been too close to a welding job. He held it up to the light. Shame. He thought again how the blueprints and the book reminded him of things that belonged in a museum display case, not carelessly left on a shelf for any Tom, Dick or Harry to paw them—or subject them to a welder's carelessness.

Mark backed in the door, hands full. In one hand he carried a bowl containing two miniature boxes of raisin bran, in the other, two cartons of milk. He plunked the breakfast down on the MAA desk and removed two bananas and a spoon from his coveralls pocket. "Didn't make it to DCC yet, but I'll go by there and get you a cup of coffee. Mess decks stuff sucks. Pick up the book while I'm there. Anything else we need?"

Steve appreciated the inclusive pronoun. "Nope. Thanks Mark. Like you said, watch out for the Cheng when you go in there."

Alone again, Steve crunched on the cereal while returning to the burned blueprint. He wondered why it was singled out for such rough treatment. In comparison, the page Peary tore out and handed to him yesterday was pristine. The only sign of age was a yellow brown line around its border, the kind Steve had seen on the older paperbacks he sometimes bought at thrift stores. But the print of the third deck was one that had been thoroughly ill-used. He turned his attention to the writing on the print. He had noticed it yesterday in DCC, but the lighting there had been much better. In the relatively dim MAA shack, he had a hard time seeing the faint pencil marks.

He held the print at an angle to the light and found what he was looking for. Slightly offset from the center of the blue-black outline of the hull, there was a roughly drawn circle made by a pencil. On the outboard side of the circle, there was a line running out to the port side of the hull with a question mark above it. There was a second line running from the forward edge of the circle to the next forward bulkhead indicated on the blueprint, also with a question mark over it. Finally, in scrawled handwriting inside the circle he made out two words: "measure" and "cut."

He was concentrating so hard on the markings on the print, he jumped when Mark threw open the doorway and announced, "I'm back!" He tossed the heavy old blueprint book on the cot next to Steve and plopped heavily into a chair. "No sign of Hiller anywhere. Don't know if I like that or not."

"Yeah," Steve said. "Maybe we should tie a bell on him." When Mark screwed up his face in his what-the-heck-are-you-talking-about look, Steve held up a hand. "Never mind. Thanks for getting this."

He picked up the master blueprint book and leafed through to the place he thought would shed light on the chiller piping. A glance at the second deck configuration convinced him something really strange had happened to *Redstone*'s chilled water system. The turn-in valve they'd retrieved from *Seahook* was right where the blueprint of *Redstone* showed it. Made sense. Sister ships would have very similar layouts, but the turn-in valve on *Redstone*'s current layout had been moved a significant distance away from the WINS chiller; a move that meant rerouting a good fifteen feet of pipe and cutting a new hole through a bulkhead where the current Dive Locker sat. Steve scratched the stubble on his chin while he thought about this. Mark munched away loudly on his bowl of cereal. Laying the book down with the second deck print spread out, he took the marked up third deck print and laid it over top of it. Yes. There was no doubt the strange circle showed a spot directly underneath the place where the valve would have been, if it had not been moved. Curious. He folded up the blueprint and closed the book. Then he took the old, ill-used print and folded it along the crease lines. He wasn't surprised to see that it fit perfectly into the back pocket of his coveralls.

Chapter 25
Jasper Running on Empty
September 1976, Atlantic Ocean crossing

The ordeal of the outchop OPPE went on for the ship's engineers like a man in a dentist's chair with an aching tooth. The team of inspectors poked and prodded and did anything but make it feel better. Failing a mainspace fire drill had been a license to dig deeper and push harder. The engineers went from typically tired and complaining sailors to a zombie-like, nearly homicidal mob. There was talk—some of it too specific for casual dismissal—of making a couple of the more malicious inspectors disappear. Perhaps tying them up inside a boiler when it was open for another of their inspections, then shutting them in and lighting it off. Being the leader of one of the two primary firefighting teams put particular weight on Jasper. Daily—sometimes hourly—inquiries from Richards about the feasibility of cutting into WINS berthing from below sandwiched between more and more fire drills had brought him to the edge of his endurance. Any hint on his part that he wasn't wholly committed to seeing the heist through to the end was greeted with increasingly harsh threats from the supply chief petty officer.

Between fire drills, more to keep Richards at bay than because he retained any true interest in the plot hatched in Riley's bar, Jasper took the double-folded third deck plan from the book of blueprints, folded it up in a pocket, and went to take measurements. To his surprise, Richards's rough calculations appeared to be right. If anything, the spot he marked was even closer to being directly below the false compartment Jasper had installed the week before the Egyptian treasure came aboard than Jasper had guessed initially. It would be easy to cut a hole and come up inside it.

But the clock was ticking, the ship moving ever closer to the end of her Atlantic crossing. In this way, the masochistic OPPE team helped him. As long as they continued to rip and tear at the engineering department, Jasper had cover. He had no legitimate window of time to complete Richards's scheme. Maybe he could run out the clock and avoid what he had decided would be a disastrous venture—a venture he was sure would end in him spending a good long time in the federal prison at Fort Leavenworth. Unfortunately for Jasper, the miraculous happened: *Redstone* passed two consecutive mainspace fire drills with flying colors. The OPPE team gave the engineering plant a two year certification and flew off on a helo to the carrier accompanying *Redstone* home.

Jasper was too exhausted to think of anything but his rack. He retired there and fell into blissful, oblivious sleep, with no alarm clocks and no thought of leaving the dark, quiet cocoon until he heard one of two things: the 1MC announcing "moored, shift colors" at the pier in Norfolk, or the final trumpet calling him to the judgment seat. At the moment he didn't care which came first.

Chapter 26
Executive Officers
1990, Pierside, Norfolk, Virginia

The weekend passed in different worlds—on different clocks. For the few who spent three days forgetting about the *Redstone*, forgetting about upcoming deployments, forgetting about the Navy altogether, it evaporated. To those for whom a duty day broke their reverie, it came and went as quickly and noisily as a trash truck rumbling up the street, unavoidably progressing, temporarily interrupting the peace, and then gone. To the prisoner, it bled away like a helium balloon slowly sinking to the floor. The end for all was punctuated late Monday afternoon by four bells on the 1MC, announcing the return of Captain Shumate.

"Ding ding, ding ding, *Redstone* arriving."

Redstone's Executive Officer, Commander Katy Kendall, greeted the CO on the quarterdeck. "Welcome back, sir. How was your weekend at home?" she said.

"Fine, Commander, fine. Not a single call from a CDO all weekend. Either things are too bad to tell me over the phone or things are too good to be true. Which do you think?"

The Executive Officer's feline face took on her much studied look of severity. "Well, Capt'n, I've been around all weekend. Things have been real quiet."

Shumate considered this lie for a moment. He knew his Executive Officer, and he knew the true interpretation of 'been around.' The woman hated the ship, the waterfront, the entirety of seagoing life and would not voluntarily spend one second more than absolutely necessary aboard ship.

Commander Katy Kendall, USNR, was a Training and Administration of reserves (TAR) officer who managed to rise to second in command of a naval vessel and the rank of commander while spending a total of 13 months at sea in 18 years of naval service. Her Navy career was an anomaly, a bubble formed in women's career paths when the political climate of the late 70s intersected the old boy network of the traditional Navy.

She entered the Navy expecting to be no nearer the ocean than her home in Iowa. TAR officers were little more than government service workers stuffed in military uniforms. They ran reserve training centers in places like Des Moines, Omaha and Cleveland, and majored in the minutia of reserve paperwork. For reservist men, officers and enlisted, the needs of the Navy frequently meant they ended up on ships. Kendall had nothing like that in her forecast. She expected to spend her twenty years pushing paper across a desk without seeing a haze gray ship. Ten years into that twenty, the defense authorization act of 1979 sent the first ever contingent of women to active duty ships with the proviso their ships would not enter combat zones. The first of those women came to *Redstone*, and, shortly thereafter, to the rest of the auxiliary fleet units.

Kendall was a wisp of a human being with coke bottle glasses, a figure to make a two by four jealous, and a perpetually sour countenance. She had no husband and no prospects, and preferred cats to people in general and men in particular. Momentarily caught up in the fervor of women cracking the Navy's glass ceiling, she forgot she knew nothing about going to sea, and spent two years badgering her chain of command to get her a billet on a ship. When her superiors gave in, it was only because of a quota issue that fell in her favor. As Congress tracked the integration of women going to sea, it created a demand for a certain number of female officers of a certain rank, and a certain number of years' service for the Navy to satisfy them that they were taking proper steps to make it happen. The number of women who fit the bill was very small, and Kendall was one of only half a dozen of them who had asked to go to a ship. She went to sea in the second wave of females in the early 80s, on a tender out of San Diego that had little room for the lieutenant commander division officer who quickly demonstrated ineptitude in everything she touched, except writing reports. Navy ships are like trees when it comes to having foreign objects thrust upon them; they will swallow them up and grow around them. On her first ship, Kendall was like a hammock hook screwed into an oak tree. In a month she was barely visible. In thirteen months the ship spit her out, profoundly unchanged, untrained and, in the way that only makes sense in the military, recommended for promotion and department head school.

She returned to an obscure reserve training center, this time in Illinois, and contented herself with wielding her red pen on her subordinates' reports. When several sets of females junior to her made it through department head school and on to the fleet with no hint of getting orders there herself, she assumed, with relief, that her seagoing days were over. But then the Executive Officer on *Redstone* watched *Full Metal Jacket* one too many times, right before the ship went to REFTRA in Guantanamo Bay.

The XO, Commander (select) Bruce Gordon, two days out from Gitmo, shaved his head, donned a flak jacket and a camouflage battle helmet and demanded that the armory provide him with an M-16, loaded and at the ready at all times, on a gun rack he installed himself on the port bridge wing. Gordon took to stalking up and down random passageways at all hours of the day or night inspecting watertight doors and hatches muttering to himself over and over again "yoke is no joke. yoke is no joke. yoke is no joke" a saying any sailor on their way to Gitmo would have on their mind, because setting material condition "Yoke" correctly and within a specified timeframe was a huge "go—no go" for ships to pass REFTRA. But the bizarre hours at which the XO walked into spaces and slammed shut watertight fittings, paired with his zombie-like expression, began spooking the crew. He walked unannounced into WINS berthing, sending half a dozen half naked female sailors scurrying like cockroaches caught in the light. He surprised a Hospital Corpsman, a green sailor who'd only been on *Redstone* three weeks as he was doing paperwork in Medical at 0500 preparing for sick call, and demanded he open the secured door to the controlled medicinal storage, insisting it was on the list of watertight fittings that had to be inspected. The XO even violated the sanctity of the Chiefs Quarters, walking in uninvited. By the time the ship made port to begin REFTRA, the skipper had been buttonholed by every department head and several chiefs about some craziness involving his Executive Officer. He'd witnessed some of the crazy firsthand on the night before reaching Gitmo.

At the evening trash dump, Gordon ordered the helmsman to come about, pulled the M-16 off the gun rack and opened fire without warning, on an old desk that was thrown over the side. He said that it failed to sink fast enough and constituted a hazard to navigation. The bridge watch was so thrown by the unexpected gun fire, the OOD called the CO to the bridge from his dinner. The Navy is full of places where crazy is excused, and the XO might have survived all of these incidents had he not topped them all off with one for the ages.

The first day in Gitmo, just as the inspection team was about to come aboard for the in-brief, Gordon appeared on the main deck with a red Radio Flyer wagon. How he'd gotten it aboard, no one knew. He was wearing his flak jacket and camo painted battle helmet. He ordered the gangway watch, a third class boatswain's mate, to pull him around the complete circuit of the main deck shouting "yoke is no joke!" at the top of his lungs. At the board of inquiry, held some two months later in Norfolk, Gordon had insisted it was his way of building esprit de corps. The Captain didn't see it that way. He relieved the XO for cause and sent him home for a Psych Eval at Portsmouth Naval Hospital.

The dominoes that fell when Gordon departed *Redstone* created a ripple in the manpower pool, eventually leading the Navy to do something it is very good at doing—covering one mistake with another mistake. The logic was that they needed a female officer to restore the morale of the crew on their first ship with women. They needed a Commander with sea experience to fill the billet, and the lot fell to Katy Kendall, who was as incompetent as Gordon was nuts.

Kendall and the new CO arrived in consecutive months following the departure of the outgoing CO and his Ops Officer, who had filled in for Gordon during *Redstone*'s recently completed Mediterranean cruise. The ship wasn't due to deploy again for 18 months; plenty of time for her new leadership duo to sort themselves out. As it happened, the two got less than six months and Kendall, the Midwesterner who could barely dog paddle, found herself in deep water.

Threading his way in and up to his in-port cabin with Kendall closely in tow, the Captain knew he was going to need some hard answers about the state of readiness of his ship and crew. His weekend *had* been disturbed, but not by anyone from the ship. Admiral Fink, Commander of Logistics Group Two, Shumate's boss, had personally called his house yesterday, to break the news. The next scheduled deployer for LOGGRU2, USS *Shenandoah*, had failed her engineering readiness exam, not once but twice. The second failure was so spectacular that *Shenandoah*'s CO was relieved of command, even though he'd only been onboard four and a half months and the problems discovered during the exam were the result of years of neglect. *The sea may be a harsh mistress*, Shumate thought, *but the United States Navy is an unforgiving bitch of a wife.*

Another ship would have to take *Shenandoah*'s place, and that ship was going to be *Redstone*. It briefly occurred to Shumate to point out the unfairness of forcing his crew to turn around and deploy after being home from her last Med cruise for less than six months. It also occurred to him that Fink didn't care and wasn't interested in having a conversation, so he gave the answer the admiral was looking for: "Yes, sir. We'll be ready to go on time. Count on it."

Over his shoulder, as he reached the door to his cabin, he said to Kendall, "We're going to need a department head meeting first thing tomorrow."

"Yes, sir, where would you like to do it and what time?"

"Come to think of it, I want to include all khaki. Better make it the flag mess at oh eight hundred."

Kendall raised an eyebrow at this. "Anything up?"

"Yeah, plenty is up, but I'm going to relax tonight and I don't want to get into it. Let's have a sit down tomorrow after quarters and I'll fill you in."

"Yes sir. Anything you need tonight before I shove off?"

"No. I'll see you in the morning, XO."

As the CO closed the door to his cabin, Kendall decided she better get on the beach and enjoy herself tonight. Something in the Old Man's demeanor made the closing of his cabin door sound like last call.

Chapter 27
The Bos'n's Key

"Everyone knows it's true," Mark said.

"I'm not sayin' it isn't," said Seaman Faith Green, "I'm just sayin' I'd like to see if that key is really there."

"You don't believe it. You're one of those who has to see for yourself. My friend works in the Wardroom Galley and he has to clean that passageway. He checked it out and there it was, the key to the Bos'n's stateroom."

"So that doesn't mean all the other stuff they say about it is true. What if he just likes to keep it there, in case he loses his keys?"

"Green, you can believe what you want to believe. I'm telling you the Bos'n lets whatever woman that gets his key and gets in his bed first, sleep with him, and there's a key hidden on top of the light right outside his door. You've seen him around. You tellin' me he doesn't talk smack with every woman he sees: officer, enlisted, contractor, anything with boobs? Tell you what else my friend up in O country says. He says there are two officers taking turns using the key and they don't know about each other yet."

Mark, never the sharpest knife in the drawer when it came to women, didn't notice the look in Green's eye or the change in her tone during this conversation.

"Who?"

"It's the two ensigns, Fratella and Pender."

Green looked doubtful. "Fratella I could see, but Pender? She don't look like the kind who'd be chasing after someone like the Bos'n."

"Yeah, well my boy up there tells me it started on the last deployment when we were in Crete. Pender got talked into going out with the dive shack gang and they introduced her to Ouzo. She didn't handle it too well and the Bos'n ended up helping her back to the ship and into bed. His bed."

"That was nice of him," Green said, this time with enough venom that even Mark picked up on it.

"Don't get mad at me, I'm just tellin' you how it happened. Maybe you need to stay away from the Bos'n and his key."

Green said, "I don't need anything like him and his three ringed circus of a bed." But her eyes told a different story.

***

The 1mc crackled, "Now reveille, reveille, all hands heave out and trice up. Give the ship a clean sweep down fore and aft. The smoking lamp is lit in all authorized spaces."

Steve opened his eyes slowly. He tried to think of a reason to get up. He knew no matter what punishment the Navy eventually rendered, it was going to involve days on end of waking up to those exact words. Two things roused him out of his makeshift rack in the Master-at-Arms office. The first was the memory of the perfume he'd smelled, both here and in his unintended collision with Maggie Freeman. The second was the folded up blueprint in his coveralls, hanging off the chair next to his cot. Curiosity over those two things convinced him to heave out and trice up. They were worth investigating.

The door to the shack shivered slightly as Chief McBurney worked his key and let himself in. "Mornin' shipmate. Glad to see you're enjoying your stay in my little hotel. Would you like me to bring you some room service?"

"Mornin' Chief. Sorry I'm dragging a bit today. I'll get up and out of here. Do you think I still need to be escorted to the head by Hayes? Or can I go potty on my own?"

McBurney snorted, half choking on a sip of coffee. "Get your ass out of here. I got my guys to muster and then we're going to see the Old Man about all this B.S. the Cheng is trying to pull."

Steve looked hard at the Chief. "You're going to go over his head like that, Chief? Think that's a good idea? I did disobey a direct order—twice."

McBurney nodded. "Carter, I thought about it a lot over the weekend. Had a come to Jesus moment. I've been in this man's Navy for over twenty-two years now. I've never seen anything like this Cheng. The more I thought about it, the more I decided I wasn't going to take it. So we're going to see the Old Man and you're going to tell your side of the story and if the Cheng and the Old Man don't like the way I'm doing business they can fire me. What are they going to do? Take away my birthday? Navy's already taken fifteen of my last twenty-two birthdays anyway. Now get out, get cleaned up and put on a sharp uniform. We'll see what happens."

Half an hour later, Steve sat upright on a chair in the MAA shack, trying to keep the military creases on his shirt from touching the chair back. He was tired from three nights on a strange bed with too much thinking and too little sleeping. He doubted today would clear up his fate, but at least he'd get a start.

McBurney shot holes in that hope as he came through the door. "Can't get in to see the Old Man," he said. "Him and the XO are huddled up in his cabin with a 'do not disturb' sign on the door. The steward gave me the 'don't try it' look when I was about to knock, anyway. I heard there's going to be an all khaki meeting in the flag mess right after quarters."

"What do you think's going on, Chief?" Steve asked.

"Dunno, Carter, but I'm going to need you to stay put here some more."

"You sure I shouldn't go on up to quarters with Engineering, Chief? I may give the Cheng something else to accuse me of if I don't show."

"No. He turned you over to me and you're my responsibility. He can't say anything about it."

Hayes gave a quick two knocks on the door of the shack and let himself in. "Hey, Steve. Morning, Chief. Anything going on? Just thought I'd check in on my way to quarters."

McBurney grunted there was nothing he needed from Hayes and departed for his morning formation. Steve decided the military creases didn't matter anymore and sat back in his chair.

"What's up Mark? I know you better than to think you're just passin' through. I can tell by your eyes."

Hayes glanced down at his watch to see how long he could take to tell about what he'd discovered. For a moment, Steve thought he might have something important to say, then he opened his mouth. "So I told Green about the Bos'n's key and she didn't believe me," he said.

Steve arched his eyebrows and said, "Please man, who cares about that? What difference does it make?" Steve said.

"No, listen," Hayes continued in a conspiratorial tone. "She didn't believe me and so she said she was going to go see for herself."

Seaman Faith Green was a relatively popular crewmember on *Redstone*, primarily for two reasons, which had magically appeared on her formerly unremarkable chest after the last deployment. Six months' worth of sea pay and two weeks of leave in California and voila, popularity, especially with her male counterparts in Deck Division, who regularly met her coming or going through the narrow passageways up forward near the paint locker, where she worked. Hayes was particularly impressed with Green's new dimensions. Steve wasn't and wished his friend would recognize that Green had no interest in him, without Steve having to be the one to point it out.

"Well what happened?" he sighed, knowing from experience that Hayes needed to get this out.

"I'm not sure, exactly. But I know this, Pender and Fratella both showed up last night after the Bos'n came back aboard and neither one got in that stateroom."

"How'd you know that?"

"My friend up in the wardroom mess said both the ensigns pretended to be going to the women's head right down the hall from his stateroom one at a time and they both came back to the wardroom looking mad. Then they sat there and watched a movie till around oh one hundred and they both went on to their own cabins."

"So what about Green?"

"I dunno, Steve. I didn't see her after chow last night."

"So what are you saying? You think Green went and let herself into the Bos'n's stateroom and locked out the two ensigns? You think she's in his rotation now?"

Mark didn't seem to like the continuation of his own thoughts as they came out of Steve's mouth.

"Mark?"

"I guess I don't want to think it's true."

"Why, Mark? You've got no claims on Green do you?" Steve let that sink in a second. "Listen. Leave her alone. Nothing good will come of it, nothing good would've come from it and nothing good has come from it. Best thing you can do is forget about Green."

Hayes checked his watch again. He looked like a kicked dog and sounded like he looked. "I better get to quarters Steve."

Chapter 28
The All Khaki meeting

The all khaki meeting began fifteen minutes after quarters. It was standing room only in the flag mess. The most senior Officers were seated around tables set up in a U. A mixed bag of junior officers and Chief Petty Officers sat in rows of folding chairs in the middle of the room while others stood and leaned against the walls. A dull murmur filled the air. The XO opened the door and shouted "Attention on deck!" in her best command voice. It came out more like a suggestion than an order. Even so, it cut off the murmuring like a light switch.

Shumate entered and squeezed through the crowd to the head of the center table. He sat down and cleared his throat. He had decided to approach his officers and chiefs like a bombing run: line it up and let the news of the surge deployment fly. When he was done explaining the situation caused by *Shenandoah's* woes and its effects on *Redstone's* schedule, he paused and scanned the room. He expected the response to be negative and would have been suspicious and worried if his khakis had been enthusiastic about a six month turn around between six month deployments. The Cheng was the exception. Shumate knew the man had no life to speak of off the ship and going to sea or being tied to a pier had less impact on him than anyone in the entire crew. The man had a strong mind when it came to keeping this old bag of bones running, though, and it immediately kicked into deployment mode.

"Skipper?" Hiller asked.

"Yes, Cheng." Shumate said.

"Have we gotten word on when we'll be able to do REFTRA?"

REFTRA or refresher training was the navy's little going away present for ships preparing to deploy. It involved taking several weeks to travel to Guantanamo Bay, Cuba where both vessel and crew would be subjected to long days of drills and inspections. It was hot, tedious and anything but its namesake, not to mention that it stole the better part of the last month a ship would be able to spend in home port before an extended absence.

"Well, Cheng," Shumate said, "I had been considering a request to Group that we be allowed to skip it or modify it to give the troops a break. Maybe get a fly away team from GITMO to come up here and do a three or four day shakedown out in the VACAPES instead of going all the way down there."

Shumate could sense an upswing of goodwill in the room. He was on their side, after all, looking out for them against those heartless bastards at Group. It was exactly what he'd wanted to have happen—let some not-so-bad news water down the bad news. A murmur of approval began to fill the room. He appreciated the Cheng giving him the opportunity to appear in this role. Hiller was still talking.

"I think we should take another look at that, Captain," he was saying, "I know we haven't been back long from the last deployment, but there's significant turnover in the firefighting teams. We've had to replace three damage control locker leaders and the number one hoseman on two teams. There's really no way to have them trained up properly without a full REFTRA."

Hiller was letting the goodwill out of the room, but it wasn't escaping into the atmosphere as much as it was being deposited in his running account of bad will with every other khaki in the room.

The XO spoke up. "What're you saying Cheng? Your guys aren't ready to fight a fire on this ship? Whose fault is that? And you want to make the whole ship go to GITMO because you can't keep up with quals in your department?"

Shumate didn't like the direction this was taking with every chief and officer present and cleared his throat to bring it to a close, but Hiller was already firing back at the XO. "Well, Commander, as you know, the manning bill and readiness of this ship is your responsibility. Every department here is supposed to be supplying bodies to the firefighting teams and you are the one who's supposed to make sure it's happening. I've got copies of three memos I've sent you in the last six weeks, informing you of the needs we have and the department heads who aren't giving up the people that I need. Would you like me to go get them?"

Kendall's face was streaked red with anger and embarrassment. She was not built for a confrontation over a late book fee with a librarian, much less with *Redstone*'s Chief Engineer on his home turf. Shumate caught Cheng's eye and silenced him with a look.

He said, "We'll talk more about the need for REFTRA. Right now, every one of you needs to get together with your troops and tell them exactly what is going on. Don't let rumors run amok. They'll have us leaving tomorrow and being gone a year. It's not good for them, so go and tell them the straight dope. Next I want a status report from every department telling me the major milestones you'll need to pass in order to deploy on time. I want it typed and on my desk before liberty call today. That's all." He got up. There was an awkward moment before Kendall realized she was forgetting her lines.

By the time she choked out, "Attention on deck!" Shumate was already halfway to the door.

He'd dropped his bomb, now he would see what happened. Getting *Redstone* to her deployment date was going to be a challenge. He needed the Cheng in order to get there and to get through it. Kendall was scurrying to catch up to him. As the door to the flag mess closed behind them Shumate said, "XO, how about getting me these memos the Cheng is talking about."

Chapter 29
Bad News Spreading Fast

News of the deployment spread through the ship like the plague, and of all the places it infected, none was more sickened than the engineering department. There were no illusions among the engineers as to what it meant to compress eighteen months of preparations for a Med deployment into three. The Cheng would live on the ship even more than he usually did, and he would have them living with him, if it could be called living. He would have them working so much that when they did manage to get home they'd be zombies—there and yet not there. For *Redstone*'s engineers, the surge deployment started at 0900 that morning, when the Cheng called an all hands meeting on the fantail to give them the word.

"We're going to take the place of *Shenandoah*," Hiller told them. "The reason we are going to take her place is because her engineers didn't take care of her. We are going to take up the slack for a ship that is twenty years younger than *Redstone*. It's going to take a lot of work to get us ready on time. We will be ready to go. As of today we are going to port and starboard duty sections. Sections Alpha and Delta will now be Port and sections Bravo and Charlie will be Starboard. All leave and special liberty requests are canceled.

You can resubmit them using your new duty sections, but let me give you a hint, ain't nobody who's not fully qualified for their in port and at sea fire party positions and for their underway watchstanding position going anywhere, so if that's you, don't bother to put in a request." He paused long enough to give them a smug grin. "Any questions?"

The formation of sailors was silent, the weight of this information squashing them into the deck like bugs on a windshield. Morale was not something the typical sailor thought about, but Hiller thought about it and knew what he wanted to do with it. He felt it bottoming out in the silent formation before him, then opened the trap door beneath them.

"I've requested *Redstone* be sent to REFTRA in Gitmo. I'm guessing we'll go there and then keep going on deployment instead of coming back here. Just be a waste of time."

Now the silence of the sailors gathered on the fantail had a sound of its own. Hiller looked them over. He had them driven down far enough. Now whatever scrap of freedom he flung at them would be scarfed up as if it were filet mignon instead of beef jerky. He smiled again.

"Divos," he said. "I want re-written duty section watchbill and muster lists on my desk by noon." He turned around and left.

No one moved for a long moment, then the three division officers, all of whom were not yet recovered from the long weekend spent trying hard to forget they were in the Navy, turned to face their respective divisions. If a division officer was supposed to be the first line of defense between a department head and his men, the men of engineering were looking at a line that had been completely obliterated in the last ten minutes. They were pale and speechless. The engineering formation wasn't dismissed, it dismissed itself silently.

***

Maggie was not affected by the news of the deployment the same way her shipmates were, but the gloom of the situation settled on her just as rapidly. The few hours she'd spent alone in the hotel room had begun a process of clearing her senses. Returning to the ship to discover Steve Carter handcuffed to a stanchion in the MAA shack... that finished it.

Detoxed. She knew the resolve to turn away from Hiller and stay turned away was in her, all she had to do was find it. She was ready to get on with it, the same way she had gotten on with ditching Dave. She decided on the direct approach. Straight to the face and straight to the point. That was Friday night. Now everything was more complicated. Hiller would be more of a presence in every engineer's life in the push to get *Redstone* to deploy on time. He would be unavoidable. Alienating him, or worse, making him an enemy, would have harsher consequences, and keeping him in check and playing him would have more rewards. She began to reason with herself. This wasn't just about her, was it? If she gave him more cause to come down on the whole division, was she being fair to her shipmates?

A flash of insight came along with this though, a possibility she'd missed. Could it be her fault that Hiller was treating Carter like a criminal? Did he think there was something between the two of them? And if he did, where did the idea come from? She had had no interactions with Carter at all. They didn't even work in the same main space. The more she thought about it, the more sure she became that there was a connection. Hiller regularly quizzed her about the engineers she worked with and for, and it always carried a twinge of the jealous high school boyfriend. Was Hiller capable of letting the green-eyed monster control him that much? Put a man in irons just because he thought that man might have designs on "his woman?" She hated the answer. No, she hated herself for the answer. Yes, he was that kind of man and yes, she'd let herself get involved with that kind of man. Stupid girl. What am I going to do now?

Hiller was a bad man. Staying attached to him was not an option, but dumping him now didn't seem like an option either. Using him was bad, but was it worth worrying about with a man like Hiller? She was sure she had only seen a glimpse of the blackened iceberg of the man. Who would blame her for manipulating him? No one. He is the type of guy who dies young and has a funeral procession of two cars, one of which is the hearse. Maybe she could use her influence to help out her coworkers and regain something she'd obviously lost with them and herself, some kind of connection.

Lost in thought, she entered the skin of the ship and started forward. An interior door to a small supply closet opened as she passed and a pair of arms swept her forcefully into the cramped space. She saw the Cheng's grin before he shut the door behind her, then they were standing in the dark face to face. He kissed her roughly.

"Where you been all weekend?" he asked. "I took the duty all alone the whole three days, 'cause I was expecting to have some fun with you... and you disappeared..."

His pause was a question. Maggie thought quickly. Dive in or dive out? There in the dark closet, another factor entered her calculations: Fear. They had been lovers, it was true, and on this very ship, but everything they'd done had been much more discreet than this. Being pulled into the dark closet could have been romantic, the action of a lover so deprived of the one thing he needed, he could not restrain himself any longer. But this had the feel of something else— the feel of a quarry and a hunter, a demand and not a desire. His arms around her back and his breath in her face felt like a snare fallen on her soul. She tried not to move, to breathe, to give him anything more than he had already taken.

"I went to see my brother." She exhaled the lie smoothly, gently, hoping to avoid further inquiry.

"In Fishersville?"

"No. no. He was up in Richmond for his work, so I drove up to see him and spent the rest of the weekend there...." She blended her last word into his mouth with a closed lip, dry kiss. "Please let's get out of here, it's creepy and I'm scared someone will find us."

Hiller's embrace loosened.

"I'll be able to talk with you later, ok?" she said.

He said nothing but she felt him nod slightly in the dark. She reached back and grabbed the door knob, pausing long enough to see if she could hear any movement in the passageway. There was none. Backing out of the closet in an awkward motion she hesitated for a moment, unsure of whether she should leave the door open for Hiller or close it and let him come out on his own. It almost made her laugh in spite of the fear she felt. She closed the door quickly and headed for the aft engine room.

Chapter 30
Baber in a Box

Chief Warrant Officer Three Pete Baber, the Diving Officer known by everyone on *Redstone* as "the Bos'n," sat alone at the corner table of the wardroom mess, drinking a cup of coffee. It was his preferred morning spot because, with a nearby porthole cover undogged and latched open, he could keep track of his divers returning from liberty. His men were amazed at his ability to come to quarters each morning and fire off a list of those who were late or missing. He thought it equally amazing that none of them had figured out his sixth sense for missing divers consisted of nothing more than a caffeine habit and a seat with a view.

Baber looked into his second cup and caught the reflection of one puffy middle aged eye. His life, already complicated with the tangled lines of a love triangle, had gotten more complex over the weekend as he fell into bed with a third woman. He mused over that. He was no longer in a triangle, he was in a box. Math was never his best subject, but he had a feeling this was not going to add up to a good outcome. Three women at one time. Every man's fantasy? He didn't think of it as a fantasy at all. He was just a guy who couldn't say no to women and women were always coming at him from one angle or another. He had been called a dog more than once in his forty-three years. He used to dislike the term, but as he began the slide through youth and into middle age, he had begun to reflect on it.

Sitting at a stop light on Military Highway, he saw a dog, a lab mix, pacing back and forth in the rear of a car next to him. The dog stuck its nose through the car's barely open windows, first one side then the other. Pete watched it move. He saw its nose straining to take in every smell. It hit him. The dog is on overload. His most sensitive part, the thing he uses to understand his world, is his nose. And there was so much to smell—too much. *Maybe I am a dog*, he thought. *Maybe it is exactly the way I am.* The dog didn't look happy; he looked busy. Pete thought if the car door were to open or the window were to be rolled down just a little bit more, the dog would be off to the races, chasing down the nearest, most interesting smell, but it wouldn't be long before he was going another direction. He'd probably end up road kill.

He pondered the path that led him to this point. Handsome by anyone's standards and raised by an athlete to be an athlete, he had just done what everyone expected him to do. He was athletic, so he played the big three: football in the fall, basketball in winter, baseball in spring. He was good looking, so he slept with girls. One wasn't much different to him than the other.

When a girl didn't accept his sexual advances, he thought of it more like a lost game than a lost cause. It was just something that happened once in a while and you didn't linger on it. So he'd developed a habit of winning on and off the field. Several offers to take his winning habit to college came in right on time and he took the one from San Diego State. It was close to home—he was living in Chula Vista—the beach, and according to the Beach Boys, the cutest girls in the world. Pete never found a reason to disagree with them on that point. His endless summer was terminated after one semester and an incident involving his Economics 101 prof, who didn't accept his offer to sleep with her if she would pass him. She probably would have let it go as a joke if he hadn't made the offer while attempting to fondle her. He thought she was giving him signs and hey, she was decent looking for a woman her age. As far as he was concerned, he was trying to get a passing grade in something he knew he could do— why fake it with economics?

His unrepentant attitude was no help with the school's athletic department, and, fearing they had a loose cannon on their hands, both the head football coach and the athletic director decided they could afford to lose this problem. Without the support of anyone in the school's administration and with the professor intending to press her grievance against him to any possible scholastic or legal lengths, his father stepped in and negotiated a deal. Pete wrote an apology to the professor and withdrew from school.

Out of school and out of organized athletics for the first November in thirteen years, Pete didn't know what to do with himself. He tried to make the best of it by finding a brainless job handing out beach rentals in La Jolla. It was there he met a group of Navy divers, who seemed to spend as much time surfing as he did standing in the cabana handing out chairs. They looked like they were happy. They made their job sound like it was fun. Over the protests of his father, who was working out a deal to get his son into UCLA, he enlisted in the Navy before Christmas, went to boot camp within a stone's throw of his home and was sent to a ship as an undesignated seaman.

An undesignated seaman is the lowest of all Navy creatures. It denotes a person who has no training beyond basic deck seamanship. Out of his recruit company, only Pete and one other guy didn't have any follow on schools. They were the Navy's version of old school G.I.'s, trained to know enough to hold a rifle and fall in ranks. But Pete wasn't in the Army and he quickly learned that trusting a Navy recruiter had been a costly mistake. Of course he was going to dive school, the recruiter had told him, just get through boot camp then apply for it and you'll be on your way. He made it sound so easy.

Of course recruiters, like all salesmen, never lie, they just move the facts around to fit the contours of the situation; strategic manipulation of the truth in the name of meeting one's quotas. While it was true Pete could apply for dive school once he finished boot camp, it was also true the Navy wouldn't wait for boot camp to end before they assigned him to a ship. And once you were on a ship, well, who was going to help out a nondescript, standard Navy issue squid? Why would anyone on the ship want to hurry him back off the ship? Who would be there to swab the decks, pull in the mooring lines, and keep a fresh coat of haze gray paint on the hull? The Navy, the real sea going Navy, needed deck seamen like cars needed motor oil. And so Pete discovered his position on the ship was untenable. If he wanted to be a diver, he couldn't afford to be a screw up, but if he did a good job, he made the people over him want to hold onto him even more. But he persevered and he put in a special request chit to go to Navy dive school, every month for a year. His dad taught him a few things over the years that stuck with him, one came to him as he struggled to get off the ship and into dive school: "Son, the squeaky wheel doesn't always get the oil, sometimes it gets the hell beat out of it with a hammer, but the wheel that doesn't squeak at all, well it doesn't have a chance either way. Might as well keep squeaking till something happens one way or the other." So he squeaked.

The Deck department head finally came and told him if he would quit writing chits, the ship would send him to the rescue swimmer school. It wasn't dive school, but it was taught by divers at the same command where dive school was taught. Pete accepted the peace offering, went to the school during the next in port period and never went back to his ship. He discovered he had his own ability to sell, especially when he was the product. He started the day he got there, with the first instructor he met, saying how he wanted nothing more than to be a Navy diver, and by the time he was done with the short two week course, he had gained the attention and sympathy of the commanding officer of the dive school. He didn't hurt his cause when he broke an unofficial school record, swimming the training pool three times without surfacing. A few phone calls later, Pete found himself enrolled in the full diver training course. It turned out to be a wetsuit fit of a career for a guy like him.

Divers had to be in shape and stay that way, and they always seemed to be around women. It was like he'd stepped into an age enhanced photo of his adolescence. Still the athlete. Still the women. Life was good. He hardly noticed twenty years passing, as he put one Navy day after another behind him. He didn't really know how he became an officer, other than it was the way to keep on diving and living the life he wanted. It was natural growth for him as opposed to any kind of ambition.

As a boot sailor on that first ship, in spite of feeling cheated, he found he liked ships and going to sea. The ocean had a draw to it he couldn't exactly understand. It seemed full of possibilities and it was, in some way he couldn't understand, cleansing. At the time he thought the only thing he would miss if he was at sea for the rest of his life would be women. Now here he was all these years later, thinking how nice it would be if this ship could take him away from women. Instead, as he had just found out in the all khaki meeting, he was going to be confined to a ship in which he was carrying on with three of them at once.

"Mornin' Bos'n."

He looked up to see the wardroom steward standing in front of him with a stainless steel coffee pot.

"Saw you sittin' here and thought I'd brew you a fresh pot."

"Thanks, Parker," Pete said. He pushed his cup forward.

"Man, Bos'n, you ever gonna wash this cup? Looks like it ain't ever been warshed."

Pete looked into the deeply stained ceramic cup. Once upon a time it had been bone white inside and out. It had his name embossed under the Navy diver insignia, an end of tour gift from his first full tour as a Navy diver. Now the inside was blackened from a thousand cups of coffee; the outside was cleaner but not by much.

"Nope. I don't wash it. I like it this way. Keeps the flavor in. Besides, if I ever run out of coffee, I can just pour some hot water in here and brew a cup from the scum on the sides."

The steward was unfazed. "OK, Bos'n. You need anything? I mean from the galley?"

"No thanks, Parker. Appreciate it."

The man, barely more than a boy, left. He sat another minute sipping at the hot coffee. Did he need anything? Yes, but it wasn't in the galley. He didn't know exactly what he needed, but this kid and his question made him start thinking of things long gone and things never seen. The weight of his whole life seemed to find its way into his hands and for a moment he couldn't lift his cup for another sip.

Chapter 31
Cheng and Mouse

Katy Kendall settled into her desk. The early morning pre-brief with the CO and the all khaki meeting had thrown off her morning schedule and set her an hour behind. Normally she met with the on-coming and off-going Command Duty Officers immediately following quarters. She liked it because it gave her a feeling of power in the sea of powerlessness she inhabited daily. Today the oncoming CDO, in light of the impending deployment, was already off and running with ship's business and begged off from attending the meeting. Usually Kendall, in the way of insecure managers in every organization who substitute rules and routine for actual leadership, did not make allowances for missing this meeting, but this was a disheveled day. She reluctantly gave in to it, leaving her one-on-one with the off-going CDO, the Chief Engineer. She summoned Hiller to her office via the Messenger of the Watch instead of phoning him. She knew this would irritate the man, but she also knew he wouldn't be able to blow her off, as he was likely to do over the phone. It was one of her best passive aggressive moves and she was privately proud of herself for discovering its usefulness.

The Cheng knocked and opened the XO's door in one motion, an act calculated to anger her and let her know he was in charge, in spite of her maneuvers.

Kendall tried to keep her expression impassive and her voice commanding. She failed at both. At best she looked and sounded like a teenaged actor trying to play her role in a high school production of *The Caine Mutiny Trial*. "LT Hiller, please give me the CDO turnover and then I'd like to talk about the manning issues with the fire parties and the refresher training." Sensing her own lack of gravitas, she played another card of overmatched managers. "The CO is really unhappy about you bringing that up."

Hiller had taken this woman's measure before she even set foot on *Redstone*, as he watched her struggle up the pier in her too clean, too pressed cotton khakis the day she reported aboard. As Kendall had made her way to the brow, a strong wind had blown her side to side like a brown paper towel ready to take flight. Lightweight. He knew exactly how to handle her. In this case, he had to walk a line between letting her feel a little control while giving up no real authority. The incident with Carter had the potential to cause him grief. Powerless little bureaucrats like Kendall lived to memorize and quote "the book." They used it as their only basis of power, and they needed to be massaged just right, or they might connect with bigger bureaucrats, who actually have a little power and are the enemies of anyone who lives and works in the real world.

"Sorry about the memos comment at the all khaki meeting," he said, putting on his most contrite expression. "I'm sure we can work that out between us." He watched her face to see if this landed properly.

Kendall grimaced and exhaled. She was thoroughly unequipped to recognize a snake, even one who'd bit her more than once.

"I'm glad," she said, unable to keep the relief out of her voice.

Bingo, Hiller thought. He quickly followed up with the card in his deck with the most influence. "Good, good. And it looks like we'll have plenty of opportunities to work on getting you qualified in engineering."

Now he had her full attention. Kendall had never qualified as Engineering Officer of the Watch (EOOW) on her first and only ship. She needed it now, in order to advance. Hiller knew better than Kendall herself that getting one rung away from command at sea made people do and think crazy things. Six months ago she may not have thought about or even desired to take command of a ship—and her prospects were nil—but here she was with her feline nose poking out over the top of that ladder. Hiller also knew she had a snowball's chance in hell of making that last step. No navy ever in the history of the world was hard up enough to put this woman in that position. No matter. He could play along and let her think she had a chance. The EOOW qual was his equivalent of catnip and there was no way Kendall was getting it without his help. He set the hook. "No reason you shouldn't come home from this deployment fully qualified for command at sea."

For a millisecond, he thought he'd played it too loose. Kendall squinted, took off her Coke bottle glasses and rubbed her nose. She sat forward with a changed look that Hiller took for suspicion. He was not on friendly terms with anyone in the wardroom; he could be more aptly described as being on business terms with everyone there, only paying attention to any of the other officers to the degree they were currently useful to him. Kendall fell into the category of officers who were 99.9% useless to him and not worthy of any energy, and from his perspective, it would be foolish not to see this clearly. But, in a flash, he realized that what he mistook for suspicion was the woman grinning.

"That would be very nice, Cheng. I'm a little green when it comes to engineering. All the help you could give would be very, very welcome. Appreciate anything you could do to look out for me. And..." she added conspiratorially, "I'd be happy to look out for you too."

Hiller smiled back at her. This was like fishing in a pay pond. He didn't need bait. Hell, he probably didn't need a hook. Kendall was ready to jump straight into the boat. He suppressed a snicker at Kendall's suggestion she could look out for him; he'd discovered long ago the ability to swallow one's pride and purge it, long before anything like true humility got into his digestive tract.

"Of course," he said. "The ship is like family." Without a pause he rolled into the real issue—his real issue. "We had a small problem over the weekend. The only matter that needs any attention from turning over the watch. MM2 Carter went missing over the weekend," he paused for effect, "twice." He put on his most grave face. "Once was bad enough—disobeying a direct order. Twice... twice is desertion. So for a time and because of the circumstances, we needed to secure him in the MAA shack." Keep the details fuzzy; another anti-bureaucratic move.

The XO's eyebrows arched up. Hiller went on without giving her space to interject. "I gave all engineering notice following quarters on Friday morning that liberty call was at my discretion... too many overdue PMS checks and quals. Only way to get their attention focused. Anyway, Carter and his buddy MM3 Hayes snuck off the ship and I caught 'em coming back myself. I was going to go easy on them. Read'm the riot act. Threaten them. Damned if two hours later Carter, didn't go over the side again. I caught him trying to sneak back aboard in the middle of the night."

Pausing and gauging the XO's expression, Hiller decided to throw in a creative touch calculated to remove any sympathy for Carter. "Had to have been a woman involved. Hayes and Carter are world class skirt chasers. Carter especially. Got to watch him with the females in engineering. Caught him putting his hands on the new girl, Freeman, not long ago."

The effect of this lie was immediate and produced the exact result that Hiller desired.

"Did she report this to anyone? Why wasn't he written up?"

Hiller had to play this part of the game subtly. "I didn't see the incident personally. It was told to me. I called her in and asked about it, but she didn't want to talk. Said it was nothing..." He let this trail off ominously.

The XO pursed her lips. The one role she felt confident about on *Redstone* was being senior female onboard. The truth was that the females, officers and enlisted, held her in contempt, even in this role, openly mocking her behind her back. Kendall was utterly oblivious to the fact. She believed herself to be the guardian of all things female on *Redstone*, from feminine hygiene products to the security of WINS berthing to policing the wearing of bras at all times, she stood her vigilant watch.

Hiller used the precise moment to drop in his bombshell. "I had to shackle the man. Flight risk and acting erratically as he was. Either that or send him to the brig. Felt like we could do without that kind of publicity at the moment."

Kendall's eyes widened at the mention of shackles, but Hiller's preparation of the battlefield made her inner conflict short and sweet. Of course the Cheng did the right thing. He was doing the right thing to help her and to help the ship.

Carter? Carter was lucky not to be in the brig, if not for going U/A, then for violating a woman.

"OK, Cheng. We'll take care of Carter at the next NJP. I think the Old Man will want to get one set up and out of the way so we can get on with prepping for sea. Where is he now?"

"I turned him over to Chief McBurney. He's been keeping him in the MAA shack."

"All right. I'll take care of it with him. Anything else?"

"No, XO. I'll take care of the watchstanding issue with the Old Man. I don't think we need to worry about that." He turned to go.

"Thank you, Lt. Hiller."

Hiller stifled a laugh at Kendall's stern expression and tone, but by the time he closed the office door behind him, he was grinning ear to ear. Yes. Like fishing in a pay pond.

Hiller had no second thoughts about sexing up the story about Carter and Freeman. He had been a witness to the collision between them outside the door to Damage Control Central. The innocent embarrassment of both of them grasping clumsily to keep themselves from falling was anything but innocent to him. He was sure he saw pleasure pass across Carter's face as he came up with a handful of soft female flesh. Touch "his" woman? He suppressed the urge to confront them right then, put the fear of God in Carter and claim what belonged to him, but it was over in an instant. The fire simmered down and he let it go. None of these knuckle draggers was stupid enough to cross him. He kept them all firmly in their places. It didn't mean anything, right? Even as he talked himself down, he admitted it gave him a twinge of something. Call it jealousy or something more primal, like a dog seeing another dog stumbling upon his bone. Hiller did what he habitually did with any incident on *Redstone*; he filed it away for future use.

When Carter showed himself resourceful enough to solve the insoluble problem of the missing valve, it elevated the sailor from a no-name, non-competitor, to someone who might think for themselves. Hiller wasn't interested in sailors thinking for themselves. It moved MM2 Steve Carter up an invisible threat matrix that Hiller carried subconsciously. Anyone stepping too far up or too far out was likely to trip a wire and set off Hiller's warning lights. Keep the people under you afraid of you and keep the people over you needing you so much they're afraid of losing you. That was his ticket. Fear was a wonderful tool. He used it regularly as he climbed the Navy's ladder. Like what he'd done to that overweight asshole Lambert. The man he'd sent to the brig with a bag full of coke. That story left him in absolute control over the engineers. They talked about him in whispers. He loved it.

Then Carter turned up U/A with that buffoon Hayes and with a valve that should never have been found. Great initiative. Good thinking. Too smart by half. Click. He could recalibrate Carter. The sexual assault angle was a pure piece of improv in front of the XO. That would get back to the rest of the ship. They would know to keep their grubby hands off his woman. The fact that no one who saw the actual encounter between Carter and Maggie could construe it as sexual assault in any way shape or form did not bother him in the least. The opportunity to put Carter in his place while keeping the XO in hers made him so happy he momentarily forgot about Maggie's rebuff in the closet.

Chapter 32
World Moving Events

Redstone buzzed with activity in the days following the announcement of the surge deployment. The weather turned hot and muggy. The air grew heavy with the possibility of afternoon thunderstorms. A crane from shore services delivered a crate large enough to hold a car. It was one of two liberty boats returning from overhaul. Deck division pulled a paint punt up under the stern where several sailors in badly stained coveralls went at the old girl's rusty derriere with needle guns. They looked like spiders hanging from the black pneumatic hoses snaking over the sides of the ship. The constant movement of people and things up, into, over and around, gave the ship the feel of a gigantic gray ant hill.

Four bells let the crew know the skipper was leaving for a briefing at Logistics Group 2 Headquarters, where he would learn of the ship's schedule more precisely; the main question centering on a "yes" or "no" for REFTRA.

It was Thursday before the Executive Officer convened Executive Officer's Investigation (XOI). There were seven cases to be heard. The sailors scheduled for an appointment before Kendall lined up outside the ship's chapel, converted into a faux courtroom for meting out Naval justice. Each of them was accompanied by their leading Chief Petty Officer and Division Officer; each dressed in the best working uniform they could find. All were nervous but doing their best not to look it. As sailors exited the Chapel, those waiting in line checked their faces to see good news or bad. If *Redstone* herself was on pins and needles, these men were feeling the point more sharply than their shipmates. Given only four weeks' notice to sail away again for six months or more, and with all leave canceled, no one wanted to get busted today and end up adding the last month alongside the pier to the long months on the other side of the pond. As it turned out, events were conspiring to cut down the wait for everyone.

Some 7000 nautical miles away, Iraqi troops stormed across the border of a little known neighboring country in their version of blitzkrieg. They were creating a 'Greater Iraq,' taking what was rightfully theirs; following the tedious claims of despot leaders from time immemorial. In a matter of days, they controlled Kuwait, and stood atop the country like a playground bully daring anyone to knock him off it. With a hawk in the White House, it appeared a bigger bully might accommodate the Iraqis.

On the same day, a Navy frigate, USS *Boone* (FFG-28), had attempted to enter the Egyptian port of Hurghada in the North Red Sea. Charts of the port had not been updated since the early twentieth century. *Boone* grounded on an uncharted reef, bent her main propulsion shaft, and tore up her propeller. Barely able to make it into port, the frigate limped pierside and tied off, unable to get underway. The United States was in the awkward position of having one of her warships in an Arab port when the possibility of hostilities between America and an Arab nation seemed imminent. The presence of the *Boone* was an embarrassment to Egypt, placing her in a forced position, unable to appear as a completely neutral, good faith partner between the Arab world and the US.

About the time that Carter, the last sailor to take his turn in front of Commander Kendall at XOI, had stated his name and the Legalman First Class had read out the report against him, the Captain of *Redstone* was on his way back to the ship with a newer, nastier surprise. Admiral Fink, Commander Logistics Group Two, was on the end of a string coming down from on high, and that string pulled his right arm up in a smart salute. Yes sir, I will have a repair ship in the Red Sea, working on *Boone* within a week. He hung up the phone, took the string and tied it around Shumate's neck, and just like that, *Redstone* found herself on the pointy end of the spear, hustling off to a potential war zone with little more than 48 hours' notice. By Saturday afternoon, she cleared Chesapeake Light, headed east, making her best cruising speed; a pedestrian 18 knots, but not bad for a 50-year-old gray lady.

Chapter 33
A Kiss in a Different Light
December 1989, North Atlantic Ocean, Course 082, Speed 12 knots

Steve looked out over the dull gray sides of *Redstone* at the deep blue Atlantic. It was a brilliant day at sea; the air itself magnified each detail of the waves and sky. He calculated that the results of Captain's Mast ultimately cost him less than twelve hours ashore during the frenzied run up to her departure.

Once the orders from COMLOGGRU Two became official, almost everyone on the ship worked around the clock to get her underway on time. All liberty was canceled. Each sailor got four hours to go home, pack, and return to the ship, carefully monitored by the quarterdeck watch. The XO approved a few exceptions. She let a man from the Operations Department spend a night ashore with his wife. They'd been married less than a month. The run-up to underway was harsh and revealing. It was a time for separating the real sailors from civilians fulfilling a four year obligation to get a little college money.

The hyperactivity of the week before leaving was followed, as always, by the surreal stillness that comes after a ship casts off the last line and begins baby stepping into her natural environment, the open ocean. The sea and anchor detail to get out of Norfolk through the lower Chesapeake Bay and out into the Atlantic lasted three hours. By the end of those hours, nose pointed east, the at-sea routine had settled in and with it, a form of peace and quiet.

Steve's Captain's Mast case was a blip on the radar. Quickly convicted of Unauthorized Absence and given forty-five and forty-five with a suspended bust to Petty Officer Third Class, it didn't sting so much out here. Everyone on a Navy ship at sea is incarcerated; all wear the same clothes and eat at the same time. The lights come on and go off on schedule. It is a jail of a sailor's own choosing.

Steve's only distinctions underway, as a restricted man, were extra duty musters and chores. As an engineer used to working in terrible conditions in the pit, he found both the musters and the chores a relief from his normal life at sea. While many around him, both his extra duty mates and his normal shipmates, were in a state of mourning over their lost time at home, Steve found himself content with his situation. The CO gave him a stiff punishment to be sure, forty-five days extra duty, forty-five days restriction to the ship, half a month's pay times two, and reduction in rate to E-4, but Shumate had also suspended the bust and the fine, on condition of Steve's behaving himself. Steve couldn't put his finger on what had transpired in front of the Captain, but he felt the Old Man knew he was being railroaded by the Cheng. It was evident in letting him keep his rank and his money, but it was also in the way he had pronounced the sentence. Steve thought he heard regret in Shumate's voice.

Now here he was, halfway across the pond. A day like this one made him forget any lost time. This was the thing he loved about the Navy. There were hours upon hours of boredom. The sea and the sky and the ship and the sounds around you became a haze gray backdrop, pulling you in and making you think the whole world must be completely empty and mind-numbing. Then you stepped onto the weather decks and saw things most of the people in the world never saw. You saw an F-18 launch off the catapult of a carrier cruising 500 yards away and watched it roar right over your head. You saw it come back for a low pass and realized it wasn't making any sound; then—BLAM!—its sound arrived, trying to catch up with its supersonic source. A pod of humpback whales appeared, spouting and herding their young along. Dolphins chose a calm day to put on a show for you, rising from water so still it appeared to be blue plate glass until the gray rockets exploded in flips and turns and dove back into the deep with only the slightest ripple. Or a day like, this when the gentle rhythm of the ship coupled with the perfect following wind and seas froze time and made you feel like you were not just *looking* at a masterpiece of a seascape, you were actually *in* one.

"Nice," he murmured to himself, and it was nice. He realized he was glad to be alive.

"Yes." A woman's voice startled him. "Almost too perfect to be real." It was Maggie Freeman.

He looked fore and aft warily, checking for anyone who might see them, then he met her eyes. "How long have you been standing there?"

"Not long. I've got a few minutes before I have to go on watch. I try to spend some time in the real world every day. And," she added with a sweep of one arm, "You don't see this in Fishersville."

"Guess not," Steve said. He fought the uneasiness rising in his stomach. This is the Cheng's woman; he knew it, everyone knew it. He flashed back to their collision-embrace, the way she felt in his grasp, softly electric to his touch. He tried to keep it out of his eyes and off his face, but failed. She moved to the life lines next to him. He noted the way she smelled. She noted the way he looked at her.

The smell! It all came back to him like a flood. The MAA shack. The door flung open in the night. He had forgotten about it, but here it was. Here she was. And he knew it had been her. She was much more than a delightful smell here and now. She was as full as the seascape. She glinted in his eyes like the sun off the waves. What was it? He thought this over for years afterward and could never fully explain it. It embarrassed him. He wasn't the type to fall for this. He settled on unexpected beauty and left it at that. Maggie Freeman would always be this to him.

"What?" she said, studying his face.

Steve flushed, unready for her perceptive glance into his mind, and embarrassed at how easily she saw into him. He hoped she couldn't see too far. "Nothing," was all he could manage to say. The Cheng's woman? This person and the Cheng. It didn't fit. She felt like, like, the ocean. Much too large and free for Hiller. He shook the thought off, again trying to keep it off his face. What did he know, anyway? Maggie Freeman was Hiller's woman, no matter how good she smelled or felt or sounded here in the seascape portrait moment with the sun shining on their faces. And that meant she wasn't, couldn't, be what she seemed, and she couldn't be trusted either.

Maggie put both hands on the uppermost lifeline and lifted her face to the sky. She smiled. Involuntarily, Steve glanced up and down the approaches to where they stood. Feeling danger, feeling exposed, but also enjoying this woman's presence. A wisp of her long hair pulled free from its moorings and whipped her face. The wind dropped. A curl lazily settled in the cleft of her white V-neck t-shirt, showing at the top of her half unzipped engineering coveralls. Steve fought the urge to follow it with his eyes. He shook his head, trying to keep the thought out of his mind. She turned toward him, brushing her hair back in place. It was an unpretentious, girlish movement, absent of fussiness or care.

"What?" she said again.

"You're beautiful." The words came without thought. His face reddened. He shrugged and held up his hands as if trying to catch the words and pull them back.

Her eyes remained steady; her expression unchanged. Steve thought she was contemplating a way to get away from him, away from the crazy words he'd said out loud. His heart, which had been so calmly beating only a moment ago, was jackhammering. She must see it through his shirt. Faster than the sun slips finally over the horizon she leaned into him, kissed him, and was gone.

The water tight door behind him clanked shut, punctuating her departure. He felt dizzy. He grabbed the lifeline to keep his balance and touched his lips. His face felt hot. Her smell lingered for an instant in the heavy air. Her smell! The same. He looked forward as two sailors from Deck Division came into view, carrying cleaning gear. They passed him laughing at some private joke, or were they laughing at him? He nodded to them and touched his lips again. He was sure the kiss was a permanent mark there, written in lipstick he could never erase.

***

Mal Hiller sat on the edge of his rack in a tee shirt and boxers, pressing his stateroom phone against his ear. "I don't give a shit what you say, MM1, go and have the watch check the line-bearing temps on the port shaft. Something ain't right. I can feel it all the way up here. Don't know how you numbnuts don't. Get back to me ASAP."

He dropped the phone back in its cradle. It rang. He picked it up again, ready to chew on whoever was going to tell him how everything in the plant was running within specs. How he couldn't possibly feel a line shaft bearing going bad, three decks up from the engineering spaces. The voice on the other end wasn't one of his engineers. He listened intently.

"Where did you see this? Uh huh. Yeah. Yeah."

He hung up again and sat, looking at the phone. It was original, he was sure. Almost fifty years' worth of phone calls had come and gone through the oversized old black handset. He was in the Cheng's cabin. It had always been the Cheng's cabin. Fifty years' worth of wake ups and break downs, complaints and orders. Bet there never was another call in all those years like the one he just received—a call to tell him his girlfriend, who was one of his engineers, was just seen kissing another one of his engineers, somewhere on the main deck. Nope. No other Cheng ever got a call like that one.

He contemplated MM2 Steve Carter. He began to think of him as an engineering problem. He wasn't a human being at all, merely something on the his ship that wasn't working the way it should work. Like the line shaft bearing going bad, sending a vibration through the steel hull; something that needed fixing so the ship could operate the way it ought. Yes. Carter was like that bearing. Maybe all he needed was to be taken out and machined so things would work again, but then again, if it couldn't be fixed.... He picked up the phone again and called the XO. *Hill Street Blues*, baby. Do it to them before they do it to you... and they were always waiting for a chance to do it to you. Always.

***

Mark leaned over Steve's shoulder. "What's got you so interested in this?" he said.

Steve stood over a makeshift stainless steel table in the lower level of the forward engine room, the creased and stained blueprint of *Redstone*'s third deck spread out before him. It was loud and hot there, normal steaming conditions for the aged steam plant. They stood close and shouted into each other's ears to be heard. He wiped sweat from his forehead with a grease stained, red mechanic's rag.

"The layout on *Seahook* got me to thinking about this," he pointed to the penciled circle he'd discovered on the print. "When they gutted this area to make WINS berthing, it looks like they rerouted a steam line, for no reason. And it's the same line that runs through the Dive Shack. The one that leaks all the time. The chief diver, McMillan, tells me the Bos'n is getting pretty sick of it."

Mark nodded. The din of machinery made him hesitate while his brain sorted out Steve's words. Steve had been waiting to tell Mark what had happened on the main deck earlier in the day and now it spilled out awkwardly.

"Maggie Freeman kissed me this morning."

"What?! Huh?"

"I was just standing there taking in some air, and she came up behind me. I told her...." He thought better of repeating what he'd said to Maggie Freeman. He shrugged. "She kissed me."

Mark's eyes grew wide. A silly grin split his face. "Shit."

Steve seconded the emotion. "Yeah. Shit. He shrugged again, not knowing anything else to say, not knowing how to make sense of it or explain it.

"Jeez, Steve. You know she's been with the Cheng. What if he finds out?" His eyes grew wider as a new thought swelled his brain. "What if the Cheng is using her to set you up? With all the bullshit they've been pushing about sexual harassment, all she has to do is say you touched her and you're screwed."

Steve put both hands on the table and bowed his head between them. For once, Mark had thought of something before he had. It had never occurred to him that Maggie's kiss was anything other than genuine. It felt real. Mark threw it into a completely different light. It could be true. She found him on the main deck alone. She initiated the conversation. She looked him in the eye. She kissed him. Was it all a set up? It wasn't as if he was a man who women went wild over. He closed his eyes and replayed the whole encounter. After a moment he realized Mark was staring at him, waiting for a response. He had none. The possibilities of love and betrayal log-jammed in his brain and brought him to a standstill. Love? He scoffed. A single kiss. That was all it was. Mark's explanation popped the foolish idea like a kid's balloon falling on a rose bush.

"You better stay away from her, buddy. You got enough trouble as it is."

Steve said nothing. When Mark pressed his face within inches of his nose he simply nodded in agreement.

Neither one of them knew how much trouble was already descending on them.

Chapter 34
Phipps Runs Out of Time
September 1976, North Atlantic Ocean, Course 273, Speed 14 knots

Getting rid of the OPPE team was like getting rid of a virus. They were gone, but the ravaged body still needed time to recover. The Chief Engineer put engineering on a bare bones watch rotation. The exhausted men fell into their racks, only venturing out of their berthing compartments for chow and to stand watch. Jasper slept 14 hours straight. *Redstone* was less than 48 hours out of Norfolk when he awoke to Richards shining a flashlight in his face in the blacked out berthing compartment.

"Rise and shine, Phippsy," he said, hissing in his ear. Jasper pushed him back, annoyed at the unwelcome guest, startled out of a dreamless sleep.

Richards caught himself on a stanchion, barely regaining his balance before landing full on the deck in a heap. He grunted, and smiled his bulging, blue-eyed grin.

"No way to treat your partner, Phipps. Time's burnin'. You think you could stall me till it was too late?"

Jasper, still stupid with sleep, gave no answer.

"I know you got cold feet my boy, but trust me, you'll thank me when it's over... when you're sleepin' on your own private beach instead in a stinking black hole like this. Jeez, don't you snipes ever bathe?"

Jasper bit off a retort about snipes being too busy making sure everyone else had hot water and air conditioning to have time for personal hygiene. Instead he said, "The most likely place we'll be sleeping, if you insist on doing this thing, is a place that's gonna look and smell a lot like this."

Richards chortled. "No chance. You and me are the only people on earth who will know what happened. Keep quiet and we walk. Now come on. I got the Suppo to ask for some help with a little 'A' gang work in one of our spaces and your name came up. The Cheng said we could have you as long as we needed you." There was that infuriating grin again. Jasper wanted to wipe it off his face. He got up with a grunt. Richards started and backed away as if threatened.

"Jumpy, Richards? Mark of a guilty conscience. Not a good sign for someone that needs to keep their cool. And you do. Don't think it's not gonna happen. This will get hot," he sighed. There was nothing for it. He was out of time. He slipped into his grimy coveralls. "Let's go."

Chapter 35
As Redstone Turns

Pete Baber was on the bridge talking with the captain. He loved the bridge. It kept a happy dumb smile on his face. The Old Man was doing what, in the Bos'n's experience, all CO's did, stressing over things well out in the future, and things out of his control.

"Bos'n, are you sure we can trust the Egyptian harbor pilots when we get to Suez? Are we prepared to go it alone?" Shumate asked, his normally droopy face drooping more than usual.

Pete thought about saying something along the lines of, "You know, Cap, there've only been about a million other ships making the passage with Egyptian pilots, and Egypt would be crazy to mess with a source of revenue like the Canal." It was a true statement, full of common sense, and also the thing a Captain of a navy ship would receive in the spirit of goodwill about once in those million times. He deferred.

"Cap, we could put our guys aboard the pilot boat, or put our boats in the water to lead us through. Take a lot longer. No one knows the Canal like their people. But we could do it. Of course, there's the chance they'd take offense at that. And there's the chance they would tell us to pound sand. Could be awkward. What do you think?"

The Captain screwed his forehead and eyes together tightly with the tips of his fingers and rubbed his loose fitting skin like his face was a pot of stew.

"Naw, Bos'n. Guess we'll go with it. Don't want to take any more time than we have to."

Baber smiled inside. Always best to let them think they were making the decisions, no matter how obvious they were to everyone else. "Yes sir. Good idea. And we've still got some steaming to do before we get there. Plenty of time to get ourselves up to speed on their procedures."

Baber was so content on the bridgewing of the ship, he was oblivious to the soap opera playing in the wheelhouse, where two of his three current lovers, Ensign Sandy Fratella and SN Fran Green stood watch together, one as the JOOD and the other as helmsman under instruction.

The deck watch on a long ocean transit was in many ways a human cruise control. No orders to the helm or engine room, the ship plowing along, steady and straight. This left plenty of time for idle chatter between watchstanders while the Captain fretted the Bos'n.

Fratella, a thick yet well-proportioned Italian girl from New Jersey, was on the verge of promotion to Lt.(jg) and qualification as a Surface Warfare Officer. She was loud talking and funny in a smug, goodfellas way. The crew, especially the male sailors, liked her because she was more a character from a mob movie than a Navy officer, and she was sexy in the way self-assured women are sexy. The female sailors liked her because she was steady and fair, not cycling with her cycle as several of the women chiefs and officers seemed to do.

Growing up in Jersey, Fratella saw her mother and older sisters—four of them, all married off in successive years—taking care of men they regularly referred to as "pigs" and "slobs," yet none of whom took control of their own life. They were content to feed the pigs, clean up after the slobs and to push out a new generation of pigs and slobs. She broke the pattern, went to college, joined the Navy, in order to leave the pigs and slobs behind. And now? Now she was stuck on a ship, fooling around with a man much too old for her, who was by any definition of the word, a pig. But she felt something inside she had missed when she judged her mother and sisters so harshly: the man was *her* pig. Damned if she would put up with someone else rolling around in the mud with him.

The key atop the light fixture outside the Bos'n's stateroom was *her* key. Keeping multiple women believing this was the Bos'n's greatest bit of debauched magicianship. It defied explanation, but in the nearly three years he'd spent bedding everything from a stuffy, married, lieutenant commander department head to a hypersexual seaman apprentice who sported breasts so large she had trouble wriggling through a water-tight hatch, the idea of sole proprietorship of the key hidden in the overhead light fixture held up. There had been close calls, no doubt, but the controlling influence over the women wasn't their relationship with the Bos'n, it was their relationship with Navy regulations. It turned out that, in general, women were much more afraid of being found in violation of Navy regs than men, so much so, they were very tight lipped about violating them by copulating aboard ship, and each one thought she was the exceptional person, willing to flaunt the regs. When two women who were sleeping with the Bos'n ran into each other in the vicinity of the key over the light fixture, they both retreated. This left the Bos'n's rack empty for a night, but it also left out drama. Until today.

Seaman Fran Green was standing easy at the helm, not minding her business or anyone else's business. Two hours into a four hour watch, she stared straight ahead into nothing, resting her hands lightly on the shiny, well-worn brass wheel of the helm. She was so preoccupied with nothing that she paid no attention when Ensign Fratella sidled up behind her. The other watchstanders, lost in their own personal monotony, ticked the minutes away in their own little worlds. The two were alone. Fratella looked the girl up and down, like a dog sizing up a stray that wandered into its yard.

"Bitch."

The word, barely above a whisper, had no visible effect on Green, who continued staring ahead.

"I saw you, you little bitch." This time a little louder, as Fratella leaned in closer to Green's ear. The younger woman started as she became aware of both the words and the other woman.

"Wha-?" she began to say.

"I saw you take the key. I saw you let yourself into the Bos'n's stateroom."

And there it was. Years of the philandering Chief Diver's dumb luck keeping all the women in the dark, blown up by a perfectly timed chance.

Several things happened at once. Green, wide-eyed, tried to sputter an objection. Unfortunately for her, her voice happened to be similar enough to Fratella's second oldest sister that no matter what she said, fireworks were coming. The voice triggered the ensign. Fratella grabbed Green by the arm, jerking her around, face to face. Green's hands went up defensively, pushing Fratella back. She stumbled, losing her balance and fell hard against the bulkhead at the rear of the bridge. Enraged, she jumped to her feet and came at Green, both hands raking the girl's face like a cat. A full-on Jerry Springer show ensued, replete with hair pulling, rolling on the deck and curses about exactly whose man was whose.

Green, the smaller woman, nevertheless gained the advantage, pinning Fratella's arms and pummeling her head on the deck between handfuls of hair, before the other crew members jumped in to break it up. The two combatants ended up facing each other, one restrained by the bewildered officer of the deck and the other by the quartermaster of the watch. The sound of the melee carried to the bridge wing, bringing the CO, XO, and the Bos'n running. Their presence muzzled the two women, who had been screaming profanity laced threats at one another.

"What's going on here?" Shumate demanded, red-faced with anger.

Both women, disheveled from the fight, at once realized their position. Caught in a spotlight neither one wanted, the tension drained out of their faces. They looked down.

"Well?!" the CO said.

The Bos'n, who knew exactly what was going on, stood frozen to the deck. The walkie talkie pinned to his collar crackled.

"Bos'n, need you in the Dive Shack," a disembodied voice said.

Shumate stared holes in the two women, who remained silent.

"XO, find relief for these two. Confine them to quarters until we sort this out!. No time for this. No time for this!" he shouted over his shoulder, as he turned his back on the scene and returned to the bridge wing. "C'mon, Bos'n."

Baber paused half a beat, trying to make eye contact with either of the combatants. The XO said, "Go. I've got this, Bos'n."

But he knew she didn't.

Word spread quickly about the brawl, with rumors of the cause running faster than the ship was making headway eastward. Baber hustled to remove the key to his stateroom from its hiding place. He remained in his stateroom in self-imposed hack for the next several days, only venturing out as far as the wardroom for meals and straight to the Dive Shack and back as duty demanded. He waited for the ax to fall, expecting a summons to the XO's quarters any moment, but none came. Green and Fratella remained mum under questioning, saying only that they had had a disagreement. He expected Fratella to hold out; it was Green he was worried about. Officers had a lot more to lose and generally knew their rights better than a newbie sailor like Green, whom he assumed would be subjected to a great deal of pressure to give up whatever she knew. The only thing Green did give up was the fact that Ensign Fratella started the brawl, and for her part, Fratella didn't deny it. She was confined to quarters until the ship reached port, with the exception of her watchstanding duties. Meals came to her stateroom. Green was reassigned from mess cranking duties in the wardroom to the crew's mess and written up, awaiting the next XOI and Captain's Mast proceedings. Eventually, Baber emerged from hiding, but steered clear of both the bridge and the chow hall. The people who knew him best, who were a small handful of divers and Chief Petty Officers, noticed a change in the Bos'n's normally cocksure attitude. To the rest of the officers and crew, he just looked older.

Chapter 36
Shaft Alley

Steering clear of Maggie Freeman was easier said than done for Steve. Under Senior Chief Snell's cross training plan, Maggie stood watches in both the forward and aft main spaces. Their paths crossed often. In the days following "the kiss," she turned up too much for it to be random. The night before the main shaft bearing incident, she cornered him as he took lube oil pressure readings on a pump, in a dimly lit section of the forward plant. He was bent over the gauge holding a penlight in one hand and the pressure log in the other while sweat dripped around the edges of his blue mickey mouse ear protectors. Unlike many of his fellow engineers, Steve strictly adhered to the mandated double hearing protection, stuffing yellow bits of foam—"yellow foamies"—into his ear canals before plopping cumbersome earmuffs over top of them. Paired with the steady thrum of the steam plant pushing the old ship over the ocean, the hearing protection gave one the sense of being in an audiologist's booth, where you strained to hear and respond to their elusive beeps.

Concentrating on getting the reading and then recording it in the log in the low light, Steve was unaware of Maggie's presence. He stood up from a crouch and, turning to go in one movement, there she was. He dropped both flashlight and clipboard. A repeat of the clumsy collision outside DC Central ensued, but this time, instead of rebounding speedily into their own private space, Maggie let Steve's arms encircle her without moving away. She put her arms around him instead, looking directly into his eyes.

"Why are you avoiding me?" she said, her mouth so close to him that he felt her words rather than heard them.

His heart was racing. He sputtered like a lawnmower trying to start. "I, I, I..."

Maggie kissed him. It was a sweaty salt kiss. She tried to make it linger. Steve, recovering his composure, grabbed both of her arms and firmly broke their embrace.

"What are you doing?" he asked. "I'm not... I don't... " He searched for words. A sheepish look crossed his face. "I'm sorry, Freeman, but I can't do this. Everybody knows... you... you... you're... " Looking into her eyes, he couldn't bring himself to say the words.

She finished for him, "I'm the Cheng's woman." She spit the words out like a mouthful of vinegar.

"I'm nobody's woman, Carter. I belong to myself."

They stood face to face. Steve searched her eyes, looking for the clue; looking for the trap, trying to figure out what this was all about. If he would have seen inside Maggie, he would not have found the answer to that last question, but he also wouldn't have found any ill will or trap. Maggie was as confused as he was about why she was standing here, kissing a complete stranger for the second time. She'd kissed plenty of men, but she was always the pursued, never the pursuer, never like this. It wasn't what she was here for; not what she left everything behind to find. The opposite was true. Get away from men. But then, there was Hiller and now.... She stepped back, shook her head and looked down.

Although Steve still had his doubts, he regretted the look he'd put in Maggie's eyes. He touched her on the arm. She looked up. "We can't talk here," he said. "Is there a place we can meet after watch? A place you're sure we are safe from...."

"Yeah. I know where we can go." She leaned in and shouted a location in his ear, again more of a vibration than a pronunciation. When his eyes questioned her, she only nodded and disappeared as quickly as she had appeared.

Steve spent the rest of his watch mulling over the strange development. He knew Hayes was giving solid advice when he warned him to stay away from the girl. It was even money at best he was getting set up, but that's not the way he felt when he looked in her eyes, or heard her voice.

He completed the balance of his duties in the main space that night on auto-pilot; an unfortunate circumstance that would come to haunt him before he was due back on watch, twelve hours later.

***

The meeting place proposed by Maggie was undoubtedly the most isolated spot on the ship, it was also a spot that left no possible route of escape if they were discovered. The climb down to the port shaft alley felt like he was descending a metallic mine shaft. The further down he went the more claustrophobic it felt. He had been down to the shaft alley many times, but he avoided it while underway. Something in the realization that this was the end of the line when it came to *Redstone*, as she plunged along through the deep ocean made it especially eerie. Coupled with the knowledge that any other human being descending to where he was going to meet Maggie would trap them, unnerved Steve. He chided himself for letting her set this place for their rendezvous. She was a newbie; green. She probably hadn't thought it through.

He reached the last rung on the ladder and checked his watch. He was five minutes late. Freeman was nowhere to be seen. Tentatively he edged forward along the whirring shaft, peering along the length of the surprisingly well-lit space. Brighter here than the lower level of either main space. No one was here. Behind him he heard the slightest clink of metal on metal and watched in amazement as Maggie emerged from a recessed panel behind the shaft alley ladder he'd just descended. She was smiling broadly.

"There are some advantages to being the Cheng's woman," she said, emphasizing the man's title.

"I guess so!" Steve said. "I didn't know that little cubby hole existed."

"No one does. And it isn't a cubby hole, it's an old damage control locker. Come and see. There's room in there for more than two."

When Steve hesitated, she took him by the hand and led him into the space. She showed him how the latch to open the door was concealed by a nondescript fitting, easily moved to one side. Inside, she closed it behind them. He was amazed by what he saw. Here was a small desk with a lamp, and on the sloped bulkhead where once had been a rack for stowing DC gear, a bed.

"This is like a secret little stateroom!" he said. Then he knew that it *was* a stateroom and who it must belong to. He turned to leave, his skin crawling.

"Don't," she said. "Trust me. I know Hiller's habits better than he knows himself. And I know he never comes here underway. He told me himself. Believe it or not," she said, grinning, "I've discovered the monster's weak point."

Steve looked puzzled.

"The Cheng's afraid of being down here underway because he says the weakest place in the hull in this old bucket is right here." She pointed to the bulkhead over the bed. "I wouldn't believe it myself, but I tried to get him to come down here once. He actually broke out in a sweat! Said he'd be damned if he ever did, underway. The shaft alley would fill up faster than you could snap your fingers if *Redstone* took one good jolt." She said this with a wry smile that didn't make Steve comfortable.

"If anyone knows, it would be him," he said, eyeing the bulkhead and thinking of the horror of drowning here before anyone onboard knew the ship had sprung a leak.

Maggie pulled out the chair from the makeshift desk and motioned for Steve to sit. He did while she leaned against the rack. She eyed him carefully. Steve started to look away, embarrassed at her attention, but something clicked in him. He had nothing to be ashamed of and no reason to lower his eyes from this girl. He met her eyes and held them.

"What are we doing, Freeman?"

"Maggie."

"Maggie. What are we doing? I'm crazy for being here. There's no upside to this," he added under his breath, "Hayes warned me."

"What? Who?" Her countenance changed like throwing a light switch. She looked genuinely alarmed. "Someone knows about us?"

Steve looked hard into her face and let out a long exhale as a teacher would for an exasperating student.

"Us?! There is no "us." I have no idea what we are doing here and why you keep tracking me down! Yeah. Hayes told me this was nuts... even talking with you is nuts." He searched her face and went on, "he said the most likely reason for you to pay attention to me is to set me up for the Cheng to really finish me." He found he couldn't maintain eye contact with her with the last of these words and looked down at his boondockers, shined to mirrors for his restricted men's musters. "As if I'm not already finished enough."

Maggie pushed off the bed and stepped to him. "Look at me," she said. "You already know that's not true or you wouldn't be here. You're too smart for that."

"Freeman, you're smart too. What makes sense on this ship? Power. Not justice. Not the way things ought to be. Power. On **Redstone**, power is stronger than smarts. And from where I sit, Hiller is the most powerful person aboard. Being smart didn't keep me out of getting handcuffed to a stanchion, did it? No. I'm giving up on smart. Me being here with you right now is proof of that."

"So why are you here?"

"I guess I decided to stop calculating and start feeling."

There was a long pause with only the steady thrumming of the giant propeller shaft filling the space.

Maggie broke the pause. "That's very interesting because I think I'm here doing the opposite. I've gone from feeling to feeling most of my life. Men especially, but other things, too. I joined the Navy to get away from a life of feeling... break the pattern; think for myself, make a new start. I did, too. Until I got here." She trailed off.

"And then?" Steve asked.

"Then I fell right into my old ways. A man pays attention to me and I like it. I like it. He says the right things and I can't help myself. I do stupid things. I sleep with him. I know it's not real, but it feels real. I look in his eyes and I see... nothing. No that's not true... I see no trace of me in his eyes.

I only see him making me into what he wants. Pretty soon I'm not me anymore when I'm with him, but even then, I don't stop. It's the attention. It's like a drug." She sighed a deep, sad sigh—a lifetime of a sigh, like the sound of a locomotive easing to a standstill.

Steve waited. Maggie sat down tiredly. He said, "I'm sorry Freeman... I mean Maggie. I am. But why are you telling this to me? You don't know anything about me. And how is this different from the pattern you just spelled out? Aren't I just another man?" Unconsciously his eyes drifted to the bed behind her. "Because I'm not going to be...." He didn't finish his thought.

"That's the point. That's the reason. Reason. Not feelings. When I ran into you that day—literally ran into you—outside DCC, there was something in the way you looked at me. I know it sounds stupid. But you did see me. I could tell. And later, when I kissed you, I was testing out what I thought about you."

"What?"

"That you wouldn't pursue me even then. You didn't even kiss me back. It was just...." She searched for the word. "It was just innocent."

When Steve rolled his eyes at the word she laughed. "I know. I said it sounds stupid."

"No. No," Steve said. "It isn't stupid. I think I see. But you're reading a lot into a little. How do you know what I'm really like? I'm not that innocent. How do you know I'm not scared of Hiller? Maybe that's why I'm steering clear of you. Maybe that's why I'm not giving you any of your drug."

"You're right. But I can see you, too. I saw what you did for Hayes. I knew what the Cheng was doing with that valve. He told me. He knew before he ever made that announcement that the valve was at the bottom of the Med.

He knew it was Hayes that screwed up. He was using the whole thing to make MP division work the weekend. He even knew about the strip ship announcement for *Seahook*. He had the long duty weekend and he wanted to knock out one of his maintenance lists. And," she looked ashamed, "he wanted to keep me aboard with him. The man has no reason to leave the ship. He's got a locker full of liquor in his stateroom and a secret chiller stocked with beer. Add those to "his woman," she pointed to the center of her chest sarcastically, "and he is fine using *Redstone* as his personal houseboat."

"He knew," Steve said, "and you did, too."

"He did. I did. I'm sorry. I didn't know what to do. Who to tell. Would it have made any difference? Is anyone on this ship going to stand up to him? But you did. You outsmarted him, Steve. That's the real reason you ended up handcuffed to a stanchion. You ruined his plans. Worse than that, you showed him up. He can't take that. He won't."

Steve got up suddenly. Anger flashed across his eyes. Maggie stepped back. He reached for the door.

"Please don't go. When I saw you there, in the MAA shack, it knocked me awake. I knew you did what you did to save Hayes and the rest of us from Hiller. I knew it was you who figured out how to get the valve. I knew you were getting punished for all of us."

"Us?!" Steve said. "I don't see how you qualify as being one of "us." You live in a different world than the rest of engineering, Freeman. The rest of *us* are on the USS *Redstone*; a Navy ship. You? You're a plaything on the Cheng's... what did you call it? Houseboat. A plaything. Willingly. Well I'm not willing to be *your* plaything. You stay away from me, understand? Get your attention fix from someone else."

He exited the hidden compartment, closing the door behind him in one motion, slicing off Maggie's protests. He climbed the thirty foot ladder out of shaft alley like a submerged man, swimming for air and daylight.

Chapter 37
The Main Shaft Bearing

The port main shaft bearing gave up the ghost around 0800 the next morning, right after the CO visited the bridge and checked his morning message traffic. The situation in Iraq was deteriorating and the tension between the US and moderate Arab nations was strained. There was talk of towing the *Boone* out to sea, bent shaft and all, and letting her fend for herself. The higher ups were wracking their brains for any other unit they could send that could ease the situation. Shumate didn't want the Navy sending anyone else. He wanted to be the white knight, even if he rode in on this donkey of a ship. *It might even be sweeter this way*, he thought to himself, as he sipped coffee from a white china cup from his mess.

While his orders told him to proceed to Hurghada at "best speed," up to now, Shumate had been prudent. Hiller warned him when he checked aboard that *Redstone* was a steady old girl who needed a gentle hand. Shumate knew he didn't know enough and never would, to challenge the Cheng's hegemony over the engineering plant. *Redstone* COs, by and large, over the last thirty of her fifty years' service, had respected the ship's foibles and did not ask questions of her that neither she nor her engineers could answer. Shumate, mulling over the messages in his hand, saw, in *Redstone*'s first war cruise in half a century, a glimmer of hope for his lost chance at a carrier, or an admiral's star. If he could get the old girl to perform where the newer ships had failed, maybe he could climb over the impossibly high wall and catch the gold ring with a fingernail. He decided to push his ship a little harder. He told the OOD to ring up 20 knots; only four knots faster than they were cruising. The order went down to main engineering, the adjustment was acknowledged and Shumate slouched into his chair on the starboard bridgewing.

The Engineering Officer of the Watch answered the bridge's order with the engine order telegraph and the throttleman eased the huge throttle valve open. Running the plant on this old ship was more art than science. She had her idiosyncrasies. Her engineers had learned and passed these down to each other over the years; things that would not be written in official operations manuals, but were nevertheless rules no one would violate. Like the peculiar vibration the engineers referred to as '*Redstone* choking on a bone' that showed up whenever she made between twelve and thirteen knots. No engineer had ever been able to find out why she did it, and the choking bone persisted even through extensive overhauls of every major system that could be producing it. Even Hiller, who prided himself on sorting out mechanical issues others claimed were insoluble, gave up on fixing it and starting calling it the chokey ghost.

The engineers knew what the book said about answering all ahead flank bells, and they knew what *Redstone* could do. The opposite of the chokey ghost applied to getting her up to twenty knots. To deal with the chokey, the engineers popped the throttle quickly to keep the vibration from having a chance to do any damage. When the ship passed eighteen knots on the way up, the book said, let her go; open the throttle up. She was supposed to answer a flank bell like any other bell; in about two minutes. But the engineers' institutional knowledge told them to never crack the main throttle all the way open without walking it up a half knot at a time, letting her settle in for a minute or so and then adding half a knot. The watch on duty began building speed the way they'd always done it.

Shumate, after restlessly slouching in his chair and finishing with his message board, bounced up and returned to the pilot house for a second cup of coffee. Entering the pilot house a full ten minutes after ordering the flank bell, he stopped to check the ship's speed, which was just edging up to eighteen knots and appearing to hold there. He checked his wristwatch and called the OOD over.

"What's taking so long? Why are we at eighteen knots? I asked for a flank bell, didn't I?"

The staccato questions stumped the OOD, whose cheeks turned the color of freshly boiled lobster. Before he could offer an explanation, the CO punched the button for main control on the nearest squawk box and keyed it up.

"This is the CO. I ordered a flank bell ten minutes ago and we're at eighteen knots. What the hell are you doing down there? Is there a problem?!"

A raspy reply started to come through the gray box, "No sir..."

Shumate cut it off. "Then answer the fucking bell. Now! And find the Chief Engineer and tell him I want to see him in my at sea cabin!" Shumate stomped off the bridge, his face as red as the OOD's.

The EOOW was the newly qualified Ensign Fratella, still in hack since the incident with Seaman Green on the bridge. The CO's voice through the squawk box in Main Control sent a shiver through her spine like the ones she got when her father had lost his temper in her home, growing up. She turned to the throttleman and shouted over the din of the engine room.

"Open it up! All the way!" Then added, "Now!" when the MM3 looked doubtful.

"Messenger! Go and find the Cheng. Tell him the Captain wants him in his at sea cabin! Go!"

The fireman apprentice was two rungs up the ladder before she finished the sentence.

Redstone groaned as the throttles opened to their stops and steam poured into the turbines. There was a faint whirring above all the rest of the equipment as the old girl stirred herself to answer the bell. Fratella removed her Mickey Mouse ears to wipe sweat from her brow. The heat in the engine room was normally too much for a standard watch, according to the Navy heat stress regulations, a fact that the Cheng conveniently ignored. But the heat stress on the watchstanders was nothing compared with the stress they felt about catastrophically breaking something. The ship settled out at her maximum speed as all the snipes eyed their respective gauges, expecting the worst but hoping she wouldn't break, at least not on their watch. A half hour into her first flank bell in many years, *Redstone* was steady steaming.

The main shaft bearing closest to the port main engine was running hot by the time the Cheng completed his visit to the CO, a visit in which he had given no ground at all but simply allowed Shumate the rope to hang himself. Unlike the line officer trying to reach his brass ring, Hiller had already reached his. He knew before he climbed the ladder to the Old Man's cabin that the ship was answering a flank bell. The messenger had filled him in on what had transpired. He also knew she would break. He wasn't prescient enough to call the exact component, but his gut told him it would come sooner rather than later and it would be a debilitating set back. He kept this to himself while Shumate ranted. Let the fool have his moment. When *Redstone* broke it wouldn't fall on his head.

The break came one hour and three minutes into the flank speed run. To the surprise of everyone in MP division, Hiller did not descend into the engine room after his talk with the Old Man. There had been the general consensus the Cheng would be the one setting the captain straight, not the other way around, and that before an hour had passed, they would get the call to walk her back down to a reasonable speed and then walk her back up a little at a time. Instead, Hiller retired to his stateroom and told the messenger of the watch, who had waited around anticipating this chain of events, that no one was to disturb him. He was going to take a nap. And he did.

It started with a noticeable shudder on the lower level of the forward engine room, underneath the main turbine. It came and went like a top beginning to lose momentum. In moments however, it became a steady shaking accompanied by the shrieking sound of metal on metal. Fratella, who had expected the Cheng to pull her from between the Captain and a hard place, froze at the switch, unable to decide what to do. The throttleman, an old hand on *Redstone* although only a third class machinist mate, shouted at the new EOOW twice before taking matters into his own hands and slamming the main shut. When Fratella failed to acknowledge the casualty, he elbowed her back to the present.

"Ma'am you have to tell the bridge we are not able to answer bells on the port screw!"

Fratella did so in halting phrases, then, snapping out of it, she picked up the phone and called the Cheng's stateroom. A sleepy sounding Hiller answered on the third ring.

"Chief engineer," he said.

"Lieutenant Hiller... Cheng, we've suffered a casualty on the port screw and can't answer any bells for now. Starboard is still ahead flank and I, ah, I don't think we should keep trying to answer that flank bell. What should I do?!"

"Have you informed the CO? Hiller said deliberately.

"The CO? No. The bridge knows. The OOD knows. Shouldn't he tell the captain?"

Hiller coughed into the phone.

"Yeah. That'll do. It's his call." He went silent.

"Cheng? What do I do?" Fratella was edging toward frantic. Someone needed to be in charge of this. She only qualified EOOW because she needed it to get her Surface Warfare pin. She never asked for this kind of pressure.

"Well," Hiller said, "If I were you, I'd wait for the OOD to inform you of the Captain's wishes." He hung up the phone with a clunk.

The number one main shaft bearing for the port main engine ate itself. Because the port shaft needed to be locked to prevent its free rotation as it was dragged along like the gnarled foot of a wounded soldier, *Redstone*'s maximum speed was six knots. The Old Man was apoplectic. The time-distance problem grew minute by minute, as his ship wallowed along at a pace comparable to the days of ships of sail. Hiller had played him. Hiller had let him run the ship into danger. It was the chief engineer's job to prevent disasters like this from happening, no matter how much a Captain pushed him. He was supposed to draw the line. It was his duty as an officer and a gentleman. These were the things Shumate told himself, the internal monologue he rehearsed for the day he might stand in front of a board of inquiry. But in the intense spotlight of the here and now, he kept the thoughts locked tightly away. In the here and now he needed an engineering miracle. And the only messiah in sight was Mal Hiller.

Chapter 38
Heroes and Goats

From the moment *Redstone's* tired old line shaft bearing failed, the Cheng did what the Cheng did best; he set out to affix blame for the wiped bearing upon someone, and determine how to best position himself as the hero of the emerging crisis. The second goal he knew would be easy enough. The first dawned upon him a few hours later, as he reviewed the previous night's lube oil logs.

Although *Redstone* carried a full complement of technical experts who could be called upon to repair almost anything a modern Navy could break, the *Redstone* herself was a relic of a bygone era. The Repair Department could work on her, but it would be like handing a sick velociraptor to a horse veterinarian.

Hiller knew the anatomy of the old girl better than anyone in the Navy, not just better than the prissy college boy engineers in the Repair Department. He had their measure anyway. In a moment like this, when careers were on the line, not one of them would voluntarily step to the head of the line. No, they'd be sure to stand half a step back and offer their expert opinions from a safe distance, like a bunch of old men, armchair quarterbacking from a safe seat in the barbershop. Hiller would take the lead. He would take the spotlight. And if one of those ninnies muttered too loudly, or tried to get too much of the limelight, he'd shove them into it and watch them scurry away like cockroaches.

The only slippery part of being the hero would be getting Repair to cast a new bearing without letting them come off looking better than necessary. He knew it was not an easy job, but in the first "head shed" meeting convened by the Old Man to sort out options for repairing his ship, Hiller had been ready, while the Repair reps were not. He laid out the steps needed to get the ship to its commitment in Hurghada on time. Without giving the Repair Officer any heads up, he mentioned the need to pour a new bearing, throwing in that it would be a "routine" evolution for the Repair Department, especially, he said, since they had no real gainful employment while the ship was in transit anyway. The Repair Officer, taken by surprise in front of the skipper, did what all these manicured fingernail biting officers did when questioned about the capability of their people; he sputtered out a quick agreement to do something he had no real idea how to do, and voila, the Cheng was set as the star of the *Redstone* wiped bearing story within two hours of the event. Now that he was the good guy in the script, he needed a bad guy; and even though he knew perfectly well it was that idiot Shumate who was to blame, he had other ideas of who to cast in that role.

Hiller called for the logs from the previous night's mid to 04 watch. He found what he was looking for immediately and dialed up the MPA, Lt.(jg) Bill Poulton, a sleepy-eyed blonde-haired college boy he generally ignored. When the MPA presented himself in Hiller's office, five minutes later, he had a hangdog expression. Hiller spit a long stream of black tobacco juice in his emptied paper coffee cup. He enjoyed the awkwardness of everyone who had to stand in front of him in this office. He let the silence grow just enough to make the man start shifting his feet nervously.

"Well MPA. It's a cluster. Your boys screwed the pooch."

Poulton, who was on the bridge as Junior Officer of the Deck for the mid-watch and had been in the forward main space since the shaft casualty, was over matched on a good day. This was not a good day. He was dead on his feet and dog paddling in a sea of engineering problems that he had a limited capacity to understand, much less solve. He learned early in his tour in engineering to keep his mouth shut, no matter what the Chief Engineer said, until it became an absolute necessity to speak. He remained silent. There were too many paths following this greeting and all of them ended up in bad places. He kept his eyes down and waited.

The Cheng enjoyed this, too. College boys. Normally useless. Unnecessary for any operational purpose. But today... today he was going to make use of the clueless MPA.

He pointed to the clipboard full of sweat and oil stained logs from the night before curled at the edges, sitting there.

"Take a look," he said. "Tell me what you see."

Poulton tentatively picked up the clipboard and flipped it right side up. The logs. It was always the logs. Every day there was a dressing down about the logs. The MPA had a degree in physics from a state school in Virginia. Books and labs and eight weeks in the Navy's Steam EOOW course in Newport, Rhode Island did not prepare him for the jumbled spaghetti of steam, water, and electrical lines in the real world of *Redstone*'s ancient guts. He stared blankly at the top log sheet and tried to keep his ignorance out of his expression. He flipped through all the logs. Nothing stood out to him, but then again, in all the times he'd stood on this spot to answer for the logs, he'd never once found what the

Cheng barked about, without it being painfully pointed out to him.

He handed the clipboard back. Today he was too tired and too overwhelmed by the main shaft breakdown to play the usual game of whack a mole, where he was the mole with the Cheng hitting him over the head with his own dullness. "Don't know, Cheng. I don't see anything out of the ordinary." Inwardly he braced for the expected put down. It didn't come.

"Yeah. That's what I see too," Hiller said with no hint of sarcasm at all. He went on, "This takes a little deductive reasoning, MPA." He pulled a single sheet off the clipboard and waved it between them. "If you look at the lube oil pressure and temperature on the main shaft bearings all night long, there's zero variance. Look at the numbers." He handed the sheet over.

The MPA looked warily at it. He hesitated, then said, "Right. But, we were steaming steady state all night. No change at all. It's what you'd expect..." there was a slight waver in his voice. Never commit yourself to any position before the Cheng stated his—the primary rule of surviving in this jungle.

"And yet we have a catastrophic failure of this bearing," Hiller said, taking back the log and stabbing the recorded column of numbers with an index finger. "Does that add up to you?"

When the dullard of an MPA failed to reply, he said, "Major components rarely fail without warning. Think of your car. You think the engine just lets go out of the blue? Hell it does. Knew a woman one time who didn't know what the red squiggly symbol on her dash meant. Annoyed her so much she took a piece of black tape and covered it over. No more red squiggly light. Engine blew. Threw a rod right through the bottom of the block. No oil. See what I'm getting at?"

"But Cheng, no one ignored any warnings. You can see right there, the numbers are all in range."

"Yes. The numbers are all nice and neat. But we know that's got to be a lie. Gets pretty hot in the main spaces, especially over by the main engines. And it's nice near the throttle board. Nice big fan. Cooler. By my way of thinking, there should have been at least eight to ten hours of increasing lube oil temps before that bearing shit the bed." Casually he scrutinized the log.

"Maybe—let's see who—maybe MM2 Carter was stayin' comfortable under the blower. You know he's pretty unhappy with the result of Captain's Mast. Maybe he isn't as motivated to do a good job. When I look at the logs, there's nothing that says he didn't do his job, but..." he trailed off, waiting for this dunce to pick up the scent.

The MPA's head hurt. He didn't like this game. More than anything, he wanted to crawl into his rack and forget he ever joined the Navy. But no one in MP division was going to be getting any sleep until the port shaft was spinning again. He shook his head to clear the cobwebs. When he realized the Cheng was waiting for him to say something, connect the dots, he blurted out the first thing that popped into his skull. "Someone gun decked the logs? he said.

If the young officer had been more alert, he might have seen a slight narrowing of Hiller's eyes, and a subtle upturn of the edges of his mouth. "I didn't say that. I just said it doesn't add up. Maybe you should do some checking around."

Hiller paused half a beat before setting the hook. "A successful investigation would help us all. We need to find out who's dragging down the division, keeping us from performing. It might help you personally. A good way to wrap up your time in engineering and get you on your way up topside."

Hiller let the last sentence dangle in front of the MPA. It was the choicest morsel and he knew it. The man was alert now. He could almost see the young officer salivating. He'd woken up this morning, another day in *Dante's Inferno* with a broken piece of gear beyond his capabilities by many degrees, the Old Man screaming bloody murder in his main space, the Cheng summoning him to his office... and no end in sight to his sentence in engineering hell. It was offering parole to a man expecting to spend another twenty years in jail. His eyes brightened at the mere prospect of escaping Hiller's masochistic fun house.

The hook was down the fish's throat. Hiller gave it one last twitch. "Yeah, last night I told the Old Man you were ready for your SWO board, as far as the engineering side of the house; it'd be a formality at this point."

The MPA said, running a greasy hand through his sweat matted hair, "Guess I'd better take these logs and have a talk with last night's watch. Especially Carter. He might have something against us, after all."

Hiller noticed the use of the word "us," and smiled. Hook swallowed and set. Now when Carter's name came floating to the top of the main shaft bearing blame list, it would come from someone other than him. "Good man. Let me know if you need any help sorting those guys out. You know they'll try to cover for each other. Don't let them bullshit you."

The MPA turned and left, now a man on a mission. Trade Carter for his freedom? Easy choice. The man had already shipwrecked his own career by skipping the ship, hadn't he?

***

The main shaft bearing fiasco seeped into the ship like a London fog. Normally boisterous sailors told their jokes in hushed tones, the wardroom was devoid of banter, the only evidence of the officers eating their meals was the clinking of knives and forks on plates. The crew's galley mirrored the wardroom as little knots of sailors hurriedly, almost apologetically, consumed their meals and retreated back to their workplaces.

Repair Department fired up the forge and created a mold from blueprints dating to just before the Second World War. Their first attempt at pouring the mercurial looking babbitt metal produced a bearing that appeared to be perfect, but when x-rayed, turned out to be riddled with internal flaws. The Cheng, shifting his attention from fixing blame to affixing glory to himself, explained to the Captain that the repair crew had not accounted for the particularly thick design of the *Redstone's* bearings, something he'd given much thought to. The truth was that Hiller, combing through old records after he relieved the previous chief engineer, discovered an exacting record of the last time *Redstone* poured a new bearing for her own engineering plant. In the record, the engineer noted the design called for a lower temperature of the babbit when it was poured into the mold and a slower, more demanding pour that had to be completed at certain time intervals to keep flaws out of the material. He kept this information to himself, holding it like a man holding the nuts from the flop in a high stakes game of Texas Hold'em.

While this little play within a play worked its way out, *Redstone* continued wallowing along, alternately trailing the lame shaft as it free-wheeled, and locking it down, dragging the stationary screw like a man walking with a clubbed foot. Each time the bearing casing was opened, it required this procedure and slowed the ship to bare steerageway. The CO grew more and more agitated as he watched the ship fall further behind her track.

Hiller, who was no navigator, had a relationship with the chief quartermaster, both having come from the same general part of Pennsylvania. Soon after the bearing gave way, he had asked for and received a "drop dead" time and position, past which it would be impossible for the ship to make up the lost miles and still arrive in Hurghada on time. Using his own calculations, Hiller came up with the perfect scenario to save the day. He let the repair department flail through the first attempt at refitting the bearing, knowing he would have just the right amount of time left to get the ship fixed and to Hurghada with a high speed run if the second pour went right. He went so far as to recommend that Shumate not to report the casualty in the mandated casualty report.

"Skipper, it's like this," he'd said, using his most diplomatic tone, "No one expects much out of this ship except what's happened—a breakdown. We can't look bad, but we can look good. Let's see what we can do before we tell on ourselves. If we get this repair done at sea and still make our commitment, it'll make us look really good. We can always send a CASREP later." Shumate, still clinging to the hope of making the right play that would get him to the top of his ladder, agreed.

Hiller personally took over the second pour and shepherded it from start to finish. Using his secret formula, the new bearing came out perfect and the process of bluing it in began. It was a tedious evolution. The bearing, which was a shiny silver half circle approximately the size and shape of a bisected tire from a full size pickup truck, had to be coated with a blue dye and slid into place under the main shaft. The main shaft was hoisted up with a chain fall, just enough to allow the new bearing in before being lowered again to its resting position. Once this was accomplished, the shaft was rotated several revolutions before it was stopped, hoisted again and the bearing removed. Observing the pattern the shaft made on the silver surface revealed if it was properly seated or if high spots remained, needing fine tooling. Each time the process repeated, the ship was brought to a complete standstill so the stricken shaft could be locked while the bearing went in and out.

"Like a fire drill in a Chinese whorehouse," BTCS Snell remarked, standing to the side of the intense work and helping himself to a generous portion of Copenhagen from his ever present can of tobacco.

Maggie was fascinated with the whole procedure. She skipped chow to watch the work. The opportunity to see a piece of major engineering gear opened where you could see its guts thrilled her in a way she barely understood. The bluing-in took seven repetitions before the engineers were satisfied they'd gotten it perfect. It was well into the mid-watch the following night before *Redstone* was making turns on both screws. The new bearing would take a while to break in, the Cheng warned, but after another six hours of taking it easy she would be ready for the high speed run that would get her to Hurghada on time. He intended to be in the main spaces himself when the ship was cleared for the run, he assured Shumate.

During the mid-watch Maggie went looking for Carter, who was on her same rotation. It wasn't until then she found that he'd gone missing.

Chapter 39
Collision Course

Carter and the MPA had a hate hate relationship that had nothing to do with each other. They both hated the Cheng and they both hated being stuck in the belly of the fifty-year-old *Redstone* with no hope of getting away from either. But, with the main shaft crisis, that had changed for Lt.(jg) Poulton, the MPA. He saw daylight and he didn't care who he left in darkness to get to it.

Poulton, MM1 Peary at his shoulder, shook his head. "Carter, no one else saw you for a good half hour in the middle of your watch. I've talked to the other watchstanders from last night and all of them are accounted for but you. There's no glitch except you. Peary here says you went to take readings and you went MIA. Now, if you've got a good reason no one saw you, I'm all ears." He hugged the engineering log clipboard to his chest as if it were armor plate, daring Carter to penetrate it.

Steve's head was spinning. He had no idea where this line of questioning was coming from. Peary, his EOOW from the night before, never questioned him when he got back from rounds; never intimated there was a problem. Often watchstanders covered for each other when one of them got a bad case of the nickie fits and slipped topside for a quick smoke. It was an unwritten rule of life in the main spaces—a wink and a nod at the official rules from a group of men and women subjected to the inhumane environment of the main spaces. He knew the official line on leaving the main space when you were on watch was that it never happened, and no one would cover for you if you got caught or if something went sideways because you weren't at your post. But he hadn't left the main spaces, and the reason he'd been a little long making his rounds was something he would never share with Poulton. Had his little rendezvous with Freeman really lasted that long? It didn't seem like it. What he didn't know, couldn't know, was that Hiller had had a talk with Peary right after he'd met with Poulton and he'd played his Jedi mind games with the not so bright MP division LPO. All it took was the suggestion that "someone" told him one of Peary's watchstanders may have been seen out of the main spaces during watch. It reflected poorly on the EOOW— might even lead to an investigation. It was a shot in the dark. Hiller had heard no such thing, but he knew enough of the engineers in his plant to know on any given night, he was likely to hit his mark. Peary turned deathly pale before Hiller asked him who his lower level man had been, because Peary himself had taken an unofficial smoke break on the night in question. He exhaled, realizing he was not Hiller's target. "MM2 Carter was my lower level man, Cheng."

Hiller had given him a knowing look and said, in an uncharacteristically diplomatic tone, "Tell you what, Peary, I'll let you handle this. Gives me a chance to see how you're coming along as a leader. If you want to put on the khaki, you've got to take care of business."

Now Poulton and Peary had their man cornered. They were both ready to lay the weight of the main shaft catastrophe squarely on the back of an innocent man. Carter had taken every reading at the correct time and recorded it precisely by the book. But a ten minute diversion in a dark corner of the lower level with Maggie Freeman had created a crack, just wide enough for him to get pushed down a very deep chasm.

Poulton was still looking at him. "Carter? Where were you?"

Steve shook himself as if waking from a bad dream. He met Poulton's eyes. "I was standing my watch, MPA. Standing my watch and doing my job like I always have. It's not true that I was missing for 30 minutes." His words were firm, his delivery monotone.

"That's not what Peary says. This is some serious shit you're into, Carter. The Cheng says there's no way the lube oil readings for that bearing are accurate. Says they must have been gun decked. And some time in the mid-watch, there had to have been a spike in temperature and a dip in oil pressure."

And there it was. The Cheng. Steve tried to think of a way out of this, a way around this tyranny of a broken chain of command. He couldn't see one. The question he had now was about Maggie. Was she part of this sickness? Had she set him up? If they hadn't had their rendezvous in shaft alley, he would have been convinced she was in cahoots with the Cheng. But in an odd way this changed his mind. If she was doing the Cheng's bidding, it was unbeknownst to her. Meeting him in shaft alley didn't make sense if the meeting in the lower level during his watch had been part of a set up. And that meant...

"Carter?" Impatient hostility rose in Poulton's tone. "You got an explanation?"

Carter was tired of fighting a fight he didn't choose and he was tired of doing it through surrogates.

"An explanation? How stupid do you have to be to believe that anyone can make a defense for something that didn't happen?! I'll answer that. Pretty stupid." He stabbed a finger at Poulton's chest. "You're smarter than this, Poulton. You're going to have to live with the things you do in this little hell the Cheng's created. And it will be right there in your heart. It won't feel good. It'll eat you. But hey, whatever strings he's pulling have got you dancing. Well, go on dancing, but I'm not dancing anymore." He simulated a pair of scissors snipping invisible strings over his head and threw the imaginary implements at Poulton's feet. He almost laughed when the man shifted on his feet as if to keep from getting hit.

Poulton started to speak, but Steve turned on his heels and walked away.

***

Steve decided he would have it out with Hiller on any ground. He went looking for him in the forward engine room, where he expected to find him hovering around the bearing repair. To his surprise, he found a handful of sailors from Repair Department buttoning up the bearing casing and a few from MP division gathering tools and field-daying the area. He spoke to the latter.

"You guys seen the Cheng?"

A weary looking fireman apprentice in a filthy set of dark blue coveralls grunted, "Gone to the bridge. Heard 'im sayin' something 'bout telling the Old Man how to drive his ship."

Carter hesitated a moment then set his jaw. If he was going to have it out with Hiller, it might as well be in the most visible place on the ship. He had plenty of time to think about what he was getting ready to do, climbing upward and forward until he was at the last ladder, one level below the bridge. He wasn't a confrontational guy. He was a 'live and let live' guy, but he'd reached his boil and there was no way to take the heat off but to cut it off at its source.

He paused at the bottom of the ladder, looked up and took a deep breath. Just as he put his foot on the bottom step, he heard Hiller's distinct snorting laugh floating down from the bridge. If he had any doubts about what he was doing, that laugh drove them out for good. He tightened his grip on the hand railing and climbed two steps at a time, launching himself onto the bridge through the hanging blackout curtains like a broaching torpedo.

His arrival was anticlimactic. It was dark on the bridge; the only lights showing were dim spots dispersed here and there: the green glow of two gyro repeaters, barely visible yellowish backlights of various dials and indicators. Steve could barely perceive the blotchy forms of the people on watch. He stood waiting for his eyes to dilate, swaying dizzily in the disorienting darkness. A voice near him said in a low tone, "What are you doing up here, shipmate?" He recognized it as a boatswain's mate he'd done mess cranking duty with; an annoyingly friendly guy with the equally annoying habit of referring to everyone as "shipmate."

Like a blind man, Steve reached for the voice. He touched a rock-hard arm that reached back and steadied him.

"Martin? That you?"

"Yeah, Carter. What're you doin' up here?" he repeated.

"Where's Hiller? I heard him. Where is that bastard?"

Martin said, "Sounds like you need to cool your jets, shipmate."

Carter's vision started to clear. He could make out Martin's serious eyes.

"I'm as cool as I'm gonna get until I set some things straight. Now, where is he?"

Martin shrugged and pointed to the starboard bridge wing.

Carter said a terse, "Thanks" and stepped behind the helmsman, a man on a mission. He never saw the angle iron, on which the ship's inclinometer was mounted, hanging in his path. His forehead connected with it in an explosion of stars inside his head; the last thing he saw before he went down like a felled tree. Two things prevented worse injury. The angle iron had caused so many head injuries over the many years that *Redstone* sailed the seas that a thick black piece of foam rubber pipe insulation had been wrapped around it, long ago. When Carter's head connected with it, with a resonant "thwooong," it was more like getting punched by a boxer with steel knuckles than brained with a tire iron. Martin, thinking Carter would walk around the helm and not behind it, had started to warn his friend when he heard and saw the knockout blow. Just as Carter's knees buckled, he managed to grab him under the arms and lower him to the deck. Martin saw Carter's eyes had rolled up in his head. He immediately called away the duty corpsman. When the Cheng and CO finished their conversation and returned to the bridge, Carter was already strapped to a stretcher with several sailors getting him ready to transport to medical. Carter was beginning to come around, wincing as the medic flashed a light in his eyes to check for dilation.

The Captain said to Hiller, "That's one of your guys, isn't it?" Looking closer, he recognized Carter but failed to remember his name. "Yes. That's the fella you sent to Mast, ah, Gary, no..."

"Carter," Hiller said.

"Carter," Shumate agreed, "What's he doing up here?"

Shumate looked at Martin, who was trying to keep his position despite the flurry of activity around his helm. He shrugged, not willing to tell of his brief encounter with the fallen man.

Shumate sensed he wasn't getting a vital piece of information..

Hiller, reading the helmsman's face, set his lips in a scowl. He knew when enlisted guys were covering for each other the way a buzzard knows roadkill. He locked eyes with Martin and put the hint of a threat in the look. Then he said, "Captain, we've got to get started breaking in the new bearing if we're going to make Hurghada on schedule. We'll have time enough to sort this out."

The mention of Hurghada immediately refocused Shumate. "Right. OOD! Get the names of these watchstanders for me and leave them on the desk in my at sea cabin. Cheng, let's get this evolution started."

Chapter 40

Coveralls

September 1976, North Atlantic Ocean, Course 256, Speed 12 knots

The two men made their way forward and up together. Jasper stopped in his shop to collect his welding gear. None of the sailors there asked any questions. Jasper was Johnny on the spot for so many jobs the Cheng wanted done around *Redstone*, either for favors or to return them, it wasn't unusual for him to come and go with his own kit. He had even managed to procure a portable set of tanks for small jobs. It was these he grabbed and took along. The presence of Richards probably meant the Cheng was paying off an exchange of goods from some shipment that made its way to engineering.

"How do you know there's nobody in WINS right now?" Jasper said, as they arrived at the door to the controlled equipage locker.

"Strange thing, these Egyptians," Richards said. "Being Muslims and all, I thought they'd turn up their noses at alcohol. But turns out they're big fans of Johnny Walker Red and I just happen to have a case of it stashed. Booze is great for negotiations." He thought a second and added with a sly grin, "Just like our negotiations in Riley's. But our Egyptian friends, well, they like the taste, but they're light weights. Been pretty much out of the game for days. Tried to keep them that way so we might avoid having to do this," he shrugged, "but they're coming around at just the wrong time. They won't go in WINS, though; too confined for the foggy headed drunks. But they're hanging close to the door up there."

He pulled out a key, unlocked a deadbolt and punched a code into the cypher lock. They went in. Richards closed the door behind them before flipping on the lights. The harsh fluorescents hissed and crackled as they grudgingly came to life, settling into a dull hum. The large locker area was laid out in a cross shape. Two alleyways bisected it, creating four squares at each corner enclosed in mesh cages. The place smelled strange to Jasper. It took him a moment to place it— it was the smell of new—very out of place on *Redstone*, which reeked of age in every nook and cranny. The four cages contained boxes, some marked, others plain, and shiny new pieces of gear for various uses. Richards walked Jasper aft, along the main thoroughfare, stopping at the last cage. He took out a jangling ring of keys and unlocked a huge brass padlock. He dropped it on the deck. It thudded dully. The door to the cage squeaked in protest as he opened it.

"Not much cause for getting into this cage," Richards said. "This is where we keep new clothes that go missing if we don't lock them up." He stooped and popped open the top of a large box on the deck, showing Jasper its contents.

"These are brand new coveralls! I've been trying to get these for my guys for half the deployment. We ruined all ours with the chipping and grinding up there." He pointed to the overhead separating them from the modified WINS berthing space above them. "And they were here the whole time?!"

Richards shrugged and wiped his mouth with his sleeves. "You need to be careful with supplies. Can't be hasty giving things out that you may need later."

Jasper stared at the man incredulously. "Need? Later? For four months I've been wearing a set of coveralls any self-respecting bum wouldn't use to wipe his ass—so dirty the grime chafes my legs. Same with all my guys and here they sit. You asshole...."

"Phipps," Richards stopped him, "That's what coveralls are for, right? To get dirty so our clothes don't."

Not for the first time, Jasper envisioned his fist poked into that smug face, shutting off the matter-of-factness that flowed from that mouth. He controlled himself.

"Help me move these boxes," he said. Glancing over his shoulder at the way they'd come into the locker, he added, "Probably a good idea to stack them up against the front of the cage. Give us some cover if anyone comes in here while I'm working."

"No chance of that, but we do need to get this stuff away from any sparks. Last thing we need is a fire in here," Richards said.

"Yeah," Jasper said. "Can't afford to burn up the clothes you need to keep in these boxes." But a thought clicked in his mind. Fire. Could he do it? It might be his last chance to get away from this maniac bent on burning down both their lives. He laughed grimly to himself. Start a fire to prevent a bigger fire. The only question was how to do it without killing anyone. No sailor in his right mind would set fire to his ship. Fire at sea was the bogeyman of all the bogeymen. No place to run but the merciless deep.

He looked up. Richards was staring at him quizzically. He shook himself. "Give me a hand, DD," he said, slinging a box of coveralls to the front of the cage.

Chapter 41
Eyes Dilating
August 1990, Mediterranean Sea,
Course 115, Speed 23 knots

The high speed run to Hurghada was going perfectly. The CO was so effusive in his praise of Hiller and his engineers that it actually led to a change of heart for the Cheng. He decided it would cheapen the sweetness of his victory and deflect attention from himself to peddle the blame he'd planned to heap onto Carter. Besides, he could let the threat linger over his man like a thunder cloud and call down the lightning any time it suited his purposes. He was sure Carter had come to the bridge to confront him. He wished the angle iron had not been there. It would have been Carter's ruination. But he had time and power on his side. Let Carter sweat. All the cards and all the chips were his.

The whack on his head gave Carter a concussion, a splitting headache, and a limited duty chit that was the envy of his main space engineering peers. The ship's doc kept him in sick bay a full 48 hours for observation before writing the chit, which kept him off watches for another week and out of any space at risk for heat exposure for twenty days. The doc also required Carter to report to sickbay each evening at taps and spend the night there. When the sailor balked, he explained that sickbay was the only berthing aboard where Carter would be assured of sleep uninterrupted by watchstanders coming and going at all hours and that the head injury required quality sleep in order to heal. Carter became a ghost for the duration of this time—any warm body not actively engaged in keeping a Navy ship habitable, moving, and afloat was a specter. By day, he haunted the fantail and the midships breezeway; by night, restless through lack of activity, he wandered the square formed by the passageways around sick bay.

The time in limbo gave him room to reflect on what he'd almost done. He felt the knot on his forehead as it slowly receded. He rubbed it like a rabbit's foot as he walked the decks. He knew it had been a life saver, and shuddered at the thought of what might have been. With Maggie standing her watches and continuing her cross training, the two rarely saw each other and then never alone. Neither could read what the other was thinking. Steve wanted to keep his distance while he healed. He was unsure what to make of her, even though the bizarre claims of the MPA and Peary trying to frame him for breaking the main shaft bearing proved the girl was not working with the Cheng to set him up. Still, he felt an unease about her.

On the third day of his recovery, Steve was walking his loop between the fantail and breezeway when the ship passed Gibraltar. He paused in his circuit long enough to appreciate the distant but clear view of the famous rock set against a robin's egg blue sky with low swatches of cotton clouds. The ship hummed under his feet, plowing out of the Atlantic across the invisible line into the Mediterranean. He reflected on the numbers of sailors who'd seen the same sight from the decks of their own ships. How long? A thousand years? Yes, at least, maybe longer. As *Redstone* slipped past the landmark he realized he was standing at the same spot

Maggie Freeman had found him and kissed him. It felt like a long time ago: another age, another person, another ship. It had been less than a week.

Releasing his grip on the lifeline, he started aft to complete another lap, mulling over how much had changed in such a short period of time. He recalled the events leading up to that kiss. The Cheng's edict about the missing valve. The trip to *Seahook*. Retrieving the valve. The forgotten ID card. Hiller catching him on the quarterdeck. The night in chains in the MAA shack. Captain's Mast. Finally, the threat of war breaking out requiring *Redstone* to make this wild run across the globe. If he didn't feel the deck gently swaying under his feet , he'd think it was all a dream. But he did feel the old girl plowing along, tired as she must be from the many times she'd crossed the pond, faithfully answering the call again. He was suddenly filled with a strange affection for his ship, as if she was a living thing with a past she remembered and a present she was experiencing along with him. He stepped around an old steel fixture rising from the teakwood deck, a two foot gray triangle. It caught his rear toe. He tripped like a drunk over a sidewalk crack. He glanced around to see if anyone had seen him gracelessly regain his balance at the last instant to avoid a face plant. No one was around but the fantail lookout, who was, at least in this instance, faithfully scanning the horizon with her binoculars, oblivious to his presence.

He turned and took a closer look at the offending support, wondering that he could step over it for twenty laps and almost bite the dust on the twenty first. It was the last remnant of the ship's rear six inch gun battery. There was another like it on the starboard side. The guns had been stripped away long ago when *Redstone* lost any semblance of being a fighting ship, relegated forever to the ranks of defenseless auxiliaries. The support was a scar, he thought, like the scar he would carry on his forehead, even after the knot went away. Evidence that things were not always the way they are now, both good and bad. The thought reminded him of the blueprint he'd used to find his way to the valve on *Seahook*. *Redstone* was an old girl with scars for sure, some of them as nonsensical as the crease he'd carry on his forehead for the rest of his life. He grimaced thinking of this and remembered the odd rerouting of the chill water piping, causing issues in the Dive Shack to this very day.

He said out loud to his ship, "You'd never know you were a warship, old girl. If it wasn't for those blueprints and some old photographs, you'd be keeping that secret to yourself and the only thing to show for it would be an odd scar here and there."

He toed the support with the tip of his scuffed black boondocker. Curiosity overcame his desire to complete his usual fifty laps around the deck. He slipped in the water tight door at the front edge of the fantail and descended into the gloomy interior of *Redstone*, his eyes chasing to catch up with the contrast of the brightness of the sea and sky above. In his momentary blindness, he collided with Maggie Freeman again.

Maggie grabbed him and righted him before he realized what had happened. He heard her and felt her hands on his arms before he knew who it was.

"Whoa." She said. "We have got to stop meeting like this, Steve. People will talk." She had a smile in her voice but shifted quickly to a concerned tone. "You all right? Are you having trouble keeping your balance? Concussion?"

In spite of nearly falling on his face twice in the past couple of minutes, Steve dismissed the thought that it had anything to do with his injury. "No. No. Just didn't give my eyes time to adjust. Bright out there. Great day."

Her smell. There it was again. It was close and nice and incredibly attractive. Her eyes were emerging from the dimness, large and wide and kind with concern. All doubt about this woman faded as his pupils brought her fully into focus. He kissed her, simply, honestly, inquiringly, like a middle schooler's passed note. I like you, do you like me? He took a half step back and waited. She answered, drawing him to herself slowly and kissing him back in kind. It was the least passionate, most passionate moment either of them had ever experienced, friendlier than mere friendship, loving without yet falling, with room and time for the intricacies of exploring deeper intimacy understood and instantly agreed upon by both.

"Well I guess that settles that," he said, more to himself than to Maggie.

"What settles what?" She said, smiling.

He looked sheepish, caught out, his internal monologue exposed to the light. "I was walking laps around the deck thinking through everything that's happened in the past two weeks. You were a big part of it. Trying to understand if you were part of Hiller's plan to ruin my life." He saw her face go sour. "No. No. I know now," he assured her. "I wasn't so sure. I admit it. But when Poulton and Peary tried to frame me for the main shaft bearing fiasco, well, I knew it couldn't be your doing. But it still left me wondering why...? How...?"

She was studying his eyes, listening intently. "Why? How what?"

"Why you seem to want me. How this is happening."

She looked at him for what seemed a long time, exhaled a long full breath and said, "I don't know myself. It doesn't make sense. I joined the Navy to get away from men, or I thought I did. I ran away and ended up right where I started. Hiller is the story of my life up till now. One bad decision after another when it comes to love." She smirked at the word. "Love. Ha! I don't know anything about it. It's me that should be asking the question. Why would you want to have anything to do with someone like me? You were right to question my motives. I don't think I would trust me either, a few weeks ago. But something happened."

She stopped and searched his eyes again as if she were standing on the edge of the high dive deciding whether or not to jump. He waited silently, sensing she needed to move on her own or never move. A tear formed and pooled in her left eye, followed by a twin in her right. They came without a blink and she made no attempt to hold them back or wipe them away. They just flowed from some deep place. She continued speaking, the flood of words matching her tears. "When I saw you risk yourself for us, for the division, but mostly for your friend, Mark... when I saw you do that I knew I was seeing love. Not the thing I've always called love, but something different and real. You had nothing to gain and everything to lose—I knew that better than anyone on the ship because I knew Hiller was setting it up for failure, that he already knew where that valve was and where to get a replacement and everything else. Then you not only took the blame when Mark should have gotten it, you took his punishment. He should have been chained to a stanchion, not you! And you took it. It just... it just did something inside me. It made me want to get close to it. To feel it. And it made me want to throw up, too."

Steve raised an eyebrow questioningly. She went on. "Because I saw all the cheap imitations of what I've called love for what they were, and I saw how Hiller was the face of all of them. It made me sick. It made me want to run, but where can you run when you live on a 400 foot long island in the sea? An island inhabited by a creature like him who seems to do anything he wants to do? I don't know why, but I felt like you were the only safe place on the island. That you

255

might love me the way you loved Hayes. Does that even make sense? I don't really know you, do I? And when I tried to get close to you and kissed you and later tracked you down and tried to make you see me, I was doing what I've always done, I guess. Trying to get love the only way I know how. But you didn't do what the others did. You didn't act like a man... or maybe you did. Maybe what you are is a man and all the others are something else. Something different. Boys. You might be the first man I've ever known."

Steve took her by both arms and held her at arms' length studying her face and finding only earnestness. He said, "Maggie, this is all really flattering, but I just did what was right. And if I'm honest, I've wondered a lot—with all that happened since—if it was right. Funny thing is," he bit his lip, "the more flack I get and the more the Cheng tries to throw me under the bus, the more I feel I must be doing something right. I don't know how that comes across outside my head. Maybe I just prefer trouble or I'm crazy."

She slipped inside his arms and started to kiss him again just as the door to the fantail clanged open, admitting a shaft of bright light, along with a sailor they both recognized from E division. They pushed away from each other as the man closed the door and dogged it shut. There was nowhere to go to avoid him without sprinting away down a passageway—an act sure to make them appear more guilty than they felt already. They stood their ground, backs pressed against opposite sides of the narrow passageway. The sailor, eyes dilated as Steve's had been, was almost between them before he saw them. A grin dawned on his stubbly face when he recognized the two of them. It wasn't a pleasant look, Steve thought. It was a look full of innuendo on a man whose mouth was likely to share what he saw with others as soon as the opportunity presented itself. He knew the man to be one of the "A" gangers in Hiller's pocket. He was a tubby EM1 who always managed to pass weight standards when it was obvious to anyone with a set of eyes he shouldn't. Another reminder of the importance of being right with the right people on the steel island. He turned sideways to squeeze between Maggie and Steve, going face to face with her, purposely drawing out the contact between them. He went on his way without saying a word. Maggie and Steve looked at each other in the wake of his passing and both exhaled, realizing they were holding their breath.

Steve broke the silence. "You think we should try to talk to him?"

"No," Maggie responded, glancing in the direction the fat EM1 had gone. "No. You go. I'm going to cut that off at the knees." She inclined her head again in the direction of the departed sailor. "He'll be in DCC before you get to your rack and he'll be telling anyone who'll listen we were making out back here with our hands down each other's pants. Trust me, I've been in Hiller's stateroom when he's taken calls from that piece of work."

"What are you going to do?" Steve asked.

"What I should have done the night I found you chained to a stanchion in the MAA shack... no, what I should have done when Hiller told me how he was gonna use that missing valve to keep everyone onboard for his duty weekend. I'm gonna go tell that sonofabitch we're through. I've been playing dodge with him since then, trying to figure a way out of this. I've been scared." She looked at him now with a fierceness he was glad wasn't meant for him. She went on, "I'm gonna end it. And," she smiled grimly, some new idea popping into her mind, "I think I see how we can turn the tables on him."

Steve raised his eyebrows. Maggie looked through him and spoke to herself, 'There may be some things he wouldn't want anyone to know about that we can use against him, like he uses lost valves against us.'

Chapter 42
Steve's Discovery

Whether or not the fat EM1 dropped the dime on them before he got to his locker, Steve never knew. It turned out not to matter. He retrieved the blueprint from his rack and paused, wavering back and forth on what to do about Maggie. Should he follow her and keep an eye on things when she confronted Hiller? How could he do it? In the end he decided she was more than capable of handling herself. He wanted to look over these prints in privacy. He considered his options. Privacy on a Navy ship is at a premium, the further down the food chain you live. The Old Man, the Exec and some of the department heads were the only crewmembers on *Redstone* who truly controlled their own few cubic feet of it, dwelling in their staterooms behind locked doors.

At Steve's end of the spectrum was a curtain drawn across the face of his rack which wouldn't keep out anyone who wanted in, as Mark regularly proved. And it was a space only suited for sleeping, not conducive to laying out and studying a three-foot-long, intricately drawn blueprint. He thought of his rack in Sick Bay but ruled it out, too. Too many people randomly coming and going all the time. He thought of

Maggie again, wondering how long it would be before she would be done with Hiller. Thinking of her reminded him of their meeting in shaft alley. That would be the perfect place to lay out the print and look it over.

He rolled up the print and stuffed it in his back pocket, then he took a walk, calculated to bring him past DCC. Before he got himself to the bottom of the long ladder to shaft alley, he wanted to get a feel for the state of play in engineering, and to see if he could catch sight of Maggie. If the Cheng was actively on the warpath, or if any kind of damage control drills were imminent, it would show up here. No one looked up when he stuck his head in and passed on by; it was calm. Good.

He continued aft, and met no one along the route. At the top of the long open trunk leading down to the repaired port shaft, he lingered, gazing down. He resisted the urge to drop something so he could hear it plink when it hit the deck, some forty feet below. Climbing down methodically, unsure of his balance since the concussion, he stepped down, two feet to each rung, two hands on each rung, reset and repeat. Even so, he still had a bad moment half way down, when the ship pitched forward at the same time he shifted his weight backward, adding so much extra force on his hands that it felt he might lose his grip. He hugged the ladder tightly, catching his breath and letting his heart rate fall before continuing to the bottom.

It took some time to find the release for the hidden door Maggie had shown him, but at last he found it and slid it away from the bulkhead with a satisfying clunk. The door swung open. He went in and closed it behind him. He sat down at the desk. The electric lamp on the corner of the desk was lit. He wondered if it was ever off or simply burned away down here, its incandescence wasted upon this secret place until the filament burned out and a new bulb was installed.

The thought of being in the dark down here, separated from everyone on the ship—more than that, separated from everyone on the ship and without a soul on earth knowing he was here—made his heart flutter as it had on the ladder. Suddenly it seemed important to know he could get light if the lamp chose this moment to give up the ghost. He was sure he wasn't the first to think of this. There would be a flashlight in the desk, or a spare light bulb. He tried the center drawer. It wouldn't budge. The two side drawers also resisted his attempt to slide them open. Locked? Who would be paranoid enough to lock desk drawers in a place like this? What would be that important to keep safe or secret? A secret in a secret place. He forgot about a backup plan for light. Curiosity took over. He pulled out his old Case knife and tried it in the shiny silver key hole. He wiggled it back and forth several times to no effect. *You don't want to break this thing*, he thought. *Don't want to leave evidence anyone's been here, do you?* It may have been the concussion or the accumulation of tensions from everything that had happened over the last three weeks; whatever it was, his normally cautious character gave way. He stood up, braced a foot against one leg of the desk and with both hands strained on the center tray drawer. It was sturdy, but old. It gave way all at once, sending Steve tumbling to the deck in a heap, its contents strewn all over the deck, several random scraps of paper fluttering lazily in the air. Steve did a quick assessment of his body. No discernable injuries, with the possible exception of a bruised ass.

As the shock of finding himself sprawled on the deck wore off, He scanned the detritus from the drawer scattered around him. At first glance it appeared to be nothing more than the typical junk that accumulates in desk drawers; paperclips, spare staples, pencils and pens. A multi-colored marble rolled slowly back and forth, mocking his carelessness, a reminder in this horizonless void that he was in a vessel at sea. He scooped up a handful of the stuff and deposited it in the gray metal drawer, which didn't look like it was much the worse for wear. He wished for that flashlight now, as the lamp didn't lend much of its light to the far corners of the cramped space, where he was sure odds and ends from the drawer must be. He used his hands like a blind man, feeling for anything he might have missed. A piece of metal scraped along the deck under his searching left hand. He pinched it up and brought it to the light. It was a key. The desk locking mechanism was the kind that released the middle and side drawers with one lock. He sat down at the desk and pulled open the larger of the two remaining drawers. Inside it was an army green file box lying on its back. It fit snugly in the drawer and he had to stand it up on end to squeeze it from its nest. He tried the key in the file box's silver lock. It turned easily. He opened it, again wondering what contents could require this kind of security. It took only a glance to see the answer. It was full of polaroid photos of women in various stages of undress.

Steve was both sickened and shamefully aroused by the pictures. He poured them out on the top of the desk. He flipped through them hoping Maggie would not make an appearance. When he recognized Fran Green, he stopped. His arousal and curiosity cut off by a familiar face amidst the anonymous pornography. It was in her eyes. They were empty, sad, and somehow haunting. He didn't want to see any more of this, didn't want images caught in his eyes when he saw anyone else, especially if Maggie were to show up in the pile. He grabbed the file box and started to put the Polaroids back when he heard a clatter from something he'd not seen in it. Reaching in, he retrieved a set of keys he immediately recognized as a set of engineering keys, the kind that included keys to lockers and spaces only an engineer would need to access. There was a dog tag on the ring. Steve read it out loud as his blood ran cold:

Lambert, Raymond T.

229642223USN A pos

Methodist

Everyone knew about Lambert—top spot on the Cheng's hit parade. He'd always claimed his set of keys went missing right before the cocaine showed up in his locker, and the locker search that landed him in the NOB brig and his Big Chicken Dinner bad conduct discharge. Steve remembered Lambert's face when he walked off the brow of *Redstone* for the last time. The eyes. They were the same eyes of Fran Green's polaroid, disbelieving, haunted. They said, "This can't be happening, but it is." Steve turned the keys over in his palm, feeling the cold metal, hearing them jingle together. His mind raced. He thought of the kind of man who would keep such trophies hidden when their discovery would destroy him, especially this set of keys. He realized he might as well be holding Hiller's balls. The thought repulsed him. He dropped the key ring in the metal box, locked it and stood up. It would be a long awkward climb up the ladder carrying it, but he knew the next time the Cheng saw the box and its contents, it would not be down here in this metal mine shaft, in the dark where people like Hiller operate. No. He was going to come out of his rat hole and Steve was going to be the one to make it happen. He smiled a mirthless smile. He'd had the right idea all along, sleuthing. He just hadn't thought to look down the deepest hole on *Redstone*.

Chapter 43

Fire in the Hold

September 1976, North Atlantic Ocean, course 274, speed 14 knots

They quickly cleared a space under the spot where Jasper would cut through to WINS berthing. He pulled the plat from the blueprint book out of a pocket and spread it out on top of a stack of boxes.

"I've done some measurements, but I want to dial it in before I cut. Our best chance is if we can make a hole inside the false compartment I made up there. Trouble is, I was in such a hurry to do that, and with all that's gone on since, I'm a little fuzzy on where it is. "Plus," he said, gesturing around, "never been in here before." He pulled out a tape measure. "Only take a few minutes. Like the old saying goes, 'measure twice, cut once.'" He handed the tape measure to Richards, who took it like he'd been handed a moon rock.

Jasper laughed at his look. "Don't worry. All I need you to do is get the measurement from this bulkhead to this wall," he showed Richards the lines on the plat. "Go out on the passageway opposite the one we used coming in here. When you get there, come aft. I'll thump the bulkhead right here, so you'll know you're in the right spot." When Richards looked doubtful, he added, "Go ahead. I'll get set up to make the cut while you do it." Jasper hoped he'd kept the lie out of his voice. He knew exactly where to make the cut. He needed Richards out of the way, just long enough to get a fire going.

Richards gave him a strange look, but obediently left, tape measure in hand. As soon as the door to the front passageway clanged shut behind him, Jasper shredded up the top of the nearest box, making a neat little pile of kindling on the deck, just below the spot he'd already pegged as directly under the false compartment he'd installed in WINS berthing. Knowing the place had been much easier than he'd thought. Just by looking at the overhead, he could make out faint burn marks in the mint green paint. It was a wonder he hadn't started a fire down here before. Setting a fire watch had not been priority when the Cheng and the Old Man set him to creating the women's berthing compartment. *A little deeper heat would've set this place ablaze*, he thought. And it would've saved him a lot of trouble now.

He stepped up on the little step ladder he carried with his gear and drew an "X" in the center of the cut he hoped he never completed. He climbed down and waited an amount of time calculated to let Richards to reach the place he was supposed to make his useless measurement, far enough away so he'd not have a chance to stop him setting his fire. He struck the flint striker for his torch over the pile of shredded cardboard, sending a shower of sparks down on it with no result. He did it a second time. A tiny ember landed in the dry paper. It smoldered slightly. He got down in his hands and knees, cupped a hand around the pile and blew gently on it. It went out. 'Why not light the torch and go for it?' he thought. Why not? Because it was counter to his every instinct to start a fire like a bed-pissing little arsonist. And he wanted something small; something he might convince Richards was truly an accident. He was so focused on the little wisps of smoke growing atop the little pyre he forgot about Richards. Two things suddenly happened at once: the cardboard caught in earnest: a bright orange-yellow dart stood up clear in the dim cage and the door to the cage clanged shut with a ringing thud, followed by the sound of the padlock snapping together.

Jasper, caught by surprise, sprang to the locked door. Thrusting his fingers through the mesh he rattled it. The door shook violently under his assault but gave no hint of giving way. Richards stood back on the edge of the cone of light from the nearest overhead fluorescent lamp.

"Richards!" Jasper's voice cracked with the violence of his scream.

Richards looked back at him, blank faced as a man at a poker table. He said, "Now, now Phipps. Don't get all heated. I thought you must be up to something. It's why I just went out and came right back in. You know it's a real good way to keep folks on their toes. Do it all the time with those slackers in the office."

Phipps rattled the closed door of the cage again, harder, straining as if he could will his fingers to stretch out to grasp Richards by the neck. "You son of a bitch! Open that lock! Open it or I'll use this torch to cut you into little pieces!"

Richards remained placid. His voice was low and steady. "Be hard to do from over there, don't you think?" He gestured at Phipps's new cell. "And I think you better pay attention to your jail cell before things really get heated."

Phipps heard and smelled the blaze behind him at the same moment Richards pointed it out. The small pile of kindling caught just enough to burn through a box sitting next to it. It was a box full of white rubber shower shoes. The flame licked at the first shoe, sending up an black stream of acrid smoke that quickly began to sting his lungs and eyes in the confined space.

"Jeeezus, Dick! Let me out!" Phipps half barked, half screamed.

The chief stood and gazed in at him with an unworried expression, as if he was watching a man in a batting cage, not a man moments from immolation. "Should've thought ahead, Phippsy. You've got to have an exit plan if you're gonna start a fire. Right now, I'd say you better douse that flame pretty quick, 'cause, Phippsy," his flat monotone finally gave way to the violence in his heart, "I swear by Christ, I'll let you burn before I let go of my treasure."

His eyes went wide, the same blue marbles Phipps laughed at behind his back. There was nothing comical in those eyes. They were filled with a menace he'd never seen in the man. He released the cage and raced to the growing flames, choking and hacking in the poisoned air. *Smother it,* he thought dimly. *Got to smother it before it smothers me.* He tore the top from a box of coveralls, took a handful of the garments and dove on the fire using them like a shield. He got a lungful of black smoke and his vision narrowed. Gasping, he stood up and caught a breath of cleaner air. The fire, deprived of air, sputtered along with Phipps, who grabbed a second heap of coveralls and threw it on top of the first for good measure.

Richards cackled. "Good thinking Phipps. Those new coveralls are fire retardant."

Panting, Jasper made his way back to the cage door. He bent over his knees and retched. After a few minutes he finally sputtered, "OK, Richards. You've made your point. I'll cut your hole. But let me go topside and get some air. I'll get a portable blower out of the spare DC gear so we can clear the smoke."

Chapter 44

In Sick Bay

August 1990, Mediterranean Sea, course 097, speed 21 knots

Steve made his way surreptitiously from shaft alley back to engineering berthing. His pulse hammered with each step. Fear of running into anyone, especially one of Hiller's stooges, like the fat electrician's mate or Peary or, God forbid, the Cheng himself, drove him along, his anxiety slamming. Sweat poured from his brow and he felt it soaking the t-shirt under his coveralls. When he'd carefull opened the door at the aft entrance to berthing and stepped over the knife edge, he sucked in a breath, feeling safe.

"Hey, Steve!"

He dropped the metal file box with what to his hypervigilant mind seemed like an ear splitting clatter. Fear and anger raced to the top of his emotions, and tied, keeping anything other than a grunt from escaping him as he crouched to retrieve the box, which blissfully, had not spilled out its damning contents.

"Whoa, brother! Didn't mean to scare you. You're wound as tight as a cat in a dog pound! Let me help you there."

Steve found his voice. "No! I've got it, Mark. What are you doing here anyway? Aren't you supposed to be on watch?"

268

Mark grinned his simple, disarming grin. Steve felt the anger and tension drain away with it.

"Had a heat casualty on the last rotation. Pushing the old girl this hard has got it really boiling in the main spaces. The Old Man told the Cheng to cut main space watch time to the regs for the heat stress program. Hiller bitched and moaned, but Magoo wasn't having it."

Steve stood up with the box, wishing he could do a Jedi mind trick on Mark that would keep him from seeing it, knowing he couldn't.

"What's that?"

"It's nothing." Mark gave him the hurt look he'd grown accustomed to seeing on his face. "Mark, believe me, it's nothing you want to know about. Trust me." To his relief Mark seemed to accept this.

"You find Freeman?" he said.

"Freeman? She's looking for me?"

"Yeah. Saw her about 20 minutes ago down in DCC. Asked if I knew where you were."

"What did you tell her?"

Mark grimaced. "I told her you were either in Sick Bay or doing your laps on deck." He nodded at the green file box. "Looks like you've been somewhere else. Admin?"

Steve followed his eyes. "Not exactly."

"How did Freeman look?"

Back to the silly grin. "Freeman? She looks good. Always. Smells good, too."

"I mean, did she seem flustered?" Steve pictured the intended confrontation between Maggie and Hiller. He was happy she was not in it any more, at least not as of twenty minutes ago.

"Not that I noticed," Mark said. "She just seemed in a hurry to find you."

"Thanks, Mark. I'm going to head down to sick bay, but I'll swing by DC Central on my way there. If you run into her, let her know to meet me there, OK?"

He started to push past him. He wanted to get the file box secured, somewhere out of the Cheng's reach as quickly as possible. As he did, he heard the clink of the ring of keys at the bottom of the box and got a sick feeling in his stomach. His rack or his locker obviously were not safe places to stow anything. Lambert probably never imagined someone would invade his only private place on this tub. Give it to Mark? No. His rack would be the next obvious choice if Hiller got wind of the missing box. And why was he lugging the box around with him? It was bulky and awkward. He decided to lose it. He went to his rack with Mark in tow, uninvited but inevitably there. He swept aside the curtain across the face of his rack. In one smooth motion he grabbed his pillow and pulled it out of its case. Before Mark could see what he was doing, he dumped the contents of the file box into the pillow case. He handed the empty box to his friend.

"Mark, I want you to take this and dump it over the side."

When he hesitated, it irritated Steve. "Take it. What's the problem?"

"Last time I got involved with dumping something over the side in the Med it caused us both a lot of trouble." Mark said.

Steve had to admit this was true. "This isn't anything like that. Trust me." He gave Mark a look intended to communicate confidence, but the sack full of evidence at his side wouldn't give him enough room to be fully in charge of his face. Mark saw it.

"What's in the sack, Steve?"

"You really don't want to know, Mark. And you really don't want anyone to see you with this box. Wait till it's dark.

Wrap it in something before you take it topside. Here, use my blanket. Throw it over, blanket and all. Got it?"

Mark looked happy to be able to do something for his friend. He nodded his agreement. "I'll take care of it, Steve."

"Thanks, Mark. I'm going to go to Sick Bay. If you see Freeman, tell her to look for me there."

He turned and left, hoping Mark would get the task done the way he'd told him to do it, contemplating what would happen if anyone saw him with the box or caught him throwing something over the side. He decided he couldn't worry about it. He needed to talk with Maggie and find out about her confrontation with the Cheng, and he needed to brainstorm what to do with the evidence now in his possession. In spite of the nondescript white pillow case he found himself cautiously padding through passageways, attempting to go unseen. He'd succeeded until making the turn onto the last passageway leading to Sick Bay, which was always busy with sailors, coming and going day and night. Still, he slipped in the door without seeing anyone who set off warning alarms in his head.

The HM1 who, during working hours, ran Sick Bay like the head nurse of a doctor's office, acknowledged him with a head nod. His feet were up on his desk and his face was buried in a well-worn copy of *Sports Illustrated* swimsuit edition. Kathy Ireland smiled at Steve as he slipped past him to the narrow corridor leading to the three tiny examination rooms, the middle of which was his home until the Doc cleared him. The smell of alcohol and the bright lights in here always triggered him and threw him back to his seven-year-old self, associating any place that looked and smelled like this as a place to expect pain. Shots. His already taut nerves tightened another notch.

He stepped in and flipped the light switch, closing the door behind him. He put the sack on the bed and let out a long breath, realizing he'd made his way from engineering berthing, mostly holding it in.

"What's in the bag?"

For the second time in the past ten minutes the fear-anger nerve endings fired in surprise.

Maggie Freeman materialized like magic. He turned on her. She recoiled, seeing the fear and anger. It quickly dissolved as Steve realized it was her.

He grabbed her and hugged her hard. "Maggie!" She was stiff in his arms, unsure of the conflicting signals.

"Sorry, Maggie. You scared me and... " he flicked his head to the white sack on the bed, "the stuff in there's got me jumpy." He felt her relax without returning his embrace. She stepped back.

"What is it, Steve?"

"Evidence," he said.

She quizzed him with her eyes. "The stuff in there will sink Hiller," he said. Maggie's face remained blank.

He went to the bed and dumped the contents of the sack. The three dozen or so Polaroids spilled out, Ray Lambert's key ring on top of the pile. Maggie looked over his shoulder. Steve instantly felt his face redden at what he'd revealed, realizing that the fleshy nakedness of the women in the pictures wasn't something he was prepared to share with Maggie, knowing she might be in them, hoping she wasn't. She picked up the key ring, fingering the dog tag as she read it silently. She pulled in her lips, biting down in a grimace. Her eyes shifted to the pictures.

Steve started to say, "Are you—"

"No. No." She looked hard in his eyes, searching, then said, "you don't know?"

The blush that had already started on Steve's cheeks blossomed to his neck. "I didn't look through them," he said. "They made me a little sick to my stomach. Nothing about this is... " he didn't know how to finish his thought.

"Sexy?" Maggie finished it for him. He nodded.

"Where did you get these?" She said.

"Shaft alley."

She nodded. "What were you doing down there?"

Steve pulled the still rolled-up blueprint from his back pocket and tapped his palm with it. "Going to look at this. Wanted a place to spread out and study it in private."

"Find anything?"

He swept a hand across the bed. "Yeah, but not what I was looking for. Went looking for a light. Broke into the desk and found all this. What happened with Hiller?"

"Nothing. Couldn't find him. Don't know where he is." She gave a little shudder. "You know what's worse than having to see him all the time? Not knowing where he may show up."

"I know what you mean." Steve reiterated the story of seeing Hiller emerge from the bilges like a ghost.

"I guess I gave you a little taste of that when you came through the door." Maggie said.

"You did. How did you get in here without HM1 seeing you?"

"Him? I'm not sure I couldn't have walked right past him, with his face stuck in the swim suit pictures. But as it turns out he is crushing on one of the new girls that came aboard just before we got underway —that little red-headed radioman. I just asked her to invite him into the p-way for a little stroll. She was glad to do it and it gave me time to slip in here and wait for you. Now that I've decided to do something about him, I, ah, I don't know why, but I'm afraid. I didn't want to be alone out there."

The look on Maggie's face made Steve's heart ache. It was pitiful. It was like the looks of the women frozen in their Polaroid poses. He started to go to her but thought better of it.

She spread the pictures across the white top sheet of the bed with splayed fingers as if they were a deck of playing cards in disarray. She began flipping them right side up, examining the faces, making quiet noises as she recognized one and then another.

Without turning around she said, "No. I'm not in this pile, but I might as well be." Her voice was low and heavy, like a black rain cloud. "He tried to get me to do it. To pose. I almost did." A choked sound came from deep inside her. The cloud burst. Tears dripped from her face and splashed on some of the pictures. Steve went to her then. He turned her around.

Through her tears she choked out, "I'm no different than any of them! We're all idiots. I'm an idiot. How did I end up in this same place... no, in a worse place than where I started?"

Steve said nothing. He held her and let her cry until she was done, her ragged breathing slowing. He talked into the side of her head feeling his words vibrating into her. Good. Let her feel this more than hear it.

"We choose. We have a choice. Choices add up. You are here because of choices. You are not in that pile of pictures because of choices. You are choosing now and those choices are adding up in a new direction. And we can add our choices together now. I will help you."

Maggie's breathing evened out more as he spoke. Her shoulders lost their tension but her arms remained around him.

"This isn't just your fight, or mine. Hiller is a bad man who's done a lot of damage, not just a difficult man who's hard to work for. He needs to be caught and stopped from hurting more people. And we're going to stop him."

Maggie leaned back, looked him in the eye and said "How?"

Steve said, "My dad used to say that evil is a parasite that can't live without good, and because of that it's always one step away from starving to death. Take away whatever good it's been feeding off of and the evil thing goes looking for something else to attach itself to. It means it's always stretching and looking, and in the end, it always goes too far. Gets too hungry. Knocks on the wrong door. Then it gets exposed. And evil can't live in the light. Maybe Hiller's been keeping these mementos to snack on and it's kept his appetite in check. I bet if he finds out someone's gotten into his cookie jar he's gonna do something stupid to find out who did it."

Maggie said, "How's he going to find out? Won't it lead him to you and me? Why not just take all this to the Old Man and expose the Cheng that way?"

"I thought about that. The thing is... I don't know if the Old Man can be trusted. I don't know if anyone can be trusted. Hiller is getting us to Hurghada on time and probably no one else could have done that. Shumate is no different than any of these officers. They want their glory. They want their feather. They want the promotion. If he thinks he needs Hiller to get him there..." Steve trailed off and shrugged.

Maggie finished his thought, "And no one else is going to step on Hiller's toes, if they think it'll get them on the wrong side of the CO."

"Right."

"So what do we do?"

Chapter 45
Hiller and the Bos'n Drink
August 1990, Port Said, anchored awaiting Suez Canal
southbound transit

It was after midnight. *Redstone* swung to her anchor north of Port Said, Egypt, the successful high speed run behind her, a trip through the Suez Canal awaiting her.

Steve got up from his rack in Sick Bay. He was unable to sleep. Tonight it would break, one way or the other. The shot he'd arranged to fire across the Cheng's bow would be unmistakable and, he was sure, would evoke a rapid and strong response. Waiting alone in the antiseptic smelling exam room that was his current berthing felt too much like waiting for the square, rusty needle his brother always said awaited him at the doctor's office. Maggie was on watch, where she could stay visible, with many witnesses, in case the hammer fell in her direction. He had taken pains to turn it towards himself, but there was no way to keep her out of it. When the Chief Engineer discovered the envelope of selected pictures that Steve had shoved under his door almost an hour ago, there was telling what the man would do.

Leaving sick bay and walking forward, he almost had a heart attack when he heard the distinct guffaw of Hiller's mirthless laugh coming from the Dive Shack. He stopped outside the door and listened. He recognized the voices of Hiller and the Bos'n, but their conversation was not loud enough to distinguish words from behind the closed, outer door to the shack. He considered trying to crack the door so he could hear, but thought better of it. His heart was hammering so loudly it was a worse impediment than the closed door. He took several deep breaths, talking it down. Been way too jacked for way too long. His bruised head ached. Gradually the noise of his heart, which he'd mistaken for the thrum of the ship, began to subside. The two men's voices were still faint but he began to make out their words. The first line convinced him no one else was in the office.

Hiller was saying, "Green is a feisty one. Held her down the first time. Little bitch kept saying 'no,' just like you said she would. But she meant 'yes.'"

The Bos'n grunted. "Hold her down? I never did that with any of 'em."

"You don't? It's more fun. Trust me. You're the one that gave me the idea for the Polaroids. Once I convince 'em to pose for one of those... shiiiiiit. I own them—make them do anything I want, whenever I want, whether they're feelin' it or not. Rough them up, hold them down? They cry or say something, I just tell them I've got a nice, pretty little picture I'd be happy to mail to mom and dad. And if that don't shut them up—if they don't give a shit about anybody at home, I let them know it could always show up on the XO's desk."

The Bos'n said something inaudible. Hiller gave another of his snorting laughs.

"Kendall? She would shit a brick if she saw one of those pics. The shock might kill her. She couldn't find her way out of a wet paper sack. Did she ever connect the dots between Fratella and Green? Hell no, she didn't.

"Doesn't mean she won't."

"What's wrong with you, Baber? You sound like an old woman. You gone pussy on me?"

Steve braced for an explosion. He'd seen enough of the Bos'n in action with his divers to know these were dangerous words. Instead of the sound of a fist hitting flesh, he heard the creak of springs in the Bos'n's worn out swivel chair and the long exhale of a weary man standing up. Next he heard the clink of glasses.

"Have a drink, Hiller. This scotch is better than sex. It might keep you from saying something you regret."

Steve thought about the irony of suggesting alcohol to take away someone's inclination to say stupid things. As muffled as Baber's voice was through the door, Steve still caught the whiff of a threat in it. He wondered if Hiller was stupid enough to poke the lion. Then, "Shit! That dripped right in my glass!" It was Hiller.

"I've been telling you, that chill water piping that runs through here ain't right. Surprised it didn't let go earlier." A pause. "Damn sorry way to dilute good scotch."

Steve missed the rest of Hiller and Baber's conversation. The mention of the chill water piping brought him back to the question of the blueprints. He had heard enough. Hiller was a bad man. He was already convinced of that, but there is bad and there is dangerous. Or maybe this is what happens to bad that's allowed to keep going. It doesn't stay bad. It keeps going right on into dangerous—like a stray dog that goes mean. What was a nuisance becomes a hazard. He knew his plan had risks. Now he knew they were high. He also knew, from the words out of Hiller's own mouth, that the pictures would work. Judge your own judgments, his father had told him. If Hiller thought he could control those women using the pictures, it could only be because of the way he thought. That meant the pictures could be used on him.

Steve slipped back down the passageway and into Sick Bay. Better to let this play out on its own and stay out of sight. It would get hot enough, soon enough, and there was another thing he'd overheard that he wanted to explore.

Returning to his exam room berthing compartment, Steve looked through the scanty pile of his possessions for the blueprint that had led him to his shaft alley discovery. He pulled it out and unfolded it, spreading it on the bed to its full size. His rack ran fore and aft, so he oriented the print that way and studied it. The Bos'n's complaint about the chill water leak gnawed at him. Still didn't make sense to reroute that piping. Now he realized the Dive Shack and Sick Bay were both modifications to *Redstone* which would not show up on this print. Both spaces were on a single starboard-side passageway, which, in the ship's original layout, had housed various shops and offices intended to support a sea plane and her complement of aviators and sailors during World War Two. As soon as the war ended, the plane became a superfluous appendage, just like *Redstone*'s guns. Steve wondered how many mods there had been over the years. Reflecting on it he was amazed that the ship itself had survived the massive drawdown of troops and ships in the post war demobilization. *Redstone*, ugly and unsexy as she was, must have possessed some magic characteristic that kept the Navy from cutting her up or selling her off. He guessed it may have been the same thing she possessed these forty some odd years later—the ability to repair the sexier and prettier ships the Navy truly loved, which were scattered across the globe and would be for many years to come.

Getting his bearings, he put a finger on the office where Hiller and Baber sat. It was the furthest up the passageway from where Sick Bay was located. The print showed the space as the Aviation Instrument Shop. Sick Bay appeared to be made by gutting three different spaces, two marked as storage compartments and one as pilots' quarters. The adjoining rooms opening off the passageway, he knew, were currently dedicated to Deck Department controlled equipage; mainly moldy-smelling, green, foul weather jackets that never seemed to dry completely, and life preservers. He had been inside the space once or twice since coming aboard and had always left feeling like he needed a bath or a shot of penicillin or both. It wasn't just the smell, it was the creepy set of cages laid out in the dim fluorescent lights, their covers yellowed by years of accumulated nicotine from boatswains' mates sneaking cigarette breaks away from the sight of their First Lieutenants. At some point the place must have housed objects more valuable than the current piles of coats and life preservers; the cages bore witness to that. No one would worry much over missing those. And these days none of the cages were locked. Even the main door to the compartment halfway up the passageway between Sick Bay and the Dive Shack was never secured.

Steve traced the light blue lines on the drawing as he visualized the new transposed over the old. It felt like he was playing with the visible man illustration he'd had as a kid, the one with plastic sheets for bones, muscles and organs you could move individually until there was only the skin-colored outline of a person left.

When he got to the circle marked on the print, he stopped. There it was. In 1939, it had been in the pilot's quarters, now he guessed it would be in one of the cages of deck gear. He had not thought of the lightly penciled circle and words since first looking at it, the night Hiller ordered him chained to a stanchion.

What did it mean? Why would this one plate be torn out of the master set of prints? Steve smiled to himself. Here I am reading when I could be looking. Typical bookworm.

Let's go see what the circle's all about. It's just around the corner. He rolled the print up, put it in his pocket and went out to the passageway. He opened the door inward and waited, listening for anyone straggling around this late at night. Quiet as a mouse, he stepped out and padded to the gray door marked Deck Storage Locker. The door had a padlock hasp with an old Navy issue brass lock hanging from it, unlocked. *Good old boatswains' mates,* Steve thought. You could always count on them to make things easier on themselves. Why lock the lock and have to hassle with getting a key every time they needed to get in there? He slipped the lock off the hasp and opened the door. Same smell as always and the lighting dim as ever, too.

He started to hang the open lock on the door hasp then thought better of it. Getting locked in here by some random sailor finding the door open freaked him out. He dropped it heavily into the pocket of his coveralls. The metal was cold against his skin, even through the cloth. Pushing the door closed behind him, he pulled out the print and studied it again.

The doorway he'd used to enter the space appeared to be original. Take a left and head aft about twenty feet and he should see... what? A circle marks the spot? The aisles between the mesh cages were clear. He held the print in front of him as he walked, keeping it folded over on the quarter sheet defining the space he was now entering. The last caged area on the left in the aft end of the storage space looked like it should be where he would find the circled area. He felt like a treasure hunter holding a map, except "O" marked the spot in this scenario, not "X".

The door to the cage hung askew on bent hinges, half open. He tried to pull it fully open. It screeched, metal-on-metal against the deck. No one had been in here recently. There were kapok life preservers scattered on the deck and some of the foul weather jackets hanging on a wire, strung port and starboard. He pushed all the hangers to one side and used a foot to slide the life vests out of the way, clearing the deck as if it was the floor of an ancient, unexplored forest. He examined the deck. Nothing. He laughed aloud at himself. What did you expect to find? A literal "O" on the deck where you'd break out a spade and dig? The lighting in this far corner was worse than any other part of the compartment. The single fluorescent light flickered and hummed, the worn out gasses in the tube spidering along towards either end. Steve looked up at it. There, in the overheard, just aft of the mostly dead lamp, was the bead of a shoddy weld job. It was in the shape of an O, about twice the diameter of a manhole cover. It had been painted over with the standard Navy white paint for overheads. Something stuck out of the sloppy weld bead at twelve o'clock on the circle, from where he stood.

He found a wooden crate in the corner, dragged it under the spot, and stood on it, tracing the circle, with a forefinger. He stopped on a bit of metal protruding half an inch from the overhead. It had an oddly familiar look he couldn't place at first, but slowly it dawned on him. It made no sense, but he was sure he was right. It was the forked end of a crow bar.

Chapter 46

Exit Strategy

September 1976, North Atlantic Ocean,
course 277, speed 16 knots

Richards didn't move to unlock the door. He clucked and wiped his mouth. "I don't think so, Phippsy," he said. "This is our last chance. Tonight. Right now. The Suppo and the lead custodian met last night. They're gonna start staging their crates for the off load. Time is of the essence. They want everything off within an hour of going pierside in Norfolk. Truck's already waiting. They're gonna inventory their stuff in the morning. When they do, they're gonna come up with an extra box that ain't on their lading list. Our box. Day after that, we make port. No. No more time, Phipps. You're gonna cut that hole now and we're gonna finish this job." The smoke from the extinguished fire rolled lazily out of the cage into the space between the two men, blurring their view of each other.

Despite his aching lungs and stinging eyes, Phipps laughed grimly. "You really are Double Dick." He spat on the deck, his mouth permeated with the acrid smoke taste. "What do you think you're gonna do to keep me in here? I'll cut a hole all right. I'll cut this door off its hinges in about two minutes. Then we'll see." He turned to get his welding rig. As he did, he heard the distinct sound of a round being chambered in a gun. Richards stepped forward through the smoke, holding a U.S. Navy issue Colt .45. He pointed it Phipps's chest.

"What did I just tell you, Phipps? Always have an exit strategy. Here's mine," he waved the gun at him. "Called in a favor with the gunner, the night you came to me crying over your change of heart. I got this old pistol he wanted to get replaced and two full clips. He got a couple of Berettas that came along with my little coffee deal in Naples. Those things sell like hot cakes in the States. I couldn't get any ammo for them... but this old girl," he suddenly swung the weapon up and fired a round, a foot over Phipps's head.

The bullet sliced a clean hole in the steel mesh door and left a fist-sized dent in the bulkhead at the rear of the cage before zinging wildly off deck and overhead as it expended its energy. The crack of the shot in the confined space deafened Phipps, who fell to the deck even as Richards raised the gun. He clapped his hands over his ears and tried to make himself small, as the slug pinballed around him. He cowered behind a box, unsure if Richards was just a bad shot or if he meant to shoot over his head. He was shaking. His ears felt as if they must be bleeding. Dully, through the slowly fading echoes of the gunshot, he heard Richards.

"Get up, Phipps."

He staggered to his feet. He was surprised at the muffled sound of his own voice. "You crazy bastard. You could've killed your own self as well as me."

"Right. Right. But I didn't. And now you understand me."

"I understand you're batshit crazy."

"Maybe. But I've got a plan. It's the only plan. No plan "B". We're getting that treasure. Now. Tonight. You're gonna cut that hole and seal up that box and I'm walking off the brow in two days with my retirement account safe and sound, inside a big metal safe named USS *Redstone*. You've got—maybe—ten minutes' work and you're finished, Phippsy."

"We," Phipps said.

Richards gave him a quizzical look.

"'We' are gonna walk off the brow. You said 'I', but you mean 'we.'"

Richards's eyes narrowed, but he said, "Right. We. Right."

***

Richards stood at the door to the cage, gun in hand, while Jasper did some quick measurements and chalked an "x" on the overhead. His well-worn wooden step ladder, as loose in the joints as an eighty-year-old man, wobbled as he climbed down to get his cutting rig. The barrel of the .45 stood out like a malicious black eye, staring at him through the still settling smoke. He knew now the man holding it never intended for him to leave this ship. The slip of his tongue had begged the question; the look in those eyes left no doubt of the answer. As he lit his torch and climbed back on the ladder to start cutting the hole into WINS berthing, he considered what Richards's plan might be. 'Always have a plan,' the man said. He had an endgame in mind, may have had one before he looked Jasper up in Riley's. What was it?

There was one obvious way to make people disappear on a Navy ship. A man who went missing over the side at night was a goner if no one saw him fall. Even if someone did, the chances of recovering a man overboard on a dark night were much less than 50-50. If no one saw it happen? A ship steaming at the speed *Redstone* was going now, a leisurely fifteen knots, could easily be sixty or seventy miles down range before a man was missed. Chances of recovery then?

Nil. Or very close to it. Jasper thought Richards wasn't the kind of man who would leave his fate up to a coin flip. He would make sure no one saw Jasper Phipps go over the side. He might even put a bullet in me—take the odds down to absolute zero.

He was a rat in a trap. His mind whirled. Richards couldn't make his move until the crate was sealed in the false compartment and they'd made their retreat. He would have to climb up through the hole he was cutting two times, up and back down. That would be the moment to make a move.

He flipped his welders' goggles onto his forehead and glanced over his shoulder. Richards hadn't moved. The gun was still in his hand, still pointed at him, but the expression on the man's face had changed. For an instant, Jasper felt as if all his internal monologue had somehow been broadcast. Richards's look was knowing.

How did I get mixed up in this? Jasper wondered. He heard his mother's voice, answer: *Whiskey.* He had to agree. Yeah. Too much whiskey and an unlucky chance that brought Richards and whiskey and a tired out, end-of-deployment, fed-up-with-the-Navy's-bullshit Jasper together in Riley's, all at just the right—or wrong—moment. He almost laughed out loud. Momma always said liquor tasted like fire, 'cause it came straight from hell and would take you there with it. She knew a little about that, having been routinely beaten by Jasper's father, whenever hell, or the devil or the liquor took him.

Jasper brought an end to that devil's reign when he walked in and found the old drunk trying to stuff his momma in a steamer trunk that sat at the foot of their bed. The woman was knocked cold. The blankets that normally filled the chest were strewn about the room. His father, bent and staggering with a belly full of Old Grandad, had her three quarters of the way into the box. He swayed as he tried to get the legs bent at the right angle to shut the top. God knew what he intended to do with it and with her, once he got it closed. There was a click in Jasper's brain. He walked up behind the man, grabbed a handful of his greasy gray black hair, and slammed his face down onto the nearest post of the solid oak four poster bed. Twenty years later, as he returned his goggles to his face and relit his torch, Jasper still felt the satisfying crunch of his father's face bones obliterated under his hand.

Yeah. No damned topside city slicker puke like Dick Richards, who never had to fight his way out of anything tougher than a bad cold, was gonna bury Jasper Phipps at sea. Not after he'd fought his way out of his own home just to have a chance to start a life.

Chapter 47

Into Darkness

September 1976, North Atlantic Ocean, Course 275, Speed 15
knots, steaming as before

The hole Jasper cut came up in more or less the perfect
spot. He held the round cut out slab of steel on his palm like
a waiter's dinner tray as he made the final cut, freeing it from
the overhead. He lowered it, carefully balancing as he
stepped down off the ladder. It was heavy. A little bigger hole
and putting it back in place would have been a two man job.
As it was, he wondered if he could do it alone. Maybe
Richards could be convinced to help, and maybe this would
be the opportunity he needed. The job wouldn't be done until
all evidence of their treasure "dig" was covered over, and he
was certain Richards was incapable of even a simple tack
weld job.

"We're in," he said. He climbed back up the ladder and
stuck his head and shoulders through the still warm square.
He already knew it, but he took a moment to admire his
work. He had cut the hole inside the three walls of the
incomplete false compartment he'd created in Naples weeks
ago. Behind and below, he heard the clinking sound of
Richards unlocking and entering his impromptu jail cell.

Jasper looked down at his feet. It was an odd feeling, standing here suspended between two decks. The future WINS berthing smelled the same as he remembered it, mostly the smell of rust, but there was also another smell. It took him a second to place it. Fresh cut lumber. He realized all the crates of Egyptian treasure must have been custom made. They were brand new and smelled it. It reminded him of home and that was odd, too. Egyptian lumber putting him to mind of cutting logs in Kentucky. Navy life. It did things like that to you some times.

The gun appeared at his feet an instant before Richards's face, peering up suspiciously. "Go on," Richards said, and waved the gun as if it was a magic wand. "Those two Egyptians are passed out drunk in my office. The MAAs are out front, but no one else can be in there but the Old Man or the Suppo, and they're not gonna be up and about for a good while yet." He checked his watch.

Jasper said, "You're gonna have to hand me up my rig, Richards, unless you want me to come back down there and get it."

"No, Phipps. Go on up and get away from the hole. Tap on the deck so I know where you are. I ain't sticking my head up there so you can brain me and take off."

Phipps took a deep breath and let it out. He locked out his elbows on either side of the hole he'd cut and leveraged himself up and into the unfinished berthing compartment. Strings of construction site incandescent light bulbs he'd strung himself while working here lit the space sparsely. He saw that the final wall plate he'd left standing innocently against the outer bulkhead was undisturbed.

"Are you away from the hole? Get away and tap the deck," Richards said. The man was getting more anxious by the minute; more dangerous. Jasper didn't like the combination: anxious -stupid-gun. He walked to the steel plate and examined its edges. He realized this adapted plan had a hole in it. He'd meant to weld in the final wall from the same place he'd welded the others, standing outside the boxy little closet, probably with Richards to help set it in place if he needed it. But now...

"Tap the deck!" He heard Richards hiss from just outside the hole. He picked up a scrap piece of steel and tapped the deck lightly.

Grunting and cursing preceded the emergence of his welding rig through the hole like some industrial parody of childbirth; the hoses and torch coming up last before the gun and Richards's head.

"Come get this shit out of my way," he said, again waving his magic wand of a gun.

Jasper retrieved his gear, placing it in the nearest cone of incandescent yellow light. Richards struggled through the opening, trying to keep his gun pointed at Jasper and mostly succeeding. When he was through and on his feet, he snapped on a battleship gray standard Navy issue flashlight. He held it in his left hand and the .45 in his right.

"C'mon," he said, aiming the flashlight in the direction of a set of crates lining the starboard side bulkhead. The weak light coming from the flashlight flickered with each step Richards took, and he shook it testily, as if it were a clogged salt shaker and he could get more light to come out of it if he knocked the holes clear. The effect of his antics was a crazy spray of flashlight beam that made your head hurt if you tried to follow it. Being out front yet not knowing where he was going agitated Phipps.

"Jeez-zus, Richards, either turn the damn thing off or point it where you want me to go and leave it steady."

Richards grunted, gave the flashlight one last shake and pointed it at the furthest crate in the line. "Think that's it," he said. "Just need to match the number."

Phipps followed the diffused watery eye of light trying to see which crate Richards meant. Although varying in size and shape, all the crates were similar in construction. The fresh cut lumber ripped and rough cut, crisscrossed with reinforcing slats. Each bore a seven digit number stenciled in black paint and an Egyptian flag. Phipps could also see pointy, spiky scribblings of Arabic lettering that he assumed to mean "fragile" and "this end up." It occurred to him—and he thought it strange it hadn't occurred to him before now to think of this—that there were several crates here which would not fit in his secret compartment. The one he thought Richards had indicated with his faulty flashlight appeared to be one that would, but it was also quite a bit larger than the sea chest sized box Double Dick had explained to him in Riley's, the day this all began. If it was too big, it would create another crease in Richard's plans; another possible point where a quick and decisive move might save Jasper from whatever fate the man had planned for him.

"That's it," Richards said, pointing at a box roughly three quarters the length of a coffin and half again as tall. He motioned Jasper to one side and knelt down, shining his flashlight beam on the box's serial number.

"That ain't no sea chest," Jasper said. "Hope it fits."

"It'll fit, Phippsy." Richards said. "And if it doesn't, you'll make it fit." He pulled a scrap of paper from his breast pocket and read off the number to himself. "Eight oh seven, seven one six six." He stood up and smiled. "You're looking at a crate that doesn't exist, Phippsy. I've done a magic trick better than Houdini ever did. All it took me was a typewriter. And I never got locked in a box." He tapped the crate with the butt of the .45, carelessly.

Phipps said, "Take it easy with that, DD."

Richards looked from the gun to Jasper. "Don't worry, Phippsy. I'm not gonna shoot you. Grab this thing and let's get it stowed."

Jasper ran out of patience for Richards's game. "And then what? You're not gonna shoot me? What are you gonna do Richards?" He tried to keep the panic he was feeling out of his voice and mostly succeeded.

"It depends, Phippsy," he said and stared out of the gloom at Jasper, his mouth set in a line as straight as the barrel of the gun.

"On what?"

"On whether or not you want to be rich. Whether or not you want to be partners." He managed a lopsided grin that made Jasper think of a stroke victim.

Jasper said, "Sure I do. Of course. Partners. Rich. All of it. Don't know why not." He tried to sound as convincing as Richard's fake grin and fake peace offering. A momentary truce by each man. Everyone move two free spaces ahead in the game without rolling the dice. Let's go easy for a second here, before the next real move. Richards lowered the gun in sign of the armistice. Jasper bent down and hefted one end of the crate. It was relatively light and came up off the deck easily.

"Grab the other end," Jasper said to Richards. "Ain't heavy at all, just awkward and bulky. Help me get it in the hideaway."

Richards went to the other end of the crate, placed the gun on top and lifted his end. The two men shuffled to the back of WINS berthing, Jasper walking backwards, trying not to trip, sure, for now, that whatever Richards had planned for him would wait. *He needs me to finish the welding and that's that*, he thought. *So I need to finish him before I finish the hot work.*

There was an awkward moment when they got the rectangular crate to the secret compartment. It was too long to fit in the space without covering the hole they'd cut in the deck, and it was almost wide enough to fill it side to side. Richards grunted as he hit the back wall, caught between the box and the metal bulkhead. They set the crate down and discovered that, when the crate was all the way into its hiding place, there would only be room enough for one man to stand in a three foot by three foot cube. They tried setting it up on end, but it was half a foot too tall and knocked against the overhead.

"This is gonna be a problem," Jasper said. "We should empty it now and cut the box in pieces."

"No," Richards said. "This stuff is old and might be fragile. I want to keep it stowed until I have another way to get it off the ship."

Jasper noted the use of the personal pronoun again and decided to ignore it. Let the truce hold. "Once I weld this last panel in, it's gonna be a chore to get out through the hole. How'r we gonna do that?"

Richards said, "We can prop up one end of the crate and crawl under through the hole." Jasper was surprised by the simple sanity of Richards's suggestion. "Yeah," he said, "That would work. Or you could go through and hold it up for me when I'm done."

Jasper could see in Richards's face that this suggestion ended the truce, along with the man's sanity. Richards retrieved the .45 from the top of the crate and pointed at him. "Smart guy, Phipps. And when I'm down the hole, what's to stop you from cutting out of here? Letting yourself out the front door? Ratting out the whole plan?" The rapid fire questions were accompanied by a wide eyed intensity.

Now, for the first time, Jasper really saw it. Richards was not a sane guy. He wasn't a normal person who had momentary slips into crazy town. No. Richards was one of those dangerous crazies, the kind that are so good at acting sane they could and did fool their own mothers. He held both hands in front of him, making the universal sign for calm.

"No problem, Chief." He used the title purposely, trying to reconnect Richards to a different reality. "It's just that when I start welding it's gonna get awful nasty in here. Hard to breathe. When I'm done and we seal up the hole, this will basically be an air tight tank. That hole," he pointed to the spot covered by the crate, "is our only ventilation." He said this as evenly as he could, watching Richards carefully. Richards cocked his head like a dog listening to human speech.

"Ok. Ok. Let's do it this way," he said, back to waving the pistol around carelessly. "You get the last wall there and tack it in place. Then, when I'm sure you can't run off, you can hold up the box while I crawl down. Once I'm down we prop up the box so you can finish sealing the wall and I can keep an eye on you through the hole." Richards seemed pleased with himself as he finished speaking, as if feeling himself exerting control over the crazy.

Jasper didn't have a reason to object to the plan, which again made too much sense coming from a loony. "Ok, Chief, let me get the plate in place and we can shove the crate all the way home."

Having set upon a course of action, the work went rapidly. Jasper retrieved the thick steel plate he'd hidden in plain sight against the bulkhead furthest from his hidey hole. It was heavy and he grunted with the effort to lug it near its final resting place. Richards made no move to help. His guard was back up and he leaned against a wall, leering at

Phipps out of the gloom. Phipps improvised a handle tack-welded to the plate, so he would be able to hold it upright while standing inside the secret compartment. In less than five minutes, he had sealed both of them inside it, tacking the four corners in place and letting the wall stand on its own. Richards sat on his fat haunches atop the crate while Jasper did the work. It was a perfect fit, Jasper had to admit, admiring his handiwork. When he completed the welds all the way around the plate, this little compartment would be all but airtight, save for the hole in the deck. Rerouting the lines from the chill unit on the deck above WINS meant there was no penetration of the walls. Acrid smoke lingering in the still air between them in the space, now only illuminated by Richards's dying flashlight, bore witness to the airlessness of the place. The slightest hint of fresh air seeped up and around the crate from the hole in the deck under it.

The final beads sealing off the secret compartment cooled. The two men sputtered and hacked. Time paused. King Tut's treasures, at least this small portion of them, were again buried in a place only the barest number of men on earth knew about.

Chapter 48

Desperate Moves

September 1976, North Atlantic Ocean, Course 274, Speed 12
knots, approaching the grand banks, barometer falling

Richards grinned at Phipps, his teeth a gray smudge in
the light reflecting from the smoke in the chamber. The next
move was the critical one. How to get the two of them out of
this space without upsetting the truce, and how to find a
window to escape the trap. The supply chief had been mum
on the point of what they'd do once they were out of here.
Jasper had assumed they would seal up the hole and
complete the cover up. Now that they'd made the
compartment and created an easy access to it, he wondered if
Richards had planned all along to leave it open so he could
get at the loot. A light clicked on. Of course he'd leave it
open! The only reason Phipps was here was to do what he
had already done: weld. Now Richards could get rid of him
and have no more need of him. He decided to test this
theory.

"Richards, we need to prop up the box now." He slapped
the steel wall he'd just put in place with a flat palm. It made a
thick *thwack* sound that went nowhere in the dead air. "You
can get behind me... there's just enough room. I'll hold it up,

and you go through. I'll finish up here and come down myself." He paused to see if Richards's face would give anything away. "And when we're both out, I'll button up the hole in the deck. Only take us ten more minutes max."

Richards sucked in his cheeks slightly and said, "Now that we've got ourselves an easy way to get at the loot, I think it's better we leave it open. No one's gonna come in the controlled equipage locker besides me and the Suppo, anyway." His voice was even but his eyes narrowed enough to tell Jasper that SKC Richards, who always had a plan, had already thought through this eventuality.

Whether it was something in Richards's tone or his look, Jasper would not have been able to say. The same click that led to smashing his old man's face into a bedpost clicked now. Enough.

In one smooth motion he dropped his torch, reached out with both hands and jerked the crate towards himself with all the force he could muster. In the confined space he only had about a foot of play. He surprised himself with his amped up strength. Richards had been perched on his haunches atop the far end of the crate, in the dim glow of his flashlight. He had just started to shift his weight forward in order to crawl over to Jasper and make his way out when Jasper made his move. The result was a cartoonish flailing by Richards. The gun went flying. A crack opened behind Richards, between the crate and the back wall. It wasn't wide enough for him to fall into and Richards would have easily regained his balance if he hadn't reached out to support himself with his now empty gun hand. He reached for a handhold on the crate but the crate was no longer there. His hand went down the crack followed by his entire arm. His face thudded against the rough-hewn wooden box top, leaving painful splinters in his right cheek. Jasper, seeing the arm go down the hole he'd created, shifted his stance and rammed the crate back the way it had come, pinning Richards's arm between it and the back wall, as neatly as a piece of sheet metal in his shop's press. Richards screamed in pain, the sound grotesquely dulled against the steel walls. The weak yellow light of the flashlight still in his left hand pointed crazily to the overhead like a searchlight.

"I'll kill you!" Richards said through gritted teeth. Several things happened at once. Both men saw the .45, which had come to rest on top of the crate between them. They locked eyes. Jasper lunged for the gun. Richards, right arm still pinned, threw the flashlight at Jasper. It pinwheeled through the space between them and connected with Phipps's forehead with a loud crack. The blow stunned him and made him see stars. A trickle of blood started from a gash over his right eye. He reeled back and fell on top of his welding gear in the neat little square of space between the crate and the new wall he'd just finished sealing up. Richards stretched out his free left hand and caught the trigger guard of the pistol with his middle finger. He dragged it to himself as Jasper staggered and fell.

Jasper shook his head, trying to get the stars to go away, but the stars in his eyes were joined by locomotive shrieks in his ears as, for the second time tonight, a gunshot went off, too close and in too small a space. Blinded and deaf, Jasper felt the crate start to move against his back and dimly realized that Richards would kill him, here and now, if he got his arm free. He was sitting in the square hole between the crate and the new wall he'd just sealed up. He put both feet against the new wall and straightened his legs as far as he could, with all the force he could. The result was a satisfying crunch and a corresponding howl from Richards, who had made just enough room to begin twisting his pinned arm from its prison. Jasper's move caught Richards just as his elbow came even with the top board of the crate. The force of the counterattack shattered the joint, breaking both bones cleanly in half and sending Richards into spasmodic pain.

Dully, through the still reverberating echo of the gunshot, Jasper heard Richards screaming.

"Awwwargh! Ooooh fuuuuucck!" Then chillingly, in a guttural growl, "Gonna kill you here and now, country bumpkin fuck. I was gonna do it the old fashioned way. Gonna make you walk the plank, but now I'm gonna put a bullet in that mashed potato brain of yours."

Jasper responded to this by pressing harder against the wall, exerting more pressure on Richards's mangled elbow. Richards let out a "Whumpf" and screamed in anger and pain.

"How you gonna do that?!" Jasper said. "You ain't gonna move unless I let you out or you chew off your arm like a 'coon in a trap."

Richards answered with another round from the .45. The bullet zinged off the steel wall half an inch from Jasper's foot before bouncing off the overhead and straight down through the top of the crate. A sound like the clunk of an old cow bell struck with a stick accompanied the splintering of a board.

Jasper yelled over his shoulder, "you idiot! You'll kill us both if you keep firing off rounds inside this steel coffin!"

"Fine," Richards said, chambering another round.

"And you'll blow a hole in your treasure too!" Jasper said. "That last round hit something inside the crate."

Even with his ears ringing, Jasper thought he could hear Richards's gears grinding. At any rate, the shooting stopped. He assessed the Mexican standoff and decided upon a plan. Once again he eased the pressure of his back against the crate. It slid towards him a quarter of an inch. He heard Richards groan with relief and immediately slammed the gap shut again, thrusting his legs full against the wall. He grunted with the effort. He felt the crate give way against his back as two boards cracked. Then, flipping around on all fours, he grabbed the crate, flipped it up on a pivot and slipped his legs over the edge of the hole below it. He reached behind him, wrenching his back painfully in the process, and in one motion, swept his welding gear through the hole before heaving himself through after it. He landed on top of his ladder and gear in a heap.

Richards was screaming, a mixture of obscenities and painful yelps. Jasper heard him crawling over the crate, searching for a way out. He set his ladder on its feet, hoisted the round piece of steel he'd cut out to make the hole into WINS like a waiter with an empty tray and fetched his torch. In seconds he'd lit the flame, leapt up on the ladder and tacked the plate back into place with four small beads. As the last bead smoldered, he saw a sight he would never forget. It was one of Richards's bulging blue eyes, now swimming in a blood red socket. It blazed through the gap at the rim of the now-filled hole, as if it could cut steel, not with heat but with ice.

Richard's pressed his mouth to the crack and screamed, "I'll kill you!" It came out as a hoarse shriek.

Jasper said, "I know you would, you crazy sumbitch. That's why you're in there and I'm out here!" keeping his voice steady with an effort. A shiver ran through him, shaking him from head to foot, a thing that hadn't happened in twenty years. He remembered it in a flash. His mother standing on the worn out porch that was painted white with too many coats of paint, screaming his name. "Jaaaaaaas-PEEEER! The shrill last note like the end of a bos'n's whistle. It always went through him, struck him in the shoulders and down through his back and legs like lightning searching for a way to ground. And he shook.

Without thinking he relit his torch, grabbed a handful of welding rods and began filling in the ragged circle edging the hole. He'd make that sound stop or stop it up so it couldn't get out at him.

Richards, his face forced from the hole by the heat and sparks flying up at him, went into a rage. Jasper heard him slamming the crate side to side, attempting to move it away from his rapidly disappearing manhole. Suddenly through the closing gap around the hole he saw the blunt nose of a crowbar. *Must have left that up there*, Jasper thought. He did not hesitate, he welded around it and only returned to the spot to fill in around it. It ceased to move as the molten metal congealed, the blunt nose of the tool sticking through.

Chapter 49
A Cut into Another Time
August 1990, Port Said Anchorage,
awaiting southbound Suez Canal transit convoy

Maggie got off watch at 0400. She went to her rack in WINS berthing, grabbed a fresh set of coveralls and underclothes and showered before slipping out and making her way to Sick Bay. Steve's eyes were intense when he let her into his room. Her heart went icy, knowing Hiller had already done something about the envelope of his secret Polaroids shoved under his door, along with the note they'd concocted. But when she said "Hiller?" Steve shook his head as if coming awake from a dream.

"What?" he said.

"Did Hiller find the pictures yet?" she said.

"Hiller. No. I don't know. Haven't thought about him all night."

"You haven't? Then you better tell me what you have been thinking about, because I haven't been able to think of anything else."

He heard the strain in her voice and said apologetically, "I'm sorry Maggie. I've just been distracted by something. I need your help to solve it. Hiller is in the Dive Shack

303

drinking with Baber. At least, he was there last time I checked, half an hour ago. Been in there all night."

"All night?"

"Yeah. So it's impossible he's found the pics yet."

Maggie's shoulders sagged. "I've been thinking this whole time he'd come busting into the main space and drag me out in the middle of my watch. I've been bracing for it, and he hasn't even seen them yet?"

"No." Steve filled her in on the conversation he'd overheard between the Bos'n and Hiller. Maggie shuddered.

"Yeah. It's worse than we thought." Steve's countenance didn't match his words. He looked excited, maybe even giddy.

"What's up with you? We've got our necks on the line and you seem happy about it. You're the one who must have been drinking."

"I haven't. Hiller is gonna do whatever he's gonna do. Our plan is still good. In the meantime, I think I may have found another secret place on the ship—if I'm right, it's one that no one will know but us. I've been waiting for you to get off watch, because I need you to help me do some measurements before I go any further."

"Further?"

"Come with me."

Maggie followed Steve to the controlled equipage locker. He showed her the ragged, welded-over "O" in the overhead, and the corresponding drawing on the blueprint. She pointed at a box and a helmet on the deck underneath it.

"What's that for? You're not planning to cut a hole in the deck are you? We've got to be right under WINS."

"That's exactly where we are and what I need you to help me with." He handed Maggie a tape measure and explained the measurements he needed her to make.

Maggie had been on pins and needles for hours. Finding out Hiller couldn't have seen the envelope they'd planted in his stateroom released the tension momentarily and immediately the clock reset; the rubber band began to twist and her empty stomach churned and growled so loudly that Steve heard it.

"Jeez Mags. When's the last time you ate something?"

She shrugged. "Don't remember. Breakfast yesterday, I guess. Not very hungry."

"You gotta eat something. You won't think straight if your tank is empty. Look, you go up and grab these measurements. Make sure you use the things I gave you for landmarks. I'll go down to the galley and grab us some beans and weenies. There's always leftovers from mid-rats. I eat them cold. That ok, or you need me to heat yours up?" Maggie doubted she'd be able to eat anything at any temperature.

"I don't mind them cold," she said. She looked at Steve closely. "Are you sure we ought to be jerking around with... ah, whatever this is," she gestured at the overhead, "when the whole world is getting ready to come down on our heads?" There was an edge to her voice that broke Steve's mystery hunting spell. He met her gaze with a look so boyish it made her laugh in spite of her tension.

"What?" he said.

"There's no getting treasure hunts out of boys, is there?" she said. "I guess all of you want to be Indiana Jones." He started to say something. She held up one hand. "Go get the beans and weenies. I'll get the measurements."

Less than ten minutes later, they were sitting, using a couple of kapoks for stools and the wooden crate as a table, as they both spooned up sugary brown beans with slices of overcooked hotdogs from a half gallon tin can scavenged from the galley. Steve had also scored a plastic jug of sugary-sweet orange "bug juice"—the shipboard equivalent of Kool-Aid. He used his welding rig to add a little heat to the beans and weenies, but it failed to penetrate far into the sticky mass. The meal tasted much better than it was, because they were both famished from missing meals and overworked nerves. They took turns shoveling in the food and washing it down with the bug juice, forgetting, for the moment, the ticking time bomb that was Mal Hiller.

"You double-checked these?" Steve asked, trying not to sound condescending, sure that he did. Maggie was nonplussed.

"I found the places you told me would be there and marked it off like you asked me to. It was dark and I had to be real quiet so I didn't wake up any of the girls, but I'm sure of these." She pointed to several numbers marked on the diagram he'd scribbled out for her. His eyes were wide again, like when she'd come to him in sick bay. "And I double-checked them, as well as looking for any kind of door or access point, like you said. There's nothing there."

"Mags, this means there is a space up there that's not on any drawing and doesn't have any way in." He nodded to the welded O in the overhead. "And that makes this even more curious than it already was." He stood on the crate and fingered the forks of the crow bar. "Let's find out what's up there." He said it partly as a question, partly as an invitation. His expression was so full of childlike enthusiasm and life, it made Maggie want to kiss him. She did.

"What can I do to help?" she said.

Steve picked up a battered red CO_2 fire extinguisher and handed it to her. "We'll have to be our own fire watch. No telling what's up there. We can clear everything away down here, but if anything in there catches fire, we need to jump on it quick."

Maggie took the extinguisher. "What makes you think there's anything in there? Couldn't it just be a mod someone out there did and then decided they didn't need? That part of WINS is close to the head. Maybe it was going to be a place for piping?"

"But that's the thing! Someone rerouted the chill water pipes that ran through that spot. You can see where they were in the original drawing. They're the same pipes causing the Bos'n problems in his office. There was no reason to do that, other than to make this compartment. And there's something about the notes on this drawing. I don't know. Maybe I'm making it up in my own head. It won't hurt to try."

For an instant Maggie thought she had snuffed out the child light in Steve's eyes and she regretted asking her question. But when she looked, she saw it was still there. He stooped to don a ratty set of coveralls and stood up, throwing his shoulders back to get his arms through. He put on a thick set of leather gloves and a set of goggles. He looked like a frog.

"Watch out," he said, lighting the torch and stepping up onto the crate.

Maggie stepped back. She pulled the safety pin out of the fire extinguisher handle and readied it. Yellow-red sparks showered down from the overhead. The torch sizzled like a cooking steak.

"I'm gonna start here!" Steve said, too loudly. He pointed at the place where the crow bar appendage stuck out. "See if it's what I think it is."

He cut a small arc around the metal fork. Maggie tried not to look directly at the blue-white tongue of the torch, but it drew her eyes like a moth. The edges glowed brilliantly. Just as Steve completed his cut, she looked down and saw the image set against her retinas. A loud thunk-dong sound echoed through the compartment. When she looked up, Steve had cut off his torch and was holding a crowbar, which at one time had been painted the same red as her fire extinguisher. It was worn and chipped. She immediately recognized it as an item similar to those found in one of *Redstone*'s repair lockers. Steve held it away from his body, staring at it like it was a meteor dropped from the sky. A round disc of metal from the overhead remained around the forked end. It smoked as it cooled slowly.

He had flipped his welder's goggles onto the top of his head and, if it were possible for Steve's eyes to grow any larger, Maggie thought they had.

"What?!" she finally said. "Isn't it what you expected?"

He looked from the crow bar to her and back. He nodded. "Yes. I guess. But, seeing it. It's different. And it's impossible. What just happened is impossible. Don't you understand?"

Maggie didn't, her face said it for her.

"I thought the fork of the crowbar might be there because someone laid it on the deck up there and it slipped into the crack while they welded up this hole. When they got to this place they were too lazy or in too much of a hurry to get it out. That can't be what happened. You saw it. It fell straight down out of the hole I just cut!"

Maggie didn't want to tell him that she'd only heard and hadn't seen it. His tone implied he needed her to affirm that he wasn't seeing things. She nodded again, still not following him fully.

"The only way that happens is that it was standing straight up when it got welded into the crack! If there's no way in there and no way out, how could that be? It can't stand up on its own!"

Maggie started tracking with him. "Ok. What if it's a prank. You know HTs are cracked. Putting their arms down toilets and climbing through CHT tanks full of shit. They would think something like this is funny. Take a guy's tools and hide them. Leave him a little clue like the end of his pry bar. Maybe they welded it in place against the edge of the hole and then put the patch in."

Steve held the still smoldering end of the crow bar up for a closer look. Examining it end on, he grunted. "Nice idea, but you can see where it was welded into the crack all at once. If it had been tacked in place first there'd be more material around one edge than the other." He showed her. "There's not. In fact, if you look closely, you can see there's less."

Maggie frowned. "So what's your idea then, smart guy?"

Steve was surprised by her agitated tone. "I think your mind isn't dark enough to guess what I'm thinking. And I'm glad it isn't." He smiled grimly.

"So what are you thinking Steve?"

He grunted, stepping back up on the crate. "I'm thinking something crazy. Probably read too many Stephen King books. Watch yourself. I'm gonna cut this same hole out and see what we see."

More orange red sparks showered down. A stubborn spark skittered across the deck, glowing hot. It settled under a dirty orange kapok. A curl of smoke rose from the spot. Maggie stepped around the crate. She lifted the kapok to see if it was on fire. A tiny black ring appeared in the material like the eye of a lizard. More sparks fell around her. She heard Steve curse under his breath as an ember found its way around his gloves and up the sleeve of his coveralls. He stopped cutting and shook his arm. He finished the circle cut, leaving two small spots on opposite sides holding it in place.

"I need some help here Maggie," he said. "I don't know how heavy this will be. Grab one of those foul weather jackets and wrap it around your arm. Yeah. Like that. Now you stand on the other end of the crate and hold up on the overhead while I make these last cuts. If it gets too heavy, jump clear, ok?"

Maggie nodded and he cut one and then the other remaining strips. On the first cut, she felt the weight of the steel disc begin to settle on her padded arm and almost let go of it, fearing it would be too heavy. But the second cut was done and Steve was holding it in one hand like an oversized discus before she could act.

Something on the far edge of the hole above their heads was smoking. Steve dropped the plate on the deck. It thwanged loudly as he snatched the fire extinguisher and shot a burst of CO_2 into the mouth of the hole. The acrid smell of hot steel and the chalky taste of the gas made both of them cough and hack.

Steve flipped on a battle lantern and shined its beam upward into the hole. The light played across the smoke that lingered lazily across its mouth like a portal to another world.

"There's a box in there!" Steve said. "It's at the edge of the hole but close enough the torch must have lit it. I'm going up."

Maggie had a vision of Steve laid out in the mysterious chamber above. "Wait! Is there enough air in there?"

Steve hesitated. "Good question, Maggs." He stepped down from the crate. It's probably air tight or mostly air tight. Let's get a ventilator out of Repair 3 just in case. You want to do it or you want me to go?"

"Maybe both of us?" Maggie said.

Steve started to argue that it was a one person job but caught the look in her eye and understood. Engrossed in his adventure, he'd forgotten about the Cheng again, and that wasn't a good thing to forget. He'd already sent Maggie traipsing around WINS berthing by herself—probably a stupid move.

"Good idea," he said. "We can swing by the mess decks and get some more bug juice to wash away this taste in my throat."

Chapter 50
Hiller's High Water Mark
28 Aug 1990, 0300, anchored, Port Said Anchorage

Mal Hiller stumbled into his stateroom. He was done drinking with Pete Baber. The Bos'n was turning out to be a pussy. No stomach for the games Hiller liked to play. Didn't want to talk about it. The man was supposed to be a big shot athlete. Happy to tell the girls how he would've been in the pros if not for this or that. Could of, would of, should of. Hiller knew why the man didn't make it. Easy to see. No killer instinct. No stomach for taking the game down, like the lions who separate out a gazelle and snap its neck. You dominated completely or you didn't dominate at all. When you had one of these girls under you, you let them know there was no escape until you were done having your fun. That was the whole point, wasn't it? Control? You either did it to them or they'd do it to you. And if you ever let them get you under their control... well he didn't expect any mercy. He wouldn't give any. Why would they? Somewhere between what his first wife did to him and *Redstone*, control and sex and power all merged into one thing, his thing. He was the Alpha now. Getting the ship to its commitment on time sealed it. He'd seen it in Shumate's eyes last night when they dropped the hook. He owned the man now. He grinned at himself in the stateroom mirror, pleased with what he saw, more sure of himself than at any moment in his life.

He sat on the edge of his rack and tried to focus on getting his boondockers off his feet. His left foot wouldn't cooperate in its usual dance of flicking off his right boot. It kept missing, slapping the deck. His bleary eyes spotted a white envelope sitting on the deck just inside his door. Was it an envelope? Or was it a tile? He tried to focus. *Haven't been this drunk in a long time*, he thought. *Might not be any more stand up in these legs. Lucky they got me up here from the Dive Shack.* He pushed off the edge of his rack and slid down to the deck. Crawling on all fours he made his way to the envelope-tile, brushing his hands before him like a street sweeper. His left hand connected with the white object and sent it spinning crazily under the desk. As it spun it spit out several smaller white-edged squares that scattered in different directions. One came to rest beside his leg. He sat back on his knees unsteadily and picked it up. He raised it to his eyes to get a better look. He fought to get his eyes to focus. When they did, he was staring at a picture of Fran Green, very naked and doing something very lewd.

"Fran? What are you doing here?" he slurred. Then he clumsily scooped up three more pictures expelled from the envelope and held them up to his face. There was another of Fran Green and two of... of who? Who was that one? It slowly dawned on his whiskey-addled brain: Fratella. He'd stolen those from the Bos'n's collection when the old pussy wasn't watching—women weren't the only ones who knew where the bastard kept his stateroom key. His knees cracked and he laboriously unfolded his legs and sat with his back against the side of his rack. What the hell was going on? These are my pictures, from my collection. How'd they get here?

The envelope caught his attention. He stretched out and pulled it to himself. There was a folded piece of paper left inside. He pulled it out and began reading. It took him three times before he got the message. That bitch, Freeman. No pictures of Freeman. She refused him. Should have known she would be trouble. There would be other ways to deal with her now. And Carter. The engineering problem he thought he had solved. Well, even the best mechanics sometimes needed to go back and tighten down a loose nut they missed. He would tighten Carter down so tight the man would never stick his head up again.

He was too drunk for anger—his normal drug of choice—to have its full effect. He shook his head, trying to clear the alcohol clouds. It only made him dizzy. He braced his back against the rack and forced one leg and then the other to support him. No time like the present, his old man used to say, any time something on the farm broke. No time like the present. Fix it now before it breaks worse or something else breaks. The fire engine red of the digital clock on his desk read 0313. He would make a little trip down to Sick Bay and see that little shit Carter. Maybe stop by and show the note to the Bos'n, if he was still in the Dive Shack. Time for him to grow a pair and help fix this problem. It was his problem too now, wasn't it? Damn right it was. The pictures of Fratella settled that. Going to take care of Carter right now, then Freeman would get hers, too. He had a few ideas about that. He stood up and the room didn't. He felt like the floor fell away from him. He went from dizzy to full on merry-go-round. His stomach lurched and he vomited a fantastic stream of yellowish liquid, which mostly hit the mirror over his stainless steel wash basin. The smell of his own puke swelled in the small space of the stateroom and hit his nose as if it were an eject button, causing him to empty the rest of his stomach's contents, this time filling the basin with half an inch of foulness that gurgled down the drain.

As his insides and his eyes readjusted, he felt the temporary relief that accompanies the release of vomit. He looked at himself in the slime spattered mirror and the anger edged up over the alcohol for an instant. He ripped his towel from its hook, ran cold water over it and wiped his face. His feet and eyes were working well enough now. 'Let's go find Carter.'

Chapter 51
Up the Rabbit Hole
28 Aug 90, 0325, Port Said, at anchor

Steve let the ventilator run a full ten minutes, one end of its yellow and black striped hose stuffed up the hole he'd cut in the deck, while he and Maggie drank down almost a gallon of bug juice. Their trip to get the ventilator and the bug juice had been uneventful. It was an abnormally quiet night with the ship swinging at anchor so far from home. The ventilator pulled the air from the mysterious compartment above. It flowed through the hose to the door of the controlled equipage locker, where Steve wedged it just out of sight. He left the door open only enough to let the air out.

Steve flipped the off switch. The machine whirred to a halt. Maggie had not realized how loud it was until the vacuum cleaner sound subsided. She shook her head side to side as if to get the remnants of the noise out.

Steve stood on the crate and pulled the vent hose from the hole. He set a beat up yellow battle lantern inside the hole. He reached into the darkness and did a pull up on the rough cut steel, hoisting his head and shoulders into the breach. It was a narrow passage. A wooden box took up half the diameter of the cut out circle in the overhead. He hooked his elbows on either side and kicked his legs for the momentum to get all the way up and into the hidden compartment. He ended up sitting on the edge with his legs dangling down.

"What do you see? What's in there?" He heard Maggie's voice rising from below, now partially muffled.

He picked up the battle lantern. "It's tight in here. Seems like the whole space is taken up with this crate we almost set on fire." He sounded excited. "Mags...."

"Yes?"

"Mags, there's no way this thing got in here through that hole! It's way too big." His legs disappeared and she heard him shuffling around.

"Hey! Help me up. I want to see." She stepped onto their makeshift crate ladder and reached for the hole.

Steve said in a choked voice, "Stop! Don't come up here." His face was framed in the ragged opening. It was pale as the white paint of the overhead.

"What? What is it?" Maggie said. Then, "Get out of the way. I'm coming up. Help me."

Steve looked unsure. She erased the look with a glare. "Help me or don't, but get out of the way."

Steve helped her. In a moment they both were sitting on the top of a rough cut wooden crate the size of a coffin. Maggie was breathing hard from the effort of climbing up into the hidden compartment. She took the lantern from Steve, who pointed to one side of the crate. She followed with the beam of the lantern. At first she thought the object he pointed to was a dead rat and she started to deride him. Afraid of a dead rat. Her eyes adjusted to the light and the thing morphed into something else. It wasn't a rat. Her mind struggled to fit it together. It suddenly clicked. It was a human hand and forearm. No. Hand wasn't the way to describe it. It was more like a claw. A shriveled bony thing like the hands of the oldest living person she'd ever seen, the skin so thin it only served to hold in the bones, plainly visible beneath.

"How?" She said.

"Don't know," Steve choked.

"Have you?" She pointed the light to the crack between the crate and the wall from which the claw arm emerged.

"No." Steve said.

Maggie got to her hands and knees and forced herself to crawl toward the desiccated hand, scooting the lantern along in front of her, warding off something worse than the darkness with its beam. Steve followed. When Maggie got to the far end of the box, she stopped and looked back at him. His eyes were wide. His face was pale.

"Is this what you were thinking? The explanation for the crow bar?"

Steve nodded and swallowed. "But it was only a crazy idea in my head. I didn't really believe...."

Maggie didn't like her face so close to the claw of a hand that appeared to be crawling out of the end of the crate. She shined the light up to see if she had room to stand up on the crate and struggled to her feet. Steve followed suit. They stood hunched over in the cramped space.

She pointed the light into the crack and they both caught their breath. A body lay there, legs forward and head aft. The left arm extended back at an unnatural angle behind its back and up onto the crate. The face was turned toward the steel wall on the port side of the tiny hidden compartment, but they could see the right side of the head. It was a man. He wore old style cotton khakis. The lantern beam played across one collar device that glinted at them.

"A chief," Steve muttered.

"What's that mark on the side of his head?" Maggie asked and focused the lantern beam on the man's head.

"Don't know. Looks like a hole," Steve said. He had a thought. "Sweep the light along the body."

As Maggie did, they saw it at the same time. A black, Navy issue .45 gripped in the dead man's right hand lying on his upturned hip.

"Bullet hole," Steve said. "Jeez."

"So he... committed suicide?"

"I don't know. This... none of this makes sense. He must have been the one trying to pry his way out with the crow bar. That's one thing. But who sealed him in here and why? And left a gun here, so he could choose how he wanted to go? Maybe I have read too many horror novels, but it seems like it's the best explanation."

"Who could do this to someone? And why?" Her mouth was set in a hard ribbon. She looked ready to cry.

Steve put an arm around her awkwardly. "Let me see the lantern, Mags." She gave it to him. He swung it along the length of the crate they stood on.

"Look at this label. And look there. Is that a bullet hole in the top of the crate?"

They both looked at the perfectly rounded hole. "We are probably standing right on top of the "why?" Mags. Whatever is in this box explains how he got here."

"We should let someone know about this," Maggie said. "It's a murder scene, isn't it?"

"I want to see what's in here," he tapped the top of the box. "Don't you? Whatever happened here happened a long time ago. The body is basically mummified! Stay here a minute and let me get a hammer and a few more lanterns out of Repair 3. We won't disturb anything much. If we report this, it'll be the last time we get anywhere near the place."

Steve sounded excited. Maggie looked in his eyes. She was surprised by this transformation. One minute he's pale as a sheet, now his eyes glittered with excitement. Boys. Men. One and the same. Steve had gone from discovering a sickening crime scene to climbing into an ancient tomb with a real mummy in mere moments.

"Ok. But I'm not staying here with that," she indicated. "You stay here. I'll go get the stuff. Be right back."

She didn't wait for Steve to respond. She stepped around him to the hole and quickly let herself down and out.

As soon as her feet hit the deck, Maggie had second thoughts. It was as if being in the hidden compartment had transported her to another world momentarily. Back here on *Redstone*, she realized she was alone and alone on this ship right now was bad. It was worse than alone with a corpse in the dark. A chill went up her back. She shook it off. She'd be back with Steve in just a few minutes. All she needed to do was find a couple of battle lanterns and a hammer.

Steve popped his head into the opening above her and said "Be careful, Mags."

She caught her breath and looked up. "You almost gave me a heart attack, Carter. I will."

The trip to get the lanterns took less than five minutes. No one was around. The decks were still as quiet as a tomb. The only bad moment came when she tiptoed past the Dive Shack. The door was open and she thought she heard someone. She waited on the edge of the light spilling into the passageway, letting her heart rate fall so she could hear properly, and as she did she realized she'd heard the sound of the Bos'n snoring. She stepped past the door, feeling like she was passing through a metal detector that would go off and alert anyone within earshot that Maggie Freeman was here. But nothing happened. 'You're as nervous as a whore in church,' she told herself. Returning to the door to the controlled equipage locker, she looked both ways before entering. Was there a shadow at the far end of the passageway? She stood still again, waiting, listening. Nothing. She stepped into the locker and pulled the door closed.

Steve helped her up after taking the lights and hammer. As he did, Maggie dropped an extra pry bar she'd taken from the repair locker. She'd forgotten it was stuffed in the back pocket of her coveralls. The steel bar thudded against the step stool crate they'd been using and then clattered across the deck with what seemed to them an earth shattering racket before coming to rest against the door to their cage.

Maggie's eyes were the size of milk saucers. She started to go after the dropped tool.

"Don't bother with it. We don't need it. I've got the lid of this thing loose already." He pointed to the old crow bar he'd cut out of the hole only quarter of an hour ago and then to his own head. "Stupid. Didn't even think about using this. I've got the lid loose. Just waiting for you to lift it off with me."

"What about that?" She pointed to the mummy claw hand. Now that they were opening the crate, it felt like the dead man's final insistence that whatever was in there belonged to him.

"I pried up this side so we can open it like the lid of a chest. Open it toward him. Didn't want to touch him."

Maggie nodded. "Ok. Let's see what's in here," she said.

They had just enough room to splay their feet out in the space between the wooden box and the side of the hidden compartment. The lid lifted easily. Nails along the far side of the box top squealed as it hinged open. There was a dry

321

thump from the far side, which Steve assumed was the dead arm finally releasing its grip on the box. He wondered briefly how long that grip had lasted.

They leaned the lid against the far wall of the compartment. Each of them shined a battle lantern into the crate. They saw a rectangle of yellow, too bright and too new in the lamp light. The smell of the stuff hit their noses at the same time. Straw. Steve tentatively stuck an arm into the packing, gingerly sweeping back and forth as if he might find a mouse trap. He touched something hard and smooth and traced its dimensions. He put the lantern aside and reached into the straw with both arms, emerging with a polished wooden box that was two feet long and a foot wide. There was a logo of some sort on its top. It had small brass hinges on one side and a brass eye and hook closure on the other. He laid it on top of the edge of the crate. It was surprisingly hefty for its size. He bent close to it to get a closer look at the logo.

"Looks like Arabic script," he said. "Can you shine your light on it for me?" Maggie did.

What he at first took for a printed label turned out to be a logo inlaid in brass on the box top. The round disc of a sun shone down with multiple squiggly beams towards three English letters S C A. Under these, upon a blue field, was an Arabic title or word. He ran his finger across it. It was fine work. Precise. The box itself was made of the blackest wood he'd ever seen. Ebony? He didn't know. His heart raced. He looked up at Maggie and gestured.

"You want to open it?"

"She shook her head. "It's all you, Indiana. You better hope there's no snakes in there."

He grinned. "Ok. Here goes."

He flipped the brass hook and opened the box. A red velvet cloth covered the full interior of the box. He peeled it back slowly and caught his breath. The weak, yellowish lantern light fell on glittering gold so bright, it was as if it shone from within itself. He'd never seen anything so shiny, unless it was a chromed piece of toy plastic jewelry, like the faux crown one of his sisters wore to play dress up. This was no toy. No piece of plastic. It dazzled their eyes. Neither could breathe.

Finally Maggie said, "What is it?"

"I think it's an arm band. I don't know what to call it. It would go up here," he touched his bicep. "Or maybe it's a bracelet." Using the red velvet cloth that covered the object he picked it up. It was heavy in his hands. Lines of light turquoise, dark blue and brick red ran up and down the band, which was an incomplete ring with an opening in back. The center of the front was a spread wing bird with a large green stone on its breast, the wings inlaid with the same dark blue as the lines around the band, and a yellow stone set over its head, as if it were flying into the sun.

"What is this doing here?" Steve said, staring at the band. "This has got to be Egyptian and it's got to be real. How'd it get here and what's the dead guy got to do with it?"

"It's treasure. Don't people kill each other over treasure?" Maggie said.

"Yeah they do, but whoever killed that guy didn't get the gold, did he?" He put the band back in the box. "Is there more in here? Seems like an awfully big crate for just this one thing. Take a look on your end."

Maggie put down her lantern and repeated Steve's careful sifting through the straw.

"Another box here," she said.

She lifted a second smooth black box from beneath the packing straw and set it in the beam of Steve's lantern. It was larger than the first, a square, three feet by three feet, and another foot deep. It bore the same markings on its cover as the first box.

"Wonder how many of these are in here!" she said, and began to unclasp the hook closure when a grunt behind her broke the spell of the found treasure. There, emerging through the hole and standing up like a specter in the light streaming through the opening in the deck, was Mal Hiller.

Chapter 52
Hiller Hunts

Hiller had stumbled upon Maggie retrieving the lanterns from the repair locker, almost literally. She was too preoccupied with her task to notice him. Even in his drunken state, his habits prevailed—he knew how to haunt *Redstone* and he knew how to see and hear while not being seen or heard. He waited in a darkened corner when he discovered the door to Repair 3 was open and that someone was rummaging around in it. He was sobering up, although still a bit unsteady on his feet, as he swayed in the shadows. When Maggie Freeman emerged from the locker, he started to accost her then and there, but his instinct for letting people hang themselves told him to wait. Battle lanterns? A hammer? Where would she be needing those? Let her go. See what she's up to.

When the girl turned up the passageway where the Dive Shack was located, he wondered if he might be getting played by Baber. Maybe that explained why the man was acting so odd. His anger; his own personal emotional jet fuel, started to flow, burning off a good portion of his drunkenness. But the girl walked past the Dive Shack. Then Hiller knew she was going to Sick Bay and remembered Carter. Carter! Her co-conspirator. Probably her lover. He'd bury them both. He'd kill them. This was his ship. His kingdom. The jet fuel burned the rest of the drunk away. He'd never felt it this hot and he knew then he could really kill. He wanted to and he would. He waited around the bend of the passageway until he was sure she'd made it to Sick Bay. He heard a door click shut. As he passed the Dive Shack, he thought of Pete Baber. The man was in it now, whether he knew or not, whether he wanted to be or not. Before following Freeman further, he let himself into the Dive Shack and the inner office where he'd left the Bos'n, it seemed like hours ago. He checked his watch. Less than half an hour had passed since he'd left the man here, passed out cold. Baber sat back in his office chair, feet propped on his desk, hands folded across his middle. His breathing was steady with a slight murmur of a snore.

Hiller went to him and shook him by the shoulder roughly. "Wake..." Hiller didn't get the chance to finish.

The Bos'n went from full repose to full alert in a flash. He sprung out of his seat as if Hiller had opened a snake in a can. Baber hit Hiller full in the chest. The 175 pound chief engineer got an instantaneous lesson in football physics as he was slammed against the bulkhead behind him. It knocked the breath out of him and he collapsed to the deck, wild eyed, clawing the air as if he could scoop it into his empty lungs. Baber came to himself, saw what he had done and knew from years of gridiron experiences how Hiller felt.

"You're all right," he said, in his best coach's voice. "Lay flat." He pushed the flailing man flat on the deck then grabbed him by the belt and lifted the Chief Engineer several times by his middle. He had no idea why trainers and coaches did this when you got the wind knocked out of you, but they always did. Maybe it was just to make you believe they could bring air back into your airless universe by this action—get your body to relax enough to start breathing again on its own. On the second up and down, Hiller took in a great gulp of air.

"Jesus! Shit!" he gasped.

"Yeah. That sure scares hell out of you." Baber said.

He grinned at Hiller's fearful eyes. "Guess you'll think twice before you mess with a man who is sleeping peacefully in his office."

Hiller grunted something unintelligible and pushed himself to a seated position.

"What are you doing here anyway? Thought you were headed up to sleep it off."

"I was, till I found this." Hiller handed Baber the white envelope. He was surprised to see he'd kept hold of it in the scuffle.

Baber took it and said, "What is it?"

"It's a conspiracy," Hiller said. "Someone wants to take us down."

Baber read the folded up note then turned to the Polaroids. He flipped through the first two then stopped and held one up in front of Hiller's face.

"Where'd this come from?" There was a dangerous note in his voice.

Hiller said, "We share the women, Baber. Why not share the pics too?" His attempt at disarming came off pleading rather than confident.

"You never had her, and you stole that from me. Fratella wouldn't come near you. She'd puke," Baber said. "Told me that herself."

He ran a hand through his sweaty hair, then fanned the Polaroids like a poker hand. He plucked out the three pictures of Fratella and tossed the others in Hiller's lap.

"Note says nothing about me. It's you they want." He stood up. "Carry your sorry ass," he said, gesturing toward the door. "And don't come near me again unless you want your breath permanently knocked out."

Hiller struggled to his feet and moved to the other side of the desk before turning around. "You think there aren't more of these?" he said, as he scooped up the remaining pictures. "Ones that can be pinned to you and only you? And," he smiled grimly, "do you think I'll go down alone if I go? Lambert thought he could fuck with me and I put his stupid ass in the brig. These guys want to fuck with me and I'm gonna put them in the ground."

"You're drunk." Baber said.

"I was," Hiller said, "but I'm sober as a priest now. And you're gonna decide if you're in or out before I walk out of here."

"In or out of what?" Baber said.

"Solving our problem. Carter and Freeman." He arched his eyebrows. Something in the look disgusted Baber. Maybe it reminded him of his old man. Whatever it was, he had had enough of this asshole. He came around the desk like he was avoiding a tackler. Hiller caught enough in his face to know it was time to go, but Baber beat him to the conclusion. He wrapped one beefy hand around his khaki belt, and used it like a handle on a sea bag, half lifting, half pushing Hiller to the Dive Shack door. He didn't stop until the man was outside in a pile on the passageway deck. He let go and stood over Hiller.

"Look at me!" He commanded. Hiller complied, and amazingly enough, when he looked up he was smiling. "If you bring me into this I'll beat you like a red-headed step child. Understand? You think this ship is your place? You'll wish you never stepped foot here when I'm done with you."

Before Hiller could utter another word, Baber turned and slammed the Dive Shack door in his face. Hiller stood up and straightened his coveralls. He wiped a hand across his mouth, checking for blood where he'd taken a shot to the face as Baber tossed him. He muttered to himself, "Pussy." Clear enough. It was him alone. Normal. He knew how to do that. What he'd always done. Baber would be easy enough to deal with, once he cut off the two loose ends trying to blackmail him. Hell, he might even give the Bos'n one more chance to get on the right team before it was all over. Give him the benefit of the doubt. Might've been the whiskey talking.

Sick Bay. There would be the two of them in there. Two on one wasn't his normal set of odds. He liked stacked decks and odds overwhelmingly in his favor. But this couldn't wait for him to work all that out. The ship would begin the transit through Suez at first light and make Hurghada by this time tomorrow. If he was actually going to do this, he needed them to disappear tonight. Kill them? Did he mean to do it? "Damn right I do," he said out loud. Two on one? He'd use another favorite technique: he'd use the threat of hurting one to control the other... then he'd hurt them both.

A quick search of Sick Bay showed him it was empty. It didn't make sense. He'd heard the door shut before he slipped into the Dive Shack. Where did she go? He let himself back into the passageway and tracked back the way he had come. There was only one other door on this passageway and he knew it was padlocked, because it was the controlled equipage locker. He'd had words with the First Lieutenant about it being a fire haz...

The hasp for the door's padlock was flat against the door. He stood looking at the place where the lock should be for a second before pushing the door open. It swung about halfway before hitting something. A portable ventilator hose? He smelled the lingering odor of hot metal. Welding? His anger at Carter and Freeman melded with his everyday anger at the dumbshit people trying to burn down and or break his ship. He was in a deadly mood anyway, and collecting reasons to keep it going.

He followed the yellow and black vent hose through the musty space like Hansel and Gretel's crumbs, the smell of welding getting stronger as he did. When he reached the other end of the hose connected to a blower from one of his repair lockers, it momentarily stumped him. A noise above took his eyes to a manhole sized hole, roughly cut in the overhead. On any day of the week this might have put murder in his heart, or something very close to it; with blackmail and a lover jilting him, this sight sent him over the edge. He jumped on the crate directly under the hole and hauled himself up in one motion, an act fueled by fury he could not have repeated, given ten more chances.

Chapter 53

A Spider in a Tin Can

Maggie and Steve were so engrossed in their discovery that the appearance of anyone in their secret compartment would have been a shock. The figure of the Cheng standing there in the disc of light shining from below was like a nightmare *Star Trek* episode, a monster teleported out of nowhere. His beady black eyes—eyes that always reminded Steve of a shark—were narrow, the whites shot through with jagged crimson blood vessels. Pure malice. Maggie sucked in a breath that made her choke.

Hiller started to say, "The fuc..." before Steve leaped around Maggie and hit him like a football sled dummy, shouldering into his midriff and stuffing him into the small gap between the end of the crate and the steel wall at the end of the compartment. For the second time in less than ten minutes, Hiller's world emptied of all oxygen. This time, white hot anger compensated for the lack of air. He brought both arms down on Steve's back with all the force in his wiry body. There was a thud, as of a rubber mallet striking a barrel. Steve gasped and tried to get leverage with his feet, which were flailing in the straw-packed box. Hiller flipped his victim around and locked an arm around his neck. He

331

began squeezing the air out of Steve's world, even as it started returning to his own.

He gulped down a breath and hissed in Steve's ear. "Pissant! Little pissant! I should've stepped on you before. But this is even better. Now I can say I killed you in self-defense! You and the whore attacked me. I had to fight you off. Kill or be kill...."

"Killed," a female voice said at the same time he felt an icy cold circle pressed to the side of his head.

"Let go. Gun's old but I'm sure it works just fine."

Maggie crouched beside him. He couldn't turn toward her because of the muzzle of the gun pushing against his temple.

Sensing his calculations she said, "Wonder if it's real?" She cycled the slide without moving the barrel from his head. As the slide slammed home, Hiller winced and released his choke hold on Steve, who fell forward gasping.

Several things happened at once. Hiller slapped the gun away from his head, taking Maggie by surprise. She jerked her finger, attempting not to drop the weapon. The gun went off with a deafening roar; a round that had lain still in the clip for more than a decade zinged off the steel walls of the secret chamber, crazily expending its energy before clipping Hiller's head, opening a gash that poured blood into both his eyes.

Steve, released suddenly from the Cheng's choke hold, spun around and went head down through the hole, unable to stop himself from falling. He crashed into the crate under the hole, barely managing to buffer his impact at the last instant by catching himself in an awkward handstand. He rolled to one side, still gasping for breath, the sound of the gunshot echoing in his ears.

Maggie, seeing Hiller's bloody head and face, dropped the gun. It clunked on the deck.

Hiller swiped palms full of blood from his eyes.

"You bitch!" he yelled.

Neither of them could hear. The sound came to them as if they were down a very long tunnel. He reached out a bloody hand and tried to get her by the throat, but the blood prevented him from getting a grip. She knocked his hand away. The lantern light shined on his face. It was a scene from a suspense movie where the bad guy won't die. Hiller's face was a mask of black blood with eye holes and eerily shiny white teeth set in a sneer.

"I'll kill you! I'll shove that gun up that cheating cooter of yours and fire every shot left in it." He reached for the dropped gun.

Maggie grabbed the battle lantern, still lying where it had fallen into the box full of packing straw. She swung it wildly like a kettlebell. It connected with the side of Hiller's head with the sound of cracking plastic and bone. He fell into the straw, stunned and bleeding, but still muttering: "kill... kill youuu... biiiiitch."

Maggie didn't hesitate. She let herself down through the hole, catching herself on the edge like doing a reverse chin up. Steve had regained his breath and his feet. He helped lower her to the deck.

"Wha..." he started to ask.

"Close it!" Maggie said, pointing up. "Close it before he gets the gun!"

It took Steve a second to realize what she was saying.

He looked up and then into Maggie's terror-filled eyes. He ran and grabbed his welding kit, picked up the cut out steel disc, then wavered. He asked her with his eyes.

"He'll kill us Steve. If you don't, he will kill us. Do it before he comes around."

Steve jumped up on the crate. "Help me," he said. "Put on one of the jackets and pull another one over your head to keep the sparks off."

He tacked the hole closed in less than a minute. They heard Hiller stirring. The sound urged Steve on.

When the plate was secured he asked, "Seal it?"

Maggie looked out from under the green foul weather jacket questioningly. Steve asked, "Should I fill it all the way in like we found it?"

Maggie understood. "Can he get out?"

Steve took an appraising look at his weld job. "I don't think so," he said.

"Good enough, then." Maggie said.

"What's wrong with your neck?"

She looked down. Her white t-shirt was stained red, in a ring around her neck.

"You're bleeding!" Steve said.

"No. Not my blood. His," she gestured upwards and briefly explained what had happened after Steve fell out of the secret chamber.

A grating sound of metal on metal caught their attention, followed by the distinct click click click of a gun, dry firing. Looking up, they saw the barrel of the .45, pressed into the gap in the weld, directly over their heads. Cursing followed. Then a grotesquely disassociated set of lips appeared where the gun had been.

"You're both dead!" Hiller's voice hissed out of the black crack, like air leaking from a punctured tire. He slapped the floor in a dull thwack. "It doesn't matter if you let me out now or a week from now, Carter. Your life is over, college boy! Both of you just handed me the keys to your pitiful little lives."

Steve stood up. "You're out of bullets, Hiller. And who said you're ever coming out of there?" He let that line filter up into the darkness, then said, "Ask your cellmate about getting out of there, maybe he has some ideas for you. Watch out, Maggie. I think the chief engineer needs a little privacy to work on his attitude."

He began filling in the black jagged circle. He left a half inch gap in the weld job, like leaving a breathing hole for a spider in a tin can. Cutting off the torch he spoke into the remaining crack. "You've got 8 hours to think things over, Hiller. I think that's fair, given the fact you chained me to a stanchion for 12. And while you think, think about this; we've got all the bullets now. We've got all the pictures of the women and the proof that you set up Lambert. Maybe we can be reasonable. That depends on you."

***

"Are you serious about leaving him in there?" Maggie asked.

They stood facing each other under the sealed hole. Each thought the other looked like they were in shock. The sweat from their recent exertions and excitements trickled down their backs and faces. Maggie's blood-stained t-shirt added emphasis to the dead seriousness of their situation.

"I dunno," Steve said. "It won't hurt if he thinks so." He piled the welding kit and the blower in a corner of the cage. "Can you go and get the vent hose from the locker door and bring it here? I want to leave all this stuff here, in case we need it quickly. Nobody will notice it's missing."

Maggie went to retrieve the hose. Steve took several of the foul weather jackets and covered his stashed gear. His back was to the cage entrance when he heard Maggie return, dragging the vent hose.

"Bring it over here, Mags," he said.

His blood ran cold when he heard a male voice say, "What are you up to, Petty Officer Carter?"

He turned to see Pete Baber standing with his hands on his hips. Maggie stood behind him, her face was an apology.

"Bos'n..." was all Steve could get out.

Baber walked to the half constructed hiding place and toed aside jackets and kapoks, exposing the welding rig. His eyebrows went up in a question Steve was unable to bring himself to answer. His eyes drifted involuntarily to the overhead, as if drawn by a magnet. Baber followed his gaze.

"The hell?" he said, and stepped under the hole. As he did a voice none of them recognized came through the burnt edges of the gap in the hasty weld job. It was somewhere between the whimper of a dog in pain and the cry of a small child.

"Letttttt meeeeeee ooooouuuuuut." It was barely audible at first, but grew louder as it was repeated several times, ending in a horrifically high pitched wail.

Baber's countenance grew deadly. Steve and Maggie drew together and stepped back, suddenly as afraid of Baber as they were of the monster they'd imprisoned above.

"Who is that?!" Baber screamed.

Instantly the wailing stopped. A man's voice barked breathlessly. "Baber! Baber! Get those fuckers. Don't let them out of your sight! And get me out of here. Get a welder. One of your guys. Baber! Baber!"

Baber looked incredulously at Maggie and Steve. "That's Hiller?!"

The voice from above grew back into its venomous fullness. "You know who it is! Baber! They've got the pictures, Baber! They tricked me into coming in here and sealed me in. They said they'd get both of us. You're next! Baber. You're next. They've got all the pictures. Yours, too! They know! They'll bring you down, too!"

Baber was watching Steve and Maggie. At the mention of pictures that belonged to him, both their faces turned white and they went more wide-eyed than they were already. Obviously, this was new information to them both. They tensed. Baber put a hand out to them. Steve's eyes darted around the room, searching for something, anything to use as a weapon against this new threat.

"Easy," Baber said. "Take it easy."

Maggie and Steve backed toward the cage exit, ready to bolt.

Baber stepped back from under the hole and away from the two of them. He said, "I don't know what he's told you, but I have nothing to do with him. Nothing."

Steve and Maggie looked at each other, gauging each other's response to this turn of events.

Hiller screamed through his insect breathing hole, "Baber, you pussy! I'll fucking kill you, too! I'll kill you! You hear me! Let me out of here!"

The whine was creeping back into the voice. And something else Steve caught now—fear. He heard it and immediately felt the opposite of what he'd imagined it would feel like to make this man afraid. He felt distaste. His stomach turned over. He was disgusted. Leaving Maggie at the gate to the cage, he pushed past Baber, dug out his welding rig and began setting it up under the hole.

Baber stopped him. "Wait. Just wait," he said, as Maggie joined them. "What are you going to do?"

"Yeah Steve," she chimed in, "what are you going to do?"

"Cut him out of there," Steve said. Even the words felt heavy in his mouth. What had he done? Sealing a man up in the dark? Threatening to leave him there with a corpse?!

Baber understood Steve's self-loathing tone. He put a surprisingly gentle hand on the younger man's back. Steve tensed then relaxed when Baber said, "We won't leave him in there long, but let's maybe go talk some things over before we get him out."

Steve looked to Maggie. She shrugged. "What do we have to talk about, Bos'n?" he said.

"A way out of this that works for all of us," Baber said, looking him in the eye.

Steve put down the torch he was about to light. "Go ahead," Steve said. He gestured for Maggie to join them.

Baber stopped her. "Let's step away from...." He looked up.

Hiller screamed, "Baber! I'll kill you. I swear it, damn you. I swear it. Let me out! Get meeeeee oooouuuuuut!" The voice cracked like a dry stick and was replaced by a gasping, choking sound. The three stepped to the exit with the noise echoing in their ears.

Chapter 54
Hiller Alone with His Thoughts… and More

Hiller pressed his face to the cool steel, straining to hear what Baber, Carter and Freeman were doing. He was hyperventilating, his heart pounding so hard he couldn't distinguish between it and the throbbing of machinery nearby. He thought he heard the clank of a door closing. He sat up. The momentary soberness and clarity attending his adrenaline and anger-fueled confrontation with the two blackmailers faded like the last of the light from a setting sun. His head swam. The thin shaft of light from the remaining gap in the floor of his cell cut the gloom like a distant spotlight. He ran his hand through it numbly as if trying to take hold of it, to take hold of something that would pull him from this darkened, tomb-like place. His eyes were not working right. Was his vision failing? He rubbed a hand across them. It came away covered in black stickiness. His head throbbed at the same time, reminding him of the blow from the battle lantern and the bullet gash in his scalp. Blood.

"Blood is in my eyes," he said to the darkness. Then he laughed. "Not going blind. Bleeding. Got to get that stopped." He looked around for something to use to apply pressure to the wound. Trying to get his legs to work was a problem. Alcohol and blood loss, maybe a bit of shock? The battle lantern, knocked away during the scuffle in the small compartment, lay inside the wooden box he leaned against. It threw its sickly yellow beam against the wall furthest from him. He tried to get up again. He managed to uncork himself from his spot between the crate and the wall and reached for the lantern. His legs gave out without warning. He pitched forward into the open wooden box, landing in the packing straw. He thrashed around in it as if he were a turtle thrown in an aquarium. The lid of the crate Steve and Maggie had propped against the wall was dislodged and fell on his head. He flailed at it, throwing it aside. Grasping the sides of the crate and pulling himself out, his left hand came away with what he thought was a piece of rotted wood. He held it up to the watery light. He saw an impossibility. A mummified human hand. He struggled to the edge of the wooden box, dropping the impossible object and picking up the rapidly-dying battle lantern. He shined it down into the gap at the end of the crate. The rest of the impossible object was there. A whole body.

Hiller tried to get his mind around what he was seeing. Someone had put a man in here and left him to die? In an instant he saw what would happen. He'd do it to them, wouldn't he? Yes he would. It was a perfect way to get rid of a problem. His mind snapped. He fell backward into the packing-straw-filled box, muttering to himself:

"Do it to them before they do it to you... do it to them before they do it to you..." But they'd already done it to him.

***

Maggie and Steve sat in Baber's office. The pictures of Fratella were on the desk between them. Baber covered them with a random sheet of paper as soon as Maggie and Steve acknowledged they were the same pictures they'd put in the white envelope. Baber seemed genuinely embarrassed by the pictures, Maggie noted, a characteristic she had never associated with the brash dive officer, the legendary womanizer. She watched his eyes carefully as he detailed his confrontation with Hiller, just prior to their own. The man was telling the truth, and more than that, she detected a hint of fear. Less than ten minutes ago, she and Steve were struggling with a mad man who would, in spite of his attack on them and threatening to kill them, hold the upper hand if he ever got out of the makeshift prison they'd put him in. She had realized the fact, even as Steve welded the jail shut and sparks fell around her. He was sealing Hiller in at the same time they themselves were being sealed out. How would they ever justify what they'd done when it came down to his word versus theirs? No one of any consequence on *Redstone* would cross Hiller. But here they were, sitting with Baber, a man who might represent a way out. It was like the Red Sea parting—a way through this mess that no one would have predicted.

As Baber finished his story, a drop of oily water fell on the papers and pictures on his desk. Without missing a beat, he opened his top drawer, pulled out a stained rag and wiped it off.

"I told you my part," he said, putting the rag away, "now, how did you two get into the blackmail business and what is that chamber you've got Hiller penned up in?"

Steve pointed to the leaky pipe in the overhead. "Believe it or not, that pipe has a lot to do with it."

He looked at Maggie again, questioning whether or not to go on. She took one more long look at Baber's face and said, "Tell him. The whole thing."

Steve did, with Maggie filling in her parts and perspectives. When it was over, there was, what seemed to her, a long silence. The three of them looked at the desktop as if the tale was a book, lying open there before them, the final pages yet to be written. Whether there would be a good or bad ending for any of them was very much in question.

Finally Baber spoke. "Let's go see the Old Man."

He paused and watched their reactions. "You were right to think the captain wouldn't help you when it came to Hiller. He needed Hiller to get us here, and there are a thousand ways the Cheng could have broken the ship, without proof that he did it. Shumate wants what every skipper wants—to look good and get promoted. The best ones keep that balanced with their crew's well-being, but it's always a close thing. This one is a pretty good one, as far as what I've seen, and two months ago I would've called him one of the best. He knew he wasn't getting promoted again and this was his last ride on the merry-go-round. The war changed all that. He's got stars in his eyes again. And who knows? He may be right. Getting the *Boone* out of Hurghada before the Arabs get angry over it being there is a mission that's got national attention. And if he pulls it off in a fifty-year-old ship with no notice and no work ups..."

Maggie cut in, "It sounds like you're making the case that Hiller is as big a deal as ever, Bos'n. He got us here even when we lost a bearing!"

Baber smiled. "Yeah, but no one knows that yet. Hiller convinced the Old Man not to report it. Probably hedging his bets, in case something else major broke. He was always going to take credit for getting us here, but he was going to do it his way. Wait for Shumate to get his glory and then steal it from him by spreading the story around about fixing the bearing. Different kind of glory a man like Hiller wants."

Steve said, "So what's different now? I agree with Maggie —the Old Man's got even more reasons to protect him."

"But everything is different now," Baber said, checking his watch. "A little over two hours from now, *Redstone* heads south in the canal. It'll take us about twelve hours to steam to Hurghada; even if we lost another shaft we could make it ahead of schedule! You see? Now, getting the *Boone* out of port is the top drawer. And that's gonna take a lot of underwater work. Now the most important people on the Shumate train to glory are..."

"The divers!" Maggie and Steve said together.

Chapter 55
Shumate's Choices

The skipper of *Redstone* was up early, having spent a restful night in his in-port cabin. He slept much better there than the rock hard little bunk in the Captain's at-sea cabin behind the bridge. He was in a great mood. On the table, beside a steaming cup of coffee and a plate of home fries, bacon and eggs, was an official record message from Commander Logistics Group Mediterranean with a cc to Commander Logistics Group Two. It was addressed to USS *Redstone*, which in most cases meant the ship as a whole, but in this instance meant Captain Ralph Shumate, USN. *I might frame this one*, he thought. *I may put this one on my 'I love me' wall.* He brushed breakfast crumbs off his khaki shirt. His wedding ring tinged off his command at sea pin. He smiled. No one wanted this pig ship. He'd known it when the detailer called and offered it to him. No one wanted the fast attack repair tender Building 20 on the NOB waterfront. A few of his academy classmates called him when he took the ship, to offer mocking congratulations. They were in staff billets, two at the Pentagon and another in San Diego at a materials command, dealing with contractors. Who's laughing now? He ran a weathered finger along the tastiest line in the "personal for" message:

Getting *Boone* out of Hurghada has the attention of the President. Counting on you to pull this off, in spite of commanding the oldest active ship we have. All resources of COMLOGRU MED and COMLOGRU TWO at your service, on request. Upon making port and commencing work on shaft, send hourly updates on progress. *Redstone* is going places.

That last line. He read it and reread it. Rear Admiral Johnson, the originator of the message, was also an academy classmate. They weren't particularly close, but knew each other. He was a "hot runner" and likely to end up with three stars on his collar before the music stopped. There were those few rare guys you could tell, even back then, who were going places. He had been one of them and everyone knew it. It became a kind of serious joke to attach the phrase whenever other middies wanted to give him a hard time. Hey Johnson, you're going places, pick me up a cup of coffee. Or Johnson, you're going places so fast, no one can see you. Of course, the places he was going were flag rank. It's where all of them saw themselves someday. Their own flag. Their own barge. Their own staff. Only, the top of that pyramid was too narrow for all of them to stand on it. Shumate was close, but wasn't going to make it. Until now. Now there was a mission that had the attention of the President and an unlikely pig of a ship to accomplish it. And there was the line: *Redstone* is going places. He was *Redstone*. That was for him. The carrot that had eluded him. The carrot cut off the string, flung far away and forgotten, yet here it was. He fingered the silver spread eagle on his collar and imagined a single star replacing it. Yes. The carrot was back, and closer than it had ever been. One task. Win or lose the game on one play. He'd win. He could taste it.

A knock at the door broke his daydream. It annoyed him. He'd told the steward not to disturb him. He began to call him off. "Go awa..."

The door opened. "Permission to enter, sir," a familiar voice called.

"Bos'n!" he said.

The dive officer entered. The man was the key to making his day dream into reality. He scooted his chair back and rose. When he looked up he was surprised to see two sailors accompanying his Dive Officer and more surprised at their identities. Not divers: engineers. He questioned the Bos'n with his eyes.

"Sir, we've got a situation. Sensitive situation. Freeman and Carter are part of it. Can we sit?"

Shumate motioned for all of them to sit. The three waited awkwardly for him to sit first, then Baber began. He retold the same story he'd told Maggie and Steve and then handed off to them; they did the same. When they finished he looked each one slowly in the eye as if he expected one of them to crack, revealing this to be an elaborate joke of some kind. They stared back evenly.

Shumate focused finally on Steve. He said, "You're serious? You are seriously sitting here telling me my Chief Engineer is right this minute, sealed in a hidden compartment along with a corpse and some, some... what did you say? Egyptian treasure?"

"I think it's Egyptian. A lot happened really fast. I, ah, we didn't get much time to look it over before all..." Steve faltered off in the withering gaze of his captain. He couldn't read the exact nature of Shumate's expression, but he suddenly felt that the less he said, the better. Shumate's use of the single word "my" with reference to the Chief Engineer stuck out like a sore thumb. Steve began to feel like he wanted to be anywhere on this ship other than here.

Shumate was calculating and recalculating scenarios that led to his own treasure. He shifted focus to Baber. "And you're telling me that you and Hiller have been using my ship to run your own personal whore house?! And there are pictures!" Baber looked at his hands before him on the table. He said nothing. Before the silence could grow, Maggie spoke up. Her voice was calm and firm. Her expression more serious than Shumate's, growing in intensity as she went.

"Yes. *Your* ship, sir. Evidently there are many things on *your* ship you don't know. Or maybe you decided not to know, because it didn't suit your purposes. I suggest you never call me a whore again or I'll show you something you can't miss." Baber and Steve looked at her with horror. Steve attempted to stop her, but she wasn't going to be stopped, and to their amazement, Shumate was now the one who looked uncomfortable.

"Everyone in this room can take some of the blame for how things stand. Me too. What's the old Bible line? All have sinned. Ok. All is all. Since we all have a part in it, let's all figure out how to fix it and not waste any more time calling names or deciding who to blame."

Baber and Steve held their breath, waiting to see what the Captain would do or say next. It felt like a long time.

Shumate said, "Who else on *Redstone* knows what you've just told me?" He spoke to them all, but focused on Maggie. She answered, "The people in this room right now are the only ones who know, Captain." The appendage of his title restored Shumate to the command of the ship. Maggie had taken it, they all knew. She returned it now, as neatly as a library book in an overnight drop.

Baber and Steve jumped in, "That's right. Nobody," they agreed.

Shumate looked at the overhead, as if appealing for an answer to appear. "Egyptian. My God, what a mess." The three looked at each other questioningly. The treasure seemed to them the least troublesome part of the predicament. To Steve, it felt like the thing that might redeem the situation, if they could find a way through the most pressing parts.

Shumate said, "I'm guessing none of you know much *Redstone* history. Why would you? But I do. I've read through a log book that's in my safe right over there," he tossed his head to indicate an old black wall safe on the starboard side of his cabin. "It's been handed down, CO to CO, since *Redstone* was commissioned in '39. Unofficial, you see. Just the things a Captain would think important. Fascinating read. Some skippers wrote lengthy passages. One even wrote a poem. Some only wrote the date they reported aboard and the day they departed, one line to the next, with all that tour compressed into two lines like a gravestone. Different strokes I guess. The Captain in '76 was almost like that. I think he wanted to be like that. His words are so sparse they're like annoyances. He wrote the date he reported on one line, the next dated entry says this: came through worst storm ever. Lost two men. Would've been home two weeks ago and missed the storm if it weren't for the damned Egyptian cargo." Shumate paused, letting the words sit on the table between them. He continued, "I got curious about this. I went back through the official record and discovered *Redstone* was tapped to be part of a mission designed to help US-Arab relations. It was a huge, high level deal. Some of King Tut's treasures were going on a tour around the States in various city museums. *Redstone* delivered those items on her way back from a Med deployment."

Steve broke in, "I saw that! My mother took me to see that at the Smithsonian!"

Shumate smiled. "I saw it too, only in Chicago."

Steve said, "You think what we found is part of that treasure? How? It couldn't just go missing without someone noticing could it?"

Shumate shrugged. "I'm just putting the pieces together in light of the information at hand. It was a big deal, this traveling exhibit. It was straight from the White House. Henry Kissinger had a lot to do with it. Middle East peace was at stake. How could we afford to lose one of their priceless works of art? Both sides had too much to lose. It was a perfectly balanced moment in time, when no one could say anything without upsetting the apple cart and probably costing a lot of lives." He studied their faces again. "Kind of like this moment."

Now the silence did grow long. Each of them struggled to make sense out of the situation. Shumate said, looking at Maggie, "you quoted a line from the Bible a minute ago. Here's another: isn't it better that one man dies than the whole nation comes to ruin?"

Baber got the gist immediately. He said, "you can't be serious!? Leave him in there?!"

"And what are the alternatives?" Shumate said. "It's a national scandal at a time we can't afford one! Do you really want more lives in Mal Hiller's hands? Let him out and it isn't our lives he controls, it's the entire country!" Even as he said it, Shumate felt the horror of his own words and knew he'd never be able to leave Hiller to die in the dark. His shoulders slumped. He sat back in his chair. Suddenly he looked much older and smaller. He muttered, barely audibly to no one in particular, "No, no, no." He fingered his collar device one more time and pulled himself out of the chair. "Come with me."

***

Steve banged on the overhead three times with a piece of scrap steel. He stood on the step ladder he'd swiped from a closet full of cleaning gear on the way down from the Captain's cabin.

"Cheng!" he shouted, through the little slot he'd left in the weld. No response. "Cheng!" Steve looked down at the others circling the ladder. All of them looked back with grim expressions.

"Go ahead," Shumate said.

Steve lit his torch. "I'm cutting, Cheng. Stay back!" he shouted. The others stepped back to avoid the orange-red shower of welding detritus.

The manhole cover sized plate came down easily. As Steve laid it on the deck, Baber said, "Let me go in first." He took the flashlight Steve offered him and disappeared up the black hole. Half a beat later his face appeared. "I'm gonna need a hand. Carter, you come up here and bring a couple of those kapoks."

Shumate said, "What is it, Bos'n?" But Baber had already disappeared again. Steve crawled up after him, slinging two of the weather stained life preservers into the hole. Maggie and the Captain waited below, straining to hear what was happening. A pair of black boondockers came through the hole, then legs clad in dark blue coveralls, the legs swung lazily as if unattached to anything.

They heard Baber grunt, "Move the ladder." He was breathing hard. A man was slowly lowered through the hole. For a brief instant Maggie had the horrified thought that Baber had decided to recover the dead body she and Steve had discovered; she did not want to see it, and started to turn away when a wheezing groan escaped the inert body emerging out of the ragged hole. Hiller! His back was to her and his head lolled forward on his chest. She heard the Bos'n and Steve straining and saw they'd fashioned makeshift ropes out of the kapok straps. One was holding Hiller's arms at his side and the other wrapped around his chest to his back to support him as they lowered away. Just before his feet touched down, he rolled slowly around to face her. She gasped. The man's face was covered in dried, blackened blood from the head wound, but this was a minor alteration in his appearance compared to his hair. Hiller's unruly mop of brown-black hair was completely white. Not a shade of gray, but utterly and shockingly paper-white. Shumate, who had been watching the evolution with arms folded, jumped in to settle Hiller on the deck.

"Grab another kapok, Freeman," he ordered Maggie. He put the life preserver under Hiller's head like a pillow. Maggie thought the man was unconscious, but when she stood over him she realized his eyes were wide open, staring into nothing. They were shot through with red streaks, the irises invisible against unnaturally dilated pupils. Shumate snapped his fingers and clapped. Hiller's eyes remained fixed. Steve and Baber let themselves down and joined the other two.

Shumate glanced at his watch. He said, "Bos'n, can you get him to Sick Bay on your own?" Baber nodded. "Ok, get him there ASAP. Freeman, go and get the Doc. He'll still be in his stateroom. Ask the mess stewards if you don't know which one it is. Tell him the Chief Engineer is in Sick Bay and needs help. If he asks what happened, tell him you don't know and someone just grabbed you and sent you to get him. Go!"

Maggie took off at a trot. Baber, unencumbered by the confined space of the secret compartment, easily hoisted Hiller onto his shoulders in a fireman's carry and headed off to sick bay.

When they were alone, Steve looked at Shumate questioningly.

Chapter 56
The Storm
September 1976, course 270, speed 17 knots, steaming into a nor'easter

Jasper stepped down off the ladder. He cocked an ear toward the overhead. Dull thuds could still be heard and a faint reverberation that must be Richards screaming, but after the gunfire, ricocheting bullets and clanking of steel plates, he felt as if he'd been plunged into an isolation booth. His ears physically hurt, in a way he'd never thought possible, and he put a finger in one and drew it out, expecting to see blood. There wasn't any. Back on his feet in the cage where Richards had tried to imprison him, he realized the ship was moving differently than it had been, only an hour before. He double checked his watch, hardly able to comprehend all that had transpired since Richards had awakened him.

Redstone was not a graceful ship under any circumstances. Her old bow looked like the nose of a fighter who'd spent too many nights on the undercard. In heavy seas, that nose would come up over a cresting wave, sniff the salt air and then slam itself down on the fist of the next wave. If she had anything over eight knots on, the result would be an awful shuddering that ran from stem to stern, as she twisted rather than knifed her way along. This night, approaching the Outer Banks of North Carolina, *Redstone* ran headlong into a Nor'easter. Winds veering around from her starboard side bent her over in the troughs of huge Atlantic breakers, coming south with a hundred miles of fetch to build their momentum. The track home was westward and the Old Man, as with all CO's, was determined to meet his ship's commitments, especially one that had the attention of the White House. He would get to Norfolk on time and make the transfer of the Egyptian treasure trove that had caused so much trouble already. Graveyard of the Atlantic be damned. His ship wasn't altering course or speed. The delay caused by all those extra drills during OPPE had put the ship at the short end of the candle; no wiggle room.

An hour after *Redstone* felt the first wisps of the oncoming storm, the ship heeled over, fifteen degrees to port, and stayed there, pinned under the press of wind and water. By the time Phipps had cut his way out of the cage that Richards had locked them both in, he had to lean into the angled deck to keep upright. The pitch of the ship, accompanied by the shudder familiar to *Redstone* veterans, made holding a straight path hard going.

Jasper paused at the door to the controlled equipage locker and gathered his thoughts. His mind had been pegged on overdrive, racing along ever since Richards zinged the first bullet a foot over his head. The horrific nature of what he'd just done seeped in as the ship swayed and creaked around him. It would be miserable in there, in that steel closet, in the dark with the ship carrying on like this. Yes. Miserable. Then, in his head, Jasper heard Richards screaming again: "I'm gonna kill you... kiiiiiilllllll yoooooooouuuuu!"

And what am I going to do? Jasper thought. *Go to the Suppo and the Old Man and confess I was planning to steal the treasure?* He saw himself in Leavenworth. Hell, the skipper might go old school, put him in irons and throw him in the brig. "God knows what Richards will say when they let 'im out," he said out loud, startling himself with the sound of his own voice. He sounded so... normal. Not at all like a man who'd just sealed up another man in a steel box. He set his jaw with decision. *I'm going to let him stew in his juices a while*, Jasper thought. *Let him feel some of the fear he's been dishing out to me. Won't hurt him a bit.* He looked at his watch again. *Give him an hour. It'll still be early enough there won't be anyone up and about but the watch.* He was about to leave the locker when he remembered something. He put down his welding gear and returned to the cage. He shuffled through the boxes he'd moved earlier and retrieved the coveralls he'd used to snuff out the fire, then he searched till he found an unopened box marked *Coveralls, Blue, Large.* He threw it up on one shoulder, paused for an instant to listen under the sealed circle in the overhead, and heard nothing. He took a last look at the work he'd done and admired it. "Damn, Jasper," he said to himself, "you can flat out weld your ass off. Except for that little nub of crow bar that looks like it belongs there." He returned to the front door of the locker, laboring against *Redstone's* wallowing motion, gathered up his gear, and opened the door.

In the passageway, Phipps had a bad moment. A shadow passed the end of the port side passageway off to his left. He realized the exposure of his position. He wanted to keep the out of control situation as controlled as he could; that meant not being discovered leaving this space with his welding gear. He did a quick assessment of the pathways back to his own territory that would be least likely to cause him to run into someone. The forward engine room damage control locker was a good place to crash while he let Richards cool off and consider his sins. The best way to get there, he decided, was to go forward and topside and come back down near the forward escape trunk. If anyone should see him along this path, he had plenty of spaces to duck into that would be unlocked and unoccupied at this hour. He shifted the box of coveralls, which was surprisingly heavy, from one shoulder to the other and set off. Ascending the port side ladder onto the level of the main deck with no free hand for the rail, he strained to keep his balance against the increasing movement of the ship in the storm. He put down the box and opened the water-tight door at the top of the ladder.

He could smell the sea, briny and turbulent, as he emerged from the confinement of belowdecks, where one could lose the sense that you were at sea, feeling instead you were in an industrial plant that occasionally swayed. Up here though, the senses of sight and sound and smell were continually assaulted by the relentless ocean. You were reminded that you were only here at her tolerance and could be wiped away if she was angry. Tonight she was angry.

Jasper let the wind slam the door closed behind him and dogged it closed. He re-hoisted the box onto his shoulder and leaned into another roll. He made it to the breezeway that bisected the main deck. The door to the ladder he needed to descend back into his world was in the center of the breezeway. The deck in the breezeway streamed with rivulets of rain water and the sea water cascading through it like a sluice of a dam.

Redstone groaned in her arthritic metal bones, pressing into the heart of the storm, taking its full force on her starboard beam, the Captain unwilling to yield and bring her nose into the onrushing waves. Just then the ship took a huge, out of sequence breaker that threw her violently to starboard. The deck came level for an instant, then fell away to port, so fast and so far, it felt as if the whole world had gone sideways. The quartermaster of the watch on the bridge, who claimed ever after that he'd hung on a stanchion with his feet in the air, suspended like a trapeze artist, when the wave hit, told the story of this moment for the rest of his life. How the Old Man turned white—white as a bucktail deer's behind—and crawled to the helm on his hands and knees, where he screamed for the helmsman to bring the ship's head into the wind. Slowly, so slowly it was imperceptible, *Redstone* answered the helm. She took a beating, bucking wildly over the final set of quartering waves before the battered boxer's nose began to rise and fall through the crests into the wind. It was 0300. *Redstone* would lose a full twelve hours to the storm, but she would make it home. Jasper would not.

As he stumbled down the slanted breezeway, the rogue wave that pushed *Redstone* on her beam ends and turned the Captain bucktail white, put Jasper on his back. He lost his grip on the box of coveralls and his welding gear. The massive wave, hitting the ship on her starboard side, looked for passage back into the sea, and found the path of least resistance in the square funnel of the breezeway. The sea burst into the gap like a flash flood in a canyon. It filled it completely, scouring it out, leaving nothing behind. Jasper flung an arm out wildly but found no handhold. He hit the port side lifelines, heaped up like a ball, the weight of the water relentlessly pushing him up and over them. With a last great effort, he snatched the top steel wire and held on, his body dangling over the edge for one terrible moment before his dropped acetylene tank connected with his forehead. He saw stars explode in his vision and released his grip on *Redstone* forever.

Chapter 57
(Un)endings

Rear Admiral Ralph Shumate looked out his office window on the Norfolk Naval Operations Base. It was a satisfying view. A smattering of destroyers, sleek and sexy amongst the decidedly unsexy auxiliaries. But the oilers and supply ships were his, and he took pleasure in them, in all their awkward functionality, as a lover comes to celebrate even his loved one's flaws. On his desk were two pieces of paper, which no person on earth—well, he corrected himself, only five people on earth would ever connect—one of whom had no capacity left for speech.

The first was the draft of a message to Bupers, clearing up a matter of reinstatement of rank and back pay for one Stephen R. Carter, USNR. The gist of the message was to restore Petty Officer Carter's rank to Machinist Mate Second Class by expunging from his record a non-judicial punishment, imposed by then-Captain Ralph Shumate. The action, dated almost exactly a year previous, would disappear; Carter would receive, not only the half month's pay times two months taken away at the time of the NJP, but also the difference in pay from his reduced rank up to the day he was honorably discharged. The message specified that the check cut to make payment was to be sent to the Navy

Reserve Center in Blacksburg, Virginia, where Petty Officer Carter was serving out two years of ready reserve duty.

The other sailors at the center wondered at the deal Carter had got. When they asked him about it, he would only say it was one of those 'one time good deals' that sometimes came around, and he was glad of it. It was a good deal. It cut a year of active duty out of his way and allowed him to go back to school at Virginia Tech earlier than he'd anticipated. He was getting paid good money for the reserves and he was close enough to Norfolk that he could cut his Friday afternoon Psych class and make it there before Maggie got off work, a thing he pulled off at least twice a month.

The other piece of paper on Shumate's desk was a memo from his boss at COMNAVSURFLANT. He was asking for Shumate to sign off on a plan to dispose of a handful of ships, in the face of the massive cutbacks in forces following the Gulf War mobilization.

"Austere" was the new buzz word around the fleet, and getting rid of auxiliaries was going to be a priority. The question was, what to do with them? Send them to the James River ghost fleet? Donate them to environmental causes where they would be sunk and turned into manmade reefs? Or sell them to foreign navies that coveted even used up US naval vessels to augment their slender forces?

There she was, top of the list: *Redstone*. She was no longer "USS". They had ridden out a couple months following the Hurghada job, anchored in Souda Bay, Crete, standing by in case they were needed. Soon they'd gotten the word: return to home port, best speed; decommissioning upon arrival.

In a most unlikely turn of events, Shumate received a spot promotion to Admiral, and Commander Katie Kendall USNR (TAR) took command from him, shepherding the old girl through her final weeks on the rolls as an active naval vessel. The Navy got to count this as a female in command of a ship, which made the quota bean-counters happy, and Kendall got to be CO of a ship with no chance of having to do anything except shuffle paperwork across her desk while every useful bit of gear on the ship made its way across the brow or out the sally ports to other ships. Everyone was happy.

Now, with the stroke of a pen, Shumate would write the final chapter in *Redstone*'s history. Sending her up the river was out of the question; too much money to mothball her and keep her in suspended animation. It would either be death and the bottom of the ocean, or rebirth under another name in another navy. Shumate looked over the list of navies interested in purchasing his ships. Spain, Chile, Brazil, and... Egypt? That would be a first, as far as he knew; no American military asset had ever been sold to the Egyptians. He wondered at the changes in the world, and he wondered at the irony. US-Arab relations always hanging by a thread. Today it was a stronger thread, and it lay on his desk. Giving them *Redstone* would make it even stronger, wouldn't it? A Navy ship is always more than the sum of its parts; more than its guns, its engines, its compartments. It's an image. It's like the American flag on the moon. It's a piece of America. It's also a woman. Mysterious. Full of secrets, and dangerous in ways no one but her lover can know.

Shumate scribbled a note on the bottom of the memo. *Redstone* was the perfect size ship for the reef the greenies wanted, off the coast of Mayport, Florida. He would arrange to get her towed down there next month, using the duty oiler that was going that way for a Fleetex. Good practice for everyone, and the cruiser-destroyer guys could use it for target practice.

He set the memo on top of the work pile for his flag secretary and smiled. Nice neat solution. Welded up tight as a drum. His phone buzzed.

"We're going to be late for Pete Baber's retirement if we don't get going, Admiral. I already called your car for us."

"Us?" he said. "You're going too, Maggie?"

"Wouldn't miss it, sir. Wouldn't miss it for the world."

THE END

ABOUT THE AUTHOR

R. Kenward Jones

Buried at Sea is R. Kenward Jones's debut novel. He is an ex-Navy officer who originally enlisted in the Navy and trained to operate nuclear power plants before receiving a NROTC scholarship and attending college at Old Dominion University in Norfolk, Virginia. Returning to active duty, he served in various roles as a Surface Warfare and Intelligence Officer, making several deployments to the Mediterranean, North Atlantic, and Barents Sea.

He grew up in Augusta County, Virginia, where his father moved the family the year after he helped coach the TC Williams Titans (remember them?) to the 1971 Virginia state football championship. Together they renovated a 150-year-old farm house and settled into country living. The hills, fields, creeks and abandoned barns of Barren Ridge overlooking the Blue Ridge Mountains became his haunts. He married his high school sweetheart in 1984, and they've lived in the southeastern corner of Virginia since then, raising two children. Currently he works as a mental health counselor, and his wife runs a daycare.

The Dragon's Breath

by

James Boschert

Talon stared wide-eyed at the devices, awed that they could make such an overwhelming, head-splitting noise. His ears rang and his eyes were burning from the drifting smoke that carried with it an evil stink. "That will show the bastards," Hsü told him with one of his rare smiles. "The General calls his weapons 'the Dragon's breath.' They certainly stink like it."

Talon, an assassin turned knight turned merchant, is restless. Enticed by tales of lucrative trade, he sets sail for the coasts of Africa and India. Traveling with him are his wife and son, eager to share in this new adventure, as well as Reza, his trusted comrade in arms. Treasures beckon at the ports, but Talon and Reza quickly learn that dangers attend every opportunity, and the chance rescue of a Chinese lord named Hsü changes their destination—and their fates.

Hsü introduces Talon to the intricacies of trading in China and the sophisticated wonders of Guangzhou, China's richest city. Here the companions discover wealth beyond their imagining. But Hsü is drawn into a political competition for the position of governor, and his opponents target everyone associated with him, including the foreign merchants he has welcomed into his home. When Hsü is sent on a dangerous mission to deliver the annual Tribute to the Mongols, no one is safe, not even the women and children of the household. As Talon and Reza are drawn into supporting Hsü's bid for power, their fighting skills are put to the test against new weapons and unfamiliar fighting styles. It will take their combined skills to navigate the treacherous waters of intrigue and violence if they hope to return to home.

PENMORE PRESS
www.penmorepress.com

Historical fiction and nonfiction
Paperback available for order on line
and as Ebook with all major distributers

The Captain's Nephew

by

Philip K.Allan

After a century of war, revolutions, and Imperial conquests, 1790s Europe is still embroiled in a battle for control of the sea and colonies. Tall ships navigate familiar and foreign waters, and ambitious young men without rank or status seek their futures in Naval commands. First Lieutenant Alexander Clay of HMS Agrius is self-made, clever, and ready for the new age. But the old world, dominated by patronage, retains a tight hold on advancement. Though Clay has proven himself many times over, Captain Percy Follett is determined to promote his own nephew.

Before Clay finds a way to receive due credit for his exploits, he'll first need to survive them. Ill-conceived expeditions ashore, hunts for privateers in treacherous fog, and a desperate chase across the Atlantic are only some of the challenges he faces. He must endeavor to bring his ship and crew through a series of adventures stretching from the bleak coast of Flanders to the warm waters of the Caribbean. Only then might high society recognize his achievements —and allow him to ask for the hand of Lydia Browning, the woman who loves him regardless of his station.

PENMORE PRESS
www.penmorepress.com

The Measure of Ella
by
Toni Bird Jones

The islands frightened her with their uncivilized rawness. They looked like a place where anything could happen, a godforsaken outcrop at the end of the world.

Sea-faring chef Ella Morgan is an honest woman — until her life falls apart. When her dream of owning a restaurant is shattered by the death of her father and loss of her inheritance, she is suddenly alone in the world. Desperate for money, she signs on as crew for a Caribbean drug run, only to find herself fighting for her life in an underworld ruled by violent men.

Set in the Caribbean, The Measure of Ella is a dramatic story of love, murder, high-seas action, and the consequences of pursuing a dream at all costs. Like Patrick O'Brien's novels, including Master and Commander, The Measure of Ella captures the breathtaking and perilous world of blue-water sailing. Like Girl on the Train, it unwinds with gripping suspense from a woman's point of view. With its brave, strong, complex female protagonist at the helm of a high seas adventure, the novel is entirely unique.

PENMORE PRESS
www.penmorepress.com

THE SIMUSHIR ISLAND INCIDENT
BY
MARC LIEBMAN

Manufacturing and selling illicit drugs is a lucrative business. But what good is being rich if you can't enjoy your wealth?

North Korean officers Admiral Pak and General Jang are in charge of an operation that produces high-grade heroin to be sold in the United States as Asian Pure. But an alarming number of high-ranking officers in the Democratic People's Republic of Korea are being accused of treason -- and not surviving their arrests. Admiral Pak and General Jang suspect it is only a matter of time before their own heads will be on the execution block, unless they can make themselves to valuable to kill off. They figure out a way to dramatically reduce costs and increase the profit margin: rent Simushir Island from Russia and manufacture the drugs closer to their market destination. They even concoct a plausible cover story of establishing a maritime base for merchant shipping. It's a great plan -- until other heads of state decide to militarize the operation with a ballistic missile launch facility.

PENMORE PRESS
www.penmorepress.com

Penmore Press

Challenging, Intriguing, Adventurous, Historical and Imaginative

www.penmorepress.com

CPSIA information can be obtained
at www.ICGtesting.com
Printed in the USA
JSHW020950070423
40065JS00001B/2